I Remember Running

Also by Vernon Bargainer

It Is Morning

At the Feet of Angels

I Remember Running

SEQUEL TO IT IS MORNING

Vernon Bargainer

iUniverse, Inc.
Bloomington

I REMEMBER RUNNING
SEQUEL TO IT IS MORNING

iUniverse books may be ordered through booksellers or by contacting:

iUniverse
1663 Liberty Drive
Bloomington, IN 47403
www.iuniverse.com
1-800-Authors (1-800-288-4677)

ISBN: 978-1-4620-3347-8 (sc)
ISBN: 978-1-4620-3346-1 (hc)
ISBN: 978-1-4620-3345-4 (ebk)

Library of Congress Control Number: 2011910503

Printed in the United States of America

iUniverse rev. date: 08/04/2011

FROM IT IS MORNING

No word, no thought, no sense of any kind could capture in the tiniest degree the impact of seeing the little round solemn face that rose stoically out of the page . . . Lorrie Dean was one of those rare little girls who was pretty—just plain pretty—even without smiling. The only difference was that her eyes shined a little brighter when she did smile. But she smiled very little. Andy hadn't thought about this as an eleven-year-old, but now as he recalled those childhood school days, it struck him odd that one so young should bear such a serious countenance. Maybe that was just part of her style.

The yearbook picture was black and white, yet Andy could see the rose in her cheeks, the dark black hair that fell just above her shoulders, the pink in her little turned-down pouting lips, the deep brown of her serious eyes. No wonder the face of Lorrie Dean haunted him so, if only on its own merits.

One of the students, a girl, came over, stood beside him, and followed his gaze. Andy glanced briefly at her and slowly pointed to the picture, "Lorrie Dean," he said, and closed the book.

1

It was almost done: the fateful marriage of Andy and Lorrie Dean, childhood sweethearts who rediscovered each other twenty years after their adolescent fling surrendered to the inexorable course of time. Their new love, so real and boundless, so full and unassuming, would be eternal—with or without the formal vows.

Now they stood beside a gazebo in a secluded park on the outskirts of the little East Texas town of Tillman. The hour was at hand. They waited, smiling humbly, resolute in what they felt for each other and for their future as husband and wife. Everything was so right as they began to seal their love in holy matrimony while a small crowd of close friends looked on.

"I do," answered Andy, solemnly.

"And do you, Lorrie Dean LeMay, take Andrew Woodson Boone to be your husband, to have and to hold, from this day forward, for better or worse, for richer or poorer, in sickness and in health, to love and to cherish, so long as you both shall live?"

"Look out!" screamed a man in the audience, as a clamoring vehicle squealed to a stop behind the last row of seats.

Two men jumped out of the car, waving badges and shouting, "FBI! Everybody stay put!" One of the men grabbed Lorrie Dean and started dragging her to the car while the other stared at the stunned little group, whipping his pistol back and forth in front of them, clearly threatening to punish anyone who attempted to interfere.

Andy Boone was shouting and flailing the air with both arms. "What the hell is this? What's going on? You have to talk to us! Stop, stop, stop it!"

While the first man started pushing down on Lorrie Dean's head to force her into the backseat, the other sprinted over and jumped into the driver's seat. Struggling, Lorrie Dean leaned out as far as she could and murmured, "I do."

In the next instant, the man shoved her all the way across the seat to the far side, and they sped away while he was still pulling his door shut.

Andy ran after the car, foolishly reaching out for it, as Kelly Surrat, his special little buddy, gasped along behind him, right on his heels. Exhausted, Andy lurched forward, floundering for more power. Mercifully, he stumbled and fell headfirst onto the shoulder of the narrow country road. Kelly fell on top of him.

Kelly rolled off and onto her back, and Andy rolled over beside her. Both stared straight up into the sky, panting and groaning. They lay on their backs, wordless, trying to catch their breath and grasp what was happening.

"Boone Woo, you're crazy," wheezed Kelly.

Frightened and stunned as he was, Andy felt comfort hearing the words *Boone Woo* arise out of the throat of his very dear, devoted young friend. That was her personal name for him, born of the will and ingenuity of this extraordinarily bright seventeen-year-old girl. She had coined it using the *Woo* from his middle name, Woodson, and backing into it from his last name. She had argued mischievously that calling him *Andy Woo* would have been too easy and too conventional. In any event, Andy and Kelly said of themselves that they were the very best of buddies.

"You're right; I *am* crazy," groaned Andy.

"Did you think you were going to catch that car?"

"I was hoping it would have a flat."

"Never give up, do you, young tiger?"

"There are two things in this world that I will never give up on: you"—his voice was cracking—"and my Lorrie Dean." He wept.

The two beleaguered racers tried to sit up, looking at each other for strength, and with much effort, finally managed to do it. Wearily, they pushed on up and stood in place for a few minutes, staring in the direction taken by the kidnappers.

"Will she ever know freedom?" murmured Andy, still gazing dumbfounded down the backwoods road.

Four months earlier, Andy had searched frantically for Lorrie Dean LeMay, his childhood sweetheart. When she learned of it, she came out of hiding so he could find her and settle his mind. She and her parents had been sequestered under the Witness Protection Program. It happened that Lorrie Dean's mother, Charlotte LeMay, had been an accomplice in a drug-trafficking operation, and she and one of the other pushers had gotten caught. On a plea-bargaining deal, Charlotte testified at the man's trial, and her testimony had put him in prison. Since the third party was still on the loose, the LeMay family went into hiding. Subsequently the third accomplice was tracked down and sent to prison.

"I don't understand," said Kelly. "Everybody's been caught and put away. Do you think somebody's still after her mother?"

"I think the LeMay family is still in danger. Apparently, Lorrie Dean's mom and dad think so, too, because they are still in hiding. But one thing I know: I simply have to find her again. She's my wife. I will!"

2

Just as Andy and Kelly turned to head back, a pickup truck came along and parked on the shoulder of the road a little ways from them. Out of it bounded Dub Grimes, Kelly's uncle from the farm. "Come on, y'all; let's go see what we can do."

Kelly climbed into the front seat, and Andy hurried to the back. Dub headed out down the narrow county road that served the park and a scattering of old homes.

"Where are we going?" asked Kelly.

"We're goin' the way they left out of here. Help me look for any, ah, well, maybe little inconspicuous side roads takin' off from this one that we can tell the police about. I expect they're already familiar with the little dead-ends off the main highway."

Everybody fell silent as they began stretching and bobbing left and right, looking for pathways or cattle trails leading away from the road. They were deep in the piney woods of East Texas, but on this heart-wrenching day, the smell of sap, normally refreshing and pleasant, was stifling. Nothing was normal about this day. It was horrifying and mournful.

Now it was looking very much like their reconnaissance mission would wind up a futile effort. They were still just poking along, and Andy was getting restless. "Ah, Dub, shouldn't we be hurryin'?"

"I figure it's all under control," said Dub. "As I headed for the parkin' lot to get my truck so I could come after you and Kelly, both Aunt Leah and that woman from your office were on their cell phones. I don't think anybody else, including us, had a phone there. Anyway, I heard Leah making the 911 call."

"Oh. Yeah, that was Paige Ivy from my office. I guess we need to be counting up everyone who was there in case they ask for more witnesses at some point. Let's see, there was Paige, all five of y'all from the farm, my mom and dad, Lorrie Dean's boss and the other two people from her office, plus the preacher and us, of course, and there were three or four from your church, huh, Kelly?"

Kelly nodded. "Four."

Andy pressed on. "And I want to talk to the people in Lorrie Dean's office to see if anybody remembers getting any phone calls asking about her or maybe trying to find out where she was going to be at any time—you know, to see if anybody was trying to find out what her plans were. Maybe some unfamiliar names or numbers were left on their caller IDs or 'calls missed.' And we also need to talk to everyone there. We'll need to form some concrete questions before we start with them."

When Andy finally wound down, Dub Grimes glanced toward Kelly beside him and then cut his eyes toward Andy in the backseat. "I guess y'all know that was *not* a government vehicle."

"Right," Kelly said emphatically.

"And they were not FBI men," added Andy. "I know how FBI agents work, and that's not the way they apprehend."

"Wonder if anybody got a license number or the make of the car," Dub ventured.

Kelly was nodding agreement before he finished. "There *was* no number. It just said US GOVERNMENT, with no numbers or letters. I know that's not right. And the car was a solid black Lincoln Town Car. I'm not good on years, so I can't tell you the model, but it looked newish, so it has to be a late model."

As solemn as life was at that moment, Andy couldn't help but grin and shake his head lightly. "I knew if anybody picked up on that, it would be my morning light," he said, using his affectionate name for Kelly. It was a title that, to him, best summarized this bright young warrior. It was an emblem of her insightful mind, her playful adjustment to life's offering, and the glow of her sweet countenance, hiding a heart full of hurt and sadness.

In a moment, Andy pulled to the edge of his seat and grasped the front seatbacks while he talked. "We've got a lot to do. I assume the Tillman police are already on it, for whatever they can do. Anyway, I have to find out if they notified the state police, since kidnapping is probably in their jurisdiction, and I have to get to the FBI."

"FBI?" queried Kelly and Dub at the same time.

"Right. They get involved in kidnappings a lot of the time, even if they don't include federal issues. Not only that, this business of impersonating a federal officer will have them stirred up big-time. Every single agent will be offended by that. So, I have to get to my friend, Agent Jarrigan, in a hurry. Unfortunately, it's going to be hard to activate very much on the weekend."

Kelly was pulling at her fingers while Andy talked, aching for him and for her best pal, Lorrie Dean. She started to speak, but her voice came out as a scratchy whisper, so she cleared the rattle in her throat and tried again. "Where are we actually going, Uncle Dub?"

"We'll come to State Highway 315 in a little while and go left, back toward the main highway to Tillman—you know, 175. I figure the kidnappers, if they got to that point, would have turned right on 315 toward I-20 so they could get up some speed."

Dub slowed the truck as they rounded a curve. Off to the right, not far off the road, stood an old, weathered, dilapidated barn, its roof collapsed almost to the ground on one end. It looked as if it had just died there in the trees, slumped down in a spotty patch of ragweed and bull nettle.

Andy was frowning. Something was puzzling about that picture. Apparently Kelly was thinking the same thing, for at that moment, she tilted her head slightly and muttered, "Hmm."

"Yeah," agreed Andy. *Buddies think alike.*

They poked on in silence. After a few moments, Andy pulled to the edge of his seat again and started to rattle. "It was such an ordeal when I was trying to find Lorrie Dean. At first, I didn't really know why I was searching for her. Then I found her, and I fell in love with her. I didn't tell everybody what I was doing. The people in the office never knew, not that they have sense enough to comprehend anything, except of course for Paige Ivy. I didn't tell my mom and dad for a long time. Mom acted strange about it all, well, I guess like mothers do . . . you know. I had this girl, Mildred—wonderful, wonderful woman—helping me in Baytown. I wanted to flush Lorrie Dean out through a class reunion. Mildred thought a fourteenth reunion was out of the ordinary, but she finally agreed that we would have a makeup reunion. Anyway . . ."

Andy cleared his throat and took a second to catch his breath and rambled on: "All this time, the FBI guy was a pain in the butt, and a couple of pathetic hecklers in my office were on my back. So I took to drink. You know, in life you can only—why are you looking at me like that?"

"Boone Woo, it's just that, well, I've never heard you talk so incessantly like that."

Andy slapped the front seatbacks and screamed, "Kelly, I'm scared to death!" Then he lost it and completely broke down, bawling out loud. Kelly twisted around and reached both arms toward him. He took her hands, and they cried it out together. Dub was stone silent, but he, too, was swatting tears trickling down his cheeks.

After a while, Kelly, still sniffling, said sweetly to her buddy, "I'm scared, too."

"I'm sorry I screamed, my morning light."

"It's okay. It's okay." She paused and then cleared her throat and started to speak kindly but seriously. "Boone Woo, I know that you've always thought of me as a little girl, and yeah, I guess I am, but I also have strength. And, please, I like being your morning light, but you need me for more. Boone Woo, you also need to rely on me partly for strength. You're going to need lot of that. I can be your strength."

Andy took her hands again and kissed them and then snuggled them to his cheek. "You're so right. I need you, and you are the very one person I do need. You know, I want Lorrie Dean, not just for me, but for her. I want her freedom, once and for all. She deserves a happy life, and she deserves every good thing in the world, as you know from your own friendship. When she finally revolted and marched out of hiding under that witness protection thing, we rejoiced because she was free. Now she's captive again."

They were at the intersection with Highway 315. There was no traffic light, which was understandable because there was also no traffic. As Dub turned left onto the state highway, he leaned back in his seat and took the steering wheel stiff-armed with both hands, apparently to dramatize a change in strategy. He drawled, "Okay, so much for that. It's on to Tillman and the police station."

"Yeah, so much for nothing," said Kelly.

"You're right, Kelly, dear, we didn't see much, did we?"

Andy curled a finger around tight lips and droned, "Nothing but that pitiful-looking old barn." All three nodded, and that was all—on that subject.

As they cruised along toward the main highway to Tillman, they tried hard to find fascination in the countryside, hoping that would take the edge off their fear and grief. There was nothing going on. Nature was just sitting there. Trees are trees, once you've been in them for a while. Finally they were served a little variety, such as it was: a few red oaks here and there, drooping over the scrub pines. Maybe the trees were weeping for Lorrie Dean. Soon they came upon a little clearing that had been cut out of the woods years ago to serve as a cotton field, but it was now dead and gone, and the barren land didn't seem fit for grazing. The once breathtaking fields and woodlands had lost their personality. At least, that's the way it appeared to the three friends on this woeful day.

Soon they turned onto Highway 175, and, not long after, they were slowing into the outskirts of Tillman. Now they were passing alongside a small lonely-looking schoolhouse with its deserted playground. Andy turned his head to keep it in view as they passed it. He shook his head as he reflected on the scene, which four months earlier had launched his determined search for his childhood sweetheart, his beloved Lorrie Dean.

Kelly had turned half aside to watch Andy as he studied this situation. She said nothing. She felt that she knew her Boone Woo, maybe better than anyone else, and she was positive that she knew what he was thinking about and that he should not be interrupted. He should be left alone with his memories, she thought, especially if they helped him cope and keep his strength.

In a few minutes, they arrived at the one-time boarding house, now serving as the Tillman police station. They parked in a lot behind the building and walked to the front. The building stood between a drugstore and a newspaper office. Across the street were a few retail dealers and five-and-dime stores and one small café, boastfully named East Texas Restaurant.

Inside the courthouse, a young man greeted the trio and advised them that Officer Foley was their one source of information about the park-side kidnapping. He invited them to wait in the adjacent room while Foley finished an interrogation already in progress.

Apparently, nothing had been done to the building when it was converted to a police station, for it still looked virtually like a classic, old boarding house. It had very high ceilings and walls of polished, hardwood paneling, which was curved where it met the corners of the room. The little room they were in had evidently once served as a small parlor, and the bedrooms were now the offices and interrogation rooms.

Andy was staring at the ceiling and frowning.

"What?" said Kelly.

"Well, it's just, you know, I don't believe I've ever seen a chandelier in a police station."

"You been in a lot of police stations, have you, Andy?" chuckled Dub.

"Good one, Uncle Dub," sang Kelly, as the three of them attempted to share a light moment.

Then they all fell quiet.

Andy noticed his little morning light deep in thought and decided not to disturb her with questions and chatter. Dub went to look for a restroom, and the commotion roused Kelly from her reverie. She looked at Andy and smiled.

"Are you thinking about anything you want to share, darling?" asked Andy.

"I was just reminiscing about the wonderful times Lorrie Dean and I spent together in just one short month. We always seemed to know what to talk about—you know, a lot of girl talk, of course, but also serious things and some fun things." Something in her memory made Kelly giggle as she continued. "We played a lot of frivolous games, like little brain teasers and what-if puzzles."

"What-if puzzles?"

"Yeah, you know, like what would you do if a certain thing happened? Like, one time I said to her, 'What would you do if you saw a vicious dog charging toward you?' Now get this: Lorrie Dean didn't bat an eye; she just said, 'I'd try to confuse him. I'd walk toward him, whistling and saying little sweet things like come on boy, commmme on, come to mommy.'"

"That's Lorrie Dean," said Andy. "Always with grace." He dropped his head into praying hands and pleaded, "Oh Lord, please bless our Lorrie Dean. Reach to her. Ease her fear and pain. Watch over her."

Just then a man came into the room. He extended his hand to Andy and introduced himself as Rick Foley. He had obviously been briefed on the purpose of their visit and began at once to explain where they were in their investigation of the kidnapping. He pointed out that law enforcement agencies were all cooperating, including the police in Jacksonville and Dallas and even the Texas Rangers who, he said, just happened to have two troopers who were already traveling I-20, where they suspected the kidnappers fled. It seemed he wanted to console his visitors. "You know, obviously they kidnapped the girl to serve a purpose, so chances are they don't intend to hurt her, at least not right away."

"Do the investigators know what they're looking for?" asked Andy.

"All we know is that the getaway car was big and black and had illegitimate license plates. Unfortunately, they probably won't stay in that car very long, but we'll be on the lookout for it, even if it's abandoned somewhere."

"Kelly here has a slightly more complete description, if that would help any," offered Andy.

"It would indeed help," said Officer Foley enthusiastically.

"It was a late-model black Lincoln Town Car with a rear license plate that looked homemade and read simply US GOVERNMENT."

"Hey," said Foley, "that's outstanding. This your daughter?"

"I wish," said Andy.

Kelly caught her breath and covered her lips at that quick, unexpected answer. For the last eleven years, she hadn't felt that she was anybody's daughter. Even though her constantly bickering mom and dad had received joint custody in their divorce, neither of them had wanted her, and so they shopped her around for the taking. Now here was a man in her life, fifteen years her senior, who clearly loved her for being herself, and she could tell by the twinkle in his eye that his love for her was genuine and everlasting.

Soon, the courthouse meeting ended, and the three friends headed toward the farmhouse where Kelly and Dub lived so Andy could pick up his Cutlass and drive back to Dallas. Once there, Kelly excused herself, indicating she would be right back—that she had to dash into the house for a minute.

Meanwhile, Dub came around and laid his hand on Andy's shoulder. "You know, Kelly's right about her strength. She's overcome a hell of a lot, as you know. I can't figure how anybody could deal with bein' rejected by both parents, one at a time, and still hold their head up and keep on tryin' like Kelly has. She is indeed strong. I guess I'll never be able to relate to my sister because of her part in this—you know, Kelly's mother."

Andy nodded, and in that moment, Kelly returned. "Boone Woo, do you want me to go back with you and maybe be some help?"

"Thanks, darling, but I don't guess there's anything two can do on a Sunday—possibly even one. I'd rather you stay here and get a good night's sleep in your own bed and be ready to help me think. You do that better than anybody I know. And, my little morning light, you're right, I need your strength."

Now they were ready to part, and Andy grew solemn. "I don't know what I'm gonna feel, what I can possibly think, what I'll do when I step into our little house where we were going to begin our lives together as husband and wife. I don't know; I don't know."

Kelly came to him, and they embraced. Then they parted and said good-bye, and Andy trudged on to his car.

Kelly watched as Andy drove away, much as she had done at their first meeting four months ago when he delivered his case of beer as a goodwill gesture to her uncle Dub. Two days before that, Dub had helped him untangle his car from their fence where he'd crashed after passing the little schoolhouse.

Now, as she watched her buddy disappear down the long driveway, she recalled how he'd conceded to her at that very first meeting, how he'd engaged in her banter so readily and so naturally; he'd accepted her on her own terms. She recalled thinking as he drove away, *There goes a grown-up who might could have loved me for me being me, but I'll likely never see him again.* Kelly shook away her reverie and braced up: *Bye, Boone Woo.*

3

Lorrie Dean fell against the door, banging her head on the window as the big cruiser whipped around a sharp curve. She tried to pull herself straight but toppled again when the car skidded into another breakneck turn and thrashed through a patch of overgrown weeds beside an ominous-looking old barn. Then it swung around behind the barn and stopped alongside a smaller car.

The other car's motor was idling. The man sitting behind the wheel stared straight ahead, never flinching or looking around to see what his visitors were up to. Clearly, he was a part of the strategy.

"Okay, young lady," said the man sitting beside her as he grabbed her arm. "We're out of here. Best you stay cool while we change cars. I'm sure you'll like this little Chevy Lumina so much better." He giggled stupidly.

Lorrie Dean obeyed, for she had already decided that the best course for her was to say nothing and avoid presenting them with anything calling for a reaction. As she twisted around to squirm out of the backseat, her bridal hat, which had been crammed between her and the door, was raked onto the floor. She glanced back at it, shrugged, and labored on with her captor. Now the driver of the big cruiser was climbing into the passenger seat of the new car.

As they pulled away, the new driver began to speak, and as he did, it was obvious that he was taking over and that he was really the one in charge of this operation. "I know you're wondering what's going on here, who we are, and what we plan to do. Well, sorry to say, you're not going to find out all that just yet, but I will tell you that we know who you are. You are Lorrie Dean LeMay. So you just be studying what that might mean while we cruise along. Think about it real hard, now, because there's coming a time when we will ask one Lorrie Dean LeMay for her help on something."

Lorrie Dean didn't respond, but she knew the score the instant they said her name and urged her to think about it. It was clear to her at once that these men would hold her hostage until they got what they wanted.

I've got news for you guys. There's no way I will ever reveal my mother's hiding place. It's my own fault that I'm in this situation. You thugs wouldn't even have had this opportunity if I hadn't abandoned my parents to seek adventure, to find out what was driving the man who was so desperately searching for me. Little did I know that I would fall in love with the finest man I've ever known. I didn't set out to have it turn out that way, but as it happened, I was jeopardizing my parents to find a dream. Stupid me.

Suddenly she froze. The full reality of her predicament hit her like a load of dirt. *I'm in a no-win position,* she thought. *I can tell them what they want to know, or I can refuse. Either way, I will die.*

Sickness hit her stomach. Her whole body tightened up like a fist. Then she began to tremble inside and tensed every muscle to keep it from showing She flinched at the sound of the driver's voice.

"Oh, by the way, my lady," said the driver, "I guess we can tell you our first names now, since we may all be together for a while." He chuckled and nudged the man next to him, who laughed with him. "I'm Frank, and the guy beside me is Tom, and with you back there is your long-time traveling companion, Bill." All three giggled like silly boys at a girl's birthday party.

Yeah, right, thought Lorrie Dean. *How convenient that all three of you have dated, one-syllable names, and how coincidental that you're all in the same place at the same time. Nice to meet you, Frank, Tom, and Bill.* She said nothing.

They were traveling down the little country road at about half their earlier speed. The kidnappers glanced at each other a few times and also remained quiet. Soon they came to an intersection and made a right turn onto a highway. At that point, the driver, the one calling himself Frank, mumbled something about heading toward I-20, the interstate.

For the first time in her life, Lorrie Dean wanted to cry aloud. She wanted to let it all out, to weep for her mother and dad and her sweetheart and her dear friend, but she knew she absolutely couldn't afford to. That would make the victory all too easy for the three thugs. But the struggle to contain it was staggering. The emotion welling inside her was almost out of control, tensing every muscle and fiber in her body and painfully straining her throat. She stiffened to keep from trembling, but that wasn't working, so she decided to pray: *Dear God, please watch over Andy, my sweetheart, and Kelly, my precious friend, and Mom and Dad. Give them courage and keep them well forever, I pray.*

As they eased along the new highway, the two guys in front—Frank and Tom, right?—started mumbling to each other something unintelligible about who was going to get the "stuff," whatever that meant. This mundane chatter went on for about ten minutes. Finally, Frank raised his voice and grumbled, "Forget it; we'll both go."

Lorrie Dean glanced at her watch from time to time, mentally trying to convert time into miles. When they came to the interstate, they ignored it and proceeded through the underpass where they picked up another highway that seemed to be heading back into the country. Then they turned onto a very narrow deserted road and proceeded into the woods. In about fifteen minutes, they slowed almost to a stop and headed left onto a dirt road, barely wide enough for one car. It was very winding and bumpy, and they seemed to be traveling at only about fifteen miles an hour. Again, Lorrie Dean was counting the minutes. This phase of the travel seemed interminable. All the while, nobody was talking. After about an hour and fifteen minutes, they came to an old, obviously abandoned, two-story frame house, which Lorrie Dean calculated must have been about five miles off the highway.

She preceded her three captors into the house at their command. As she entered, she glanced all around, taking in details she might need to recall at some crucial moment. Overall, the house appeared remarkably well maintained considering its remote location and the obvious absence of permanent tenants. They were in a large, formal living room with an unusually high ceiling and papered walls that angled at each of the four corners. Two doors opened at the back wall, one apparently leading to a hallway that predictably contained stairs to the upper floor. Furnishings were sparse—one long couch, one upholstered and one straight-back chair, and a short, square table shoved against one wall. There were no decorations at all—no wall plaques, no pictures, no adornments that would normally give a house personality.

"Sit in this chair," said Frank, touching the straight-back.

Lorrie Dean glanced toward the other, clearly more comfortable, seat but did as ordered. She winced as she settled into the wooden chair, for it was hard and she was stiff and road weary.

"Want to tie her up, Bill, while we're still here?"

Lorrie Dean gasped at the thought and stiffened as the man they called Bill hunkered down and handcuffed her ankles together. She kept staring down at them after he got up and even as they continued talking to her. *What would Kelly do? What would Andy do?* At this point, she could faintly hear Frank's voice. She could tell he was jabbering some kind of mischief, but it sounded far away. She was still thinking of her Andy, as if in a dream, while Frank's voice floated in the air around her. His words just sounded like they were blowing in the wind. Suddenly, his voice erupted and shattered her dream.

"So, Lorrie Dean LeMay," snarled Frank, emphasizing her full name, "how long you stay here is entirely in your hands. Tom and I have an errand to run before we get down to business. It may take us a couple of days, but we're leaving you in the able hands of Mr. Bill and his dependable .45. Just hope it doesn't go off in your direction."

Lorrie Dean nodded lightly, holding firmly to her trademark composure and noncommittal expression.

"Are you understanding me?" asked the boss man, somewhat angrily.

"Yes," said Lorrie Dean, and the two men turned and strutted out the front door.

"Well," said the guard, as he pulled the better chair around so it faced Lorrie Dean, "it's just us now. Woo-hoo, huh?"

Lorrie Dean nodded.

"Listen, young lady, I don't know what your game is, but it's not gonna get you anywhere if you play close-mouthed all the time. That won't cut it, and you'll lose quicker that way. So you better open up and save yourself some real trouble and, I might add, much pain."

"I understand. Surely you must know that I'm frightened, and it's very hard for me to talk or think or do anything. I'm at your mercy, and I know it. Also, I've never been one who talks very much."

"Yeah, right. Aren't you even curious what . . . err . . . Frank and Tom have headed out to do?"

"Of course." She dropped it at that. It would be illogical for her to feign indifference, yet she would not press the matter. She was consumed with curiosity about their mission, but disclosing strong interest in that issue might leave the impression that she would be easy prey.

"Well, okay, have it your way—for now." He leaned way forward in his chair toward Lorrie Dean, smiling awkwardly, and drawled, "Hello there, y'all, my name's Bill, and I'll be your guard for the evening. Just let me know if you need anything."

"Cute."

"Uh-oh, little shut-mouth is a smarty pants."

Lorrie Dean said nothing, and her guard let it go and fell silent, himself, for a while. Finally, Lorrie Dean decided she would begin a campaign to distract Mr. Bill from his commitment and perhaps lead him to some doubts about their situation. When she cleared her throat, he looked up, and she spoke matter-of-factly, her voice deliberately denying any intonation that might reflect judgment. "So, Bill, is this a pretty good life for you?"

"It's the best. What do you care?"

She shrugged. "Just curious. I mean, you don't look all that comfortable to me."

"Again, what's it to you?"

"Okay, I withdraw the question."

"Don't think I'm stupid, old girl. You don't see *me* tied down in a chair. So I happen to know what you're trying to do. You think you can get cozy and throw me off . . . weaken my devotion so I might make a mistake. So there! Am I smart or what?"

"You are. But be assured, that's not what I'm trying to do. It's just that, to me, you look out of place in this drama. So I was just wondering, that's all. Forget it. I'll shut up."

"I've never felt more sure of anything in my life. This is the best."

"Okay."

"Okay? That's it? Okay? Surely you got something else to say."

Lorrie Dean shook her head and said no more. *It's working,* she thought.

"So what makes you think I look out of place?"

"Oh, it's just that . . . well, you don't seem quite as tough as your two pals."

"Tough?" he shouted. "You want 'tough.' I'll show you 'tough.' You mess with me and I'll knock you out of that chair and tell them you tried to get away. And while you're down, I'll beat the hell out of you. Look at my eyes. Still think I'm not tough?"

"No, you just convinced me. I'll give you no trouble."

"So with all that cleared up," he snarled, "what do you now think I am?"

16

"A jerk." *Oh boy, wish I could get that one back.*

Bill, supertough guard that he was, cocked his head and drilled his eyes straight into her, scowling. His brow was wrinkled, and she could see the pulse pounding in his neck. He held it that way for a few moments. Then he pooched out his lips and frowned as if he'd just swallowed a wooly worm and slowly settled back in his chair. He dropped his contemptuous expression and whispered, "That didn't work either, my dear."

She decided to let him have the final word. This was the politically correct thing to do, considering her predicament, she thought. Even though he was making his case, she had been successful in causing him to defend his choices in life. He could have dropped the matter in the very beginning when she did, but he continued to toss out little excuses. *Surely,* she thought, *I have aroused some doubts.*

Darkness had now settled over the old house like a heavy blanket. Lorrie Dean shivered at the eerie mood gathering around her. The night seemed so dominating and scary. There was only one dim source of light in the house—a lamp on the table across the room. Lorrie Dean was beginning to wrestle with the question of when, where, and in what position she would be sleeping that night. Also, she was worrying about getting stiff, since she had been sitting for several hours. She needed to stay in shape for any possible—though at this point, unlikely—opportunity to run. She had to find a way to exercise without it being conspicuous. She forced a loud cough, and Mr. Bill looked up.

"You still here," he mocked, snickering like an idiot.

"I need to go to the bathroom."

"You gonna take a bath, darling?"

"I have to pee."

"Let's see if I can find a bucket for you."

Oops! She didn't answer. But for some reason, he didn't move out of his chair. Perhaps he was afraid the problem was too big for him to solve with a bucket.

"Okay, my young captive." He picked up the pistol leaning against his foot and pointed it at her. "Surely you know you'll be shot dead in your tracks if you try anything. See, darlin', I hold the high card here. This buddy of mine here, this Colt .45, is loaded, cocked, and ready to fire all the time."

"Absolutely, I know there's no chance for me to do anything. Please, I just want to pee; it's been about fifteen hours, and I'm about to explode."

Pistol still in hand, he stood up, fished a key out of his pocket, and walked up to her chair. He handed her the key. "Unlock your ankle cuffs while I hold the gun to your head!"

She did as told and handed him the key. There was no use resisting that obvious requirement. Besides, returning it so promptly would show continued subordination, giving him nothing to be concerned about. From this point on, she would try to establish a track record of cooperation that should make future requests easier for her.

"Now stand up, turn half right, and start walking toward that wall. Go slow and when you get to the door, stop."

"Ouch." She was indeed stiff, much more so than she had predicted. Walking was grueling, but she trudged on. She stopped at the door. "Now what?"

He stepped right up to her, the gun actually touching her back. "Walk through the door slowly and turn left, then head for the door in the middle of the hall."

Inside the small toilet, Lorrie Dean held herself high above the bowl, so her captor could hear the sound of pummeling water, thus legitimatizing her request. In a few moments, she called out, "Wait a second, I have to do more." She began doing knee bends and then stretching her legs while she braced against the sink—all very, very quietly.

"What's going on in there?"

"Okay, I'm through." As the door opened, she deliberately adjusted her underwear by pinching through the ankle-length bridal gown. At once, Bill handcuffed her wrists, without explaining the change in procedure from ankles to hands.

Back in their chairs, Lorrie Dean asked, "Are we having something to eat tonight? It's been a long, tiring Saturday for both of us."

"Yeah, soup. Are you ready?"

"Sure, when you are."

Guard Bill made her go back to the hallway while he followed close behind. There, he opened the door to a cabinet mounted on the wall and pulled out two cans of soup. He turned to face her and popped the tabs on each. "Sorry, Your Majesty, but we don't have any dishes or spoons or anything."

"Ohhh—kay." This came as shocking news, but she swallowed hard, set her chin, and squelched the temptation to make an issue of it. She preceded Bill to their chairs at his demand. Then he unlocked the cuffs and returned them to her ankles. *How sweet and thoughtful.* "Any crackers?" she asked.

"Nope."

"Maybe an olive?"

"Nope."

When they finished eating—that is, drinking—Lorrie Dean asked, "Where will I be sleeping?"

"You're there."

"Here, in this chair?"

"Yep."

"What are you going to do?"

"I'm going to turn you facing the couch. I'm going to sleep there with the gun in my hand. It'll stay there. I've done that many times before. Not only that, Miss, I will first fix a cow bell to your chair. So, really now, try to stay quiet tonight so I can get some sleep—okay?" He chuckled and slapped his knee.

This guy is a laugh a minute, thought Lorrie Dean. Momentarily, Bill came over and affixed the bell and started toward the couch. "Wait a minute," said Lorrie Dean. "I can't sleep sitting up in a chair like this."

"Then don't sleep," he growled and fell onto the couch, holding his gun high in the air for a few seconds and then bringing it down to his side.

Lorrie Dean shook her head and then closed her eyes and began to mull over her situation. It was going to be a long, weary, frightening night. Who could sleep? Somehow, she had an absorbing sense of needing forgiveness, though she had done nothing wrong, at least not of her own volition. Still, something was working on her conscience. For now, she would try to sleep, for she had a wary sensation that, in the hours ahead, she would need every ounce of energy she could muster.

4

Young Kelly Surrat, loyal friend of Andy and Lorrie Dean, was up before dawn Sunday morning. She was the only one up at that hour. The family usually slept late on Sunday mornings because worship services at the little Tillman Baptist church didn't begin until 11:00 a.m. At the dining table, she scratched out a short note to the others, letting them know she was on her way to help her Boone Woo in Dallas. She had decided, during her near-sleepless night, that if she was to be strength for him, she needed to be at his side as he wrestled with the staggering challenges he faced.

She yawned down at the clump of French toast languishing on her plate and shook her head. She squinted at it and poked at it a few times with her fork, halfheartedly. Then she wrinkled her nose and laid down the fork as she continued to gawk at her nondescript breakfast. Finally, she picked up the fork again and raked out a few bites. The stuff was mushy and tasteless, mostly because she didn't feel like eating. She was much too sad and nervous to do anything. Besides, she had to get it on. On that thought, she pushed back from the table, grabbed her purse, and hurried away.

The ramshackle old garage, a converted tractor shed, was far enough from the house that the noise she would be making shouldn't disturb the others. She strained at the heavy door, which sagged precariously on one side and, grunting and puffing, finally got it high enough that she would be able to back out. Then she raced to the car, jumped in, cranked the engine, and turned her head half around to watch her way out. At that instant, the teetering door banged back down to the floor.

Kelly flung open the car door with the engine still running and leaped out to rescue the tumbled-down garage door. As she twisted desperately to hurtle past the open car door, her head struck the pointed, outside top edge of it. She fell to the floor, unconscious.

*   *   *

Andy's early morning trip to the federal building in Dallas yielded nothing. The office he sought was closed, but it displayed a sign, offering an emergency number. When he called the number, he learned they had no information on the matter. Later, he learned that the FBI had no word on the subject of abductors impersonating federal agents in Tillman, Texas. The police were obviously concentrating on the kidnapping aspect of the crime and hadn't informed federal authorities. His efforts to locate names of the two agents he knew, Chad Jarrigan and Terry Aylor, were also unavailing, so he headed for the little house that was to have been their castle, his and Lorrie Dean's.

As Andy passed the phone near the front door of his house, he noticed that the message light was blinking. He ignored it, for he had altogether too much to do and think about to waste time fiddling with what was very likely an unsolicited phone call. He tried again to locate a phone number for federal agent Chad Jarrigan, using AT&T's information service. No luck.

Weary and discouraged, he decided to give himself a break for a little while. He plodded into the kitchen, got a drink of water, and strolled stiffly back to the parlor where he would rest and try to think. Rarely in his life had he felt so helpless. He'd always found something he could do to solve anything, but this time, he was so overcome emotionally that he couldn't even think straight. He had taken for granted that nothing bad could ever happen to so fine a woman as Lorrie Dean, who was the epitome of grace and refinement. The memory of a childhood incident involving the two of them had driven him to search for her. When she found out about his search, she emerged and let him find her. That was an act of sheer grace, for little did she know that they would fall in love.

He rose and strolled toward the front door, where he planned to check the lock and return to his recliner. It was all coming down on him. He simply had to find a way to rest if he was to give a good fight. As he passed the blinking phone, he shook his head and pressed on. Then he hesitated; the pestering message light seemed to beckon, relentlessly. There was something eerie about this scene. It was as if the irresistible light was calling out to him, so he backed up a few steps and reached down to push the PLAY button.

*   *   *

Andy slammed his Cutlass to a jarring stop in the parking lot of Trinity Mother of Saint Frances hospital in Jacksonville, Texas, about fifteen miles from Tillman. He threw open the door and ran toward the entrance. He used only a minute to get directions from the receptionist.

Now he was looking down at his precious buddy, passed out in a hospital bed—and this grown man doubled over and cried his heart out. He didn't let it last but a few seconds and quickly clenched both fists, stretched tall, and braced up. That done, he chastised himself. *Knock it off, Andy, get straight. This time your morning light needs* your *strength.*

At that moment, Dub Grimes walked over from where he had been seated across the room, laid a hand on Andy's shoulder, and stood with him. Words could never say as much as his presence beside his friend.

When Andy finally sat down, Dub said kindly, "You were really cryin' for *two* girls, weren't you, my good friend?"

"I was indeed—yes, for Kelly and for Lorrie Dean, the two dearest people in my life. Seeing Kelly unconscious there brought the whole thing storming into view. You know—you know, Dub, 'cause these two extraordinary human beings are eternity for me."

Andy and Dub fell silent and just let the moment have full sway. Every now and then, they would look at each other and nod, each accepting that there was nothing to say. Andy made frequent trips to Kelly's bedside, each time whispering "I love you" and pulling away, praying privately for his sweet girls. In a while, a couple of young men came in and Dub stood to greet them and called them by name, saying, "God bless you. Thank you for coming."

When Andy stood, Dub introduced the two farmhands, Rick Gonzales and Sol Millick. As the two men moved solemnly toward Kelly's bed, Dub said to Andy, "Rick is the one who found Kelly passed out in the garage. He was headed for the henhouse to gather eggs—you know, we share eggs and vegetables with them. Anyway, this fine man flat jumped into action. First, he turned off the engine, and then he picked up Kelly and carried her, runnin' dead tilt all the way to the house. We took over from there, but Rick hung around for, as he put it, 'any way I can help Miss Kelly.'"

Andy got up, walked over to Rick Gonzales, and touched his arm. Then he reached out to shake hands. As they gripped strongly, Andy said, "Thanks, Rick. We owe you big-time." Rick smiled timidly and nodded.

The young men stayed for two hours and left out about 6:00 p.m., pledging to return. Dub and Andy thanked them again. A few minutes later, Dub looked at his watch and said, "I thought surely the doctor would have come in by now, but it's lookin' like it may be late tonight before he makes it here. Andy, I guess I better mosey on back. You want to come on out to the house and have some supper?"

"Thanks, Dub. I'll just grab something out of a vending machine or somewhere. Thanks again."

Dub nodded. "I fully understand, Andy. Are you plannin' to stay late?"

"All night," said Andy.

Dub nodded agreeably and drawled, "See ya, buddy." He turned to move on and then stopped abruptly. "Oh, by the way, just so you'll know, I called my sister, Rosalea—you know, Kelly's mother. We're not really speaking, but I thought she ought to know. After all, she is the mother, no matter what." He turned and walked out briskly.

For a moment, Andy thought back to that day, weeks ago, when Dub talked to him privately about Kelly's heartbreaking situation. He said that after her parents divorced, the dad sailed off to work at some dinky little job in Europe, and her mother started asking around for anybody in the family who would take Kelly. Grandpa, father-in-law of Dub's sister (Kelly's mom) reached out to Kelly and eventually adopted her legally. Dub said that the mother refused to explain her actions to anybody. *Why so secretive?* thought Andy. *How could any mother give up this little jewel? How could anyone not want her?*

Andy was shaking his head in anguish as he pulled a chair right up to Kelly's bed and made ready to spend the night there—with her. There was nothing he could add to what the police were already doing on this Sunday night in the search for Lorrie Dean.

At about nine thirty, a physician came in, walked straight to Kelly's bed, looked closely at her, smiled at Andy, and said, "Mr. Grimes?"

"No sir, Dub Grimes went home about six. I'm Andy Boone, and thanks for coming in."

"Sure," said the doctor, "I'm Louis Landly. You her dad?"

"No, I would be honored if I were. She is just my dearest friend in all the world. Dr. Landly, Kelly Surrat is my morning light."

"And lucky she is to have you."

"Thanks."

23

Andy moved his chair back and remained standing. Dr. Landly studied Kelly for a long time, checking her pulse, listening to her heart, and once, touching her eyelids.

"Is she going to come out of it, doctor?"

"She should." He turned to face Andy and offered, "If you'd like, I'll explain a little about where we are."

"Oh, thank you Doctor Landly. I would really appreciate that."

"Okay. The thing is, as you probably know, she was subjected to carbon monoxide poisoning, and she took a pretty hard blow to the head. Although it doesn't present a very visible injury, it was the concussion aspect of it that's causing trouble."

Andy was squirming and struggling to keep from breaking down again. The doctor seemed to recognize this and paused for a bit while Andy regained a measure of composure, slight as it was.

"Sure, she has suffered some denial of oxygen to her brain," the doctor continued, "but I really don't think it was for a critically long period. We're pretty confident there won't be any brain damage. And actually"—he paused, wrinkling his brow—"she really should be coming out of the coma by now. We'll just have to watch her."

"That helps a lot, doctor. Thanks for taking the time to explain it." Andy smiled and said cheerfully, "I'm glad her brain is going to be okay because this young lady may well have the best brain in the world—and the biggest heart."

"Well, it's going to help that she has someone who cares for her as much as you obviously do."

"Thanks. She has a great support group in her corner."

"Glad to hear it. Take care, Andy."

"Good night, doctor."

Andy had dared not leave the room lest he miss the doctor's visit. At this point, he felt it was late enough that he probably shouldn't be eating anything. Still, he had a tiny hunger and so argued with himself that surely a little nibble wouldn't upset his metabolism or keep him awake during the night. For that matter, he didn't predict that he would get much sleep anyway. Sleep was not the priority! So, he slipped away briefly and got some cheese crackers and a Snickers from the vending machines.

Back in the room, he stood for a few minutes, watching his buddy sleep. In a while, he found a pillow in the closet, dropped it in the seat of his chair and pulled it up to her bed. Then he lowered himself into the cushioned chair, leaned in, and laid his head on the bed. He was just dozing off when a nurse came in. As he raised his head, she apologized for disturbing him.

"Oh, not at all," said Andy. "I'm glad you came in."

The nurse looked at Kelly for a while, just as the doctor had done. *What can they tell from just looking?* wondered Andy. She continued to just stand there, looking at her patient. Andy studied her facial expression the whole time she stared, hoping for a sign of what she was thinking. There was nothing there. She deftly checked the IV and oxygen and the small bandage on Kelly's forehead and then shifted her shoulders around a little. Finally the nurse stood up straight and continued to look at her patient before turning toward Andy and asking, "Has she moved at all since you've been here?"

"Not at all."

"You didn't notice her eyelids twitch or try to move, even if just slightly?"

"No. I've noticed not a glimmer of anything going on in her that shows life except, praise God, she's breathing."

"I see." She looked at Kelly again and then hesitantly turned toward the door, wrinkled her brow, and said, "But she will. We just don't know when." With that, she breezed out of the room.

Andy reclaimed his place at the bedside, rested his head on it as before, and closed his eyes. Now his mind was filled again with thoughts and pictures of Lorrie Dean. He felt totally powerless in finding a way to rescue her. But he absolutely had to. He couldn't just leave it in the hands of the police, able as they were. He had to be a factor in finding his beloved wife. Now his thoughts were getting hazy and not making much sense.

Andy awoke and resumed worrying consciously. He glanced at the clock and winced from the sudden zing of a crick in his neck. It was two o'clock Monday morning. He shouldn't be sleeping anyway. His girls needed him, and he needed to be awake and alert to any development calling for his help. He gazed at his little comatose buddy, doubled his fists, and swallowed so hard it pinched his throat. Then it hit him! There was something he *could* do for his buddy and his wife. "Why did it take me so long?" he whispered to Kelly.

He had made a decision. At the nurse's station, he explained that he would be away for about an hour. He walked confidently out of the building and strolled to his car, got in, and drove away.

Andy slowed as he approached the little Baptist church in Tillman. It was, of course, deserted. A couple of cars sat in the parking spaces, but he figured they stayed there day and night. He parked and ambled toward the front steps, ever so slowly. At the door, just under the awning, Andy knelt, lifted praying hands to his chin, and prayed aloud in the dark:

"Oh divine Lord, I know you listen to prayers, that you are merciful, and that you love me and that you love all others. And I know you're watching over Kelly and Lorrie Dean. Please, Lord, hear me praying.

"I pray that you will be with Lorrie Dean wherever she is and that she feels your presence with her. Help her to stay clear of mind and be able to think straight, scared as she is. Protect her from the evil of those who would harm her. Help her to find that one chance you hold out to her for escaping. Please give her also the strength, energy, skill, and soundness of mind to defeat her captors. If she gets a chance to run, Lord, please run every step with her.

"And, oh Lord, by your own will, may the will you've given Kelly rise up within her and thrust her back to conscious living. We need her. The world is so much better with Kelly in it. She teaches so much by the way she lives, overcoming cruel and merciless abuse without bitterness and with her head held high. Reach to her with your healing grace and bless those who minister to her. Save her sharp mind and kind heart and lift her up to fullness again, I pray. Please have mercy on Kelly and awaken her.

"For me, oh Lord, I pray, please help me to serve. Help me to find ways to attend these two beautiful souls I love so dearly. And finally, please know I pray all these things humbly and with trust in you. Thy will be done."

As Andy drifted toward his car, he glanced back at the church from time to time. In a moment, he eased into the driver's seat, gently pulled the door closed, and slumped over the steering wheel for a few minutes before leaving.

Back at the hospital, Andy greeted the two people at the nurse's station and proceeded to Kelly's room.

Kelly still lay perfectly motionless except for the faint, rhythmic rise of her chest. Andy resumed his watch at her bedside and prepared to relax, using her bed as his pillow, as before. At once, something caught his eye, or he thought it did. For one instant, he thought he detected a slight movement in her eyelids. He stared straight at them for a long time, but it didn't happen again—if indeed, it had happened at all.

He took a long, deep, cleansing breath and as it faded it appeared to him that Kelly had taken a breath by her own will. It was very brief, but it was spontaneous, and there was a faint change in the sound of her inhaling as if she had actually reached for a breath beyond her reflexive breathing.

Andy continued to watch his dear friend, his morning light, but failed to see a repeat of the movements he thought he had witnessed. Perhaps it was just his imagination, born of his prayerful hope that these signs of conscious life would show up that night. After a good half hour of waiting and watching for the miracle, Andy dropped his head and closed his eyes. *Good night, little buddy.*

5

The grim clang of a cowbell shook Lorrie Dean from a night of faltering sleep. When her eyes popped open, she was stunned by the sight of her guard jiggling the leg of her chair. *Bastard.*

"Soup time," he blurted, over a dumb-looking grin.

"Do we have to?"

"Hey, girl, that's up to you. For me, I choose not to starve."

"See what you mean," she conceded, calmly. At some point in her restless night, she had made what she hoped was a strategic decision to change her style. During one of those fitful periods, when she sat helplessly awake while her mind raced, it came to her that *smart girl* wasn't working and that *sweet girl* might play out better with her goofy guard.

"Okay, you know the routine," said Bill as he handed her the key to the cuffs. "Get loose and go ahead of me to the big hall."

"Okay, I got you," said Lorrie Dean amiably.

Shortly they were in the hall. While Bill was fumbling around in the cabinet, Lorrie Dean surveyed the area as fully as possible, mentally logging in everything about it, noting particularly the one lone window. This was working well, as Bill seemed to be having trouble transacting what should have been the simple little task of retrieving two cans of soup. He was frowning when finally he drew out a couple of cans.

Back at the fort, during their so-called breakfast, Lorrie Dean chuckled merrily and said, "I don't know about you, Bill, but right now I'd walk a mile on my hands for a cracker."

Uncharacteristically he chuckled and said, "No joke." Then he stared down at his can and started shaking his head. "Damn that son of a bitch! He could have left us something at least to make a sandwich with. I'm like you. I'd kill a cow for a hamburger right now."

"Really," agreed Lorrie Dean. Then, yawning and stretching, she said, "I'm so tired; could I sleep in a real bed if you still have me here tonight?"

"No real beds around here. There's nothing upstairs but old barn wood and other rubbish. And, don't you worry, you'll still be here at least until tomorrow, maybe even most of Tuesday. Then it's up to Frank. But get ready; he's going to be asking you for something that only you know."

"Well, I'll try to cooperate. I just wonder why they didn't already ask me."

"They want the stuff here in case you present a problem."

"I'm generally not a problem, but what's this thing about stuff? What stuff?"

"Well, let's just say it's the latest generation in a certain line of special devices designed to help people cooperate." He giggled and said, "But ask me no more!" With that, he looked away, staring vaguely across the big room.

What a bomb! Yet, it was no more than she had expected. Clearly, they were gathering torture devices to force her into disclosing her mother's hideaway. But they were in for a huge surprise, because there was absolutely no way they could ever inflict torture brutal enough to make her betray her mom and dad. *I'll die first. Please hear my prayer, dear Lord. Help me think; help me find a way to get away from here, because I don't want to die. Please, dear Lord. But if it is your will, then I pray let my Andy find someone else and be happy. No one in this whole wide world deserves a good, love-filled life more than he does. And my dear buddy, Kelly, may she have peace, goodness, and good will in all her life. And bless forever Mom and Dad. Praise thee in all things.*

While her captor was reading a magazine he had fished out from under the couch, she continued to search her mind for inspiration in scheming a way to escape.

Time's running out. I have to do something. If I have to give myself up, I will. I cannot continue being who I am and stay alive. I have to give up those things Andy so admired in me. So, good-bye grace and poise—good-bye Lorrie Dean. There will never be you again.

I'm so afraid. Oh, no! Please, please God! I'm getting hysterical. I feel the trembling, and I can't let him see it, but I can't stop it. All I can do is pray. Maybe a little forced yawning will trick me into feeling sleepy.

*   *   *

"You've really been conked out, old girl."

Lorrie Dean awoke at the sudden intrusion of a man's voice. "Oh, I guess so."

"Yeah, you've been out for about three hours."

"I guess I needed it."

"Anyway, it's time for dinn-dinn. Here's the key, let's get it on."

After a couple of choking swallows from her can, Lorrie Dean grumbled, "You know, this really isn't soup we've been having. Actually it's just broth."

For some reason what she thought was a little innocuous observation hit him the wrong way, possibly because he was still ticked off that the guys hadn't left him something decent to eat. He lurched forward in his big chair, drilling his eyes right at her nose, pointed a shaking finger at her, and stormed, "You start bitching, and I'll flat take you out of the play. You get it?"

She nodded. Normally under her new style, she would have said "Sorry," but something about the change of mood there in her prison suggested it might be time to make another adjustment. But right then was probably not the right time.

*   *   *

And so it went for another day. The rest of Sunday pretty well followed the pattern of Saturday afternoon—more soup and other discomforts, griping about her restroom needs and a cowbell for a good night's sleep. Then it was Monday morning and that, too, fell into the same miserable routine.

This is it, thought Lorrie Dean. *Time for another change of strategy.* She would have to become competitive instead of cooperative. The innocent, nice-girl approach had served its purpose. Although it had been appropriate at the time, the situation had become very tenuous and demanded an all-out campaign to level the playing field. A little taunting might even be in order. "So, how much soup we got left, Bill?"

"What's that supposed to mean?"

"Well, you know, you seem as annoyed about it as I am."

"Just be glad we're feeding you at all."

"That makes you pretty proud of yourself, doesn't it?"

"I don't need that to be proud. I'm great, and I know it. And listen; don't go getting sarcastic with me. I'm warning you."

"Really, now. Are you all that sure of yourself?"

"Of course, and there you go again. I just got through warning you not to mess with me."

"Okay, okay. It's just that you don't *look* all that confident."

"Don't kid yourself. You're the one acting superior—right from the beginning. You try to act so sure of yourself."

"Well, as a matter of fact, I'm fully confident in my self-image."

"You're conceited, that's all."

"And what are you?"

He got up and took two long strides to reach her and poked his face right down into hers. "I'm mean, and I'm strong, and I don't put up with anything. Know why? By damn, 'cause I don't have to." He continued to snarl and breathe his hot breath over her face for a while. Finally he just grinned like a clown, shuffled around in front of her a few times, and strutted back to his chair.

Lorrie Dean just smiled and said nothing. She felt that was a better form of aggression than some smart, insulting retort.

Mr. Bill also fell quiet, but it was evident that he was working on something in his head. His expression seemed to reflect that he was plotting something. Finally he lifted his chin and looked straight at her. "You ever been raped?"

Lorrie Dean cringed and then laughed.

"Funny, huh? Well, my dear, you didn't answer the question. Have . . . you . . . ever . . . been . . . raped?"

"It's never been necessary."

"Oh, so you're that easy, huh?"

"No, I just have my man, that's all."

*   *   *

That night, after soup and while-away time, the guard started hustling around getting his couch ready for bedtime. In light of their contentious afternoon, it came as a major surprise when he asked, "Would you be more comfortable sleeping on the floor tonight, you know, lying down instead of sitting up in that hard chair?"

Lorrie Dean instantly smelled a rat. "Oh, that's okay, I've gotten used to it now."

He bounded over to her and snarled, "Well, I want you sleeping on the floor." He grabbed her arm, pulled her up to him, and kept squeezing all the way to the bone.

"Oh, oh, you're hurting me. Please."

"So, get down on the floor."

"No, I can't. I'll be all right like before," she pleaded, scared to her gut.

"This is your last chance. Now lie down on the floor with your feet facing the couch."

"No!"

In a split second, he slung her around and slammed a fist into the side of her neck so hard she fell to the floor, banging her head on a leg of the couch. Instantly, he dropped down beside her, pounded her in the stomach and dragged her body around on the floor until her feet were at the couch. She was gasping for breath and writhing with pain in her head and neck as he shackled her left ankle to a leg of the couch. Then he was on top of her. At once, he bounced up and dropped his pants. Then he was back, lifting her gown up to her head while she pleaded and wailed. Then he was in, and all the while he executed, he was wadding her hair in his hot hand and pulling it around over her head. Then he heaved, and it was over.

While tears washed down her face, he stood over her. She could not see his expression through the tears, but his posture seemed to signal less than full confidence in what he had just done. In a moment, he turned slowly and strolled over to the hard chair.

Lorrie Dean prayed that she would go to sleep, and so she did.

*   *   *

She awoke at dawn the next morning, Tuesday, the third day since her busted wedding, and the target day for the return of the hoodlums with their torture machines. She pleaded with her guard to skip soup hour and was given that privilege. The floor was wet around her head where tears had settled. In a while, she asked if she could go to the restroom.

As they came into the hall, a cell phone began ringing. Her escort grabbed the phone from a nearby wall shelf and answered.

"Yeah," he said. "Fine, but why the hell didn't you leave me with something besides that blasted soup?" He paused, obviously listening to a long, drawn-out speech. "Okay, we'll be ready." He hung up and returned the phone to its shelf. Then he pushed his gun into her ribs and motioned her to the restroom door.

Inside, she limbered up again as she had done every other time she had been privileged to visit this private little cell. Oh, how it hurt where he had pounded her stomach, and the pain in her head was getting worse instead of better.

"Let's go in there!" yelled the guard.

He was standing a ways back when she opened the door, and as she emerged, he motioned her toward him.

As she stepped up to him, she glanced at the far window and gasped. In that instant, the guard, too, spun his head in that direction. When he did, he placed his ear directly in front of her mouth, and into that ear, Lorrie Dean LeMay hurled the loudest, the wildest, the most bloodcurdling scream possible for human lungs.

He lurched backward, waving his arms to keep from falling, and she rammed a determined knee into his groin—twice. The gun fell to the floor, and as he scrambled to reach it, she let him have one more, from behind, for good measure, and he tumbled forward.

Lorrie Dean grabbed the gun and the phone and turned to run as her adversary sprang awkwardly toward her. When he did, she shot his right knee. He crumbled to the floor, bellowing, but managed to rise up again. She could feel him lurching along behind her, cursing and gibbering nonsense. Then she slowed, deliberately taunting his pursuit. She swung open the front door with him close to her heels, and as she started through it, she turned and fired again, blasting his other knee. He fell into the open door and strained his wobbling head back over his shoulders to watch her begin her getaway.

She ran with every ounce of grit she could manage, burdened with a gun in one hand and a cell phone in the other. It was painful and extremely difficult to run in high heels, but she recalled hearing of high-heel marathon racers who did it by lifting up on their toes. It worked somewhat, but it was wearing her down fast. Fortunately, her wedding gown was just an ankle-length dress and not a factor in her speed. She was counting on her ex-guard watching her disappear down the dirt road that had brought them in. In a while, she came to a curve and after she was a ways into it, she looked back to ensure that she wouldn't be visible from the house. Satisfied, she turned and ran into the woods.

The plan was in motion. Lorrie Dean was making her way through the woods back toward the house from which she had just escaped. She remembered a conversation once with Kelly in which it came out that sometimes you have to move toward danger in order to escape it. She figured the house was the one place they would never think to look for her. *Oh, for a pair of old jeans and some tennis shoes,* she thought. It would take a while to work back to the house, because navigation was trickier through the dense woods and also because she was out of gas. She felt that she had not an ounce of energy left. Her head was throbbing, and it felt like a spear in her stomach, but she trudged on, still carrying the gun and phone.

In a while, she simply had nothing left, so she sat down on a log covered with fungus and began to catch her breath. Then she whispered to the woods, "Andy, please find me again."

As she rested on the merciful, old, fallen tree, she stared at the gun, shaking her head in disbelief. *I can't believe I did that.* After she reset what she hoped was the safety, she rested her chin on praying hands and whispered, "Thank you, O Lord, for giving me the chance and the energy to escape, and, Lord, thank you for rest."

After pausing for a while, she began to stumble on through the dense woodland, she hoped toward the old house that, though seemingly neutral, had held her prisoner for four days.

Something's wrong here, she thought. *I can't believe I ran so far away from the house. God, I hope I'm not lost. Have I misjudged that curve where I left the road? Maybe it took me farther into the woods than I thought.*

Lorrie Dean adjusted her course, and a half hour later, still dragging along, she sensed that the house was nearby. Indeed, she was there. As she peered through thick, vine-tangled underbrush, she studied the structure in detail—the walls, the doors and windows, and especially, the cone of the roof, which revealed the top of a central chimney rising from the back side. It was now time to make her 911 call. She had deliberately delayed doing so until she felt safely located fully outside the predictable search area. As she palmed the phone and keyed the numbers, it beeped and warned of a low battery. *Oh no!* She hung up instantly, so she could create a brief message to transmit in a hurry and beat the batteries to the finish. In a couple of minutes, she keyed the numbers again.

"Nine one one."

"Hurry—hostage bride—about 65 east—ask the morning light!" Ten quick words stood between Lorrie Dean and her rescue.

In the next moment, she heard a car coming up the road. Seconds later, she saw it rumble up to the front door. Out of it scrambled Frank and Tom.

"What the hell!" shouted Frank. "What's going on, Jarred?"

"Help me, Mason! The bitch shot me! Hurry, hurry, hurry!"

Frank—or rather, Mason—and the other man raced to the door. "My God, you dumb son of a bitch, you can't even guard a helpless woman. Which way did she go?"

As best as she could make it out, Bill, alias Jarred, was rocking his head up and down as if pointing down the road with his chin.

"Sorry, but we gotta go," said Mason. "Help me drag him to the couch, Sidney!"

Lorrie Dean sighed with relief as the two men raced out of the house, slamming the front door, jumped in the car, and sped away, leaving poor Jarred to his endless cursing and insane jabbering. As distressing as it was to do, she took a moment to whisper, "Dear Lord, bless that man, and I'm sorry, Lord. Please forgive me, because I really don't feel like saying that."

Now was the hour. It was time to carry out the final phase of her escape plan, the part she was counting on to deliver her rescue. Lorrie Dean moved along the edge of the woods to a point near the back corner of the house where she once noticed a sagging door that would no longer close completely. It was there. She eased into the side yard, looking in all directions. Then she crouched to the ground and crawled to the door. She waited patiently, listening for any sound of Bill/Jarred moving around, although she was virtually positive that he would not be mobile for a long time.

Lorrie Dean continued to wait and listen. This was no time to rush things. After a while, she tugged gently on the door, sorely afraid that it would squeak. Mercifully, it did not. She tucked the cell phone in her bra, pulled off her shoes, and, ever so slowly, crept into the familiar hallway that, among other things, opened to the stairs. She eased the door shut and, taking slow, short steps, padded toward the stairwell.

On the stairs, Lorrie Dean paused after every step to avoid creating a rhythmic sound that would suggest the actual movement of a person. After she reached the upper floor, she tiptoed around the piles of junk and soon found a transit to the loft. She held her breath, hoping against hope that what she predicted would be there would in fact show up. Then she caught her breath. *Thank you, merciful Lord.* Her experiences at Kelly's farmhouse had taught her that these routes were possible in old estate homes. She crawled through the small gable opening onto the roof, slithered up to the chimney, and prepared to wait it out.

b

Andy's eyes opened gradually, and he lifted his head to look at Kelly. Disappointment smothered him. She was the same. Nothing was going on except the involuntary processes of staying alive. He sat back in his chair, prayed briefly, and moved out of the way as nurses and housekeepers hustled in and out. It was almost nine o'clock Monday morning.

The day was to be uneventful except for Andy's irritating call to his boss and the brief visit of Dub and Mom, during which time he rushed to the cafeteria for a quick lunch. The two farm visitors didn't stay long because nothing was happening with Kelly.

While out for lunch, Andy called the Employee Relations Division at Clay Cutter Industries, his employer. After he had been on hold for ten minutes, his boss and former adversary, Kirk Daniels, answered.

"What's up?" barked Daniels.

"Hey, boss. Well, a tragedy struck me Saturday. Maybe you've heard about it. Paige was there—at the wedding, that is. Anyway, my wife was kidnapped Saturday just at the end of our wedding ceremony." Andy paused for Kirk's sympathetic response.

"So?"

Damn, thought Andy, *how callous can you be?* "Well, I also have a very dear friend lying in a coma at a hospital in Jacksonville. The whole thing is, Kirk, I need the week off. May I have a week of vacation time?"

"Andy, this is sudden, and sure, go ahead and take the day, but I don't think we can give you the week."

"Come on, Kirk. What's the big deal? I'm not at a critical point in any of my projects."

"Well, you just haven't been here long enough to qualify for that much unscheduled leave. Sorry, buddy."

"I can't believe you came out with that, Kirk. My leave time accrues with the company, not the local office. I already had a week accrued before I was selected for the job here, and even so, I've been here in the region for four months. So, what the hell are you talking about?"

"Settle down, Andy. The point is that Wade Boliver, you know, the director, retains personal authority in your case."

"Okay, boss, okay. Just tell his Honor, Wade, that it might appear pretty cruel and trivial for this reputable company to deny one of its employees a week of leave after his wife is kidnapped."

"Okay, Andy, take the day, and I'll get with Wade. Call me this afternoon."

"Right," said Andy as he hung up, mouthing, "Shithead."

That was the scintillating highlight of the day. After Dub and Mom left, Andy rested in his chair at Kelly's bedside for the rest of the afternoon. She didn't stir. He was now certain that the brief episode when he thought he had heard her trying to breathe voluntarily was sheer fantasy on his part. At the very tail end of the afternoon, he called his boss again as promised. It was actually gratifying to hear him say sarcastically, "Okay, Andy, Wade says take the damn week, but you better have your butt here next Monday."

And so to bed, with fervent prayers for his Kelly and Lorrie Dean. He awakened several times during the night, mostly when nurses came in, but also by reflex just to check on his buddy. He was awake to stay at seven the next morning, Tuesday, the third day after thugs had snatched his soul mate.

In a moment, Andy heard scuffling and mumbling at the door, and shortly thereafter, in walked Dub and Grandpa from the farm family. They all greeted him quietly and, while Andy backed away, his two friends paused for a few moments at Kelly's bed.

Grandpa was shaking his head. Andy knew he was deeply touched, but he was a strong man and generally philosophical about adversities. Although his faculties tended to drift in and out at times, Grandpa was characteristically very sharp. In the farm family of five singles, he was known as the professor.

The two visitors took up chairs near Andy and began to talk about what happened. At one point, Grandpa's face flushed with outright anger, and he began to reveal all he had done to the garage door that had trapped Kelly. "Andy, I was downright primitive. I know I acted like a wild, dumb animal. I beat the hell out of that door. I smashed it with a maul till my arms hurt. I hurled big rocks into it, and at one point I stupidly beat on it with my bare hands. Finally, it was smashed to smithereens and I just sat down in the middle of the rubble and cried. We are going to hire somebody to professionally install a new door."

Dub was just shaking his head as Grandpa confessed his sins. Then he lifted a finger toward Andy and said, "You won't believe this one, Andy. Yesterday afternoon, I got a phone call. Guess who it was?"

"Can't imagine," said Andy, trying to grin.

"Andy, it was Rosalea, my sister. She hasn't taken the initiative to call me in three years."

"Wow! What prompted this unprecedented contact?"

"You ready?"

"Yeah, fire away!"

"Her first words were, 'How's my baby daughter?' I said, 'Rosalea, your deserted baby daughter is still in a coma.' She said nothing and then I heard sobbing, and finally she was crying outright. She tried to talk but couldn't. I just waited. After a long time, she managed to stammer out, 'I'm sorry; good-bye!' That was it. She hung up and so did I."

"Oh my, you think the suddenly solicitous mom wants to be reinstated?"

"Don't really know what to think. But enough of that. Have you had breakfast?"

Andy shook his head and said, "That's okay."

Grandpa chimed in, "Go on down and get some breakfast, Andy; we will be here for a while."

"Okay, I'm gonna take you up on that one. See you in about, what, twenty minutes?"

"Don't hurry," Dub reassured him.

By the time Andy reached the cafeteria and smelled the hot bacon and eggs and sausage gravy, he was burning with hunger. For the brief time he was savoring hot food, he somewhat suppressed his anxiety. Somewhat.

As he was returning to Kelly's room, he saw something comically weird that made him chuckle, in spite of the somber times. When he passed the visitors' lounge, he saw two eyes peering over the top of a magazine, otherwise hiding their owner's face. It was a woman in a gaudy, loud dress. Andy snickered as he strode on toward Kelly's room.

"That was a welcome break," he chimed as he entered the room.

"Great," acknowledged a glowing Grandpa, who then whooped, "Andy, I can positively assure you Kelly is going to make it. She *will* come out of this. There is no way she can not come out of it."

"Believe me, I share your confidence, but it doesn't keep me from being scared and worried."

"Well, now wait a minute, we are also going to get your Lorrie Dean back."

Tears gathered in Andy's eyes, but he didn't cry visibly. "Yes," he blurted out. "We have to get her back for her—for herself. Right now, that's all I care about in her case—that she will live and be free and have a happy life. Please, dear God, make her free." In that moment, Andy thought of Lorrie Dean being denied freedom all of her adult life. Having to hide out under the Witness Protection Program for all those years had effectively held her captive. Now, after only a short reprieve, an outrageous kidnapping would hold her hostage for who knows how long, and, while Andy firmly believed she would be rescued, she would still be a prisoner of the horrible memories.

For a while, the visitors all remained comfortably quiet. Dub kept glancing at his watch. Finally he said, "Andy, the police in Tillman want to talk to you, the one who briefed us last Saturday after the kidnapping. He said you could call him, but he'd really like to see you."

"Okay, but I wonder what's up."

"He wouldn't tell me, but said he'd like to talk to the husband first. And Andy, we'll be here all day, if necessary. We'll watch for the doctor and get all the information we can. So, feel free to drive over to Tillman if you'd like."

Andy didn't answer right away, but rather got up and strolled to Kelly's bedside. "I'll be back soon," he said softly.

Andy was met promptly by Officer Foley at the Tillman police station. "Glad you could make it, Mr. Boone. We have some developments in your wife's kidnapping and also some questions only you can help with."

"Okay, I'm here to do whatever I can."

"Splendid. Okay, we found the initial getaway car behind a barn on the county road out there. Obviously, they changed cars so we couldn't track them. Here's the puzzling part: we found your wife's bridal hat in that car. Do you see anything significant in that?"

"No, not especially. Lorrie Dean wouldn't leave a message so indefinite as that. Knowing her, I'd say it probably was left unintentionally."

"Okay, that's the sort of thing we need to know."

Andy nodded. The remainder of their consultation covered points of procedure the police were following and a summary of what they had done so far. It was encouraging to learn that both the Jacksonville police and the Dallas police, as well as the Texas Rangers, were actively involved in the investigation. Also, Officer Foley informed Andy that the FBI had been notified, but he didn't mention Chad Jarrigan, Andy's acquaintance. Andy left with no particular sense of the progress in the matter. He was no less frightened than ever.

Back in Kelly's room, Dub and Grandpa told Andy that the doctor had come in but had no particular defining information. "He just shrugged," said Dub, "and said something like, 'She ought to be out of this by now.'"

Andy's farm friends stayed while he had lunch and left about 12:30 p.m. "Take care," they said, amiably. "We'll be back."

Still no change in Kelly. Andy remained in a chair near the wall and waited patiently. About midafternoon, a female stranger sauntered into the room. In a flash, Andy thought of the visitors' lounge spy. The loud, ugly dress looked familiar. It was a one-piece cotton thing that was way too long for a hot August day, and the flashy, orange, flowered print was shocking. The woman was well groomed otherwise, her curly blonde hair was fixed just right ("coiffured," Kelly would have said), and she had a somewhat pretty but bleak-looking face. Andy thought that, without the forsaken damn dress, she would have been downright appealing.

She glanced at Andy and then just sort of sneaked up to Kelly's bed. Andy was unable to interpret anything about her facial expression, except that it was slowly changing. After a few minutes, he could see strain in her countenance, and she had begun to bite her lip and shake her head. In a while, she looked a little toward Andy but not right at him. She seemed reluctant to make eye contact. She looked back at Kelly, who still lay completely motionless.

"Friend of the family?" asked Andy.

"Ah, from the church," she said hesitantly. She continued to stand stone still, looking bewilderingly at his buddy. In a while, the woman began shifting in place, and all at once, she turned around and stalked out of the room.

"See you, Church Lady," smirked Andy when she was beyond earshot.

Andy moved to his customary spot at Kelly's bedside. At that moment, he was strangely captured by the essence of Kelly. The vibes seemed stronger, more real. He stared at her, spellbound by this shifting presence of his beloved buddy. This time, he was positive that he wasn't imagining things. This was no aberration.

In a few moments, Andy's heart jumped, and he caught his breath. His morning light had just worked her eyelids. They remained closed, but there was definite movement in them. Then it was over, and she slept on.

Now Andy was cheering silently, rocking his arms in excitement, thoroughly animated: *Come on, Kelly, you can do it, come on, buddy, come on, come on! Go Kelly, go girl, you can do it!* Suddenly his hand flew to his mouth, and he froze.

The morning light's lips parted, and there was a slight quivering of her body as if she were struggling to say something. Then it happened, and Andy fell out of his chair. That prompted him to stay on his knees and prop his elbows on the bed, "Thank you, Lord. Oh, thank you, thank you, thank you."

Kelly had actually murmured, "Ba . . ." Andy waited. Kelly raised her head as if that would help her speak, and it came again, "Ba . . . boo . . ." She was straining to say a word, but weakness and the long sleep were weighing against her. Still she kept trying. Andy just waited, saying nothing, for he was afraid that talking to her would be distracting for her rather than encouraging.

This went on as Kelly kept trying, and Andy remained quiet. Clearly, this little miracle was not giving up. Andy leaned closer to her. Kelly was rocking her head gently as she tried to cry out. Then, ever so softly, she whimpered, "Boon . . . boo . . . Boone Woo?"

Andy touched her hair and caressed her brow and, holding his head close to hers, he said kindly, "Always—always, my morning light."

Andy saw the smile of life slowly materializing on her pretty, sweet face. Then Kelly raised her head again and started trying to talk, "Lor . . . Lor . . . Lorrie . . . Lorrie lee . . . Lorrie Dean?"

Andy was squeezing her arm gently as he replied, "We're searching and trusting in God."

Kelly lowered her head back to her pillow, looking serious.

In a while, much to Andy's grateful delight, Kelly murmured a short sentence, and a few moments later, another one. At this point, Andy began to talk with her, also in short sentences. By and by, they were actually carrying on a conversation. Admittedly, there were long intervals between short expressions, but they were having a live dialogue.

After a brief, silent period, Andy saw a full-fledged smile break across Kelly's face. He was thrilled because it was her trademark mischievous, totally disarming smile. She looked him in the eye and then stretched her smile and chortled, "Boone Woo, I'm not keeping you up, am I?"

Andy doubled over laughing. Now he had his face buried in the mattress and he was pounding on it two-fisted as he laughed fervently. That got Kelly to laughing with him. They both just carried on, laughing, while three nurses stood in the doorway applauding.

When it was over, Andy and Kelly winked at each other and grinned. Then they began to talk again, and their conversation was really beginning to flow.

Suddenly, a nurse hurried into the room, looking alarmed, and said, "Mr. Boone, there's a call for you at the desk."

"Okay," said Andy. As he walked away, he looked back over his shoulder and called out to Kelly, "Save my place!"

When he answered the phone, an urgent voice declared, "Tillman Police, Mr. Boone. We need your help quickly."

"Okay. I'll do it. Anything. Tell me!"

"A very cryptic 911 message was just relayed to us. We understand part of it and part, we don't. Listen carefully. This is what it says: Hurry—Hostage Bride—About 65 east—Ask the morning light."

"Gotcha."

"Does that morning light part mean anything to you?"

"I know exactly what it means. Call me back in ten minutes on this number!" Andy read the number to the phone in Kelly's room.

"Will do."

Andy sailed into Kelly's room and exclaimed, panting, "Listen to Lorrie Dean's 911 message and tell me what it makes you remember or think." The instant Andy repeated the message, Kelly startled him by rising full up in bed.

"Yes, yes, Boone Woo, I know. Here's what." She swallowed hard to get her mouth in gear and began to rattle out what had to be done. She was thoroughly animated and into it. Andy listened intently, swelling with gratitude and pride.

Clearly Kelly was back. She was needed, and she was energized, and she was all the way back. Nothing energizes like being needed.

"Tell them Lorrie Dean is on a rooftop. I'll explain later, Boone Woo, but right now just get them going with this. They can launch the helicopters. Andy, I'm sure of it."

At that moment, the phone rang. Andy picked it up and gave the word.

7

Lorrie Dean had given up, slumped against the chimney, frightened and exhausted, so very sad and distraught. It wasn't going to happen. She shifted her weary body around over the craggy roof. "Not so," she whispered to herself, "I will never give up!"

Suddenly, her head automatically rocked back at the sound coming from overhead: whop whop whop whop . . . She bowed her head humbly and, still looking down, raised a hand to the heavens, as far in the air as she could reach. The whop-whop grew a little louder and was staying in place high above her head. It came on down, ever closer, and started to hover only a few feet above. Then a rope slowly wound its way down to her.

*　　　*　　　*

Andy walked briskly into Kelly's room early Wednesday morning after a partial night's sleep at the farmhouse. The first thing he noticed was the merciful absence of the oxygen and IV equipment.

"Hi, Boone Woo," sang Kelly as she sat up and raised both arms in the air for a hug.

Andy rushed to the bed and took her in his arms as much as he could with her in a sitting position. Their embrace was genuine, warm, intimate, and lasting. As they eased apart, they nodded to each other, and Andy crooned, "I love you so much, and I am so very proud of you."

Kelly nodded tearfully and said, "I love you, too, Boone Woo, and I think I will never love anyone else so much as I do you." At that, they smiled together and then sighed and started chattering as only two steadfast buddies can do.

"Tell me, my little morning light, what makes you think Lorrie Dean will be on a rooftop?"

45

"Oh, yeah. Okay, you remember me telling you how we used to do brain teasers and what-if puzzles?"

"I do. Let's see, I remember you're telling me about one of your what-if teasers. It was something like what can you do if a vicious dog is running toward you."

"Right, and Lorrie Dean said she'd walk right toward him, whistling. So that's the idea. Well, it just so happens that . . . okay, first of all, we had been reading in the paper about a young girl getting taken hostage for ransom, and she broke loose and ran away, but the abductors caught her before she got far enough and brought her back."

"You know, I think I remember that case."

"Okay. So, in our game, we asked each other what we would do in a situation like that. Lorrie Dean said, 'It's like the dog thing. I'd run a ways and then sneak back to the place where they had me. That's one place they'll never look. When you keep running, you face the risk of not being able to run far enough.' Then she said, 'Remember, sometimes you have to move toward danger in order to escape it.'"

"Hmm, interesting. What does that have to do with rooftops?"

"Because I asked Lorrie Dean what she would do when she got back to the house where they'd held her. She said glibly, 'I'd climb up on the roof and flag a helicopter.' Sounds like she was jesting, but when you reported that 911 message, I knew at once that she would actually try it."

Later, after a long, delightful visit, Kelly narrowed her eyes as she looked straight toward Andy, visibly very serious, "Now, Boone Woo, I have some instructions for you, okay?"

"Sounds like I'm not gonna have a whole lot of latitude in what's coming."

"That's close. You're not going to have *any* latitude."

Clearly, the morning light was in charge here. Andy grinned and nodded.

"So, okay, here are the instructions: You are to leave here early this afternoon, go home to the farmhouse in time for supper, retire early to bed, and have a long, restoring night's sleep. Do you understand me, Mr. Andrew Woodson Boone?"

"Quite so, my dear." That was the end of it.

After an early dinner with his dear farm friends, Andy joined Dub on the rambling front porch for quiet-time and classical music. In a while, Andy said to Dub, "We had a very weird visitor yesterday afternoon. This strange woman came in, stood at Kelly's bed and stared down at her, all the while sort of biting her lip and slowly shaking her head. When I asked her if she was a friend, she claimed to be from the church, but she didn't sound very convincing. Then all at once, she just fled the scene. Strange. Actually, I had noticed her in the visitor's lounge because she made herself conspicuous by trying to hide behind a magazine."

"Hmm. Andy, describe this woman for me."

"Well, she was a little plump, somewhat pretty, but her face was kind of drawn. She's a blonde, and her hair was styled well and it was curly. She was about, I'd say, five feet six. But let me tell you about her dress. Dub, you should have seen this, ah, thing—yes, thing. Everybody should suffer the punishment of having to look at a thing like that at some time in their life."

"You really got my attention on that one, Andy. Please rave on."

"Dub, that dress—that dress was right on the edge of being the ugliest dress I've ever seen in my life."

Now Dub was grinning from ear to ear. "Tell me more."

"It's just that—see, the dress was way long, and it had these huge, bright orange flowers strewn all over it. Ugh!"

"Go no further, Andy! That has to be my sister. Rosalea always dressed in those gaudy, wild-looking—actually offensive—long dresses. Don't ask me why, because she was mostly otherwise well groomed and neat. Andy, there is no question about it; that was my sister. That was Rosalea Grimes Surrat."

Suddenly, the farm family's designated Mom banged through the door onto the porch, visibly concerned and shouted, "Andy there's a phone call in here for you, and it's the police."

Andy stumbled in behind her, scampered to the phone, and answered. "This is Andy Boone."

"Mr. Boone, this is Officer Foley in Tillman. They have picked her up! Don't respond!"

Andy almost fainted and desperately reached for the wall to steady his reeling. Nothing in all creation, for as long as he would live, could ever again have the overwhelming impact of that simple statement: They have picked her up. He stammered into the phone some kind of gibberish that even he couldn't understand.

After a short pause, Officer Foley continued. "But don't broadcast this! Tell only close members of the family, and swear them to secrecy.

I'm sorry, but you will not be able to see her right away. She will be in protective custody for an undetermined period of time. We'll talk about that and some other developments when I see you, hopefully early in the morning. I'm at home right now, but I just got this word. By the way, that word came in by a phone call from your FBI agent friend, Chad Jarrigan. It is the FBI that has ordered protective custody. That's all I can tell you on the phone. Can you come to my office at eight thirty in the morning?"

"Yes, yes, I'll be there. And thank you for getting this to me right away. I can't tell you . . ."

"Excuse me, Mr. Boone. It's better not to say anything else on the phone."

"Right. See you in the morning."

By the time Andy hung up the phone, his friends had assembled in a circle around him. He broke the news to them the same way it had been given him. "They have picked her up."

Mom and Aunt Leah stumbled to chairs, crying, while Grandpa and Dub were high-fiving, and Andy was praying. Then Andy called for their attention and explained the absolute necessity for secrecy. All agreed, smiling broadly.

Looking very concerned, maybe even a little scared, Andy said, "Now I am about to commit the unpardonable. I will have to violate Kelly's last order to me before I left the hospital today. I just have to get this word to her, even if she scolds me furiously. She and Lorrie Dean are not just ordinary friends. They are indivisible. So, I just have to do this."

"I'll go with you," Dub assured him. "I'll do my best to provide whatever protection I can, but it won't be easy."

Everybody cheered and huddled up and started chattering like newborn chicks.

"On second thought," said Dub, "why don't we just call her?"

"Police don't want us on the phone about this. Besides she'd have to get out of bed to answer it because it's across the room on the window sill."

"Oh, well, suppose I do this for you, Andy, so you can get to bed early, and so you won't be punished for violating sacred orders."

Andy chuckled. "You're a wonderful pal, Dub, but I want to be with her when she gets the news."

So Dub and Andy scurried away and headed for the hospital. When they shuffled into Kelly's room, she sat up instantly and hooted, "What?"

"They have picked her up."

She shrieked and threw her arms straight up above her head as though in a touchdown signal. Then she started to sway, waving her arms from side to side and chanting, "This is for you, Lorrie Dean." Dub and Andy looked on, grateful and proud.

The men told Kelly they didn't have details yet and that they had been asked not to tell anybody else about this development, probably as a precautionary measure to protect Lorrie Dean. Kelly nodded and placed a finger across her lips as a sign of their pledge to secrecy. The guys lingered with Kelly for only a few minutes. Mercifully, she refrained from scolding, possibly in deference to the compelling event.

Andy was in the Tillman police station by eight o'clock the next morning. Officer Foley came out promptly, and the two of them went into a small conference room. "Thanks for coming in, Mr. Boone."

"Sure, and call me Andy."

"Good, I like that. Okay, here's where we are. Your wife is safe. That's the best part. She was picked up from the rooftop of an old, vacant estate home way out in the country, about twenty-five miles east of the intersection of County Road 3127 and I-20."

"Fantastic!"

"Well, it is fantastic, due in great measure to the help you provided in interpreting the 911 call. At this point, the FBI has pretty well taken over. Only they know where the helicopter landed with Lorrie Dean or where she was taken afterward. As I indicated last night, she will be in protective custody for a while. We don't know how long: days, weeks, months, or what. I'm confident that FBI officials haven't even tried to determine this yet. Also, you won't be able to find out where they're keeping her, not for a little while, anyway . . . Oh, I'm sorry. Did you want to say something?"

Abruptly, Andy felt tension in his brow and realized that he probably had a very uneasy, puzzled look on his face. "It's just that I wonder when she will ever be free. Sure, I ache to see her and hold her—believe me, and I realize that's selfishness on my part. Still, as important as that is to me, it isn't the main thing I'm grieving about right now. I just—I just want her to be free. She had to hide out under the Witness Protection Program for fourteen years, for something her mother did, then she's kidnapped by witless hoodlums, and now she'll be confined again. Officer Foley, will this innocent, deserving woman, this precious human being, ever know freedom?"

"She will, Andy. She will, but we just don't know when, at this point. For now, please know that I sympathize with you."

"Thanks. Sorry I interrupted."

"Hey, no problem. Anyway, moving along, I can tell you that she will be treated properly, and they will work hard to make her comfortable. First, they will get a thorough medical evaluation to make sure she's not hurt in any way and to see if she needs any treatment for anything. And, frankly, Andy, they will do a lot of interrogating so they can go after these thugs. I'm sure that will be painful for her, but it just has to be done. Then they will determine when and where she can see her family. And let me say this, sincerely, although I won't be involved much after this week, I sure would like to be looking on when you two are reunited. I really respect you both."

"Thank you for that. You all have been diligent, skillful, and unrelenting in handling this tragedy. I just want you to know that this kind of excellence will not be forgotten."

"Good of you to say that." He took a deep breath and, looking sympathetic, said, "I guess that's about it for here. From this point on, you'll need to be in touch with the FBI in Dallas."

*   *   *

In the helicopter, Lorrie Dean turned to the police officer beside her and, without a word, handed him the cell phone and the gun to which she had clung tenaciously as they lifted her with the rope looped under her arms. Next, she wrote on a little scrap of paper the license plate number of the Lumina that took her to her prison. In a moment, struggling to talk but remaining calm, she softly spoke three names: Jarred, Mason, and Sydney. Then her lips tightened, and she mumbled, "Jarred is still at the house with his knees shot out."

The officer squeezed her arm gently and immediately got on the phone. When he hung up, he touched her shoulder and said, "You're beautiful. Few people in this world could handle a staggering personal tragedy like this with the composure you're showing. Bless you. Now, I have to ask you this, 'Are you hurt?'"

Lorrie Dean shook her head, but tears betrayed her.

"Do you have any urgent needs? You know, like what do you need or want most right now?"

"A shower and a change of clothes—and some aspirin."

"What size are you?"

"Twelve."

"Got it. I'll relay that in just a minute. Anything else?"

Again, Lorrie Dean just shook her head.

"Well, okay. Ah, I have to tell you this: you are going to be in protective custody for a while. Apparently, the FBI sees broader implications in this kidnapping than meets the eye. Anyway, that's what they have ordered. As yet, my pilot and I are not privileged to know where we will set down, and I have no idea where they will take you. But there's one thing I can positively assure you: they will treat you right."

Lorrie Dean listened intently as the officer explained the situation. Somehow, the question of what they were going to do with her just didn't matter. She couldn't care less. In fact, it was frustrating and saddening just having to listen to jabber about such things. How she would be treated in the future was not the uppermost thing in her heart and mind in this dreadful hour.

8

Lorrie Dean didn't recognize the place where they were landing. Nothing about it looked familiar. It was a tiny clearing completely hemmed in by tall trees.

She stepped stiffly from the helicopter with the officer holding her arm. On the ground, they walked through the trees to a little one-lane road where a car was waiting. The officer stopped there, still holding her arm. "Stay here in the edge of the woods. I have something for you."

From the trunk of the car he lifted a large shopping bag and some kind of collapsible contraption. He walked past her a few feet back into the woods. Then he unfolded the mystery object and stood it up so that it made a small three-sided screen. He handed her the sack. "Try this on," he said. "I'm sorry that we can't accommodate the shower yet, but they will, ma'am, I'm sorry. You go ahead with that and I'll wait by the car. Come on over when you finish."

Lorrie Dean stepped carefully into the little dressing stall. She fumbled around in the sack and lifted out a simple pair of brown cotton slacks. She laid them across the top of the sack, then removed her bridal outfit and set it aside. The slacks fit okay, as did the long-sleeved, purple cotton blouse. The house shoes were a bit large but fully acceptable and greatly welcomed.

Fully dressed, she stood in place for a few moments, trying to fathom her situation—indeed, her life. She leaned forward and slowly lifted the bridal outfit, the simple, ankle-length sweetheart gown. She brought it up to her chest and sobbed as she folded it into a little wad and held it way out, as if offering it to the gods. The fallen sweetheart gown meant so much, said so much, but it and all that it stood for were now gone forever. *What does this mean about life for me now?* she pleaded. *I'm sorry, Lord. I'm not complaining. I just don't know what to do. Please, Lord . . . Please.* She placed the gown gently into the shopping bag, lifted her head, and walked away, swinging it by her side.

When she emerged from the woods, the police officer again helped steady her as she worked her way into the passenger seat. As they pulled away, she heard the helicopter lifting. That was one airborne ride that would forever be etched in her memory.

There was no talking between them as they idled along. Later, as they rounded a bend, the trees thinned on one side, providing a picture-window view of a rolling, grassy meadow caught briefly in the late-afternoon glow. It was a captivating sight, and she slowly turned her head to follow it for as long as she could, until it disappeared behind a curtain of trees. How refreshing it was to look out across these fields and marvel at something so vast and seemingly vulnerable, yet unmolested by infighting and malice.

As she reflected on the tranquility of that peaceful setting, she began thinking of her sweetheart and of her buddy, two people in her life whose love was unconditional and would never waver. *What a contrast,* she thought, as her throat started to tighten and tears began fighting to come through. Now, her struggle would continue at a different level. How could she ever again accept with a free heart the loyalty of these two devoted friends? They would be the same, but she would never be the same again.

In the short span of one afternoon, she had slipped from the loving, caring, tender arms of a good and kind man into the monstrous grasp of a degenerate pig. She had descended from holy matrimony to brutal captivity. Now she was shaking her head as her mind lurched on, *Somebody, please explain life to me; I think I don't understand.*

She could hold back no longer, and tears flooded her cheeks in one big gush. She had never experienced tears coming in such an avalanche as that. She slung her head back and forth, trying to shake them away, but on they came. She gave in and placed her trembling hands over her face and sobbed into them while her body quivered and jerked.

The officer rested his hand on her shoulder, just briefly. In a moment, he said, "I'm so very sorry. No one should ever have to suffer what you've been through. Life owes you one!"

By and by, Lorrie Dean settled somewhat. She glanced at her driver, smiled graciously, and said, "Thanks for understanding."

They traveled on, and soon hooked up with a highway where signs pointed to downtown Dallas. In a couple of minutes, they were in the big city. At this point, the officer evidently decided it was time to talk, for he began to rattle off all kinds of stuff about procedures, conditions, and other technicalities, none of which aroused even the slightest curiosity in Lorrie Dean—well, that is, except for the mention of her imminent meeting with FBI agents Chad Jarrigan and Terry Aylor, names she remembered from her Andy's past dealings.

Soon they pulled in front of an antique shop in a small section of Dallas that Lorrie Dean recognized as Deep Ellum. They parked, and the police officer led her into the shop and proceeded toward the back, where two people stood up and smiled toward her. The man stepped forward and said, "I'm Chad Jarrigan, the guy who broke the news to you that a young man named Andy Boone was madly searching for you, and this is my colleague, Terry Aylor."

Lorrie Dean was nodding agreement as he talked, and when he paused, she extended her hand calmly to each of them. "Yes, I remember you both. Thank you for what you did." She curtsied and tried her best to smile.

"Okay, let's have a seat over here," said agent Jarrigan, "and we'll kind of let you know what to expect in the days ahead. So, what's in the days ahead? Terry, want to tell her what to expect?"

"Sure. First of all, Lorrie Dean, I know you're aching to reunite with your husband, but that won't . . ."

"Fiancé."

"Oh, I thought . . ."

"It was never pronounced."

"All right. So, I'm really sorry that we are unable to let you meet with any family or friends for a while. Now, how long that lasts depends on a number of variables, one of which relates to the progress we have in apprehending your abductors. Fortunately, thanks to your own alertness and heads-up thinking, we have some very good information. I will be working with you personally and I'll try to keep you informed. We'll get you together with your loved ones just as soon as possible."

"I have a very dear friend who would be a great help to me in this time," said Lorrie Dean, softly. "If only I could be with her for even just a little while. Her name is Kelly Surrat, and although she's only seventeen, she is one of the most astute people I've ever known. And of course, well, you know, she's a woman."

"I understand. We'll try to work on that as a priority while still protecting your safety. Oh, and yes," she began, as she cut her eyes toward Agent Jarrigan, "a woman needs a woman at times like this. That's why

I'll be your primary agent along the way. Now, as a matter of routine, we'll have a medical professional look you over and alert us to any urgent medical issues. On that point, let me ask this: are you personally aware of any injuries or other medical problems?"

Lorrie Dean didn't answer. She shifted around and looked away, gazing vaguely through the little shop. The agents waited patiently. She turned back to face them and just looked imploringly from one to the other, hoping they wouldn't press the question. The agents continued to wait politely, letting her deal with the enormity of her situation.

Finally Agent Jarrigan excused himself, saying, "I think you two have this well in hand. Lorrie Dean doesn't need two of us hounding her. I'll just kick around in the shop until you need me."

Lorrie Dean raised her head to make eye contact with Agent Aylor, trying to be resolute, which wasn't working. Terry Aylor waited, looking supportive. Finally she spoke kindly. "You need time more than anything right now, don't you?"

Lorrie Dean nodded. Then she cleared her throat and said, "I'm sorry I didn't answer your question."

It was the agent's turn to nod.

Lorrie Dean squirmed a little and then looked again at her agent. "Miss Aylor . . ."

"Terry."

"Terry, thanks. Ah . . ." She glanced down at her quivering hands and shuddered at the growing weakness in her stomach. She tried to shake it all by sheer willpower. She swallowed and began again. "Ah, Terry, I . . . ah . . . ah . . . I was raped."

Agent Terry Aylor stretched her arms across the table and took Lorrie Dean's hands, squeezed them, and continued to hold them as she talked, "We can help you on that. I know that is an overriding concern for you now, larger even than the vicious kidnapping, larger than the fear and pain they dragged you through, and larger than your miraculous, gutsy escape. It's bigger than anything in the world to you right now. It looms there between you and life itself."

Lorrie Dean was vigorously gesturing her agreement. "You're so very understanding, and thank you for that. A man just wouldn't grasp the horror of that brutal situation."

Terry nodded. "Now you will need some professional help that the FBI can't provide, but we can get you to the people who can. First of all, are you aware of any physical injuries or—let me put it a different way: were you subjected to physical stresses there that could have been harmful physically? That is, is there anything we should be checking out immediately, before we bother with other issues?"

Long question, thought Lorrie Dean. "When I was assaulted, that savage slammed his fist into my neck so hard it knocked me off balance, and I fell. I didn't know why he chose the neck, but he did. Right now, my neck is a little painful but not as much as in the beginning. When I fell, I hit my head, and I'm still having headaches. That's the one that worries me the most. He also punched my stomach a few times, but it's much better now. That's all, really, I can think of. I might mention that I had nothing but chicken broth to eat for four days."

"Glad you mentioned that point. So, renourishing you will be our top priority. Meanwhile, I'll report all this to the medical doctor so he'll know where to begin."

"Thanks."

"All right, you know, you also need to be tested at intervals for any possible diseases that could have been transmitted during the intercourse."

"Yes, yes."

"We'll arrange that. Now I'm sure you're curious to know more about protective custody and what it entails. Although you'll be confined, it won't be anything like prison. You'll be quartered at an undercover facility we have near Kaufman. It's sort of a small hotel, but heavily guarded. I think you'll find it okay, and they'll treat you right, but obviously your lifestyle will be greatly restricted. We will take you out there tonight."

"Okay. I understand," said Lorrie Dean, "and I accept all that, and I will cooperate fully." She paused. "There's just one thing."

"Sure, go ahead," said Terry.

"If I could please just see my friend, Kelly, she would be enormous support and comfort for me." Then she chuckled—a totally unexpected reaction in this tough situation, unless you understood that one Kelly Surrat could destroy the strongest inhibitions in a heartbeat. Still snickering, Lorrie Dean continued, "She would know exactly how to handle me."

"Okay, we'll push for that. For now, let's get you out to the facility where you can have that long-awaited shower and, let's hope, a restful night of sleep. Tomorrow, agent Jarrigan will be in touch with Mr. Boone and have him gather your shoes, clothes, undies, combs, brushes, and whatever other personal items you want. He will be instructed to bring them to a certain location. Shall we be away?"

*   *   *

Of all that can happen in the course of a day, nothing is as calming or fulfilling as a warm, lasting shower at bedtime. For Lorrie Dean, it was the only truly genuine taste of freedom she'd had since that saving lift into a helicopter. Even that didn't have the sensation of freedom. It was essentially procedural. And even with this present uplifting, she knew full well that this, too, was transient. She would always be a prisoner of the outrageous rape of her personal dignity, perpetrated by a pathetic, loathsome worm. *Surely,* she thought, *I was not born to be free.*

Lorrie Dean fell into bed, and the gods were merciful. She slept soundly until ten thirty the next morning. Sitting on the edge of the bed, she yawned and stretched and then bowed her head in prayer. Then she began looking around her room which, in her misery, she had hardly noticed the evening before. Surely it seemed to have all the necessary appointments. Still, no matter how accommodating and natural it looked, nothing could take away the nagging sense of confinement it boded.

During Terry Aylor's brief afternoon visit, Lorrie Dean again asked for Kelly, but the agent didn't seem as optimistic as she had earlier. "We're going to have to get at least through the weekend before we know much on that," said Terry. "I know it seems irrational to you, but in cases of *protection*, as we call it, we are purposely overcautious."

Lorrie Dean tightened her lips and started shaking her head. Finally, she looked wistfully at the agent and mumbled, "Okay."

After the agent left, Lorrie Dean prayed and returned to bed. Later she had a sandwich and scoffed at the collection of magazines presumably intended to distract her from her anguish.

As time dragged on, she continued to brood, and the more she fretted, the more nervous and anxious she became. *What's ahead for me? My nightmare is just beginning. Stepping out of character worked, but where does that leave me, now? And what about my Andy? I can't have him suffer.* "The really tough times are just ahead," she grumbled out loud.

And time did drag on painfully. Finally Monday morning came. Lorrie Dean slept late again. She was grateful for sleep—eternally grateful that God had given her this consummate blessing at the very time she needed it the most. Sleep had become the only ally she felt she had, so she indulged it to the maximum.

That afternoon, she was aroused by a favor that, by now, she had dismissed as unlikely for the foreseeable future. Terry Aylor burst through the door smiling brightly and whooped out, "Good news! You are going to get to see your friend, Kelly."

Lorrie Dean shrieked and cried out, "Yes!"

Agent Aylor's smile hung there as she began to talk. "Lorrie Dean, that is the first real smile I've seen on you since we met four days ago. We are attempting to work it out for tomorrow, and she will have to come here, and she will have to do it alone. Can she do that?"

"Yes, she has her driver's permit and access to a car."

"Great, we'll give her full instructions. Now, tell me, where does our Miss Kelly live?"

"On a farm in Tillman."

9

At the top of the Grimes farm driveway in Tillman, Texas stood a huge sign: Welcome Home Kelly!

It was Saturday, the big day! At once, the four welcoming revelers began to cheer as Dub Grimes drove his beloved niece, Kelly Surrat, up to the majestic old farm house. She had just been released from a week-long, initially very shaky, stay at a Jacksonville hospital. Laughter, hugs, and playful teasing took the day. In a while, they all marched merrily into the house and assembled, still chattering, in the ever-popular den.

The farm family was a unique unit of five, somewhat related, singles. According to Kelly, this presented a logistical problem, requiring too many bedrooms because, as she put it, "Nobody sleeps together." In any event, it was a pieced-together family, a collection of refugees from other disrupted family situations, and its hardworking, tenacious, good-humored members were bonded by love and loyalty.

Now Kelly was home. The family was complete again. While Aunt Leah was unusually excited—for her, that is—Mom was the most animated of all. Andy stood quietly, his unexpressed pride revealed only by a timid grin, which Kelly knew was a loving smile.

"Have a seat," said Mom as she scooted a chair beside Kelly.

"Thanks, Mom, but I guess sitting is the last thing I want to do for a while. But I'll gladly take the chair to stand behind and lean on."

In time, the jabber and commotion subsided, and Kelly could sense their sneaking little covert glances at the bandage on the right side of her forehead. It really was a somewhat small covering, and she couldn't quite figure why all the fascination with it. But she decided they were probably just trying to spare her having to talk about things she preferred to suppress. She just kept grinning and then mused to herself, *If Lorrie Dean were here, she would say simply, but graciously, "How's your head?"*

"Okay, everybody, I want to know about Lorrie Dean. What's going on with her? How's she doing? When can we see her?"

Strangely, a hush fell over the little platoon, and everybody just looked toward Andy.

Andy cleared his throat, unsuccessfully, and stammered, "She's okay. That's the main thing; she's okay." Total silence continued to absorb the little band of close friends. At once, Andy realized that this terse explanation would only arouse stronger curiosity in the mind of his very bright, unusually perceptive little morning light. So he confessed the full limits of what he knew: the promising indications, as well as the uncertainties and mysteries and just plain frustrations with how it was all going.

"Kelly, we honestly don't know a thing about her real condition. We don't know what she's feeling or if she's injured or simply emotionally broken down or anything else that we are pining to know. They won't tell us anything, yet. They just keep saying, 'hold on a while,' and they won't let us see her—for protection, as they put it. She is essentially confined."

"Confined?"

"Well, restricted is probably a more palatable word. They are holding her and at the same time shielding her. At their request, I have gathered a lot of her clothes and personal items and taken them to a drop-off place. That tells me we still won't see her for a while."

Kelly shook the chair and exclaimed, "Boone Woo, we have to see Lorrie Dean. I'm sure they're trying to keep her comfortable, but they don't love her. Only love can fill what she needs right now."

Kelly and Andy both broke a little. How could they not? But they recovered quickly, and Andy said resolutely, "Why don't we all amble down to Kelly's Cove and pray together?"

"Good idea," mumbled Grandpa.

"Right on," agreed Mom. "Andy, you and Kelly head on down there, and we'll join you in a few minutes."

*   *   *

At the cove, Kelly and Andy assumed their traditional positions. She sat on the backless bench, and he sat across from her on a stump, cushioned by a feed sack stuffed with rags and hay. This cozy little chamber was but a man-made inlet into the woods, just off a wide pathway that led to the fields. It was about the size of a double garage and looked as if it had been carved out of the thicket of ancient trees with a plan in mind. It had a natural roof, provided by age-old trees that completely engulfed it. At some point, Andy had named it Kelly's Cove, in honor of his very special buddy.

They didn't say anything for a while. They just sat there calmly letting the solitude and magic of their peaceful sanctuary settle their tensions. Finally Andy spoke.

"Kelly, something just isn't right about this. There has to be a problem they're not telling us about. Personally, I don't buy their assertions. Really, now, they could let us see her and still protect her. I mean, police are always transporting inmates and witnesses and others from one place to another under guard. This don't track."

Kelly looked at him sadly and muttered, "I know." Then she smiled, uneasily, and tried to sound upbeat. "On a brighter note, Boone Woo, this place holds a lot of treasured memories. This is where you told me all about your determined search for Lorrie Dean, your childhood sweetheart you hadn't seen in twenty years. It's also the place where you first told me that you loved me."

"Those *are* treasures. This place is everlasting. It's been laughed in and cried in, and it's stood waiting for two denied lovers to find it. And, my little morning light, it's a place of honor, for it bears your name."

Kelly bowed and smiled broadly. "It's *my* honor. In a way, this is kind of our place. We ought to make everybody else get our permission to come in here."

"Right on," exclaimed Andy, fisting the air exuberantly. They giggled. "I like that idea. Reminds me; you know, we did a lot of friendly teasing in here, you and I. That has always been our very own bond; nobody else was privy to share banter with either of us the way we held it for each other. And, you know, we probably solved a few world problems in here also."

Kelly was nodding all the while Andy talked. Then she leaned toward him, pointed to the bench she was on, and said, "And, mind you, this is where you proposed to Lorrie Dean, and it's where she and I began our friendship. We had instant rapport somehow. Lorrie Dean is so accepting, and she is the epitome of grace. I don't know of another woman quite like that dear lady in the whole world."

"Just you, my darling," said Andy.

"Thanks, Boone Woo, that's very humbling." She glanced around the cove, musing, finally wrinkling her brow in readiness to say more about it. "And this hole in the woods is very humbling."

"Know what else?" said Andy. "To my knowledge, it's never been fussed in. I mean, you don't come to a sanctuary like this to gripe. Yep, this little nook may be small, but it has its own very special ministry."

In about an hour, the rest of the family strolled in and joined the reverie and ruminations. Not long afterward, they all moseyed back to the house where they separated into different directions. Soon, Dub asked to talk to Kelly alone for a few minutes, and they retired to the front porch.

"Kelly, there are some things I need to tell you, and they have to do with your mother. Are you up to listening to that kind of talk?"

"Sure, I'm a big girl. Fire away."

"To make a long story short, your mother wants to talk to you. She hasn't told me why or what about, but then again, I haven't asked her."

"You're kidding! Somebody's biological mother wants to talk to her discarded daughter? Wow! Does she need money or some big favor?"

"Somehow, I just know it's nothin' like that. First of all, I took the initiative to call her when you were hospitalized. She's my sister, and, although we don't speak, she is your mother, and I thought it would be unpardonable if I didn't at least let her know. Please forgive me, Kelly. I didn't do that to bring any discomfort to you. If it does, all I can do is plead for your forgiveness."

"I understand, Uncle Dub."

"So, movin' on—the day after I called her, she called me back to see how you were doin' and I told her you were still in a coma. At that point, she started cryin', and we both hung up. Now, here is a real interestin' part: she came to see you in the hospital one day, ever so briefly. Andy was there. He described her, and I know it has to have been my sister."

"My, my, the plot thickens."

"It does, indeed. Yesterday, she called again, cryin' and pleading for me to intervene and get you to talk to her. Be assured, Kelly, I am not gonna make any such plea to you. But it would be irresponsible of me not to make you aware of these things. I love you, and I think you at least have a right to know."

"I see." She said no more but fell into deep thought. At a point, she smiled faintly at her uncle Dub to let him know that what he had done was okay.

Dub didn't press further. After a few moments, he excused himself and went inside.

"I thought I'd find you here," said Andy, as he pulled up a rocker to sit beside Kelly.

Kelly smiled and said—almost inaudibly—"This is the place."

Andy didn't push. Clearly his morning light needed some time, and he was pretty sure he knew what for. If he was right, she didn't need anybody asking heckling questions or volunteering shallow advice. In a while, she reached over and patted his arm.

"Boone Woo, may I talk to you about something that's bothering me?"

"Always, sweetheart."

"It's about my mother. Uncle Dub says you saw her at the hospital."

"Yes, I did, last Wednesday."

"Will you describe what she did?"

"Sure. She came in the room just a little ways, saw me, nodded without a word, and stood in place for a few minutes. Her facial expression looked like she didn't know what to think. All this time, she was just staring at you. Finally, she started moving toward your bed, very hesitantly, sort of creeping along. When she got to you, she stared down at you for a long time. She looked strained, and she was biting her lip. She began shaking her head. Then, all at once, she just hustled out of the room."

"Is that all?"

"Yes, except at one point, I asked if she was a friend, and she just said she was from church. Those were the only words spoken. Later, I told Dub about it, and he said it was positively his sister."

"She's trying to get in touch with me. What do you think I should do?"

"I can't tell you, Kelly. Here's why—I don't know what your feelings are and without that, I might wind up suggesting something that would hurt you more than it would help you. I'm sorry, dear friend, but you have only yourself for this one. It's big, very, very big, and anybody's advice may be disaster for you if you follow it. The trouble with well-meaning advice is that it never considers how it will wear on the personality that adopts it. I love you too much to tell you what to do."

"I guess I needed that."

They fell silent. Abruptly, Kelly twisted her rocker around a half turn and looked away from her pal.

While Andy was gazing out across the fields, he began to feel nervous, as if something had changed. He looked toward Kelly, and something was indeed different. As best he could make out, with her back turned toward him, she was leaning over. Now, he could tell that the rocker was shaking, and at once he knew that she was crying. His precious little buddy was trying to handle it alone. Andy pushed up and walked over to stand beside her. Then he knelt in front of her and touched her hair.

"Quit!"

"I'll quit *that*, but I won't leave you."

She raised her head and cried out, "I don't know what to do, Boone Woo, and you won't help me."

Andy had never seen her so thoroughly broken. "I'll do anything for you, my sweet. Just tell me."

"No, you won't." She slapped a hand toward him. "You won't even help me with my mother. You won't tell me what you think."

"Oh, me, I thought I was helping, but I was actually letting you down, wasn't I?" He cleared his throat. "Okay, here's what I think: in my heart, I want you to talk to your mother. You will not likely be at ease about it until you do, and—well, you just never know."

Kelly tried to smile through her tears. "Thanks; I'm sorry I had to fuss that out of you. I so wanted to know what you really think."

Andy rocked back on his heels, set his jaw, and raised his brow. "So, there! Being pals is tough work, ain't it?"

Kelly nodded, shuffled around, and leaned out to accept Andy's reaching arms, and they hugged—as only buddies can.

As Andy started pushing up, he said, "Sweetheart, what you need is unqualified respect from all of us in your support group. You deserve the very best of us, not just impulsive advice and clever suggestions."

"So, I guess I'll just think about it," said Kelly, now fully composed.

"Good. You need and deserve time to think. Nobody thinks better than you. Now, I know somebody who would be a great sounding board, and you could fully trust her to be both honest and considerate."

"Lorrie Dean! I simply must see her."

*   *   *

Andy stayed overnight, attended church with his friends Sunday morning, and headed back to Dallas right after lunch. Time was up. He had to get his head set for going back to his stimulating job at Clay Cutter the next morning.

Kelly saw him off and then watched him disappear down the long driveway, her heart pleading.

Then it was Monday, and Kelly was trying to stay busy with totally unnecessary things, but it wasn't working. Her thoughts kept bouncing between Lorrie Dean's predicament and her mother's hounding. *What a contrast,* she thought. *One gracious, caring friend and one self-centered, irresponsible mother.*

School would be starting in three weeks, but the prospect of returning for her senior year offered no consolation. She had broken up with her boyfriend last semester, so there was nothing to look forward to there. As her Boone Woo said, all she had was herself.

Then the phone rang, and Kelly picked it up, since she was standing near it. "Hello." There was no response, but she could hear breathing. "Hello—hello." Then she heard a faint grunt.

"Kelly?"

"Uh-huh, this is Kelly Surrat." She waited, but there was no response. "Are you there?" Heavy breathing, but no response. "I'm sorry, but I can't hear you."

"Kelly . . . this is your mother."

Kelly hung up, clutched the phone to her chest, and cried softly. In a moment, she turned away, disappointed with her impatience. *That's not what Boone Woo wanted me to do. Why can't I get myself together?* In a moment, she threw up her hands and started to busy herself with small, useless endeavors.

After lunch, while Kelly was doing the dishes, the phone rang again. She let it ring. There was no way she was going to put herself through more misery with her mother. It kept ringing, on and on. Finally Mom entered the room, frowned at Kelly, and scuffled over to answer the insistent phone.

"Hello . . . Yes, it is . . . Okay, hold on." She called out, "Kelly, this is for you. It's Ms. Terry Aylor from the FBI."

10

Lorrie Dean stood in the middle of her hideaway room, looking expectantly toward the door. Her breathing was labored, and she felt the tension in her shoulders, which she had instinctively been holding up. She relaxed them, shook her arms about a few times, and let them dangle straight down by her sides. Then she drew a deep breath, lifted her chin, and swallowed.

Even with all that preparation, she jumped at the knock at the door. Seconds later, Lorrie Dean and Kelly strolled arm in arm into the room. They paused there, and, facing each other, smiling, just let the moment transcend their problems.

Lorrie Dean pointed to one of the two facing chairs and chortled, "Pull up a sandbag, good buddy, and I'll tell you a war story."

They laughed together, and when they were seated, they took some time to reckon with what all was happening in their lives and gain their composure. After all, they were friends and knew they would start talking when it was time.

In a while, Lorrie Dean looked quizzically at her friend and said, "What happened to your head?"

Kelly forced an awkward chuckle and said, "That's a long story which I'll tell you about sometime, but for now, be assured that it's just a little injury that's healing well. Thanks for asking."

Lorrie Dean nodded.

Kelly dropped her eyes and gazed into her lap for a few moments. Then she lifted them and said, "Lorrie Dean, what can I do?"

"Talk to me . . . Help me understand . . . Listen."

"You got it. I guess it's okay for you to know this—and Lorrie Dean, what I'm going to say is not meant to make it hard for you, but as you asked me, perhaps it'll help you understand. The thing is, your Andy is really struggling hard. It's heart-wrenching to watch him grieving."

Lorrie Dean apologized and wept.

Kelly was struggling, too, but she was supposed to be the strength here, so she braced up and pushed ahead, hoping maybe, as a starter, she could lighten the mood a little. "Lorrie Dean," she began, "well, what I'm going to tell you is really kind of funny in spite of our grave situation. Now you know Andy, right?"

"Yes, totally."

"Okay, this is just a little humorous because, well, you know, it's Andy—our little boy."

"I can't wait," said Lorrie Dean, smiling mischievously.

"Okay, you ready?"

"Shoot."

"Well, on that horrible day when those low-livered, wretched sons of . . . those maniacs snatched you away and sped off in that car, your Andy broke away and ran after that car."

"He chased the getaway car?"

"Chased the getaway car—on foot, mind you. And Lorrie Dean, he wasn't just kind of trotting along; he was giving everything. I know, because I fell in behind him and couldn't come close to catching up. He was running with all his might. Finally, we both ran out of gas and fell down on the shoulder of the road, exhausted. I guess that doesn't sound very funny."

"It sounds very Andy," sobbed Lorrie Dean.

"So, here's the funny part. I asked him if he actually thought he would catch that car. Guess what he said?"

Lorrie Dean just shook her head, looking serious.

"Well, without batting an eye, our man said, 'I was hoping they'd have a flat.' He was dead serious."

Lorrie Dean laughed spontaneously. Shaking her head, she kept laughing. Kelly laughed with her, and they laughed right into crying. Then they smiled their way out of it. Kelly chuckled and said, "So, he ran—and he gave it what he had."

Lorrie Dean managed a modest grin and said, "Did you ask him what he planned to do if he caught that car?"

"Naw, I was afraid it would hurt him."

"Good point. You're a very kind friend. You know, it's like Andy to try. He takes nothing for granted."

"Right you are. People say Andy Boone marches to a different drummer, but that's not the point at all. Andy doesn't even have a drummer. Besides, he's not a marcher; he's a dreamer."

"Yes," said Lorrie Dean, "and it was his dream that he could catch that car. He had to try."

At that, there came a period of uneasy silence. Now and then they would look at each other and tighten their lips. Finally Kelly decided this wasn't going anywhere. "Lorrie Dean, do you feel like telling me about your horrendous ordeal? It might help."

"Yes. You're right. So here goes." Thereupon, she told the whole story except for one thing. Amazingly, she held together pretty well during the recounting of her captivity, all the while looking down as she talked. She told everything she could think of, how she slept, the unmerciful soup diet, and the scheming for a way to escape that pervaded her every waking moment. She told of the pivotal wild scream right into the ear canal of her guard, her unexpected eruption of violence when she shot out both his knees. And she told of running for her life. When she finished, she said, "There's one other thing that happened, but I just have to wait a few minutes until I work up enough nerve to talk about it."

"My dear Lorrie Dean, there is absolutely no rush for anything, so don't you worry about it. I'm your friend, and I care very deeply about everything you have to say, but you tell me only whatever you're comfortable with. I will not pry."

Lorrie Dean was gently shaking her head and smiling meekly.

"Why are you shaking your head?"

"At the marvel of you, my friend. It's something Andy sort of taught me. He said it expresses fascination and admiration."

"Oh, well, okay. That's good, then, I think—right?"

"Right." Lorrie Dean shifted a little, rested her chin on a fist for a moment, and then slapped the arm of her chair. "Okay, I have to do this!" At once, she blurted it out. "Kelly, I was raped!"

Kelly jumped as if she'd been shot from behind. Then she pushed up, went to her friend, and hugged her. In a moment, she stepped back and sank slowly into her chair. "Lorrie Dean, the words *I'm sorry* just aren't strong enough. In fact, they don't say anything. They can't begin to cover what I feel for you in this moment."

"I know. I don't expect you to say anything. There is nothing in all this world that can be said, but I wanted you to know, because I know you'll be discreet about it. Well, that's one thing, but the main reason is that it'll help you understand why I'm not Lorrie Dean any more. I'm a different friend. That beast stole my identity; he took my life, destroyed my dignity, raped my marriage."

Kelly cringed and then caught herself and tried to look serious without looking startled. She began rubbing her hands and started to speak nonchalantly, as if just academically rolling things around in her mind. "I wonder what a rapist thinks after he's done it. Is he proud, really pleased with himself? Is he even satisfied? Does a rapist actually feel brave and powerful? Do we just excuse him, willy-nilly, believing primitive instincts overpowered him for a moment? Poor baby, right? Does it ever occur to him that it's really dumb? You'd think nobody wants to be thought of as dumb."

"Those are penetrating questions. I guess I don't let myself think of them, because I don't want to think about the rape."

"I don't have an inkling of the answers to all those questions. But there is one thing I do know, absolutely and positively: it is one of the most heinous crimes ever committed."

"It's just so destructive."

Kelly held a finger in the air to pause their conversation, while she thought for a moment. She was searching for a way to neutralize her friend's sudden doubts about herself without sounding argumentative. Finally she said, "It was the most horrible thing imaginable, but, Lorrie Dean, it may have changed how you think of yourself, but it didn't change who you are. You're still Lorrie Dean to Andy and me, and you'll always be Lorrie Dean."

"I don't believe I want to think about it anymore right now."

"Take some time. I'm your friend no matter what may ever change about you. But please, don't issue such an unequivocal verdict as that till you see how the world—the people in your life—react to what happened to you. We'll change with you, if necessary. Then we'll try to restore you."

"It seems freedom will never be mine."

"Only love can set you free, and it will!"

After another long, fully accepting, mutual quiet-time for the two ardent friends, Lorrie Dean pleaded, "What am I to do, Kelly?"

"You're going to start by holding your head up, lifting your chin, looking straight ahead, defiantly. Begin now, Lorrie Dean. Lift your head!"

She lifted her head halfheartedly, meekly smiling and trying to have it appear that she was endeavoring to cooperate, while all along knowing she had lost the ability to think of herself in a positive way.

"That's a start. It all begins there. Never give up, and keep reminding yourself that if you accept fear and anger as your enemies, it'll get you nowhere. Use them; make them your friends, as silly as that sounds. I mean, let them fuel your efforts, help you conquer."

"Wow, I'll have to think about that one for a while, but I guess you've been there, haven't you, dear Kelly?"

"You bet I have, and I didn't start out right. When my mother tossed me up for grabs, I was madder than hell—excuse me. I was mad for years—still am—and I was afraid for what I was going to do, what would happen to me. Then one day, I set my jaw and swung into action. I'll tell you all about that another day."

"I would like to be as determined as you were, but I don't know if it'll be possible for me to hold my head up again."

"So there you go; you're giving in. You don't have to die at the hands of that lowly, slithering idiot. He will flat-out not win this! We will not concede that power to him. Always remember, there are people in your life who want to support you, and these people need you, really need what you have."

"Do you need me?"

"Oh boy, do I ever need you. I need the kind of help only a true friend can give. Boone Woo is helping me, but I need you because we women just have a sensitivity about relationships that men don't have. So will you help me?"

Lorrie Dean shot out to the edge of her chair, thoroughly activated. "Yes, Kelly, tell me, tell me!"

Thereupon, Kelly related everything about her accident and recovery, including how Andy hung at her bedside day and night, all the while checking constantly with the police to find out about his sweetheart. At the end, she told of her mother's efforts to sort of reunite.

"But don't worry about it. All that stuff is over, you know, the hospital and accident and so forth," said Kelly, waving it away as she flat-handed the air in front of her. "That part is past history, and I'm fine. It happened, and it's done. But, dear friend, this business with my mother I need help with."

"Be perfectly assured, Kelly dear, we can handle it together. We'll just be cool and not be startled into a fit about it. As I've heard you say, cool, calculated, and calm."

"Good start," said Kelly. "Thanks."

"Okay, Kelly, to begin with, there is no way I'm going to tell you what to do as far as meeting with your mother is concerned. No way. But I will pose only this: it might just be interesting to see what she's up to—just a thought."

"Hmm. See what you mean."

After a while, Kelly looked at her watch and said, "Well, I guess I better be getting ready to mosey on. They told me they were granting this as a privilege, and I couldn't stay long."

"Fiddle."

"Yeah, I know. Tell me, are you going to tell Andy about the rape?"

"Not right away."

"I don't blame you."

"But, wait Kelly, there are some things I have to say to Andy, and it's going to be really, really hard. It's going to be the hardest thing I've ever done in my life."

*   *   *

"Why are you keeping us apart?" asked Andy of agent Chad Jarrigan as they nibbled on ribs and French fries at Tony Roma's in the West End.

"It's all in the name of protection for your wife, Andy. It's not an effort to keep you apart. Rather, that just happens to be the unfortunate price of protection. For that matter, we initially contemplated confining you also, in case there would be a criminal effort to reach her by using you."

"I guess I just don't understand the system, but I accept that you have to do what you have to do. It's just that I'm worried about her. I ache for her, knowing she's hurting and maybe injured, or just so many things that could be bearing in on her. You know, she's my beloved wife, and I want to see about her, touch her, say something kind and loving to her, do something for her."

"I know. The system can be pretty cruel, I guess, but every necessary thing has a downside, and a price. I'm sorry for what you're going through, and we'll try to work it out for you at the very earliest time possible."

"Okay. I guess."

"With that said, Andy, here's something else you will probably have trouble accepting or even understanding, but again there are practical reasons behind this as well."

"You're really tapping my curiosity with that one, Chad. What else could there be? I mean, what else could matter?"

"The fact is that, probably at this very moment, her young friend, Kelly Surrat, is sitting with her at her place of confinement. Now, before you scream discrimination or subterfuge or whatever, hear me out! I don't even have to tell you this, but I admire your dedication and sense of logic, so I believe you deserve to know. This young girl is not seen as being affiliated with Lorrie Dean as you are, and we just don't believe the risks are there. Also, your wife is still in shock, and experts believe that a woman can help a woman more effectively in such circumstances."

"As much as I pine to see my beloved wife, actually I can understand that. Also, I know that young lady, Kelly, maybe as well as anyone, and she's my friend, too. I can tell you that she has had a lot to overcome in her own young life, and she made it with her head held high. So, yes, I can easily see the support and comfort she can be for my Lorrie Dean. No, I'm not screaming foul on that one. It's okay. It's okay."

"That's encouraging to hear, Andy. Now, on the positive side, or should I say on the more positive side, we may—just may, now—be getting close to apprehending the kidnappers. Thanks in great part to the astuteness of your wife, we had an early advantage in this investigation. Your Lorrie Dean LeMay didn't miss a thing during her captivity, and that's absolutely amazing, considering she was under extreme duress."

"Chad, this lady is all class. One of the things that captivated me about her right from the beginning was her unswerving grace and presence of mind. She is truly a jewel."

"Hey, I believe you. Andy; she not only identified the make, model, and license plate number of the car, she kept these details in her head for four days. Now, listen to this, she gave these facts to the officer in the helicopter two minutes after they rescued her. She also handed over a cell phone and a gun that she very wittingly confiscated before her miraculous run for her life. She also, very calmly, gave the first names of the three men involved. You're right, she is truly a jewel. Anyway, we got excellent leads from the cell phone. Not only that, we got a fingerprint, not off the grip, but, mind you, off the barrel of the gun. Apparently, her abductor palmed the gun by the barrel at times. You see, these guys really aren't all that bright. But they never are."

"Did I hear you say she ran for her life?"

"Yes, but I'll have to save that for after we capture those thugs. As a matter of fact, I can't even tell you why they took her at this point. We know, but we can't divulge those details quite yet."

"Why?"

"Details, Andy, details. Any revelations related to her capture and escape might jeopardize our investigation."

"So, I just have to wait."

"Right. The very minute we get a break in this thing, I'll expedite the reuniting of you two."

As Andy drove away from the restaurant, he began talking to himself, aloud—as was his habit. "I can accept that, life being what it is, bad things sometimes happen to good people. But why do they have to be this bad and last this long? Will my Lorrie Dean ever be free?"

11

Oh, the crushing burden of good news! Stark reality gripped Lorrie Dean as an excited Terry Aylor burst into the room and whooped, "Good news, you're going to see your husband, I mean fiancé, tomorrow."

Lorrie Dean gasped and instinctively slapped both hands over her face as she started to tremble. Then she began struggling for breath, and at once, the shaking collapsed into all-out convulsions, as a frightened Terry Aylor looked on.

Agent Aylor bounded over to Lorrie Dean's chair, dropped down in front of her, and gripped her shoulders. "Lorrie Dean, what's wrong? Shall I call for help? Have you had this before? Maybe I can get you a sedative. Let me help you. Tell me what's happening, if you can."

Lorrie Dean was shaking her head violently while Agent Aylor tried to comfort her. Then Terry unexpectedly released her grip on Lorrie Dean's shoulders, sat back, took a deep breath, and seemed to relax a little.

At that, Lorrie Dean hugged herself as tightly as she could, straining to defeat the raging spasms. It seemed to help that Terry had chosen to acquiesce. This set a new mood for Lorrie Dean and a new course for her mind to explore. So, she tried to curb her own outrage, dropping her hands to rest in her lap, taking full, deep breaths, and shifting her mind to other subjects. She reflected on the gentle voice of her friend, Kelly, calmly saying, *Hold your head up, and don't let fear and anger conquer you; if they just have to be there, use them.* Now, she was beginning to calm down somewhat, and, although she was still frightened by the sudden prospect of having to face her Andy Boone, her acceptance of this certainty wedged its way into the center of her mind.

Now smiling sympathetically, Terry said, "I have to confess that I was kind of scared for a bit there, but when you started to relax a little, I was reminded of your trademark composure and just knew you'd restore yourself."

"Thanks for understanding. Somehow I had repressed the idea that someday, I would have to look my sweetheart in the eye and unload all my horror on him. There's so much to explain, not just what they did to me in my captivity, but what I did to myself."

"You did what you had to do."

"No, no, that's not it. Getting out of there the way I did is the easy part. I don't like what I did, but I have fully accepted it. But there is something I did that I can't come to grips with and I never will. Terry, I surrendered the things Andy adored in me the most—my personal dignity, my character, and any semblance of grace. I changed. Do you hear me? I changed."

"Even so, I still say you did what you had to do. There's no guilt in that when you're under severe duress the way you were."

"I'm having trouble with that. I understand the concept, but I'm having trouble with it. I tried to outsmart my guard, and it backfired on me. I should have known you can't outsmart someone who's not playing a cerebral game. It only made him fight back like an animal; that's the only weapon he had, and it's the only one he needed. He trumped my arrogance in a heartbeat. How stupid of me—a helpless captive, bound and under armed guard—to think I could win with my brain. That's when I ceased to be Lorrie Dean. I don't know how I'm going to tell Andy all of this, but I have to."

"Only if he really needs to know. We do what we have to do and think of it in the best light we can. You don't have to tell him all about your hindsight, and your analysis of your own behavior. Please dump those wretched guilt feelings. Right now, they're holding you captive. Really, Lorrie Dean, you don't have to spill everything. It's okay to think of yourself and to see after your own mental health. Be patient; just do what you're comfortable with. He'll understand."

"No, I have to tell him."

"Please tell me why."

"Because I love him."

"I see." That seemed to be it. Neither said anything for a few moments. Then Terry asked, "Are you okay now, for sure? Seriously, do you need anything?"

"No, I'm okay."

"Would you like to call your friend, Miss Kelly?"

"No, thanks. I wouldn't do that to her right now. She's too good. I just can't burden her with this. She's got too much on her own shoulders, some serious domestic issues, and needs all the support we can give."

"Well, all right. It was a thought. I remember you seemed to enjoy some genuine relief having her around. I could see it in your eyes, your countenance. Your face looked softer, and you weren't so nervous."

"You're right, very perceptive of you. I guess part of our alliance rests with the fact that we need each other. That takes nothing away from our deep caring for each other and our devotion, but we do, indeed, need each other. And, you know, Terry, I guess that's partly what friendship thrives on—knowing you have a role in meeting at least some of the needs in the life of someone else. I have my obvious problems, and Kelly has some tragedies from her own past, weighing heavily on her. Still, friend that she is, who's she worrying about? Me!"

"Let her do it, Lorrie Dean; that's the way she wants it. Don't deny her the sense of belonging that it gives her. Let her help! Don't just automatically think you're bothering somebody if you ask for their help. You know very well that you're going to do all you can for her when it's time. You just said it yourself, said it all, very astutely. Remember the things you just told me about friendship. Whether you're Lorrie Dean or somebody else is a choice you make. You have more freedom than you think you do. I guess I'm pressing a little hard here, but only because I admire what you did. By golly, you made it work. You are a very impressive person, a standard setter, if you will. Among other things, you have character, or you wouldn't even be worrying about what others have to go through." She paused. "So, head up! Tell your Kelly what you're worrying about in confronting Andy with all this. She seems well qualified to hear it all."

"Yes, Kelly is an extraordinary young lady."

"And friend?" chided Terry, lifting her eyebrows.

"Come on, Terry, you're pushing. I will not burden—my friend—with this."

"I understand. Okay, that's that. Now, tomorrow afternoon, someone will drive you to downtown Dallas and let you out on Commerce near Neiman Marcus. You can go in and browse around a bit, but keep track of the time, because at three o'clock, you will need to exit Neiman's onto Main and wait there. A taxi will pick you up—it'll be our car, but it'll look like a regular taxi. Don't worry about your suitcase. The taxi driver will make that transfer before he comes for you." She wrinkled her brow and paused. "Something wrong?"

"It's just that . . . well, I was wondering: if it's all over, why so much precaution?"

"Just one last insurance step. We want to make sure you will not be followed, you know, in case there's another element out there we don't know about. So, anyway, the taxi driver will take you to your house. And then, you're free."

"Wanna bet?"

"Ooo. Sorry, sore spot."

"Forgive me. I'm being unfair to you, and you don't deserve that, Terry. You are a super professional, and I'm grateful for all you've done and all your effort to understand."

"Thanks, Lorrie Dean. I wish you the best, and hear this: someday, somehow, you'll get your self-esteem back, and you'll hold your head up again, and . . . hey, I like that smile. It looks downright natural."

"You just said something that I recall hearing my friend say. See, two against one. Guess I better pay attention." She chuckled and that surprised her and made her chuckle again, louder.

"Well, those who love you are not going to let up on you, so get ready!"

Upon that remark, Lorrie Dean grew solemn again and stared into her lap for a while, without a word.

Soon, Terry began to gather her things and shuffle around in readiness to leave. "Go ahead and pack your things and be ready to cut out of here early tomorrow afternoon. Any last requests?"

"No, and thanks again. The world is better because it has people like you in it."

"Wow, what a sweet thing to say. Thanks. I wish you ultimate freedom and no more shocks to make you suffer and lose it the way you did earlier."

"Yeah. Right. Well, in fairness, you might as well know this: another thing that happened that totally unnerved me during that shocking breakdown was a flashback to my horrifying nightmare. Still, as horrible as that was, it won't be nearly as hard to deal with as what I have to tell Andy and one devastating thing I have to do *to* him—really for his own good. That part is really going to hurt me—and him."

*   *   *

The uneasy promise of good news also fell on Andy when Agent Chad Jarrigan called him at work and broke the good news that he and Lorrie Dean would reunite the next day at their house.

"I've had a pretty positive sense about this for the last three days," said Agent Jarrigan. "Last night, we got the break we were looking for."

"Does that mean you caught the hoodlums?" asked Andy.

"Yes. That's exactly what it means. They were apprehended, actually by local police in another state."

"I can hardly even reckon with this moment, Chad. Lorrie Dean is my life, and you've been the key person in fixing it so I can have her, first by helping me find her during that mad search of mine, and now by restoring our lives together."

"My pleasure, Andy. We both owe Lorrie Dean for her alertness and conscientious efforts in this whole thing. Most people under duress won't notice little details the way she did. Believe me; those details gave us a head start on finding those guys."

"I'm not one bit surprised at Lorrie Dean being able to keep her head and stay cool during that ordeal. I'm so very proud of her. Those screwballs didn't know who they were messing with, did they?"

"Right on, Andy."

"How'd y'all do it?"

"Okay, glad you asked. On that point, I would like to have you and Lorrie Dean come to my office next Monday afternoon at four o'clock. I need to give you a sort of debriefing on this whole thing, and I'll explain some things you're probably curious about."

"Monday at four."

"Yeah, that'll give you and Lorrie Dean some time together before you have to deal with any technical stuff."

"We'll be there."

"Fine. Good-bye."

Andy hung up and sat stone still, patiently waiting, trying to comprehend what was happening. Surely, he should be absolutely euphoric at this moment, and indeed, he was tingling with anticipation, yet some ominous dread was gnawing at the edge of his excitement.

In a while, in the solitude of his office, he began to murmur to himself, asking questions: "Will I be up to the caregiving in case she's hurt? Will I have the sensitivity, the perception, to understand all that she will need? I have only my love."

Andy decided to avail himself of the wise, no-nonsense counsel of his business friend, his company hero, as he called her, Paige Ivy.

"Come in, Andy," Paige greeted him.

"Thanks. Do you have a minute?"

"For you, I always have a minute."

As they crossed the room toward the small conference table, Paige kept looking quizzically at her visitor, prompting him to exclaim, "What?"

Paige chuckled and said, "I'm having trouble reading your face. Usually, I've got you pegged by the time you take the second step through the door, but I'm seeing an expression on your face I've never seen before."

"See, I knew I was coming to the right place, for there is never any pretense in you, my candid and very sharp colleague. The fact is, Paige, I'm sort of in a trance, trying to find reality. Here's what's happened. You ready?"

"I'm ready."

"Lorrie Dean and I will be together again tomorrow afternoon."

"Yay, Andy, that's great!" She stepped forth and hugged him. "Congratulations! I'm thrilled. Goodness, I am truly happy for you two."

"Thanks, Paige. Well, I need your cool head to guide me, or just help me figure out why I'm not jumping three feet in the air and clicking my heels."

"Don't you know, Andy? This is much bigger than that to you. Your emotions are way beyond heel clicking, and it's no doubt preying on you subconsciously as to how you're going to react to each other after such a tragedy as you two have been through."

"That's it, Paige; you've put words to it for me. Honestly, as much as I ache to see my sweet wife, I can't predict what it'll be like. What are we to say to each other? What are we to do?"

"Andy, my dear, trusting colleague, just let it happen! You can't plan anything. Okay, already?"

"Okay. I knew you'd be candid with me. Thank you a hundred times."

"You're welcome."

"Well, okay, I'd better cut out. I've interrupted you long enough. Paige, most people live out a complete lifetime without having a friend like you. God bless you and your family!"

"That's good of you to say—and to wish God's blessings on us."

En route to the door, Andy paused, smiled, and chortled, "Try to look busy, Paige."

"Yeah, right."

"See ya."

"Remember, Andy! Let . . . it . . . happen!"

"Got it."

Andy's drive home after work was more eventful than it should have been. He was engrossed in visions of what might be, at one point drifting out of his lane and incurring the wrath of an angry truck driver. Fortunately for the other commuters, he was home way before he knew he was even close.

Inside their small, sparsely furnished, five-room house, Andy chewed up a burrito and sat down to call his morning light, Kelly.

"What's up, Boone Woo?"

"Dear buddy, Lorrie Dean and I will be together—here at our home—by this time tomorrow."

"Hooray! That's super wonderful. Now, don't you go gettin' drunk, Boone Woo!"

"Don't worry. I wouldn't dare touch even a beer. Our reunion needs my best. Sure, it sounds so simple, like just relax and reunite. But dear Kelly, it's not simple—not simple at all."

"I know. I've already sensed the nervousness from my visit with Lorrie Dean last Tuesday. She's also apprehensive, like you. Boone Woo, please give her time. Don't ask questions. There's so much she's going to need to tell you, and all of it will be painful for her. So, again, don't ask questions; she'll get it all out in time. Just, you know, be gentle with her."

"You don't have to ask that, Kelly. There is no way I could be any way but gentle with her."

"I know, but I just had to say it. You know, us girls have to stick together. Sometimes that makes us say unnecessary things."

"Okay. Thanks for the tip. That's why I called you. I think I trust your judgment and your insight more than my own."

Kelly chuckled. "So, do I have acumen or what?"

"My dear, you have everything. Before we finish, tell me, do *you* need anything?"

"No, thanks, I'm fine."

"Any more developments with your mother?"

"One, but I'd rather wait a while before I talk about that subject."

"All right, sweetheart. Whatever you say."

After his talk with Kelly, Andy sat quietly in the dim light of a single lamp, just across from the chair reserved for Lorrie Dean, his beloved wife. He was trying to gather a sense of what it was going to be like when Lorrie Dean would come to sit beside him. Then the words of Kelly saying, "Just be you," and Paige insisting, "Let it happen," returned, and soon he fell asleep in his chair.

12

Lorrie Dean waited near the front entrance of Neiman Marcus in the heart of downtown Dallas and watched her FBI chauffeur pull away in the traffic. She started slowly toward the entrance, looking down, watching her feet make their way along the sidewalk. She strolled into the huge department store and instinctively raised her head and then deliberately lifted it higher at the echo of Kelly's words, *Hold your head up.*

The store itself was a bright greeting, orderly and neat, inviting as a satin pillow. It had an ambience of majesty, awesomely high ceilings, restful lighting, classic furnishings, and tasteful decorations. It was a showcase of fashion, artfully displayed along routes leaving generous room for shoppers to navigate. Sales associates were obviously well trained, knowledgeable, and gracious. It was essentially a wrinkle-free store, an icon of good taste.

For Lorrie Dean, it was refreshing just being among people politely accepting life's offerings, respectfully meandering along the aisles, admiring things, and smiling as though grateful to be sharing the world with others.

She shuddered at the stark contrast with her morbid prison dungeon of just two weeks earlier. Neiman's was clearly the high ground, her brutal hostage cell, the gutter. In that hole, she had felt like a witch in Hades; here she felt like Alice in Wonderland.

Unconsciously, Lorrie Dean just seemed to gravitate toward the shoe department. She felt an obsessive repulsion to high-heel fashions, and she felt dread at the notion of ever having to walk in them again. At once, she shook her head at her own concocted absurdity, making her think, *Really now, what are the odds of being kidnapped in high heels a second time?* On that thought, she frowned and whispered to herself, "Not funny, Lorrie Dean."

As she turned away and started toward business attire, she glanced at her watch. *Oops, time to go.*

Only seconds after Lorrie Dean walked out the back entrance onto Main Street, a taxi pulled up and double-parked right in front of her. The driver got out, walked over to his supposed passenger and muttered, "Lorrie Dean?" She nodded, and he opened the passenger door, holding it for her.

As they headed out, Lorrie Dean glanced thoughtfully over her right shoulder toward Neiman's and nodded.

Twenty minutes later, they were in the suburban town of Mesquite, approaching what was to have been the dream house for Lorrie Dean and Andy. That dream and all others were now vague, unexciting memories. At the house, the driver unloaded Lorrie Dean's suitcase, wished her luck, and hurried away.

Moments later, she was nervously rambling around in their little five-room house, trying to find something to do, but there just wasn't anything that needed attention. So, she began to ponder the house itself, its meaning in the new context, its purpose from this point on. The exhilaration she had felt when they bought the house and first stepped foot in it was dead and gone, surely never to return.

She started retracing her steps through the house, slowly this time, hoping for inspiration. She stood for a while in each doorway as she passed from room to room. There were two bedrooms, one a small guest room, the other a master with only a dresser, a queen-size bed, and two lamp tables. This room, like the entire house, was just basic: two closets, a bathroom suite, and a small vanity area. Lorrie Dean lingered in the master bedroom for a long time and then passed on through the doorway, shaking her head, and into the short hallway that led to the guest bedroom and the main parlor, or den, as they sometimes called it.

She glanced around at the sparse furnishings in the den—a couch, two recliner chairs, and one thirty-inch, outdated television set. They had agreed to wait until after their formal marriage to select the main inventory of furnishings. She began slapping her legs as she entered the adjacent dining room and on into the kitchen for a tall glass of water.

The water did nothing to break the spell. That left her with no alternative but simply to accept her circumstances as stoically as possible. Thereupon, disappointed and irritated, she stalked back into the parlor and plopped down in her recliner.

*   *   *

Andy was at his desk, opening and closing drawers, shifting stacks of manuals and file folders, trying to stay physically busy. Mental concentration, no matter how focused, was no match for his edgy nerves at this hour. By now he had repositioned his in-basket about nine times.

He was on the threshold of reunion with the love of his life, following the supposed resolution of the heartbreaking catastrophe that had dragged them through a short but painful separation. "How do you get ready for this?" he muttered to himself. Then he rapped the desk with a fist and declared, "You don't get ready; you let it happen." Thus spoke Paige Ivy, his company hero.

Throughout the day, each of Andy's five coworkers dropped by to congratulate him and offer their moral support. They were affable and seemed genuine in their expressions, and it was the best thing Andy had encountered so far in lifting his spirits. Strange thing, though: everybody congratulated him, but nobody wished him good luck.

Then along came Kirk Daniels, his laughable boss. On the surface, this seemed way out of character for Kirk, who had been Andy's self-appointed adversary back when Andy was *his* boss. Their contentious relationship hadn't changed much after they traded jobs, to make Andy's search for a missing Lorrie Dean easier. No matter, Kirk was conspicuously polite—at first.

Soon, Kirk's agreeable countenance began to fade, and in his old customary style, he chided, "Hey, look at you, Andy! You should be smiling big-time, old sport, but there you sit, looking like a forlorn old hound dog."

"Oh, not at all," snapped Andy. "I'm just touched by your kind words and vigorous support."

"Yeah, right. You're holding back. You don't fool me." Then he leaned way over toward Andy and rolled his lips like some kind of freak. "Come on, Sport, get happy!"

"Gotcha."

On that profound note, Kirk rose to leave. As he reached the door, he hesitated, turned half around, and said in a sincere-sounding tone, "Seriously, Andy, congratulations, and I wish you luck."

Goes to show you, thought Andy, *even a card-carrying bonehead has a little dribble of compassion—or was that little dance just protocol—cover-your-butt protocol?* Surely, within the history of their contentious, near comical relations, Kirk had learned one vital lesson: never underestimate a forlorn old hound dog. For that matter, Andy had learned not to underestimate the power of corporate politics.

The day proceeded in this general fashion and mercifully, it got to be three o'clock, time to leave the job and head home and into the arms of the dearest woman in the world. Kirk had gratuitously urged him to "just go ahead and take off an hour early, Andy—on the house." *The guy is all heart.*

As he was pondering these awesome questions, others of the staff, even outside his division, dropped in and politely wished him well in his reunion with—as some of them put it—his woman.

*   *   *

Lorrie Dean was in the parlor, resting quietly in her recliner, when she heard Andy's car drive up. Moments later, the front door eased open, ever so slowly, and in stepped Andy Boone. She rose from her chair and stood in place, breathing heavily, and waited.

Andy pulled the door to behind him and, with his hand still holding the doorknob, turned and faced his beloved Lorrie Dean. He could feel pounding in his chest and the relentless nagging of nervous breathing.

They stood, motionless, gazing across the space at each other. Surely, it was happening, yet this long anticipated moment, which should have been liberating for both of them, was mostly scary and uncertain. Even from across the room, Andy could tell that his sweetheart was not well.

Neither smiled, but they understood what was going on. They were granting life time to emerge, letting this awesome moment have its way. Their patience conveyed their respect for each other, their acceptance of the situation, and the right of each to have deep, personal, yet very different feelings. They were not rushing anything, for time would never again be a factor in anything in their lives. So, they waited for the gods to push them together.

Andy released the door and, after standing in place for a few moments, started inching toward Lorrie Dean, and she in turn moved slowly toward him. Andy instinctively rushed the last few steps, as Lorrie Dean waited in her ever-gracious way. There was only one truly defining point that could be made about their embrace. It was love.

Little did Andy know, nor did he in any way suspect, that this unbridled love was earmarked for a grim trial. For now, they held on.

As they held each other, they prayed for God's grace, each knowing they already had it. There was not the slightest impulse to break their humble embrace. After a while, and still unhurried, they drew back just a little, raised their heads, and looked straight into each other's eyes. Their expressions were solemn but puzzling. In a moment, Andy reached for Lorrie Dean's hands, pressed them together, folded them inside his own and held them that way for a few moments. Then he lifted high their joined hands as though in a ritual resealing their bond.

Lorrie Dean continued to stare into her lover's face, knowing that her own expression was clearly loving but also sad and futile. Andy tilted his head slightly to meet her gaze. In a moment, they spontaneously pushed apart. Lorrie Dean glanced vaguely away from Andy, swallowed hard, and cleared her throat, preparing to speak. Andy indulged.

"Andy, do we have to talk for a while? I feel so weak, and there's so much to say. Could we, like, just rest for now?"

Andy gently wrapped her in his arms, tapped a little kiss on her forehead, held a light kiss to her lips for a moment, then eased back and smiled.

Lorrie Dean managed a thin little grin and mumbled, "Good answer."

Later, with a little more animation, they agreed to take up positions in their easy chairs and watch TV. When they were snugly moored, they twisted around to face each other, and, with furrowed brows, just let their looks reflect the question, "So what are we going to watch?"

"Suppose," began Andy, "we tune in to an easy listening music channel. That way, we won't have to listen to silly jabber."

"Sounds right."

In a couple of hours, they roused themselves and agreed to go out for dinner. They settled on baby back ribs at Chili's and found, to their amusement, that the noisy but cheerful banter of young people was actually uplifting. In fact, just being out in the regular world, immersed in the predictable, seemed to ease, though slightly, the apprehension of these curiously frightened lovers. Things that used to annoy them were now welcome relief; they were dependable and nonthreatening.

"Andy, I know there are things you want to ask, but I just need a little transition time. As I'm sure you can tell, I'm in shock and just incapable of making sense right now. Are you okay with that?"

"I am indeed, my love. What you have to say is worth waiting for." Then he frowned, looking worried, and said, "There's just one thing."

Lorrie Dean didn't respond for a moment. Then she said, "Okay, what?"

"I just have to know if you're well. I mean, are you hurt anywhere? Should we be seeing a doctor?"

"No, I'm fine. They had me examined when I was in protective custody, and all they found was some dehydration. So, I'm okay, now, Andy—I'm okay."

They ate quietly, occasionally murmuring bland observations, neither of them broaching anything personal or making any reference to their sad nightmare or the prospects in their future. It was not time yet, and these two people were fully prepared to endure the psychological delay reality was dictating in this critical time.

Again, the presence of the young people in Chili's and the charm of the servers had a relaxing effect on them. They actually caught themselves chuckling merrily at times. This was good. They smiled their approval toward the tables of uninhibited high schoolers having fun. After all, they were making life work. *God bless you all.*

They left the restaurant feeling some relief which, though superficial, still had value. Job talk escorted them home. Andy told of the well-wishers from his office and even boasted of the biting me-too sentiments of his old nemesis, Kirk Daniels. He conceded that he had not anticipated such all-out support of the company people and eagerly suggested it was a credit to their character. Somehow, Clay Cutter, with all its shortcomings, had managed consistently to attract outstanding people.

Lorrie Dean smiled as often as she could and tried to be a functional player in the conversation, even though a nagging little worry hung in a corner of her mind. When Andy fell silent, she decided to test him with her concern. "You know, Andy, I guess I better find out if I still have a job."

"You haven't checked on it, yet?"

"No, they wouldn't let me have any contacts in Protective."

"Oh yeah, that's right." He thought for a moment and then said, "Tell you what, why don't you go ahead and dress for work Monday and just show up, as if there's no question about it?"

"Andy, you're such a dreamer. But you know, I think you may have something there. Showing up ready to work may well offer all the leverage I need." She slapped his shoulder playfully, and at once, her own little reflexive gesture startled her. "Thanks," she said.

Back in their house, full and lazy, they yawned their way into the shower stall, in turn, and savored the incomparable, restorative power of a nighttime bath. That done, they resolved to gear down and settle in for the night.

In their chairs, again to the accompaniment of soft music from the television, each started to nod, and this made them giggle at each other. Actually, this wasn't quite the breakthrough Andy was looking for, because their snickers were a bit flat and somewhat perfunctory, not actually reflecting much real amusement. But after all, that was a start; any chuckle is a chuckle.

Lorrie Dean finally yawned and suggested, "I think I'm about ready to retire. I'm so tired I don't know if I'll ever catch up."

"I'm with you. I'm ready to hit the sack, too."

As they stood to begin their short stroll to the master bedroom, Lorrie Dean stepped politely in front of Andy to delay him a moment. "Andy, I, ah, well, I feel I should mention something here. See, I know that you might feel like getting amorous tonight, and I'd love that, too, but I just—I don't know how to explain it . . ."

"Sex?"

"Yeah, right, sex! There you go." She managed a thin smile. "So, the problem is that I've been so tense, so stunned and scared for so long, I don't think I would be good. You know? Could we just rest tonight and not do anything else?"

"My precious Lorrie Dean, I fully understand. Thank you for caring so much as to consider my feelings that way. But it's okay, sweetheart. It's okay. One day, we'll embrace again in that wondrous sexual passion that only we know so profoundly. So, for now, we'll just sleep."

Emotion welled in Lorrie Dean, but she would not let herself show it. She did hug him, however, and they made their way to the sleep chamber. After a good hour of twisting and floundering about, they both gave out and dropped off to sleep.

Breakfast the next morning seemed like old times. Andy had made sure they had fresh eggs and bacon and bread and milk. As they were sliding their chairs away from the table, Lorrie Dean patted Andy's shoulder and said, "Get some rest, Andy, while I run to the store and get you some groceries."

"Get *me* some groceries?"

"Well, you know, restock our shelves."

Andy stifled the temptation to frown, and asked, "Why don't I go with you and give you a hand?"

"Not necessary. I'd sort of like to do it alone."

"You feel like driving?"

"Sure. Actually, I want to drive, you know, do something useful."

"Be careful, sweetheart."

"Okay. Oh, before I forget, could we possibly go to the farm tomorrow?"

"Sure, absolutely. I'll give them a call."

En route to the store, Lorrie Dean's thoughts turned again to the ominous task ahead of her. She was mostly questioning herself, which was a way of asking God for help. When would she begin to tell him? Where should she start? What would happen to him once she revealed the monster now controlling both their lives—the hideous, senseless rape? What would he think of her? What would he think of himself?

How about the other huge question, the one that loomed as a cruel, life-changing issue for both of them, something she hadn't even hinted to her best friend, Kelly? Would someone come to care for Andy the way she did? As she reached the parking lot, she was trembling again, much like she had at the onset of her breakdown while in confinement. "Enough!" she shouted aloud.

When Lorrie Dean returned, Andy helped her put away the groceries. They didn't talk much during this routine. Andy was feeling satisfaction because this was something husbands and wives do together. Lorrie Dean was pining because she knew she would never get to do this as a wife.

After lunch, while they were resting in front of the TV, Andy asked, "Sweetheart, it doesn't matter, but I was just wondering: any special reason you wanted to go to the farm tomorrow?"

"The people."

13

They were on US Highway 175, a familiar East Texas trail that held poignant memories. Once before, they had traveled this route as forbidden lovers destined to part unfulfilled, because Lorrie Dean would be returning to hidden protection. Those were heart-ripping, sad hours for the two of them. Déjà vu.

They cruised on in silence, drinking in what healing the country scenes had to offer and, unlike before, refusing to let their mood dictate their reaction to the beautiful, enchanting meadowlands and woods. Lorrie Dean suppressed an onrush of butterflies in her stomach when they passed through Kaufman, site of her recent hideaway, and again when they passed the intersection with the narrow county road where she was kidnapped. She noticed that Andy also shielded his vision with one hand when they sailed past that point.

They felt some peace when they finally turned up the driveway to the Grimes farm near Tillman. Soon they parked beside the stately old house, alighted, and moseyed up the steps onto the magnificent front porch and on over to the main door. Andy pressed the doorbell button as he and Lorrie Dean glanced expectantly at each other.

An adorable, young Kelly Surrat opened the door and smiled mischievously. "Good morning, folks. New in town?"

Andy and Lorrie Dean cut their eyes toward each other, conjuring divine help. After a brief pause, Lorrie Dean said, "No, I'm not new in town, but this guy is; he just got out."

Struggling to keep a straight face, Kelly chortled, "Well, this is a little irregular. So, do you have a permit?"

Andy, looking meek, lifted his eyebrows toward Lorrie Dean as if to say, "Take it."

Lorrie Dean tightened her lips and worked her mouth a little and then chided, "No, ma'am, I'm afraid we don't. See, we didn't have money to cover the fee for a permit. I spent every nickel I had making his bail."

At that, they all lost it, and these three clowning buddies, bonded as they were by harmless teasing and enduring love, scampered giggling into house, seemingly without care. En route through the front room, trailing somewhat behind their host, Andy whispered close to Lorrie Dean's ear, "She's trying, isn't she?"

Lorrie Dean nodded.

The moment they came into the all-purpose den, dining, and sitting room, everybody rushed for Lorrie Dean, hugging and praising, while Andy and Kelly stood back, smiling proudly.

When all the commotion finally settled, Lorrie Dean, humbly brushing away tears, waved a hand to everybody, and they all started shushing each other. Bolstered by the receptive hush of otherwise excited friends, she started to speak.

"You all are absolutely the greatest, and I want you to know that I understood, from our very first meeting, why Andy is so devoted to you. Now, I have to confess that when I asked Andy if we could come here today, I was looking forward to those hugs and warm wishes. But y'all . . . you know . . ." Her voice was beginning to crack, but she pushed on. "You know, it's therapy for me to watch you all indulging in each other." She chuckled and continued, "It's really fun to be a spectator in this crowd." She paused a moment while they all laughed. Then she turned from one to the other, saying, "Mom, Aunt Leah, Grandpa, Dub, dear Kelly, you are the real thing. Thanks for having me."

Everyone in the cozy little clique said "Thanks," each with a personal way of expressing it, while Andy gave a thumbs-up to everybody. When he glanced at Grandpa, he caught a faint glimmer in his eyes, something he'd never seen before in the face of the resident professor, as they affectionately called him. *Lorrie Dean does that to you.*

Church services were inspiring and uplifting, and that helped to bring into view a comforting sense of God's mercy. Worshipping together with others seeking the truth about the promise of life provided a comfort to them not available in any other kind of experience.

The experience of lunch was also uplifting. Mom and Aunt Leah had teamed up on this one, Aunt Leah on her specialty, peach cobbler, and

Mom rolling out the meat loaf, fried corn, baked potatoes, and a vegetable medley casserole, which she had invented herself. But the main course, the part giving something eternal, was the friendly interaction among close friends.

After lunch, the family broke down again into individuals, fully restored in every way, now scurrying off to engage in personal activities. Grandpa sauntered to the front porch to read his Bible, Mom and Aunt Leah started washing dishes, and Dub headed for the grain barn, with Andy chasing after him, somewhat late because of preoccupation with his two girls. They had begged for a little private time together and so sailed off in the direction of Kelly's Cove.

Before he cut away to join Dub, Andy stood on the back steps, watching his girls amble on down the path toward the cove. Smiling to himself, he yelled out, "Remember, girls, no cussin' in the cove."

Kelly turned around and bowed, still backing away in stride. Lorrie Dean, without looking around, waved a hand high above her head.

Andy continued to watch as they toodled on down the way until they were taken by a bend in the path. Then he hurried off to find Dub. Among other things, he was anxious to find out about any further developments with Kelly's mother.

In the cove, Lorrie Dean and Kelly sat on a bench near the back of the encircling wall of trees. They shifted slightly so as to sort of face each other. Both sighed as if to ask, "Where shall we begin?"

"Are you doing okay, Kelly?" asked Lorrie Dean.

"Oh yeah, but more important than that, are *you* doing okay?"

"Well, I have to admit that I'm struggling with some things. So, I guess there are a few issues I wanted to sound out with you to help me along with . . . ah . . . well, to break things to Andy—and I also want to find out about your mother."

"Sure. Let's start with the sound-out part first."

Lorrie Dean recounted her days in captivity, going far beyond the general summary she had given Kelly during their meeting when she was sequestered in protective custody. She told of her questionable fencing with the jerk guarding her and her ineffective tactic of randomly changing her manner of dealing with him, wherein she literally took on different personalities. She shuddered when she told of the morbid broth diet, the pain of sleeping in a chair, the torture of hand and ankle cuffs, and finally the brutal rape. She also told of the bloodcurdling scream into the wretched ear of her pathetic guard, her resorting to violence, her running away, her praying in the woods, and her making the 911 call. By this point, Kelly had taken Lorrie Dean's hands and was holding them and letting her countenance reflect support.

"I remember running," pleaded Lorrie Dean. "I remember running for my life. In fact, that's when I learned *how* to run. Have you ever thought of having to run for your life? Nobody does. I guess that's something we don't have to plan for. God gave us instincts for survival."

Kelly listened intently and sympathetically, never once interrupting. Lorrie Dean was shaking her head as she considered the miracle of her friend, the marvel of her maturity at only seventeen, the indulging sensitivity that most grownups haven't even mastered. She knew that Kelly fully understood that she didn't need advice; she needed to talk. And so she did.

"And I remember the disgusting, totally repulsive rape. Even in that horrendous time, I wasn't thinking about being raped. Actually, I was thinking about you and Andy—what would you do?—what would you think of me? See, Kelly, I am no longer Lorrie Dean. I don't have the things about me that you and Andy so treasured in me. I'm not Lorrie Dean—I am not—I am not!"

Kelly so wanted to respond to that one, to find some words to soothe her friend's frantic withdrawal, her desperate sense that she was not herself and therefore was worthless. She knew, however, that there were no such words, that nothing from outside Lorrie Dean would heal her of these deep wounds. She couldn't resist the temptation to take a stand on one point, but for the moment, she would continue to allow her friend time.

When she thought the time was right, Kelly leaned close to Lorrie Dean and declared, "Whoever you are, I know you, and whoever you are, Andy and I will always love you. I know I can't change your mind about how you feel about yourself. At the same time, there's nothing you've done or can ever do that has any power to change how we feel about you."

Sobbing and wringing her hands, Lorrie Dean murmured, "Thank you."

"Let's just meditate here in this precious sanctuary for a few minutes. If there's more, then let it out when you want to, when you feel like it. Remember, no cussin'."

Lorrie Dean smiled reflexively. "You little rascal."

When Lorrie Dean felt she had some composure back, she began to sound out Kelly's thoughts on a related matter, even though it was obvious Kelly was there to give support, not advice. "Now, I've got to figure out how to tell Andy all these things in a way that upsets him the least. Of course, that's not really possible. Still, I don't know when or where we ought to be when I unleash this story on him."

"You know," began Kelly, "I'm somehow convinced that you'll know when the time and place are right. Trying to plan those details will only stress you out. I believe when that moment is right, you'll just instinctively know it, that some impulse will show up in your mind and say, 'Now.'"

Lorrie Dean was half-smiling and shaking her head. "One thing you have to give me credit for is I know how to pick my friends. Now, heck! Enough of that. It has helped me greatly to hear myself talk about it, to describe not only the details of the experience but my feelings during them. Kelly, you're such an absolute jewel."

"We're friends."

"Okay, now, tell me about your mother. Your Boone Woo is very worried about this business with your mother. As you probably know, he has a very protective nature about him. So, be ready, dear friend, he's going to ask you about it."

"If you insist. Anyway, the thing is, my mother is wanting to meet with me. Can you help me with that?"

"I'll try. What's the latest?"

"I have actually exchanged a few words with her, by phone, of course, and she insists we need to meet, that she has some things to say to me. So, in a nutshell, she wants to meet—and I don't want to meet. That's where we are."

"She doesn't want to say her things on the phone?"

"No." Kelly found it hard to sit still in this moment, but she confined her battle to twisting her fingers around each other, over and over, while staring into her lap. "What do you think, Lorrie Dean?"

"Well, it sounds like there's some urgency with your mother. Maybe she has some revelations that would actually give you closure on something she thinks is bothering you, maybe some unknowns she figures have hounded you all these years."

"You think?"

"Well, it's possible. Are there, Kelly? Are there some things you wish were answered for you? Is there anything you want to know?"

"Only why she didn't love me."

They embraced and cried softly together—friends. As they began to calm, Lorrie Dean sensed that Kelly really did expect her to do some talking. "To reassure you, Kelly, I would say just let your heart, your own judgment, guide you. But you know what? Well, it's perfectly all right to be selfish about this thing. You know, it's just possible you might get some real answers. Maybe she can speak to some matters you've long wondered about. I don't know. Just thinking."

"Maybe so." After a long pause, Kelly looked directly at her friend, lifted her eyebrows and said, "Hmm. Something just struck me; you never talk about *your* mother."

"That's just me, part of my bearing, I guess. Andy says that I never talk about myself."

"See there? You're still Lorrie Dean, right up to now."

"I don't know about that. I've done a lot of talking about me since the . . . since the rape."

"Would you like to talk about that now? I'm ready to listen."

"No."

"Okay. So, tell me about your mother. Seems to me she had something to do with the predicament you're in."

"Not totally. It was my choice to come out of hiding. But, okay, whatever. Since she paid the price for her crime—and even before—my mother has been a very indulging parent."

"What do you mean, indulging?"

"She has always been good to me. She looked after my every need and really tried to teach me principles of proper living, even as she was misbehaving, herself."

"Doesn't make sense, does it?"

"Well, I think that sometimes, mothers—at least, some mothers—just try too hard. They panic, trying to be a perfect parent. See, neither my dad nor my mother had any specific skills that would help them land good-paying jobs. My dad worked out on a dredge boat, and for a long time, my mother worked at a dairy doing menial jobs. All the while, she was obsessed with making sure they would be able to send me to college. That was very big with my mother. Her parents couldn't afford a college education for her, so she was determined to see to it I got one. As I say, she panicked, quit her puny job, and started dealing in drugs. Two of her old high school cronies got her into that. And I must say, it was very lucrative for her, and true to her word, she was stashing all the loot into an escrow account for me."

"She was willing to break the law to look after you?"

"Well, it seems that way. Of course, I've had to suffer for her crimes. Anyway, it took all the savings she had set back for me to pay her fines, her lawyer and move across the country."

"And you're not bitter?"

"Of course, I'm bitter, and I will never forget it. But I can't say that she totally failed me. She did teach me the importance of good character, grace and respect for others. She kept reminding me that I was a lady and that poise and good bearing are what make you a lady."

"How did she teach you these things?"

"She would sit me down and drill me. At church, she would point out refined women and comment on how everybody seemed to admire them. Oh, and she delighted in dressing me up, making me look pretty for church, and it would thrill her when people would make a fuss over my appearance."

"Really, Lorrie Dean, that *is* admirable . . . for whatever reason she did it."

"Oops. Do I detect a little chiding in that comment?"

"No, no. I'm just thinking that nobody can really second-guess a parent."

"Really,"

*   *   *

At the grain barn, Dub and Andy were tugging on a homemade chain lift, trying to hoist a heavy door up to the loft near the cone of the roof. When they had it high enough, Dub directed Andy to take the stairs inside up to the loft while he climbed the ladder outside. Working from both sides, they wrestled the door into place, and Dub nailed on the hinges.

Back on the ground, sitting on tipped-over buckets, they began pattering about ranch and farm issues. Then Andy brought up the subject of Kelly's mother.

"Andy, I really don't know what the deal is, because I refuse to carry on much conversation with my sister. I'm pretty sure, though, that Rosalea has saddled herself with naggin' guilt feelin's. She is probably just plottin' to get Kelly to say she feels wonderful and is havin' a fine life."

"Do you know why her mother turned her away, eleven years ago, or whatever it was?"

"Yeah, about eleven years ago. Sure, I know why. It was just plain out-and-out selfishness."

"How old was she when she had the baby?"

"Nineteen. Not ready to be a mother, was she?"

"Wonder if she believes she is now?"

Dub shrugged. Neither said anything for a while, letting the whole problem weigh in. After a while, Dub started up again. "Andy, I don't like this, because it's keepin' Kelly nervous and upset. Rosalea calls every day or two, cryin' and beggin' Kelly to meet her somewhere."

"Where does she live?"

"Shreveport."

"Well, I guess you know whose side I'm on," chirped Andy. "I just don't want Kelly to be under stress."

"Me neither."

"Do you think it would be in order for me to talk to Kelly about it?"

"Of course. In fact, I kinda think she wants you to show an interest."

"That's all I need to know. Let's go home!"

Coincidentally, Andy, Dub, and the girls all arrived back at the house near the same time. Grandpa buttonholed Lorrie Dean to solicit her help with a crossword puzzle while Andy and Kelly stood in place, waiting.

When it was clear that Lorrie Dean would be occupied for a while at Grandpa's indulgence, Kelly looked at Andy, nodded toward the porch, and headed that way. Andy followed.

In a couple of minutes, Kelly and Andy were seated in rockers, with one vacant rocker between them, reserved for Lorrie Dean. At once, Kelly blurted, "Boone Woo, we have to talk!"

"By all means. Hit it!"

"Okay, keep this kind of between us. I'm only doing it because I love you both." She paused and then rattled on without a break. "There are some real tough things Lorrie Dean has to tell you, that is, that she wants you to know. Right now, she can't seem to come to grips with how and when. She hurts, Boone Woo."

"I know, and it's tearing my heart out, but I think it would stress her more if I pushed."

"How right you are. I knew you would see it that way. Thank you, my Boone Woo. So, anyway, I know a lot of the things she has to say to you, but I'm under oath not to disclose them to anyone."

"And I don't want you to. I will not pry. Of course, I'm curious and disturbed, but first and foremost, I want to honor that gracious lady in all her needs. There's time—plenty of time."

"Well said."

Andy got up and walked to the edge of the porch, gazing out toward the horizon, trying to reckon with his own heartaches for his wife. In but a few minutes, he turned back and came to stand in front of a very serious-looking Kelly. "What can we do to make it easier for her?"

"There's nothing we can do that will really make it easy for her. But we can embrace her with our love and understanding, and not go to pieces with her."

They fell silent. Andy returned to his rocker, leaned forward in it, and rested his chin on a propped-up thumb. Kelly quit rocking and stilled. They let it go that way for several minutes.

Finally, Kelly began to stare at Andy, and when he looked up, she asked kindly, "Boone Woo, what are you thinking?"

"Just trying to figure out what's the first thing she'll need when she finishes telling me. What's the best thing we should have ready to catch her, so to speak? Should we go to bed—go see a movie—hit the park—throw rocks at the sunset—what?"

"All I got to say is, you'll know. When it's done, it will be very natural for you to do the best thing. I'm not worried about that. I'm just worried about Lorrie Dean getting through it."

"Kelly, my incomparable little lady, thanks for being Lorrie Dean's friend."

"My honor."

At that moment, Lorrie Dean eased on to the porch to sit between them. She glanced from one to the other, trying to smile.

"Did you get Grandpa straightened out?" piped Andy.

"Some, maybe, but he knows a heck of a lot more about crosswording than I do."

"He likes you, Lorrie Dean," said Kelly. "I think he just wanted to be with you for a little bit."

"Well, he's smart and polite."

At once, Dub and Aunt Leah shuffled in and took up rockers. There followed a little symphony of subdued chatter. Soon, much to their disappointment, Andy and Lorrie Dean apologized that it was time for them to get back and be ready to hit their jobs the next morning.

On the road again, husband and wife, or fiancé and fiancée, depending on your viewpoint, tried to be stoic. They were nervous and frightened, and each knew that about the other.

"Good visit," said Andy, finally breaking the gloomy silence.

"Sure was."

"Yep."

They traveled on. At one point, Lorrie Dean flinched, and Andy asked, "Are you okay?"

"Actually I'm having quite a bit of discomfort, and I'm thrilled about it."

"Okay, give me a few minutes on that one. It may take me some time to comprehend."

She giggled, slapped his shoulder, and chortled, "Well, this really isn't news, but it confirms news I got earlier after that medical exam while I was in protective custody. The fact is, Andy, I'm having my period!"

"That *is* good news."

"Yes. Now, you know, thinking back on our visit, I believe you're right that Kelly was doing whatever she could think of to try to help me. I enjoyed our little comical banter at the front door when we first got there, and it made me laugh. Then I wanted to cry, because I knew I'd not be a part of that much longer." She paused for a moment and then sobbed, "But it's all my fault."

14

Conversation at breakfast Monday morning was restrained—not unfriendly, but noticeably subdued. When they were finished, they sat placidly, waiting for the spirit to kick in, each clearly deep in thought. Simultaneously, they laid hands on the table, ready to shove back. Upon that patently decisive gesture, they looked at each other, dead serious, and winked.

As they set away for final touches in getting ready for work, Andy was musing to himself about the wink. Not that it was all that special; it was just your basic regulation wink, yet somehow, its offhand occurrence was surprising. *I don't think I've winked or seen a wink in twenty years,* he thought. In any event, a wink can't really hurt anything. In their case, it might well reflect a new level of acceptance of reality—and it might not.

Time to go. When Andy glanced at his beleaguered young partner, still looking very pretty and adorable in her tailored, soft blue, silk dress, he caught his breath. "You look so very pretty, my Lorrie Dean."

"Thanks. Shall we go?"

Andy nodded and stepped outside, holding the door for Lorrie Dean. After he locked the door, he said, "Oh, don't forget, we're supposed to meet with the FBI agent at four. You want to just meet me at Chad's office, since you'll already be downtown?"

"Sure. Have a good day."

They drove off in separate cars. Andy headed for his Clay Cutter job in Las Colinas at the edge of Dallas, while Lorrie Dean drove toward downtown Dallas where she would report in, still an employee, she hoped, of "We Party," a fairly new event-planning service.

Lorrie Dean sucked in a few deep breaths and then nervously and very slowly opened the door to the "We Party" reception room. The instant she stepped in, she was startled by the exuberant voice of the receptionist, whooping, "Yay. It's Lorrie, everybody!" The woman scooted from behind her desk, stumbling over a misplaced chair, and dashed up to Lorrie Dean, holding wide her arms.

Lorrie Dean was already weeping by the time the others rushed into the room, applauding. Her boss, Jan Merrit, hurried over to her, hugging and consoling her. "I'm so sorry, so very, very sorry. Just let us know what you need. Consider us your rooting section."

"Thank you all so very much," she sobbed. Then, smiling through tears, she said, "I didn't know if I would still have a job or not, but I figured even I got fired, I ought to be dressed for it."

Everybody laughed. Then Jan took Lorrie Dean's arm and headed toward an interior door. "Come on into my office and relax for a few minutes."

Comfortably seated in Jan's office, they chatted excitedly about current workload and special activities. Mercifully, Jan didn't ask Lorrie Dean one word about her ordeal. The subject didn't even come up. After they wound down, Lorrie Dean said, "Jan, to you and everyone here, I just want to say, I owe you big-time."

"Not at all. The fact is, life owes you one, and we are a very proud part of your life."

Lorrie Dean nodded and tried hard to smile.

"So," snapped Jan as she started to stand, "shall we go to work?"

"Yes, yes. Lay it on me."

"Okay, you can work with Shirley on a bridal shower she just received late yesterday."

"Great. Thanks again." As Jan patted her shoulder and turned back to her own duties, Lorrie Dean was thinking, *A bridal shower. Wouldn't you know it?*

All in all, the day went well, and Lorrie Dean reached the office of FBI Agent Chad Jarrigan a few minutes before Andy arrived.

Chad welcomed them enthusiastically, offered them seats at his conference table, and sat down at the head of it, holding a handful of papers. "Okay," he began, "this should be helpful to you and maybe ease your minds somewhat. First of all, do I understand, Lorrie Dean, that you, of your own volition, have chosen to reject protection and discontinue using an alias?"

"Yes. That's correct. I want to continue as Lorrie Dean LeMay." *Oh, how I long to be Lorrie Dean.*

"All right, let me give you some details of where we are and how we got there. Most of this is public information, but be discreet about it. This is not something you really need to pass along to anyone else."

"We're pledged to hold everything you tell us in complete confidence," said Andy, as Lorrie Dean nodded her agreement.

"To begin with, I must turn to Lorrie Dean and say this: you are magnificent, and I salute you and thank you for all you did in laying the foundation for our investigation."

"Thanks," said Lorrie Dean, smiling bashfully.

"Well, here are some things you did which helped us. First of all, that '65-mile east' tip you put in your 911 call is absolutely amazing. I don't know how you did that, since most of your travel was over little obscure country roads with no mileage signs. But, thankfully, you did."

"I just estimated our speed and counted minutes in my head." She glanced toward Andy, and he was smiling and shaking his head, his trademark sign of approval.

"Well done," said Chad. "The cell phone you captured and miraculously managed to keep up with was absolutely invaluable. Thank goodness for Caller ID. We called ourselves on that phone and got names from the ID. We also used the phone to call numbers in its memory and happily, heard nitwits answer with such things as, 'Hey, Mason, what's up, buddy?' I think we already told you, we got a print off the gun you promptly handed over in the helicopter."

"Chad, this lady is one in a million," interrupted Andy. "Does all this help explain why I searched for her so hard?"

"It does, indeed. Of course at that time, you probably didn't know all these characteristics of the young lady you were trying to trace down."

"I knew there was something compelling about the girl I was determined to find. I just didn't know all that it encompassed."

"Okay, you guys, that'll do," said Lorrie Dean with a chuckle.

"So, moving right along," snapped Chad, "we got a head start when you told the officer in the helicopter that one of them was still in the house with his knees shot out. State police swarmed that house and picked up that bird and rushed him to the hospital. En route, they interrogated him with absolutely no resistance from the guy. To put it simply, he squealed on his buddies."

"He actually ratted on his buddies?" asked Andy, squirming excitedly in his chair.

"Exactly," said Chad. "This was their biggest mistake, leaving this guy there to die. And that was the crowning blow for one Mr. Jarred E. Lynch. He apparently decided that revenge was all he had to live for, if he lived at all. So he told us where they had likely gone and what they were planning. Fantastic! And, by the way, Lorrie Dean, you're a good shot."

"No. No, I'm not. I'm not a good anything. If I was good, I wouldn't have had to shoot."

The room was silent. There was nothing more to be said on that subject. Andy felt the overwhelming sorrow welling inside, but said nothing of it, in deference to what he knew would be Lorrie Dean's wishes in this matter.

Agent Jarrigan just sat still, looking serious and sympathetic. In a few moments, he cleared his throat, awkwardly, and looked anew at Lorrie Dean. "I'm aware that they had you believing they were out retrieving some kind of special torture equipment. Well, there was no such thing. They were actually off on another job, part of a smuggling operation, code name, 'stuff,' as they referred to it. Your torture, Lorrie Dean, was their leaving you there with that clunkhead with nothing to eat for three days. Obviously, they knew you were a very strong, dedicated person, so they left you there in that horrendous situation to soften you up."

"Soften her up for what?" asked Andy.

"Well, that brings us to the climax, and this will explain why we had to take you into protective custody, Lorrie Dean. The drug dealer your mother's testimony sent to prison died there about two weeks ago. Now, he has a brother named Mason Lee Fuller, the ringleader of this present operation. He swore to cohorts, including Jarred Lynch, he would find your mother and take her out or die trying."

Andy and Lorrie Dean stared at each other, stone serious, shaking their heads grimly.

"Okay," resumed Chad after a few moments, politely offered for the comfort of his subjects. "There are just a couple of points I need to cover concerning, I guess for lack of a better word, personal obligations you have for your own welfare. Okay?"

"Sure," said Andy as Lorrie Dean nodded.

"The whole point of this experience is that you should concentrate on training yourselves to be alert at all times, no matter where you are, who you're with, or what you're doing. Be ever conscious of your environment, your surroundings, wherever you go. Teach yourselves new habits, so that surveillance—as we say—becomes a conditioned reflex for you. This is not meant to scare you, because we believe the danger in this present matter is all over. Nevertheless, this is what we all should do in our lives anyway. It's unfortunate that it has to be that way, but it is. I bring it up here simply because you've just had an experience which is there to teach."

"I understand," said Lorrie Dean. "Your counsel is especially relevant to me because I'm out in the open now—now that I chose to come out of hiding."

"Good point, but let me reassure you that we have good reason to believe this gang that your mother was connected with is now history. Nevertheless, as I noted, we should all live cautiously, constantly perceptive of our surroundings. This doesn't mean you're paranoid; it just means you're alert."

On that note, the meeting ended, followed by appropriate courtesies, and Lorrie Dean and Andy left the building. Andy walked Lorrie Dean to her car, where they had a brief conversation and agreed to meet at Luby's cafeteria on their way home.

Dinner at Luby's was intentionally light and very refreshing, but with little talk. *How can we go on like this?* thought Lorrie Dean. *We're both running. Will we ever stop? This mutual hold-off will destroy us both if we don't face things soon.* On that bite-the-bullet resolution, she vowed to have it out the next day after—she hoped—a good night's sleep.

Just outside the cafeteria, Andy swung an arm out in front of Lorrie Dean, essentially holding her back. She glared at him, quizzically, and he hurried to explain.

"Shall we give ourselves a lesson in—what did Chad call it?—personal surveillance?"

Lorrie Dean shrugged as if to say, *Don't make a hoot to me.*

"Okay, let's hold up here a little bit, rather than just jumping headlong into the parking lot and dashing for our cars. Instead, stand here and look out across the lot, all around it, from one side to the other. See if you notice anything out of place or maybe a person who just looks suspicious because of what they're doing or not doing. It'll take less than a minute."

"You're serious about this, aren't you?"

"Well, duh! Shouldn't we be? Remember what happened at our wedding?"

"Touché!"

"Now, if you do spot somebody looking or acting suspicious, dig out your cell phone, hold it to your ear and appear to talk into it. Be conspicuous about it; let them see you doing it. Watch what they do and take it from there. It'll either scare them off or have no effect. Either way, chances are, they won't be a threat. Next, we'll walk into the lot, keeping our cars in our peripheral vision, while we continue surveillance of the surroundings."

"Oh, I know what," exclaimed Lorrie Dean. "Let's don't walk a direct line to the cars and just cut over to them when we get close."

"Right on! The whole thing is to pay attention, stay alert. Admittedly, that's not natural. We're conditioned to live as though everything's going to be okay."

"True, and it's okay, because when we put ourselves in God's hands, we still have to keep our wits and act responsibly. You know, I think God expects a little help."

"Really. That's not asking too much. So, okay, it'll take a little work. As I say, it's not natural." He chuckled. "Notice how most of us usually push into the parking lot, looking vaguely down at the shopping cart, as if we expect something to happen there and want to be ready for it?"

"I think we're afraid something's going to jump out of it," chimed Lorrie Dean.

"Very likely," said Andy. "So, shall we run through this exercise and head for our cars?"

"Onward!"

With that, the born-again scouts struck out into the lot and walked to their cars, confidently and cautiously—sort of.

Back home, following meal and drill, they settled into their chairs in the parlor. In a while, Lorrie Dean left the room. When she returned, she was wearing a pullover shirt, slacks, and tennis shoes.

"You going for a workout?" asked Andy.

"No, just a little stroll. It'll be sundown in a couple hours, and I think I'll walk over to the park and just, you know, amble around in there for a little while."

"Sounds good. I'll go with you."

"You don't have to; you can rest."

"Oh, that's all right. I like the idea. I really want to go."

Lorrie Dean shrugged and waited while Andy changed clothes. The park entrance was a reasonably short walk from their house. In time, they were in the park, each thinking different things, personal matters they seemed to be having trouble sharing with each other since their reunion. In fact, their uneasy relationship, following that event, was one reason, at least unconsciously, that they sought out the park. They hoped the serenity of the peaceful woods would have some restorative power for them.

Ultimately, it didn't seem to have that sought-after effect, as their communication continued to be bland and evasive, polite but definitely inhibited.

Now and then, someone would walk by or pass them, oddly more girls than boys and, only rarely, a couple walking together. Without exception, they were walking briskly, obviously on the pathways for reasons of fitness and general exercise. Lorrie Dean and Andy's mission wasn't nearly so focused as that. They were there to breathe, to get away, to seek solace in nature.

After some time, Lorrie Dean wanted to wander over by a group of trees off the beaten trail. Andy agreed and followed, looking a little baffled. Lorrie Dean picked up on his puzzlement and decided to explain. "You know, Andy, we're not in here for the same reasons as these other people, so we don't need to feel confined to their patterns."

"You got a point there. We both know what's going on with us. We are not in here for exercise. And, my Lorrie Dean, that's perfectly okay—that's okay."

"Thanks. See, the pathways are great for their purposes, but that's too much structure for me. I want to be freer than that."

"Understand, my love."

"You know, Andy, you don't have to keep saying, 'my love' and 'my sweetheart' and 'my Lorrie Dean' and all that."

"What in the world is that supposed to mean?"

"No, now, it's okay, but I don't need that emphasis, and you seem to be obsessed with it."

"Well, *excuse* me! I'll see if I can settle down a little," grumbled Andy, clearly annoyed.

"Sorry."

Andy shrugged, and that was the end of it.

They lingered under the cover of age-old trees for quite a while—no more arguments, no more posturing or placating. Then their conversation waxed a little melancholy, as they talked of times back in their childhoods when their families would have picnics at the edge of the woods and invariably make that annual trek into the timbers, seeking their Christmas tree.

"It always felt special, somehow, when we would have these little outings, if you can call them that," said Lorrie Dean.

"Yes, yes—I think it was partly because we were doing things together. We were recreating as a family," offered Andy.

"Recreating?"

"Well, okay, maybe that's not a word, but we were teamed up, embraced in a common effort, if you will."

"My Andy, how you do run on," chuckled Lorrie Dean.

"'My Andy'?"

"Touché!"

With that, they agreed it was time to rejoin the pathway and head home for showers, pajamas, and snooze land—preparation for a new day of fun and games in their fascinating vocational worlds.

As they moseyed back toward the beaten path, gazing alternately up through the lofty old trees, Lorrie Dean muttered, "Wouldn't it be delightful to be in here some morning just at sunup?"

"Oh, wow, yes. I think it would be absolutely enchanting."

"Andy, let's sleep in separate beds tonight, so my restless pitching and wallowing won't keep you awake."

"No problem. The way I feel now, I'll sleep like a log, no matter what goes on. But if you need me for something, pound on my shoulder. Pound as hard as you can."

"We'll sleep in separate beds."

15

Tuesday morning started with a bang for Lorrie Dean, a totally unexpected shocker. Her boss, Jan Merrit, was in a desperate frenzy. Just as Lorrie Dean got settled at her desk and started reviewing the bridal shower file, Jan flew into her office and breathlessly started rolling out orders like a machine.

"Listen, Lorrie, take the shower party project all the way. It is now yours. You know what I'm saying? Shirley called in sick this morning, and the people want this thing wrapped up and invitations in the mail by tomorrow morning. It's all yours. I have two people on hold—gotta run!"

Jan didn't wait for an answer. She turned and sprang away, blurting, "I'm sorry, Lorrie," as she dashed into the hallway.

"Ah . . ." That's all Lorrie Dean was able to get out as she watched the tail of Jan's long dress fly through the doorway as though sucked into a wind tunnel.

Actually, this bridal thing was not so much a shower as it was a VIP women's bash. Lorrie Dean was nodding as her mind grasped just exactly what was intended here.

The clients wanted something totally unorthodox. This was not to be a relaxed little party with affable guests politely passing out place settings in the bride's chosen pattern and state-of-the-art toasters, oven mittens, and detergent dispensers. Rather, this was to be a jaunty social, where highly motivated participants would babble and frolic, play games, applaud entertainment, and somewhere along the way, work in the laying on of gifts. In that last part, they would hand over things like season tickets to Cowboys football games, subscriptions to health magazines, and cruise ship reservations. The clients also expected "We Party" to design an announcement that would be more of a press release than an invitation. Finally, they wanted some kind of light entertainment.

Undaunted by this seemingly formidable task, Lorrie Dean got busy. By midmorning, she projected that she would be working a little late getting everything wrapped up. That decided, she phoned Andy at his job and suggested he not wait for dinner with her. "Go ahead and have dinner wherever you want. I'll just get something out of the fridge when I get in." Andy acknowledged this without actually making a bona fide commitment on the subject.

Things went better than she expected on the project. Little pieces kept falling into place. In the course of this concentrated—indeed exciting—effort, she began to feel a sense of relief. The work needed her. She was worthy. It dawned on her that in these moments, she was not so staunchly devoted to the tragedy in her life. When the old, foreboding impulse bullied its way back into focus, she shook herself vigorously, chasing away the reverie. This left her to face once again the really big event that was yet to come—her full confession to Andy Boone. The sheer dread of that huge load had led her to procrastinate on it for several days since their reuniting. Lorrie Dean threw out her hands, figuratively slapping away these morbid thoughts. She set her jaw and plunged back into her work.

At day's end, the arrangements had all been made, and Lorrie Dean actually felt herself smiling. She had crafted party invitations brimming with inducements and suspense. She also nailed a local female string trio noted for its chamber music style and its preference for light classics. As a final touch, she booked a ballroom in the Hyatt Regency.

Driving home, Lorrie Dean reflected on the day's unexpected turn of events, proudly musing over her own achievements. As she approached their driveway, she sighed, suddenly aware that she was very tired and somewhat hungry.

Andy hugged her at the door and started to kiss her, but she pretended to be distracted by something, so he didn't manage to do it.

"Have you eaten?" she asked.

"Uh-uh. I wanted to wait and have dinner with you. I thought you'd be weary after a long day and need a hot meal, so I cooked us some . . . well, you'll see. Shall we?" he said, as he motioned toward the dining room.

Andy had cooked hamburger steaks, fried potatoes (not French fries, he insisted), and green beans. As it turned out, the steaks and fries were way overcooked, and the green beans were undercooked and tough. But Lorrie Dean, chewing vigorously, just smiled sweetly and said, "Good job."

It was in moments like these that she felt his love for her so strongly. It was so distressing to think that soon she would destroy that love. Just how soon, she didn't know. Still, the longer she waited, the more stressed out she became. It was always there, like an endless nightmare.

When they finally claimed victory over their challenging dinner, Andy said, "I got the dishes; go sit down, sweetheart."

"Thanks. If you insist, I think I will." She headed for her recliner.

After Andy finished rinsing dishes and packing the dishwasher, he headed for his own recliner. Comfortably seated, he said, "I think we need to check on Kelly."

"Indeed. Yes, we should. How about I call her?"

"Great." *Perhaps*, he thought, *a round of girl talk will do you both good.*

Lorrie Dean returned in about twenty minutes and filled Andy in on their conversation. "We had a good phone visit, but Andy, she sounded down."

"I don't like that. She needs us. I want to help her."

"Me, too. Maybe we can run down one day after work and visit a couple of hours. Oh, one thing nagging her is that her mother is still trying to see her. And Andy, I got the definite impression that she is about ready to concede on that issue."

"Seeing her mother face-to-face, getting that all over with, might actually release some of that anxiety she's having," said Andy.

"Right. The last thing she said was 'Tell my Boone Woo hello.'"

The next day on the job was routine for both of them. Not long after their early dinner, Lorrie Dean started pushing out of her recliner and said, "I think I'll go to the park for a short while."

"Sounds great; let's go," whooped Andy.

"Don't you have anything else you can do?"

He didn't answer—just kept looking at her as he thought: *The operative word in her question was* can. *She could have said, "Anything else you'd* rather *do or* want *to do?" The bottom line is she really doesn't want me to go with her.*

"Andy?"

"Okay, I get the message."

"And that is?"

"You really don't want me along."

"I guess there are things still working on me that I feel I have to shoulder alone, that I have to study out by myself."

"I understand, sweetheart, but please, just let me go with you and look around over there, like Chad said we should always do before moving out. If it looks okay, I'll just sit down on a bench in the pavilion and wait there for you. Honestly, I don't want to hamper you in your private thinking, but I worry, sweetheart, I worry."

"Well, okay, that'll be fine."

Lorrie Dean stood in place under a giant red oak, looking up through its mighty limbs. When her neck began to feel strained, she lowered her head and started looking all around, staring out through the woods from one side to the other as if casting about for a source of inspiration. Something wasn't working. The rapture was missing. She looked at her hands, and they were trembling a little.

"This is not what I'm here for," she whispered to herself. The peaceful country scenes were supposed to heal, not hamper. Then it occurred to her that she was imposing her hysteria on the innocent wooded park when, in fact, she had come there for it to work its magic on her—ease her tensions, all her cares. Now it was clear that her trauma had advanced to the point where even the tranquility of nature had little persuasion. "This has to stop," she mumbled.

She strolled back to the path and on to the entrance to join Andy, who sat on a weathered bench, waiting patiently. He rose when he saw her and smiled like it was their first date. How she ached to rush to him and wrap her arms around him and hold on to him. But she was fighting a daunting monster that wouldn't let go.

"Andy, dear, let's go home."

That night, they slept in separate beds at Lorrie Dean's request. During the next day, Andy methodically transacted the duties of his job while Lorrie Dean mindlessly plodded through the hours, thoroughly lost in what she knew was an impending disaster. She prayed and ultimately headed home at the end of the day, still lost.

Friday was equally uninspiring for both. When the work day was done for each of them, they arrived at their house very nearly at the same time. After a tedious dinner, they sat back to listen to their favorite music channel on TV. In a short while, Lorrie Dean ambled into the kitchen for a drink of water. As she started back through the dining room toward the den, she stopped and lingered there in the doorway.

When Andy casually glanced toward the doorway and noticed Lorrie Dean just standing there, he somehow felt the totality of her, the consuming presence of this lost but very dear young woman. She just seemed to be waiting there for something to happen, motionless, arms straight down by her sides, her expression pensive and far away. He eased to the edge of his chair, pushed against its seat cushion, and slowly rose to stand and face his soul mate. She continued to wait, perfectly still, while he crept toward her. When he was right before her, she lifted her eyes and just held his gaze, waiting for—he knew not what. In that inexplicable moment, Andy saw, in her eyes, the heartbreaking look of a lost soul.

This was a moment that had to be honored. They both felt that. Now Andy reached to take her, and she stepped back.

Lorrie Dean cringed at the stunned look on Andy's face. Then, as she held her hand up to hold him back, she said resolutely, "Okay, Andy, I'm ready to talk. Here's the big news."

"Let's sit at the dining table."

"Okay," said Lorrie Dean as she poked along toward the small table.

They sat in chairs flanking a corner of the table, even though Lorrie Dean would have preferred to tell her tragic story from a distance. Andy prevailed on this one.

"Okay," began Lorrie Dean, "here goes." She cleared her throat to continue, but it still choked, so she cleared it again—and again.

"There's no hurry," said Andy, as he laid a hand on hers.

Lorrie Dean jerked her hand away. "Andy, you've already heard from the FBI pretty much all about the old abandoned house, and that stupid guard and the other two pathetic characters. That's just the technical stuff. I'm beyond all that, even the merciless broth diet. But what I want to . . . I just think I owe you an explanation of my behavior there, my feelings and—actually my misbehavior."

"I don't picture you misbehaving, sweetheart. The normal rules of behavior don't apply when you're scared to death and fighting for your life."

"Wish I agreed with you."

Andy lifted his eyebrows but said no more.

"Listen, Andy, I did a lot of things, thinking I was smarter than my guard. I thought I could trick him, confuse him, or distract him to the point where he would concede or make a fatal mistake. I kept changing my character from day to day because nothing was working on this guy who I thought was dumber than me. Are you understanding this?"

"Absolutely. You did what you had to do."

"No, I didn't. I was rapidly losing my identity as Lorrie Dean. I gave up my character. I tossed to the dogs the girl you searched for and fell in love with."

She was struggling to stay composed, to keep from breaking down entirely. She could tell that she was on the verge of losing it, so she rambled as rapidly as she could. She described the different personas she tried to assume and the strategies she employed, trying to stay in shape for a dash to freedom. And, through tears, she told of the excruciating pain of sleeping in a chair, of gagging down the nauseating chicken broth, of faking trips to the toilet, and of the devastating fear that she was just hours away from agonizing physical torture.

Andy was shaking his head and blotting tears, but he didn't interrupt. His sweetheart needed to get it all out without comments, questions, or any other kind of prompting.

"So, that went on and on until the beginning of the fourth day and then I was morbidly aware that it was now do or die. To this minute, I can't even believe I actually did all the things I did." She paused for a few moments, drawing in a new wave of energy.

"Would you like some water?" asked Andy.

Lorie Dean shook her head and continued. "See if this sounds like Lorrie Dean to you. In that last desperate hour, I screamed at point blank range right into the ear of that dumb guard. Andy, this was not a human scream. I don't even know where it came from. Thank you, God! It was the vicious, spine-chilling squeal of a wild animal. When he went off balance, I rammed a knee into his groin, twice, swinging my leg with all the might I could muster. Then when he was gasping and weaving around, trying to retrieve his fallen gun, I picked it up like a piece of cake and blew his knees away."

Again, Andy tried to cover her hand with his, but she shunned it each time. Now he was looking at her as if to say, "Go on." In a moment, he opened his mouth to speak and she jumped ahead of him.

"Then I ran! Okay?"

Andy nodded.

"I ran! I will remember screaming and shooting a gun for a long time, but it's the run that will go with me forever. Andy, I've never held a gun in my life; I've never even looked at one. And I always believed that the height of cruelty, the absolutely unpardonable assault on a man, would be striking him in the groin."

Andy grimaced and managed a sneaky smile. He said nothing. She seemed to be on a roll and didn't need interruptions.

"All of that misery seems to be bottled up in my running. Every wretched, hideous moment of all four days has been sucked into that desperate run, somehow. And now, in my every waking hour, it flares up and grabs my mind and sticks on it like a leech. The run is my monster."

"When it flares up, are you able to dismiss it in a few minutes?"

"Not entirely, and for some reason, dismissing it doesn't stop the pain. I can't argue myself out of it, Andy. It's a force of its own, and my mind can't stop it."

"Lorrie Dean, may I just say one thing? I'll keep it short."

"Sure."

"You *had* to run! Thank God, you did it. God gave you a life to *live*, and you honored that merciful giving. You did what you had to do. When your life is on the line, it is your obligation to save yourself, whatever you have to do. Oh, but my dear sweetheart, it's terrible what you're having to go through, remembering. But you're working on it—I can tell."

"Well . . . but I did some things that there's no excuse for."

"Well, it's done, precious. It's history."

"Oh, no, it isn't. That's not all of it." She began to cry aloud and started scooting her chair back and shoving against the table. Now, she was tangled in the chair, stumbling around, trying to get all the way up, all the while shaking hysterically and moaning and beating on herself.

When Andy shoved back and started toward her, she threw her hands at him to keep him away and shouted, "No!" Sobbing, she tried to gain control, and the harder she tried, the more she shook, until she was on the verge of convulsions.

As Andy started toward her, she backed away until she backed into the wall. Then it came. In one all-out staggering surge, Lorrie Dean shouted, "I was raped!"

There was no holding him back this time. Andy would go to his beloved, whether she liked it or not. He reached her in three long strides. He tried to take her, but she moved away. Still, he reached for her, this time more determined, and caught her. As he was drawing her into his arms, she was trying to wiggle out. But he won out, at least for the moment, and held on tightly.

"Stop it! Stop it!" she shouted, slinging her head and trying to twist away.

"Lorrie Dean, *you* stop it! Don't fight me. I love you. Please let me love you."

"You can't. I'm not fit to love. It was all my fault."

"Oh no! No, no, no—No!"

"So now, do you understand? I did it."

"I'm dead sure you didn't invite the guy to rape you."

"Course not, but I still caused it by trying to outsmart him. I guess he showed me." With that, there came a new outburst of crying and tremors.

Andy eased his hold on her. "My dear Lorrie Dean, girl of my life, we will surmount this—you and I."

"Easy for you to say. Besides, you're just being philosophical." Flinging her arms about, she wailed, "There's one more zinger. You ready?" she shouted.

Andy nodded.

"We can't go on together. It's over for us, Andy Boone."

Andy would not let this frantic decree go unchallenged. He lurched forward to take her again, but she managed to wobble away, bawling and flinging her hands at him. "Go away! Go away!"

Andy tried to take her flailing arms, but she threw them behind her back. When he reached to her again, she jerked backward and hit the wall behind her.

Andy pleaded, and Lorrie Dean cried. They were both exhausted emotionally and physically. Andy was at a loss as to how to console her. And, at this moment, Lorrie Dean was whipped. Each prayed silently.

Then it started again. Lorrie Dean stammered, "So, get this, Andy: We . . . can't . . . go . . . on. So, please just go away."

"Lorrie Dean, that's enough! Say whatever you want, do whatever you will, but I'm not leaving you."

That avowal hit her like a missile, and she staggered away from the wall, shouting, "Go away—Go away—Go a-*way!*"

He stepped toward her, and she whirled away and then stumbled over her own feet, lost her balance, and fell.

Andy was beside her in a heartbeat, banging his knee against the floor as he swooped down. He felt a little pain shoot up his leg, but it mattered not. His sweetheart was down. Then the phone started screaming unmercifully.

16

Kelly was near panic when she heard the number she'd dialed ring for the eighth time. Still, she held on, listening and hoping. "Come on, Boone Woo—Lorrie Dean, pick up, please. Please!" She stood up and started pacing and pleading, "Why doesn't the answering machine kick in?" After twelve rings, she hung up and dropped into the nearest chair. Then she slapped her forehead with the palm of her hand and at once, saw her Uncle Dub standing in the doorway.

"Kelly, dear, what's wrong?"

"I wanted to tell them about my decision to meet my mother person—so to speak—but they don't answer."

"Meaning Andy and Lorrie Dean?"

"Right. I was kind of nervous about the whole thing, and I just wanted to share the news with them, but they don't answer."

"Maybe they're just out."

"Well, of course, Uncle Dub," snapped Kelly. "I can figure that out, but their voice mail doesn't pick up. Something isn't right."

"I'm sorry, Kelly. That *is* kind of worrisome."

"Yeah, that's the point. It doesn't bother me that they don't get the big news, but when I couldn't get them . . . Well, Uncle Dub, that worries me."

"I understand. We'll just keep trying."

"I'm already nervous about it all, but I was trying to get excited over it. That's why I wanted to tell them. I know Lorrie Dean would have been pleased, and she could cheer me up."

Dub let it drop, because he knew his niece fared better left to think for herself. In a couple of minutes, Mom strolled in and pulled up a chair across from Kelly. Trusting her instincts, she, too, elected to sit quietly, because she could read in their faces that something serious was at hand,

and this was the way they were dealing with it. Finally Kelly caught her eye and smiled.

"I just dropped by," began Mom, "to see if you need any help getting ready for your trip to Wills Point in the morning."

"Thanks, Mom. There's really nothing to do, since I'm just going there and back in one day. Who knows; I might be back here for lunch tomorrow."

"Let me say again, Kelly, I'd be glad to go with you," offered Dub. "I could stay in the background somewhere."

"Yeah, me too," echoed Mom.

"No, no no. Please, everybody, let me do this alone. I don't want to have to be preoccupied with the idea of a chance encounter between you and her. Please! I can handle this."

"Okay, okay," grumbled Mom. "Do it."

"I'm sorry, Mom—Uncle Dub. Forgive me. I think the adrenalin is just messing with me."

Mom reached out and touched her hand, and Dub nodded genially toward her. "We understand," said Dub.

"Yes," said Mom. "And now, on a lighter note—maybe I should say technical note—how are you supposed to recognize each other?"

That little query brought a defusing smile to Kelly's face. "Are you guys ready for this? Don't answer." She giggled and touched two fingers to her lips. "Okay, I gotta look for a blue straw hat and an orange umbrella. I mean, really, how long has it been since you saw a woman in a straw hat? And I didn't even know they made orange umbrellas."

Mom and Dub laughed and then Mom said, "Well, at least that ought to be easy to spot. Not a lot of women in Wills Point are gonna be outfitted like that."

"Good point," agreed Dub. "By the way, they are calling for chances of rain in and around. What's plan B?"

"I asked her that, and she said, 'Bring an umbrella.'"

After the dinner dishes were cleaned and other incidental chores attended to, the family of friends visited, as often they did on Friday nights. They babbled about the week's achievements and challenges on the farm, chuckled about the little mishaps, and waved away any real concern about the big stuff. They avoided the worrisome issues and stuck to trivial matters, things fun to talk about. It was just a lighthearted flurry of chatter among friends who had long ago accepted that life isn't perfect and that, to be really happy, they had to learn how to enjoy its uncontrollable downside.

Kelly sat quietly, at times simply offering a brief, patronizing smile. Nobody pushed her to talk; neither did they pick at her for not talking. They all understood. Theirs was a camaraderie imposing no protocols. Kelly wanted to be with them and gratefully accepted their indulgence.

When the banter wound down, Kelly excused herself and picked up the phone to try her call again. All remained silent while she waited. When Kelly calmly hung up the phone, she glanced around the room and shook her head. They all nodded their sympathy. Grandpa broke the silence by clearing his throat and uttering, "Heck, it's Friday night; they probably were just tired after a hard week of work and went to bed early."

Kelly shook her head as if to say, *It's a mystery, and something just isn't right.* Nobody said any more on the subject. Her friends were trying to offer logical excuses, all of which Kelly felt she was perfectly capable of figuring out herself. Still, they were trying, and she loved them for that. Finally they all scattered to their respective bedrooms, filling the house with routine but sincere "good nights."

On her knees at bedside, Kelly prayed. She asked God to bless Boone Woo and Lorrie Dean, to guide them, watch over them, and lead them to victory over the formidable horror that had invaded their lives. She also asked God to bless her and also the strange woman she was soon to meet, and to make their meeting what it ought to be.

In bed, she continued to think of her friends in Dallas. *There's something ominous about an unanswered phone,* she thought, *especially considering their seemingly impossible situation.* She knew they were facing the severest trial they would ever have in their lives. Their enemy was so relentless, and unmerciful.

Kelly pitched and tossed in bed, frantically deferring sleep by worry over the fact that she wasn't getting any. She was thinking of her own situation. She shuddered at the memory of her personal self-punishment, right after her mother literally kicked her out when she was six years old. Her self-esteem was destroyed in an instant. She had raged and wept and finally scolded herself. At that time, she thought it must be her own fault. Surely, she had to be a bad, unworthy little girl, because no mother would cast away her own child for any other reason.

She lived with her guilt complex until one day she stamped her foot hard to the ground and shouted into the air, "No more! Whatever, no more! Do you see me now, Mommy? See me holding my head way up high like this? It's over, Mommy." She also recalled summoning all her might and nerve and bracing against the temptation to cry. After that, she still hurt, but she quit crying, and she held her head up and went on to conquer.

As she lay awake in bed, thinking back on her own battle, she murmured, "You're facing the same thing, Lorrie Dean. Your enemy is your own feeling of guilt. I wish we all three could be together right now, in this instant, to console one another. Please answer the phone. Please be okay." These last words came out a little dreamy, as the young warrior, thinking about friends, finally fell asleep.

Kelly was up early the next morning and hurried in to breakfast. She was just picking at her food: eggs, sausage, pancakes, and fried apples. Mom had laid out the big spread, boosting Kelly for a hard day's work. In a moment, Kelly caught herself and, in deference to Mom's effort, dived in. Actually, it was pretty darn good, and she flipped a thumbs-up to Mom who chuckled proudly. Grandpa bragged on it, too, and toasted her with his almost-empty glass of orange juice.

After breakfast, Dub walked to the garage with Kelly and tarried just outside of it while she scooted on in. With a hand on the driver's door, she turned toward Dub and smiled. "Are you here to monitor the operation of the garage door, sir?"

"You bet I am. I still have nightmares over what happened to you."

"That's sweet of you, Uncle Dub. Bye!"

As it turned out, everything performed as it was designed to work, and a waving, grinning Kelly was out and headed toward the top of the driveway in less than two minutes. As she reached the front of the house, she spotted Grandpa, beaming and waving both hands in the air, and a little ways from him stood Mom, waving her hand close to her chest, ladylike, and there, running across the yard, an overslept Aunt Leah bounded to the front and waved vigorously. By that time, Dub had also made it to the front. He waved once and watched her drive away, destined for a miraculous rendezvous with his sister, Kelly's . . . err . . . mother.

Kelly waved an arm through the window, acknowledging her cheerleaders, and drove on. Now, she was rocking her head side to side and slapping the steering wheel as she chanted, "I'm not bad after all. They love me. I must be a good girl. I am."

The drive to Wills Point, forty-seven miles from the farm, was delightfully uneventful. *This is one day when I don't need any unexpected events*, thought Kelly. *If I can just slip through this big one, I'll be a happy camper.*

As she continued to cruise along, Kelly was trying to anticipate: Who would say the first word? Would her mother have questions for her? What's going on here, anyway? The curiosity alone fueled Kelly's resolve to meet her so-called mother. After all, she had her own questions. *So get ready—Mom!*

Then, without warning, her mood shifted. Worry struck as her mind suddenly turned to her Boone Woo and Lorrie Dean, her two best friends in the world, totally unassuming, totally committed to her, expecting nothing from her and offering everything. They gave her the best they had, their love, with no strings attached. She pondered aloud, "Would y'all be proud of me for this? Will it make you smile when you hear about it? Is this what you would have me do?"

Knowing of her worry, Dub had tried to reach Andy and Lorrie Dean just after breakfast, with no luck. Kelly had just hoped she might get their blessings for what she was doing. Even though she knew she already had their blessings in all things, it would have been so uplifting to hear them say the words. How reassuring it would be to hear Boone Woo's kind voice saying, "Good luck, my little morning light."

Now, the sunlight was beginning to fade in and out, as hovering clouds drifted by, intermittently hiding the sun. Soon the clouds won outright, and the sun was gone. Wills Point was only ten miles away. With the threatening deterioration of weather and the sheer weight of her mission, Kelly was growing tense again. Then, as though by the will of God, her own words came rushing back to her, "Hold your head up!"

As she drew near the city, Kelly prayed aloud, "Dear Lord, please make this what you want it to be. Guide me; help me to know what I should do, what I should say, and although I don't feel one bit good about this mother, lead me away from using up our time in anger. And, oh Lord, that's going to be the hard one."

Parking was easy, and Kelly was soon walking along the street only a block from the rendezvous point. She had followed the very explicit instructions the mother person had given her. She was to remain on the sidewalk across the street from the actual point where they would meet.

When they recognized each other, that would be the signal for her to cross over and meet the woman.

Kelly flinched at a rumble of thunder. A few minutes later, the wind slapped her face with a sprinkle of rain. The sky was turning darker, and swirls of wind started to scatter trash that had blown up against the storefronts. Kelly twitched her nose at the smell of dry dirt that was just beginning to touch the dampness. She longed for a deep breath to keep her composure but was afraid to take one lest street smells overcome her. Still, she trudged on. In a moment, she moved over to let a couple of teenagers, their heads strapped with earphones, dawdle by.

At what she believed to be the right place, she stopped and backed up against a storefront for a little shelter from the drizzle. Shielding her eyes with one hand, she scanned the sidewalk on the other side, concentrating on the designated meeting place. No one was around that spot. Then a woman walked into that area, bent into the wind, looking down the walk. It must not be her contact, because this woman seemed disinterested in looking anywhere but straight ahead. The woman jerked her head in Kelly's direction and instantly whipped it back again.

Something seemed wrong with the mystery woman. She looked frazzled and desperate. One point, however, was undeniable. This haggard woman, who looked somewhat older than she was supposed to be, was sporting a blue straw hat and carrying an orange umbrella. Otherwise, she looked confused, uncertain of her bearings. She hesitated and kept looking down at the sidewalk as if checking her location. Kelly could not see her eyes, but at one point she had the distinct sensation that on one of her sweeps across the sidewalk, the woman had cut her eyes toward Kelly without turning her head.

Kelly held a hand high in the air, waiting for her to look around.

When the woman did glance in her direction, she pretended not to notice Kelly and took one long, awkward step forward. She glanced toward Kelly's side again, and then took another giant step forward, inelegantly stomping the sidewalk with her lead foot. She stopped, turned to face Kelly, and started raising her hand, ever so slowly. Then she dropped it, and her expression became secretive, as though she were on a clandestine assignment.

As Kelly continued to watch this inexplicable drama, she snickered to herself, because the woman looked halfway comical. She was reminded of Andy's description of this woman wearing a gaudy, loud dress seated in the hospital waiting room. She recalled that he had said he had seen two eyes peering over the top of a magazine, otherwise hiding their owner's face, and the sight of it had made him chuckle.

After Kelly regained her composure, following this little humorous interlude, she raised her hand again and stepped into the street. At that moment, two men veered around the woman and skipped on ahead. At that, the straw-hat lady swung her head side to side as if looking for another intruder. Kelly began walking across the street when, suddenly, the woman jumped and then, shuddering and swinging her arms, started to stride urgently down the walk. Kelly followed from her side. When the woman looked over and saw her, she picked up her pace and soon, she was running full tilt into the rain and wind, eventually disappearing around a corner.

With that, Kelly lifted her head to face life's most perplexing question, "Now what?"

She stepped back to the sidewalk and stood in place for a while, trying to fathom all that was happening. What was her mother trying to pull? Did she really know what she was doing? She looked like someone who had completely lost touch with reality. She'd actually looked frightened, as though something had spooked her. However, that kind of explanation didn't seem to fit with the efforts she'd made to bring off this unprecedented meeting. Why had she been so persistent in trying to meet her long-ago discarded daughter, only to run away when the big day came?

Suddenly, the rain became really serious. Kelly opened her umbrella, ceremonially pointed it toward the heavens, and traipsed stoically down the walk, holding her head high. *Come on down, rain!* Actually, she was stunned, but she moseyed on toward her car as if she didn't have a care in the world. After all, this nonchalant attitude had worked before when she was trying to take control of her situation. Still, she pondered, if only intellectually, what had made the mother person get cold feet.

Kelly pulled away from the parking space and drove around the block where the woman had disappeared and on to some adjacent streets. No sign of the blue straw hat. Somebody must have picked her up. *Does mother person have an accomplice?* Shaking her head, she started out of town. In a moment, she mused at her reluctance to refer to the woman as her mother. It was just a hard word for her to say. So, now, on to Tillman to tell her story.

17

Andy was on the floor, keeling beside his fallen sweetheart. The phone was ringing relentlessly, and the insistent squeal of it was drilling into them. Lorrie Dean lifted her head and began raising her knees so she could pull up to a sitting position. Moments earlier, she was virtually delirious from outrageous feelings of guilt. She had vaulted into a self-deprecating fit, shaking and railing against herself, denying Andy, and making desperate assertions about her life, her presumed sin, and their futile destiny.

Now she was subdued, yet still sobbing and trembling a little—clearly defeated. What a wretched shame that it took a crash like this to quell the brutal pain of raw fear and anguish. But it did happen, and that's where they were, and that's where they would have to pick up from, at this heart-wrenching hour.

Andy's heart was crushed. To see this blessed, blameless, deserving young woman so stricken was ripping into him.

"Easy," pleaded Andy, as Lorrie Dean tried to sit up. "Do you hurt anywhere?"

She shook her head. She had stopped crying and nearly gone into shock. When she looked into Andy's face, the shock faded, and she began to weep again. Andy wrapped her in his arms and just held her, with no urge to hurry. He was frightened that she might be hurt physically. Lorrie Dean, still sobbing, her head hung low, did not return the embrace.

"Sweetheart, I want to get you to your bed, but let's make sure first that you didn't break or sprain something."

Shaking her head, Lorrie Dean began to brace herself in readiness to stand up.

"Hold it," commanded Andy. "I'm going to pick you up and carry you to bed."

"That's okay, I can . . ."

Before she could finish, Andy had cradled her in his arms and was pushing up. Standing, he jiggled her around to make sure she was secure in his hold. Satisfied, he started toward her bedroom.

"Wait, Andy, put me down! You're limping. Put me down!"

"No. It's just a little catch in my leg. It'll work out."

From her resting place in his arms, snuggled against his chest, Lorrie Dean looked at him and frowned. Andy smiled at her. He knew that, although she was frowning, it was a caring frown. He limped on and soon was at her bed. He gently lowered her to sit on the side of the bed near the foot. As he moved to turn down the bed, Lorrie Dean squirmed around and pushed up.

"I can take it from here. Really, I'm okay." She flipped back the covers and slipped into bed with a deep sigh.

Finally, the phone stopped ringing. Weakly, Lorrie Dean asked, "Did you unplug the answering machine or something?"

"No, but I'll check on it. Right now, that can wait."

Andy hurried away and returned with a glass of water. As he held it toward her, Lorrie Dean was thinking, *The absolute last thing in the world I want right now is a glass of water.* She took the glass and teased out three little sips and handed it back to him. "Thanks."

Andy pulled a chair to her bedside, eased into it, gave her a summoning look, and asked, "What can I get you, darling?"

"Nothing. Aren't you going to bed?"

"Sometime, maybe. For now, I want to be here."

"Go to bed, Andy!"

"Later."

Thereupon, Lorrie Dean, weary and broken, tried counting herself to sleep. In a while, she was losing track of the numbers and drifting into incoherent, fragmented thoughts. *Good night.*

Now, Andy sat on the edge of his bed, rubbing his knee. Then the phone started ringing again. When finally it stopped, he twisted around and poked his feet under the sheet.

*   *   *

The phone rang again early Saturday morning, but the two worn-out sufferers didn't budge from their beds. An hour later, Lorrie Dean rolled out of bed and headed for the shower. Although it didn't produce the renewal she'd hoped for, it was somewhat refreshing. She cleaned her teeth, brushed her hair, vigorously, patted on a little makeup, got dressed, and headed for the kitchen.

The breakfast experience was a treat, both for Andy and Lorrie Dean. Andy savored the food, simply because it was absolutely delicious, and he was hungry. Lorrie Dean treasured the sight of him relishing something she had tried hard to make first-rate. They smiled at each other and chatted throughout this healing event, transient though they knew it was to be.

Good times did indeed begin to wither shortly after breakfast. The old devil was back. As they sat quietly, both afraid to attempt conversation, Andy became increasingly restless, leading Lorrie Dean to clear her throat loudly and frown in his direction several times.

"Okay, this isn't getting us anywhere with the things we need to solve," exclaimed Andy. "First of all, my dear, innocent lady, I love you."

"I love you, too, Andy, and it isn't easy to love you and do what I have to do. That's the whole point of it. My love for you is so strong that I know I have to set you free from the likes of me. I want you to have the best and be happy."

"I will never be happy without . . ."

Lorrie Dean held her hand up to keep him from going any further. "I'm not finished. All I ask is that you don't argue with this and . . ." She started crying—this was the hardest part so far. "And don't make me talk about it again. Okay, Andy? Please?"

"I will only do whatever is best for you, but I promise not to bring up this particular subject. But I have to tell you, Lorrie Dean, I will do my best to win your heart to the point where you don't feel that way . . ." He couldn't go on, for he was crying, too.

So they cried together, knowing they faced a common enemy and knowing that each had to face it alone. No doubt, each was asking the same question: how can this be? It defies explanation and mocks the best of human promise.

Soon, Andy settled enough to talk, and he sorely hoped he would be able to tender to his woman genuine help rather than hindrance. "Okay, I'll do what you say about that, sweetheart, but I'll look after you, whatever you say or think. But right now, we need to get you to a hospital. We just have to be sure you're okay in every way."

"No, Andy, I'm not going to the hospital. They checked me out and didn't seem concerned about anything. So I must be okay."

"I just . . . Please, Lorrie Dean, that little routine was probably very superficial, you know, just a quick check. We want a thorough medical exam, one that checks for all sexually transmitted diseases, not just the HIV thing. And we want one thorough enough that they can say positively you're not injured internally in any way. If there is anything, then we can correct it. Wouldn't it be a great relief to know you're clear and you don't have to be anxious about that anymore?"

"It's all done; that's all I know. I don't want to go through anything more. Can't you understand that? Why are you bothering me with all this?"

"You don't know?"

"No, I don't."

"Well, that disappoints me."

"Sorry."

"All right. All right for now, but I'm not going to give up on this. Okay, there's another critical issue here. I'm sorry to have to bring this subject up because I know it's traumatic for you, but it's your life, sweetheart . . ."

"Don't do it, Andy. Don't go there."

"I'm sorry to defy you, but this has to be done. You were raped, and you need help on that in the worst way."

"No, no, I said don't go there."

"I'm already there. We must get you in touch with the rape crisis people."

"Andy, why are you being so difficult?" Sobbing and raking both hands across her face, she turned her back to him. *Why doesn't he understand? Can't he see that it hurts too much? Do I have to tell him all the gory details to settle this with him?*

"Okay," conceded Andy as he sucked in a deep, fluttering breath. "But you know, I'm not a disinterested bystander here. I love you."

"I know you do. It's just too overwhelming. Can you accept that? Why do you even want to persist?"

"Because," Andy blurted, "you are in a deep crisis, Lorrie Dean, a dreadful, disabling crisis, and we're not going to let that take over your life. If I have to make you hate me to save you, I will!"

"Andy, there's no way I could ever hate you."

"Well, like I say, I'm not giving up—ever. But let's get off this, for now, anyway. Let's go to the park. I promise not to shadow you while we're there."

127

Lorrie Dean surprised herself when she answered instantly, "Okay."

"Good." As that word left his mouth, the ever-present phone rang. Andy strolled over and picked it up.

"Hello. Oh, hi, Kelly . . . huh? . . . right here all the time . . . hold on, let me check." In a moment, he came back on. "Oops. The answering machine is unplugged. Well, I mean not all the way, but the plug is just hanging there, not firmly seated in the socket. I don't know what happened—I'm so sorry, Kelly; I should have checked it . . . yeah, we were here, but we had an accident . . . uh-huh . . . uh-huh. Oh, no! I'm so sorry. We needed to be with you. We three really need each other . . . yes, darling . . . always. Sure, she's right here. Oh, while I still have you, well, okay, here's the thing: I love you, my little morning light. Here she is."

As he handed Lorrie Dean the phone, he mouthed, "I'm going outside." Lorrie Dean would be more at ease talking with her buddy if there was nobody around to overhear and inhibit. He hustled on out.

"Hi, Kelly," sang Lorrie Dean. From that point, the two talked and commiserated as to their individual dilemmas. Guilt feelings were building in Lorrie Dean as she listened to Kelly tell of her distressing experience. It hurt to think that she hadn't been there when this little jewel really needed her. They talked for several minutes and ended their visit genially. At the end, Lorrie Dean said, "I'm sorry I wasn't there for you." Kelly replied that it was okay and that she was sorry she hadn't been there to support her and Andy during their crisis.

Lorrie Dean sat quietly, reflecting, the phone still nestled in her lap. Somehow, it came to her that the three of them were invincible when they were together: she, Andy, and Kelly. She pondered whether she should confide more details to Kelly, especially the hard reality that she and Andy couldn't go on together. What would that do to Kelly? Her allegiance to Andy was so strong. *Why, Lord, why?*

When Andy returned, they said not a word at first. They just shook their heads, a sign of agreement that their hearts were with their friend. After a few minutes, Andy sighed and said, "Shall we go on over to the park, now?" Lorrie Dean nodded, and they took off. In the park, they went in different directions, as Andy had promised. It concerned Lorrie Dean that Andy was still limping, but she knew better than to suggest a doctor.

As was her custom, Lorrie Dean wandered away from the beaten path and stood inside a thicket of trees that included the big red oak of which she had become very possessive. In a while, she sat down beside it and wept. Although she and Andy had been together as sweethearts for only a few months, she felt everything for him. He was the love of her life. So strong was her devotion that she was willing to give him up for his own good. That had to be done, and they could not go on living together. They would simply have to separate.

Whatever her life would amount to from this point on, she couldn't care less. Maybe this peaceful park and her encouraging job could be her salvation. For now, she had to quit crying, dump this self-pity, and go find her man. Even though they were now earmarked for separate lives, he would always be her man. When she found him, he grinned as usual, and they strolled back to their house as if they didn't have a care in the world.

Back home, they enjoyed a light lunch and set about to relax and read. Andy was lost in a novel he'd borrowed from one of his coworkers. Lorrie Dean finished scanning the newspaper and picked up her Bible. When Andy noticed, he exclaimed, "Let's go to church tomorrow."

"I'm not fit for church."

"Hoo, boy. How are we going to get beyond this? If you're not fit for church, nobody is. There are no qualifications, no entrance exams. You don't have to fix anything. We go just as we are. If it wasn't that way, I couldn't go either. Nobody could. Besides, I don't know of anyone who lives Christian ethics better than you."

"Hmm."

"Hmm? That's it: hmm?" When she didn't answer, Andy rattled on. "We could recapture those blissful times when we'd sing in church and people would applaud our harmony. Well, truthfully, I'd sing and you would make the harmony. Then we'd drive along country roads singing 'My Bonnie Lies over the Ocean' and other stuff. It was so much fun, Lorrie Dean; we'd sing and laugh, sing and laugh. It was us. Then there were all those . . ."

"Andy? Excuse me, Andy? All I can say is just try to understand."

"Okay." They fell quiet for a half hour or so and then Andy said, "What do you think if we slip down to the farm tomorrow afternoon and visit with Kelly in the cove for a while, and talk to Grandpa and Dub and everybody, and find out if they all need anything? We could wait until they've had plenty of time to finish their lunch following church and rest a bit. That way we wouldn't be imposing on them."

Lorrie Dean nodded and said, "Let's do."

*   *   *

The tripartite meeting at Kelly's Cove got underway cheerfully, despite the woes of its visitors.

Andy let the two girls do most of the talking and loved it. He was in fairyland, seeing these two incomparable women conquer the good and the bad. He just sat on his stump, grinning and shaking his head while these two ardent friends rallied around each other and pretty much solved everything. At least, they tried. They dodged no challenges. *These are* my *girls,* he thought. *Everybody else, back away!*

After a while, the two girls fell silent simultaneously and looked over at Andy. He grinned and said, "I take it by your pointed looks you are saying, 'Okay, Boone Boy, you can go now.'"

The girls responded by jabbering flippantly with each other. "Not him," one said. "Oh no, not at all . . . that's not what we're saying, right?" Still, they carried on with their jesting. "We're just catching our breath and looking at him, the old man on the stump," said one. "Yeah, 'cause we have to look somewhere," said the other. They were nodding playfully as they babbled and chirped like mischievous little girls.

"That's okay, my loyal, devoted fans," chortled Andy. "I've got to go anyway, because sitting here like this, I'm getting a severe case of stump butt. See ya." He waved ostentatiously as he high-stepped out of the cove like a circus clown. As he set away, he whispered to himself, "We're good for each other. Thank you, Lord, for us."

Moments after Andy left the cove, Lorrie Dean smiled at her friend sympathetically and asked, "How can we help you with your mother, Kelly?"

"Just listen. Just listen and tell me what you think. Help me understand what's going on."

"Yes, Kelly, I'm with you on that. I'm ready to listen any time. I'm so sorry we didn't answer the phone."

"Oh, no, no, no, Lorrie Dean, I didn't mean that. Believe me, I perfectly understand."

"Well, we just want to always be here for you. Your Boone Woo felt very bad about our missing your calls."

"That's okay. Well, anyway, the lady called not long after we got back from church today. She apologized for our botched meeting. She kept saying it was interrupted. She wants to try it again, and I told her I would not go through that again. That's where we left it. So, she started crying, and I hung up."

"I see. I'm sorry you're going through this, Kelly."

"Thanks. What do you think?"

"Well, I think you've been very rational about it all—very brave, in fact, and I think you've been accommodating."

"I flat know she'll call again. What should I do, just hang up?"

"I wouldn't just pell-mell hang up; you might miss something you'd really want to know about, simply because she's aroused your curiosity. Just listen. Find out what you can. Use her. Ask questions. Put her on the spot."

"Lorrie Dean, I'm so glad my Boone Woo found you. Thanks for being my friend."

"Hey, I'm the lucky one here."

"Okay, that's that. Now, tell me about you and Boone Woo?"

"That's a sad story for both of us. We're living together, but not for long."

"What?"

"Yes. Surely you can understand, you being a woman, that I'm damaged goods, and I will not subject our beloved Andy to such punishment. Do you understand? Can you please understand? We have to part."

Kelly was stunned speechless. She felt as if life itself had just drained out of her. How could she live if her two heroes deserted each other? She tensed her whole body and raised her head adamantly and exclaimed, "No! Lorrie Dean, don't say that! Don't ever say that! You don't mean it."

"It's all for Andy."

"Bullshit. Pardon me. Anyway, I don't buy that. You're on a self-punishment binge, and I won't feed that for you. I love you both so much." She broke down into uncontrollable anguish, weeping and shaking and wringing her hands.

Lorrie Dean reached to her. They embraced and cried together, two staunch friends, united in strange circumstances, but forever united.

Finally, Lorrie Dean braced and declared, "Okay, let's don't try to tackle all this at once. Let's just give everything some time, for both of us, Kelly."

"Okay. I agree. Let's give it rest for a while. Meanwhile, if Boone Woo should happen to catch me alone some time, he'll probably ask me what we talked about. If that happens, is there anything you especially want me to tell him?"

"Just say that you can tell that I love him dearly."

"Okay, but . . ."

"But what?"

"How's he supposed to take that?"

"I don't follow you."

"Boone Woo *knows* you love him. How will that reminder comfort him, knowing you're parting? Isn't that just sort of rubbing it in?"

"So, you want me to have you tell him I don't love him?"

"Never. But your question makes me wonder whether my mother is hounding me because she loves me or because she doesn't love me."

"I think we're trying too hard to make this an intellectual puzzle. I guess love just won't stand to be measured by brain waves."

18

Monday morning at We Party was a dance—a very delightful one. It was busy but not frenzied. Jan, the boss, was breezing around, checking project status with each planner, cheering them on and offering assistance. On course, she flitted into Lorrie Dean's office, applauded her progress, visited with her for a minute, and then waltzed on out. She did stay long enough to say, with believable sincerity, "It sure is good to have you back."

There's something about the buzz of a busy office that holds ordinary worries at bay for a while, giving the psyche a chance to rejuvenate. Lorrie Dean was grateful for the three projects assigned her, especially since none of them involved anything directly related to a wedding. To her, it was thrilling to work up events aimed at honoring and respecting people held as special. She laughed aloud as she turned to one that was, as far as she knew, unprecedented. She was organizing an evening serenade for a young man seeking to honor his wife on their first anniversary—first month, that is. "Oops!" she grumbled. "That does relate to the subject of weddings and marriage." However, it was so novel and priceless that she decided she wouldn't be derailed by it.

Meanwhile, Andy had hit the ground running at Clay Cutter. By midmorning, he had already bailed his boss out of a jam by dashing off to host a crucial labor union meeting. It happened that the officer assigned to that all-important exercise had called in sick. Andy's old boss and nemesis, Kirk Daniels, actually made a production out of expressing his gratitude, even rapping him on the back as he said, "You really came through there, Andy, my boy. Way to go, and thanks."

That accomplished, Andy had a compelling personal matter that was about to get top priority. As he reached for the phone, he muttered, "Andy Boone, this may well be the single most strategic call you will ever make in all your life."

"Rape Crisis Center, this is Debbie Sills, how may I help?"

"Yes, thank you, this is Andy Boone, and my wife was raped a little over two weeks ago, and I need to know how to help her, because I can't get her to contact you."

"Sure. Okay, first, have you gotten her to a doctor?"

"I'm having trouble there, too."

"Okay, let's keep trying to get her together with us. If we can, we'll serve as her advocate in the medical matters."

"I sure will. As a matter of fact, she was checked over right afterwards and allegedly found to be okay. But, Mrs. Sills, I don't have a lot of confidence in that cursory exam."

"I see. Okay, can you come to our office, yourself?"

"Yes, yes, that's why I called. I need some coaching on whatever I can do. I don't know what to do."

"How about tomorrow morning at eleven o'clock?"

"Great. I'll be there. I'm working at Clay Cutter in Las Colinas, which isn't far from you."

"Okay, fine, Mr. Boone, we'll see you then."

Andy and Lorrie Dean dined at the cafeteria that evening. Since each had had a very heavy day, they opted to fall asleep in their recliners, half-watching TV, and then dragged on off to bed.

Tuesday morning offered them the same level of satisfaction as the day before. For Andy, it meant the pursuit of a grave mission, possibly the one gauntlet of his life. His still-grateful boss agreed to let him have an extended lunch break beginning at 10:30. At that hour, Andy was off to the Rape Crisis Center.

At the center, Andy met Mrs. Debbie Sills, who greeted him politely and escorted him to a small, private room. She interviewed him for basic information and then invited questions. Clearly, she was professional. Though she smiled pleasantly at times, overall her expression was serious throughout their very productive meeting. Even so, her tone and manner conveyed a strong sense of optimism. She chose words and points of emphasis that portended definite promise in solving the crisis.

After the preliminaries, Debbie Sills lectured Andy on the principles of rape crisis counseling, always with an earnest, yet very positive tone. In the course of it, she invited him to make notes, using a pad and clipboard that she furnished.

"Obviously, we can't make you a crisis counselor in one morning, Mr. Boone, but we can certainly teach you some fundamentals of support. Clearly, there is room for initiative on your part. In that regard, there are some positive things you can do, and there are some other behaviors you definitely want to avoid. Now, mind you, these are not theoretical points. They are the dictates of experience, and they've been validated in years of practice."

"Thanks for that assurance, Mrs. Sills. I'm convinced I'm in the right place. I just wish I could get my wife in here."

"With your help, I believe we will. The first thing we want to do is convert your wife from victim to survivor. You'll be her principal support, but her friends, family, coworkers, and others in her life will, we hope, also serve as a vital part of her support."

"Is it okay if I pass along some things I'm learning here to close friends so they'll present the right attitude to her and, you know, interact with her in a helpful way?"

"Indeed. Tough love will be at work here. Fortunately, our rape victim, soon to be a survivor, has a husband who not only cares but insightfully recognizes this for what it is—a genuine crisis."

"Thanks. Let me mention she has one very steadfast friend, a young lady, who will be the strongest factor in her recovery. My plan is to coach her on all the points you're teaching me."

"Great. Mr. Boone, I'm glad you used the word recovery."

"We will get this done," insisted Andy. "My wife is no ordinary person. She is the most deserving human being I've ever known, but right now her self-esteem is shot. Not just that, she hates herself to the point she wants to be punished and she seems bent on doing that herself. So we'll . . . you're shaking your head."

"Simply because your insight amazes me."

"Oh, well, ah, you know, she's my wife."

"Right on. Now, you are going to do a lot of listening, and it'll make you restless, trying to resist the natural temptation to give advice. Mr. Boone, just don't do it! She doesn't need you to tell her what to do. Rather, she needs you to listen. Ideally, when she hears herself describing her experience and all the trauma and her feelings about it, she'll know what to do. Be sure to impress this on her close friend."

"Yes, definitely. That dear friend already has the acumen and perception of a lifetime."

"I see you smiling. She must be your friend, too."

"Yes, indeed. Kelly is our really special buddy, our comrade. We love her so very much, and she has been a godsend to my wife."

Their meeting lasted almost two hours. As he was leaving, Andy looked straight into Debbie Sills's eyes and, nodding, said, "I owe you big-time."

Back in his office, feeling ever so encouraged, Andy reflected on his meeting with the rape crisis counselor. One last expression stuck in his mind. It was the picture memory of the counselor leaning forward in her chair, looking him in the eye, and proclaiming, "Mr. Boone, this is going to work."

Before he got back into his work, he ordered two books. One was a rape crisis text that contained technical material, statistics, and the results of surveys and special studies. The other was a crisis recovery manual, which contained clinical instructions very much like those offered by Debbie Sills. He had these materials earmarked to be delivered directly to Kelly at the farm. Then he started thinking, *Am I being sneaky? If I am, so be it—whatever it takes.*

That done, Andy decided to tackle another matter weighing heavily on his mind. Even though Lorrie Dean insisted it was something that had been firmly resolved, he was not so persuaded. Her own references on this subject were a little vague, and she seemed all too anxious to drop the question. Andy was convinced that nothing had been firmly established by competent medical authority concerning the specifics of Lorrie Dean's physical condition. First of all, this question had been covered only superficially during their debriefing with FBI Agent Chad Jarrigan. Even so, Andy considered this perfectly understandable in view of their mission, which rightfully focused on law enforcement.

Andy also felt it important that the crisis counselor's first question was, "Has she seen a medical doctor?" Everything considered, this matter had to get first priority in whatever he, Kelly, and anyone else could do in helping Lorrie Dean. In his mind, it was altogether too urgent to dismiss casually, as she seemed to want. He would call his friend, Agent Jarrigan, at once.

"Hi, Andy. Thanks for holding," answered Chad cheerfully. "How's it going?"

"Chad, I wish I knew. I'm feeling pretty helpless. Lorrie Dean is very much in shock, and I've been unable to move her to see either a medical doctor or a crisis counselor."

"Andy, unfortunately, I don't think this is really unusual. I also have an opinion based on my experience watching people come away from different kinds of disasters." He chuckled and added, "Of course, we all know what opinions are worth."

"Chad, I value your opinion, because I know it'll be realistic and unbiased. So please, let me have your opinion."

"Okay. I just think that, often, it's the people who've always been the strongest that take it the hardest. For a woman of Lorrie Dean's extraordinary bearing and strength, I think it hits harder. But whatever it is, Andy, I'm sorry, genuinely sorry, for both of you."

"Thanks. I know you're busy, so quickly, here's the reason I called: I'm aware that Lorrie Dean was examined while she was in protective custody, but I don't know the specific findings. Can you tell me anything?"

"Just a little, and this really simply refers to our standard procedure. She would have been checked for evidence of any serious injuries needing immediate attention. Also, in her case, they would have tested her for sexually transmitted diseases."

"Okay; that makes sense, but I still feel compelled to have her get a thoroughgoing medical exam. What do you think?"

"Good idea. You know, Agent Terry Aylor was with Lorrie Dean throughout her protection. I'll have her call you. She can be more specific than I've been."

"Yes, I'd appreciate it, and Chad, thank you for your time and your interest."

Andy sat at his desk, nodding approval of himself, gloating over his achievements. He'd put things in motion calculated to rescue his sweetheart from her hell. His contacts in her behalf had been positive, people were cooperating, and all the pieces just seemed to be falling into place. "What a day," he said, heartily pumping a fist in the air. All at once, he stiffened and pounded the desk with that same fist, which had suddenly turned angry.

"That son of a bitch," he shouted. Still seething, he lowered his voice and continued to grumble. "I need to go down there and clobber that idiot monster where he lies on his hospital bed, then snarl over him as he writhes and begs for his life—let him know what it feels like to be assaulted when you're already helpless." Holding his head in both hands, he raved on. "I want this guy to hurt forever. He robbed my little jewel of her dignity, and I want him to pay for it, and I want to watch while he suffers."

Andy continued to let it all out. He'd been able to contain his fury while he focused on helping his sweetheart survive. Now, with some pleasant relief in that mission, his suppressed anger had vaulted to the top. Even so, Lorrie Dean's personal welfare was still the priority, and in a few minutes, that reality started to soak in and quell his instant rage. *Don't have time for this,* he thought. *Can't let it steal my energy. Lorrie Dean must come first, no matter what I have to do. There's no justice in revenge anyway, mostly 'cause you can't undo the bad thing.*

That evening, after an uneventful dinner, Lorrie Dean and Andy lounged idly in their recliners, playing job-talk. Lorrie Dean felt truly relaxed, telling about her day; it was a day fun to talk about, and her Andy seemed totally absorbed in her stories. As she described her serenade project, she was aware that her face surely must be aglow. She was smiling and nodding, and really delighted to have it to talk about. Andy was smiling and nodding with her.

In a while, their conversation shifted to more ordinary domestic issues. From that point, Andy kept listening for a key word or expression that would give him an opening to ask Lorrie Dean if she wanted to talk about her feelings. Ultimately, he decided to abandon that scrutiny, because she'd clearly had a good day, and there was no way he was going to screw up a good day for her.

They babbled on, and in a while, Lorrie Dean was feeling the day coming down on her. The adrenaline from all the excitement was draining away, leaving her very tired. Apparently, Andy didn't pick up on that development because he kept rattling on.

Oh, how I wish he would just shut up. All that jazz he's coming up with is just pure trivia. Looks like he could tell that I need to simmer down from a really good day and just enjoy its afterglow, quietly. Why is he suddenly so hyper, anyway?

Andy babbled on. He seemed to be picking up steam from the sound of his own voice.

Okay, Andy, I didn't really want to do this tonight, but if you want conversation, I might as well use it to accomplish something. Maybe it's just as well. At least I won't have the dread of facing you with it hanging over me any longer. Like, who needs to sleep, right?

Then Andy fell silent. Breathing a deep sigh of relief, Lorrie Dean decided to put it off until another day.

That day came two days later, Thursday evening. They were still sitting at the dining table after their dinner. Andy knew something was up by the ensuing sense of unfinished business they seemed to share. Missing was their customary post-dinner chatter, leading usually rather quickly into nightly routine. They just sat there at the table, awkwardly staring past each other, occasionally working their lips and sometimes lifting their eyebrows. Andy sensed that Lorrie Dean wanted to be the one to start a conversation, so he said nothing. The waiting was beginning to weigh on his nerves when suddenly it happened.

"Andy, we have to get serious about something. We can't keep it shoved back any longer."

"I'm with you."

"The whole thing is that I've got to reckon with my life. No one can help me with it, not even you, as much as you love me and care about me. I have to do it by myself, and I refuse to let this whole thing be a burden on you."

"What burden? Sweetheart, I'm your husband. We're just one. Your life is my life."

"No, well, we'll talk about the husband issue in a few minutes. Right now, I just want you to understand that I can't live with myself right now, the way I am."

"Please, sweetheart, maybe it would help if you tell me all about your feelings, going back to the horrible things that happened and . . ."

"No. Listen, Andy. When I was running from that horrendous nightmare, running for my life, I was running away from everything. Of all the horrible things that happened to me, and of all the terrible things I did, the thing that sticks with me the most is the running. Oh, how I remember running."

"And you haven't stopped."

"Right. But don't you understand? I have no control over it, and all your loving kindness has no effect. Do you see?"

Andy raised a finger to begin his answer. At once, he felt the disappointment of failing his first attempt at crisis counseling. Then Debbie Sills' words rushed back to him: *Don't push!*

"Andy?" prompted Lorrie Dean. "Are you there?"

"Yeah, I was just thinking, trying to digest it all. But, okay, the answer to your question is yes, I do see."

"Good. So, okay, as I said, I just have to deal with this alone. I can't have any distractions. My sense of guilt is so overwhelming, and it will only get bigger and bigger if I know you're having to deal with it also—because it's not your problem."

"Sense of guilt, sweetheart? Do you want to talk about that? Would it help you?"

"Uh-uh."

"I don't want you to feel guilty. You have absolutely no reason to."

"Andy, dear Andy, you just don't know what all I did."

"I know you're here now. So, Lorrie Dean, get real. You must have done everything right or you wouldn't be here."

"Not that simple. We're wasting time on that. Let's get back to the husband/wife thing. On that, you know, Andy, I think we're not married."

"Of course we are. We both said 'I do' in answer to stated marriage vows in front of witnesses. We heard you say 'I do' as you strained toward the window of that car, just before it spun away."

"But did the preacher pronounce us? No, I don't think so. And, we didn't do the rings—don't you have to do those?"

"I'm sure he pronounced us. And I think the vow is the binding thing, not the rings."

"Okay, Andy, okay, I'm sure you could go and have the preacher pronounce us married, after the fact, in front of some witnesses who were there. And that would make us technically married."

"No way! I'm not going to pursue a technicality that would put me in the role of your opponent. No, forget it. We'll be whatever you think we are. All I know is that I feel like I'm your husband, and I like that feeling."

"Then that's settled," declared Lorrie Dean, as she instantly felt the sting of her own words. She was having trouble bearing up, and she could feel the tickle of initial tears. She braced hard against the pain throbbing inside her, for she could not live through another blow like the last time she tried to press this point—that awful night when she fell. She folded her arms, grasped her elbows, and strained as hard as she could. Finally, she jumped in headlong. "Andy, that means you're free."

"I'll never be free until I have you and until I know you're free. Neither of us will be free until you stop running."

"Oh, Andy, there's so much that if only you knew. And I just can't tell it to you."

"Lorrie Dean, go to the park, to your favorite spot, there in the woods, and tell it to the trees. Tell it out loud. I'm dead serious; this is not meant to be funny."

Lorrie Dean started to respond and then stopped abruptly, her mouth still open. As she let it close, slowly, she was thinking, *Hmm, my little boy dreamer has a point. I really could do that. Maybe I should hear what I've got to say. I could try it in that tranquil, friendly place where there are no contests going on.* Reflexively, she winked at Andy and said, "Good point. I just might do that." His instant smile was broad and joyful. It felt really good to see it. Unfortunately, her next words would kill it stone dead. *I'm sorry,* she thought, *but this has to be done—for you, my man.*

"One other thing, Andy."

"Okay."

"Under the circumstances, realistically, we have to separate. I'll get an apartment and you can stay here."

"Whoa, wait a minute! That doesn't follow from all we've been saying."

"Yes it does. That night I fell, I was trying to tell you this. If I was still Lorrie Dean, you could live with me, but I'm a stranger, Andy. Don't you see that? Just try to understand where I am." As she listened to her own words, it proved, to her satisfaction, that she wasn't her old self. If she were, she would not talk to the man she so dearly loved in such a way as this. *Who am I? I think I've gone crazy.* "So, Andy, I'll be moving out."

"No. If this has to be, you stay here; I'll move."

"But this is your house. You're making the payments on it."

"That has no weight here. It's for us." Then he sighed and took a few deep breaths. "Okay, Lorrie Dean, I'll do what you say, but hear this: you are suffering unnecessarily. Sweetheart, we . . . can . . . get . . . you . . . help."

"Not now."

"Can you give me a few days to find something?"

"Oh sure, sweetheart." Instantly she gasped, for it had been so natural, so instinctive to call him sweetheart.

"Okay," grumbled Andy. "Meanwhile, I have a suggestion that I think will help us both and help our beloved Kelly, too."

"We all get together, right?"

"Well together separately, if that makes sense."

Lorrie Dean leaned over the table a ways and propped her chin on one fist, looking halfway excited. Any thought of Kelly held great magic for these two. "So, like what, Andy?"

"Here's what I'd like us all to do. First, I need to pay a visit to my mom and dad in Dibol, preferably this weekend. So, I could drive down there, stop at the farm en route and visit briefly with all of them. Then—see what you think of this—Kelly could come here and spend the night with you and you all could go out and demolish the malls or whatever. Huh?"

"Andy, I think that's brilliant. Wait a minute; I believe Kelly starts school next Tuesday, so she may have things to do."

"Well, she'll have Labor Day as a buffer."

"Let's call her!"

19

Kelly could hardly contain her excitement. She was scooting around, making jokes, jabbering merrily, and delighting her farm family with everything that came up. Soon, she would be with her Boone Woo, and not long after that, she would spend hours with her best friend. She couldn't recall a more heartening time in her life.

For this special occasion, Kelly had elected to dress a little *up*, as she called it, not evening-at-the-opera up, but definitely upscale business. After all, she didn't want to look like a tramp on a hot August day. Grandpa once said, "Don't dress sloppy on a hot day. If you do, you give nothing to the day, and you look like a tramp."

So she slipped into a black, mid-length skirt, tucked in a cameo-pink, braided-neck blouse, and topped it off with a black onyx choker. Since she and Lorrie Dean would be hiking the malls, she opted for black pumps and elected to carry a small clutch purse. Rarely did she use makeup, but this time, she decided to pat on a faint layer of rouge and apply a little light rose color to her lips. "There now," she said to the mirror, "take that!"

Kelly stepped away from the mirror and ambled toward the formal living room, a truly inviting, exquisitely furnished chamber at the front of the house. As she approached the plush couch, the doorbell rang, and she changed her course without breaking stride. She strolled toward the front door in short, graceful steps, her chin lifted proudly, like a model at a ritzy fashion show. She eased open the door, and there stood a youngish-looking man, grinning like a backup clown.

"Good morning, sir. I remember you."

"Oh yes, I'm him all right."

"Did you drop by to repay that cup of sugar you borrowed?"

"The thing is, ma'am, that's what I came here to do, but I forgot to bring it with me."

"Are you telling me you came all the way over here just to say you're here to repay a cup of sugar you didn't bring?"

"Sad, ain't it? But, you know, it's a tough old world out there. It's hard to keep rolling on."

"Well, roll on in here, Boone guy, and we'll see if we can find you some help."

As Kelly led the way, Andy said, "Excuse me, Kelly, could you hold up a bit?"

She hesitated and turned half around and then flinched as Andy exclaimed, "Wow! You . . . look . . . beautiful. Really, Kelly, you look so pretty. You're always pretty, but that outfit is you."

Kelly curtsied and purred, "Thank you, sir."

In the den, there was Mom with her signature, totally accepting smile, still in her apron from breakfast. She hugged Andy and said everybody else was out at—not down on—the farm. She invited him and Kelly to sit at the dining table, because she knew they had work to do. Andy had foretold that in his early-morning call.

At the table, Andy laid out all the materials from his large, brown envelope and proceeded to brief Kelly on the guidelines given him by Debbie Sills, the crisis counselor. "Here are all my notes for you to keep," said Andy, as he shuffled through them.

"Don't you need them?" asked Kelly.

"No, I've pretty well memorized them, and I still remember the things she stressed. I've already tried to use a couple of the techniques, and it didn't work." He paused, pressing a finger to his chin, and looked up toward heaven, apparently for inspiration. In a moment, he continued, "There *is* one point I offered, and she actually seemed to be considering it."

"What was that?"

"Lorrie Dean just doesn't want to talk to me about all the traumatic events and her feelings about them. Anyway, at some point, I said—seriously, mind you—'Maybe you could tell it to the trees when you're in the park some time.' Surprisingly, she seemed open to that."

"Yeah, as I understand your instructor, it doesn't matter how or to whom she expresses all the stuff, just as long as she gets it out."

"Right. So I wanted to suggest she write it down, just write to herself . . . or whatever. But Kelly, I never got an opening I could rush through with that one, probably because I'm not clever enough to know an opening when I see one."

Now Kelly was thumbing her chin and looking up, the way Andy had earlier. In a few moments, she drawled, "I'm getting an idea." Soon she slapped the table and whooped, "Yes!"

"Great!" blurted Andy. "Don't tell me. Just do it." They raised a thumbs-up to each other, and that was done.

Andy slid all his notes back into the envelope and handed it to Kelly. It was time. Hence, the two buddies moseyed back through the formal living room to the front door and on out to the porch.

"Well, this is it, I guess. Kelly, please drive carefully."

"I will. You, too."

"Will do. I wish you two girls a great time together. That reminds me, did you all have a productive visit in the cove last Sunday?"

"We did. Uh-huh. And you know what, Boone Woo? I want to tell you this . . . one thing is for sure . . . that is, I could tell from all the talking Lorrie Dean did that she truly loves you."

Tears hit Andy's eyes instantly as if they were waiting there for a reason to leap out. He reached to his precious buddy, hugged her, turned away, and stalked out to his car.

Kelly stood in the doorway and watched Andy as he headed down the driveway, as she had done every time from their very first meeting. She raised her hand high and waved to him, knowing full well that he couldn't see her. As she was lowering her arm, she was thinking about their peerless relationship. Their silly front-door banter was a constant for them. In fact, these two were, in all things, constant for each other, and although that running banter of theirs was not inherently funny, it was dependably real—and every word of it said, "I love you."

The drive to Dallas, in and of itself, was easy and stress-free. Kelly just tried to relax and engage the beautiful East Texas scenery. It seemed to work better, now that she was the driver rather than a passenger. When she was the passenger, she always seemed to be given partly to sightseeing and partly to worry about the driver's driving. In about an hour, she came out of the woodland country with its shaded highway, and emerged into the wide-open, sunny prairie lands, closer to Dallas. Then she set in to thinking about the challenge facing her. There was no way to shinny around the hard fact that she and Lorrie Dean each had problems, and this meeting surely would involve mostly those problems. Then she prayed silently. *Guide us, dear Lord; bathe us in your light, I pray.*

Forty-five minutes later, Lorrie Dean opened her door, and the two pals stood face-to-face, smiling amiably, yet fully ready for the tough work of devoted friends.

"Hey, Kelly," sang Lorrie Dean, gleefully. "Come on here." With the door open barely wide enough, they embraced. Then, arm in arm, they walked through the front room to the parlor. They stood briefly before sitting, each admiring the tasteful dress and countenance of the other. Lorrie Dean had also chosen to dress up a little. She looked really chic, in her brown, dressy slacks suit.

They sat and visited breezily for a short while and then relaxed over a light lunch, which Lorrie Dean had prepared the night before. It was a cool, very tasty meal, dominated by fruits, melons, and tuna fish salad, rich in chopped celery, onions, and sweet relish. Kelly praised not only the refreshing fare but also Lorrie Dean's foresight in preparing it ahead.

After lunch, they cruised out to North Park Mall on Central Expressway. It was a huge, forty-six-acre, fully enclosed rectangular shopping complex with a sweeping promenade around the entire interior perimeter. It was a dazzling city, replacing a one-time cotton field, now a premier center, showcasing a spectacular collection of retailers, world-class art, and remarkable landscaping. Indeed, flower beds, fountains and pools, lush tropical gardens, and spacious courts—all immaculately maintained—were scattered along the clean, wide promenades. Mingled among them were stunning sculptures and enclaves of modern art. Major department stores anchored all four corners, and the galleries offered a full mix of retail shopping opportunity and fine dining.

North Park mall was also a social center. Shoppers ambled along its galleries, jabbering, laughing, and just all around visiting. Surely this was a popular meeting place. Lorrie Dean and Kelly joined the crowd and its mood, tripping along with no particular store in mind, just enjoying their visit in this very conducive environment. They did pick up a couple of clothing items each and eventually settled down for a delightful dinner at Maggiano's Little Italy.

At dinner, the two seemingly carefree friends continued their exciting fellowship, scarcely a harbinger to what was waiting when the euphoria would wear off. Right then, it didn't matter. Friends were frolicking, playing, engaging in their friendship. All else could wait.

Back home, the two young women agreed to wait until the next day for their serious talk. For now, they would listen to Andy's favorite music channel on TV and reminisce over the day's pleasantries. By ten o'clock, they were laughingly trying to talk through their yawning, probably the last humorous moments they would share for a while. So, they arose and plodded off toward their bedrooms, stretching and grunting. They bade pleasant dreams and good night and then hit their beds, to the sweet smell of freshly laundered sheets.

After breakfast Saturday morning, they returned to take seats at the dining table, which seemed to be a perfectly instinctive move for each of them. It was natural to seek this setting for a serious discussion. There's just something about having an inanimate prop to steady the nerves when compelling issues are . . . err . . . on the table. The two parties shifted about for a bit, batting their eyes and looking expectantly at each other. Finally, Kelly broke the spell.

"Why are we sitting at this table?"

They chuckled and then turned serious as Lorrie Dean said, "I guess each of us is expecting to hear a serious question."

Kelly nodded. "Yes, that's it."

"Kelly, I don't want you to feel under obligation to talk about your mother, but if you want to, please feel free, because Andy and I care very much about your feelings."

"Oh, I don't mind. Sure, you're right; it is something I'm having to deal with that is really . . . okay, very unpleasant and upsetting. So stop me if you get tired of listening to this mess." She chuckled, but it sounded phony.

"Take it all the way, Kelly. I'll never tire of hearing of things that are important in your life."

"Well, okay. I think you already know what took place in my early childhood before my mother put me up for grabs."

"Pretty much, I think. Andy has filled me in on those dreadful years. I'm sorry."

"Thanks. Actually, it was hard but not too long and drawn-out in my getting over all the bickering and insulting between my mom and my dad. As I say, that was hard, but I got beyond that pretty well. But when neither of them wanted me around, preferred not to have to look after me—well, that was devastating. I was just six years old, and to suddenly be shocked by news that you are so unlovable that neither of your parents even want you around . . ."

Lorrie Dean watched, exuding sympathy, knowing that her buddy was steeling herself against the overwhelming temptation to cry. In a moment, she leaned slightly forward over the table and murmured, "Please take your time; you are loved here."

That dear comment did it, and Kelly gave in long enough to cry ever so briefly. Soon, she muttered through a breaking voice, "Thank you. I know y'all love me. And you know what, Lorrie Dean? I've always yearned to be needed. Now, with you and Boone Woo, I feel needed for the first time in my life. Thank you for loving me." As she swatted the tears under her eyes, she smiled weakly and added, "And I know your love is real."

"You bet it is. Our love for you is forever. And, Kelly, we feel your love. How lucky *we* are."

"Me, too. Okay, I was six years old when my mother discarded me, and I went to live with Uncle Dub and Grandpa and them. They loved me, and it was genuine, I think, but I could never tell if it was just sympathy they had for me. Anyway, they've been the best in the world. They are fine, fine people."

"I know."

"So, I was just six years old, just starting to school. I didn't know how to read or write. Then, I was suddenly in a place where the adults in my life acted like they wanted me around and wanted to help me learn. The teachers treated me so wonderfully, and all the other little kids, too."

"Yeah, your Boone Woo says that grade school is the best thing in our lives."

Kelly nodded and continued, "Well, one day, I got mad and said to myself, 'They're not going to treat me this way.' Lorrie Dean, when I say I raised my head, I mean I literally took both hands, pushed up on my chin, and stretched as tall as I could. I said, 'They will hurt me no longer,' my mom and dad, that is. I said that out loud, that they would never hurt me again."

"So, you feel that now, your mother is trying to hurt you?"

"Actually, I'm not sure of that, but let me tell what I did. The best part is coming up in just a minute. So, okay, I held my head up and set about to learn everything I could—six years old, mind you. I plunged myself into studying every way I could. Lorrie Dean, I begged my teachers for homework. Is that crazy or what?"

"It's admirable and brilliant."

"Well, by the third grade, I could read and write . . . well, you know, we knew basic words, and we knew how to make a simple sentence. Then, sometime during the fourth grade, just out of the blue, I had this weird impulse. It was like a voice saying, 'Write it down.' *What?* I thought. Let me tell you, I started, not a diary, but a journal of all that had happened to me in my life, and mostly every time I wrote something, I would add some stuff on how it made me feel."

"I think that is absolutely miraculous, unbelievable, almost."

"Believe it, Lorrie Dean. Well, so that all has helped me, and that's why I guess I'm so afraid my mother is going to tear all that down. And, I'm just not going to let her." She took a deep breath and declared, "There! What do you think?"

"I think you already have experience with what works. Write it down, Kelly, and put down what your mother is making you feel like. Then read it over and over, and perhaps that'll give you your answer as to what to do."

"Write myself a letter, right? Yeah, if I write me a letter, then that way, I'll put it all in perspective."

"Right. Actually, that's what you were doing with your journal. Ingenious."

"Okay, by golly, I will."

"And in all things, please always let me know how I can help."

"I promise. Now, Lorrie Dean, it's your turn."

"To write myself a letter?"

Kelly shrugged and endured the awkward silence while Lorrie Dean waited for an answer.

"Ohhh-kay. So what can I say about my terrible situation? I can't really talk about it. Andy has tried, in subtle ways, to get me to bring it all out, but something is just boring in on me, frightening me about how it'll all sound. I just know that the whole thing changed me, and I'm not what Andy had."

"You don't think you're Lorrie Dean anymore?"

"That's right."

"Do you love Boone Woo and me, and do you care about how we get along?"

"Yes, of course."

"That's Lorrie Dean."

"That won't work, Kelly. In fact, I love Andy so much that I don't want him to have to live his life with the likes of me."

"You are on one huge guilt trip! You are making of yourself a colossal martyr." With that, Kelly began crying. "I'm sorry, Lorrie Dean, I had no right to say that. Forgive me."

"You say anything you feel about it all. We're friends. But I'm not on a guilt *trip*. I am indeed *guilty*. I egged that rogue on until he got the idea he could rape me, and I wouldn't care. I tried all kinds of ways to trick him, and my tricks only landed me under his wretched body."

"Why were you trying to trick him, or whatever?"

"I was trying to get an advantage over him so I could get away."

"You were trying to save your life?"

"Yes. I know what you're doing, Kelly. I see where you're going with this. But nothing excuses me from what I did."

"Okay, Lorrie Dean. Whatever you say."

"Oh, Kelly, I'm sorry. It's just so hard to talk about it to anyone."

"So, write a letter."

"Maybe I will. I won't let anybody see it, because I might even say some hurtful things."

"You? Of all people, I don't see that happening; you're not a hurtful person."

"See there. That's because you think I'm still Lorrie Dean."

"Everything about you seems like Lorrie Dean to me."

"Well, I'm not. And that's another thing. I can't understand why Andy is so ready to take me back, or stick with me, knowing what I am now—an unclean woman. I'm so surprised in him. Really, doesn't he have any standards?"

Kelly didn't answer right away. The two just stared at each other, their tearful eyes pleading. In a few moments, Kelly cleared her throat and moaned, "Well, if Boone Woo doesn't have standards, then who am I?"

Lorrie Dean looked startled for a moment. "I can see that I've got a lot of thinking to do, my dear Kelly. Since it's on my mind all the time anyway, I might as well make something constructive out of it. Meanwhile, I want you to let us know how it develops with your mother, and if you need us to go with you to meet with her or anything, please let us know. We love you, and we want to help."

"Thanks, Lorrie Dean. I love y'all, too, and your situation hurts me way down deep. Now, like you suggested to me, are you going to write all this down?"

"I wouldn't know where to begin."

"I didn't find that a problem. It doesn't matter where you begin, as long as you get everything in that's relevant."

"Perhaps it *would* help me. I'll think about it. I know Andy wants me to write down all these ugly memories I have told him about."

"Here's to you, Lorrie Dean. Please let me know if I can help."

"That's a deal." At once, Lorrie Dean struck a pose of someone deep in thought, as if trying to solve a vexing puzzle. Kelly just let her think. In time, Lorrie Dean said, "Tell me, Kelly, if it comes down to it, could you forgive your mother?"

Kelly blinked, lifted her head slowly, and answered as politely as she knew how, "Right now, I don't see me doing that. Have you forgiven your mother for getting you into the dreadful situation you're having to live with?"

"Yes. My dad and I forgave her right away. She paid the price of her misdeeds and asked for our forgiveness. She was foolish, irresponsible, and yes—definitely selfish. She really fouled up big time, but she paid for it."

"I understand," began Kelly. After a brief pause, she continued, "Ah, just one more thing."

"Shoot."

"Could you forgive your rapist?"

20

The next day, Lorrie Dean and Andy managed to tough out a typical Monday at their jobs and, remarkably, arrived home near the same time. Neither was motivated to dive into a heavy dinner, so they shared an apple and chomped on cold turkey sandwiches. Andy was noticeably nervous, prompting Lorrie Dean to ask, kindly, "Are you okay?"

Andy looked at her strangely, shook his head, and kept chewing as if to avoid answering.

"I'm waiting."

It was time. "I've found a place to live," he blurted out. "Guess I'll be moving out tomorrow."

Lorrie Dean looked up and nodded. Then she bowed again and started twisting her fingers, hardly able to reply. In a while, she mumbled, "That was fast."

"Sweetheart, it seemed to be what you wanted."

"I can't say that, in my heart, I wanted it, but it has to be, no matter . . . no matter . . ." She was unable to finish.

"Will you let us date from time to time?"

"Yes."

"Get ready, my little symphony," he said, smiling broadly, "'cause I'm going to court you all over again."

"Andy, I think you're a glutton for punishment."

"That's not it at all. I am just not going to let this devil steal our love."

"No, dear Andy, you're taking this like it was nothing." She threw her hands out at him and shouted, "I was raped! Do you hear me? And it was my fault, and I'm no good to you anymore!"

"I know, darling. I know, I know. You were sexually assaulted, but you yourself didn't have sex. It was just a procedure for that idiot hoodlum whose life's work is dominating helpless victims. Hear me: It . . . was . . . not . . . your fault! I said that before, but I must say it again, because it's still in your head."

"What do *you* know? You weren't there."

Andy sucked in a deep, heavy breath and heaved it sputtering through his lips. "I'm sorry, sweetheart. If it looks like I'm getting worked up, well, I am." Then he leaned in close to her and spoke calmly. "You're right; I wasn't there, but I fully understand what you had to do. When you were toying with your guard, you had no other option. The adrenaline took over and made the decisions, and that is a God-given protector of life."

"Oh, me, Andy. That sounds so easy."

"Okay, okay. While we're on this subject, I have to ask you something."

"Don't hurt me, Andy."

"I won't push it, but I just have to ask this one thing. Are you going to file charges against this Jarred guy?"

"No. I don't want to make a spectacle out of it."

"Perhaps I could file in your behalf."

"All you have is hearsay. True as it is, it's still hearsay coming from you."

"I could get Agent Aylor to testify with me since you told her also."

"Andy, once you told me you wouldn't do anything that made you my opponent."

"Okay, I'll drop it, but I'd still like to see that SOB suffer."

"Sorry if it puts you under a strain, Andy."

Andy shook his head, drew a deep breath, and said no more. In a few moments, he reached for Lorrie Dean, and she started to shy away, but relented and let him take her in his arms. In truth, it was somewhat healing to cry on his shoulder.

In a while, Andy eased away and looked at her through his own tears. "My darling, whatever can be said about your undeserved ordeal, I want you to know this: I'm so very sorry you had to suffer through that wretched nightmare."

"Thanks, Andy."

"Will you grant me one request—just one request?"

"Whoa, I'm leery of that kind of question. You know I would do anything for you, but how can I give a categorical yes to that question?"

"Please. I'm only asking for one thing—just one. You can do this one; it won't enslave you."

"Oh, well, okay, I'll grant you one simple request. Go ahead. Ask me."

"Okay, this is my one request: please don't surrender to that barbarian pig who brutalized you. Let him go. It's done. My beautiful symphony, it's time for the triumphant part."

"I'll try. And I'm sorry you're having to go through this yourself. I know you're hurting, and I know it's because you care."

"I don't mind anything I have to go through for us. It's not just that I'm afraid of losing you; I'm afraid of your losing yourself. I will not stand by and idly watch that happen. That's the one thing that hurts the most. You're important in this world. We need you, and I'm so glad you did whatever you did, because, sweetheart, it means you are here, now. Praise God! We still have you."

All of a sudden, Lorrie Dean felt herself smiling ever so faintly and her shoulders started to relax a little. "Let's go to the park," she exclaimed. "I want to talk to the trees." Then she chuckled and joked, "Will you stay out of my way?"

"Will you scream if you need help?"

"Of course."

"I'll get my hat."

At the park, Andy took his regular seat in the pavilion and started playing with a pine cone, rolling it around in his hands, hoping for some kind of reportable sensation. As it developed, he found there is not a lot of inspiration in a dead, dull gray, craggy, pine cone. As he continued to fumble with this ever-loving pine cone, he was looking far out, watching Lorrie Dean until she disappeared in a curve of the pathway.

Lorrie Dean sauntered along the cultivated path to her favorite turnoff spot. Then she tramped on over to the little thicket that embraced her favorite tree, the red oak—"Big Red," as she called it. In but a few minutes, she felt tension draining away and even a sense of wanting to smile.

Going into the woods, in and of itself, seemed to be an element of coping for her. She felt freedom. It also helped to hear the hikers and joggers cheerfully greeting each other as they passed along the trail which, though totally obscured from her location, was really only a short distance away. Most of them were complete strangers to each other, yet their spontaneous greetings carried a tone of complete acceptance. The park was good therapy for all.

As Lorrie Dean thought of these subtleties, she stretched tall, straightened her shoulders, held her head high, and looked proudly up into her tree. "Hey, Big Red, how do you keep peace around here? However you do it, I'm impressed. I don't see any turf wars raging out there—no pun intended, Mr. Red." She chuckled and kept chattering about the harmony in nature. "Where's all the political posturing and jockeying for position out here? Don't you guys have any fun?" Now she was chuckling at herself as she talked to her tree. "Oh me, if anybody hears me talking to a big red oak, they'll think I'm crazy—or at least silly." After she finished her speech, she sat down under the tree and totally relaxed. In a while, she rose, slapped the trunk of Big Red, and set off to rejoin Andy.

Back home, they seemed to be naturally at ease with each other. They interacted politely and lovingly. Each felt genuinely at ease—that is, until Andy brought up a dreaded subject.

"Sweetheart, I haven't mentioned this matter in a while because I know it upsets you to think about it. So I know it's risky for me to do this."

"You're going to break up my euphoria?"

"Yeah, I'm afraid it will, but out of love, I have to. The point is that while the park is wonderful therapy for your emotional needs, it can't doctor your physical injuries, in case you have any."

"That's enough, Andy. Forget it; I'm not going to a doctor. I would if I could see a basis for it, but I don't. So, just save your breath."

"There *is* a basis for it. You must quit running from it."

They continued to argue, waxing foolishly academic at times, both saying things they hadn't thought through. Mercifully they were interrupted by the ringing telephone.

Andy picked up. "Andy Boone."

"Hi, Boone Woo. Is everybody okay?"

Andy motioned for Lorrie Dean to pick up the extension as he chimed, "Hey, morning light. Sure, we're okay, but how about you?"

"Fine."

"Hi, Kelly; I'm on," chimed Lorrie Dean.

"Wonderful. Is this what you call a conference call?"

"Indeed," said Lorrie Dean. "It can be whatever we want it to be. How's everybody there?"

"Everybody's good." She cleared her throat pretentiously and chortled, "It's okay for you to talk, too, Boone Woo."

"Oh, I will, I will. But I know who the priority figures are in this three-way huddle."

"Figures? Did you hear that, Lorrie Dean? Priority figures? Are we figures? Is that a status symbol? If so, I'm honored to be one."

"No, but your Boone Woo makes up a lot of things. So, just make allowances and humor him."

"Bless his heart. So, while we're humoring around here, how about saying a little prayer for me."

Lorrie Dean squealed. "Don't tell me—you're going to meet your mother."

"I second that," said Andy. "Are we right?"

"Yes. You got it," droned Kelly. "Forgive me; I know I should sound more excited."

"We understand," said Lorrie Dean. "Just know that our spirits are with you."

"Thanks. Actually, that's why I called. See, I've really been kind of edgy about it, and I do want you to say a prayer for me."

Andy and Lorrie Dean answered at the same time, pledging their blessings and their prayers. "When is this coming off, and where?" asked Lorrie Dean.

"A week from Saturday, at the same place, Wills Point. By then, I should be fully settled in the routine of school—my senior year, you know. Woo-hoo."

"My Kelly, I feel good about this," Andy assured her. "Me, too," chimed Lorrie Dean.

"Now," began Andy sternly, "we will be there for you. Can you give us some directions to the actual place you're meeting?" Lorrie Dean was agreeing in the background as he spoke.

"Thanks. Believe me, I'm grateful for that. But you don't have to be there. I really just called to hear you say you're with me. That means so much to me. I get pretty anxious when I think about the whole screwy thing. But if I can hear your voices, something good just happens inside me and I feel better."

"We get the same feeling hearing yours," said Lorrie Dean. "And, Kelly, please, we *will* be there for you."

"Thanks again . . . but I'm afraid something might slip up again. She might get spooked or whatever. So, y'all don't come. Okay?"

"Well, whatever you say," said Lorrie Dean, diffidently. "We'll pray, and my dear Kelly, you have our blessings."

"I know, and that lifts me. Believe me. I guess the main thing that worries me is that she'll run again. But anyway, thanks to you, my dear, best friends."

Their visit ended cheerfully, and when Andy and Lorrie Dean hung up, they walked straight to each other and embraced. It just happened, spontaneously. In fact, when they eased apart, they looked surprised.

The night passed on, and then came the day for Andy's departure.

Packing was tedious and aimless. His shoulders sagged, and his body felt like a sandbag. His work clothes, coat-and-tie apparel, as he called it, were all hanging on a rod he'd fixed above the backseat of his car. All the other stuff was just dumped in two suitcases. He didn't have to take everything he owned. After all, it wasn't like he'd never be back to stay. Besides, it was his conviction that he wouldn't be gone for more than a month.

The more he packed, the more his nerves pestered him, and he started dropping things, and that made him mad. Well, something was making him angry, so he began to ponder the chicken-and-egg question: *Am I getting angry because I'm nervous, or am I getting nervous because I'm angry?*

Whatever the real problem, Andy felt he was losing control; perhaps his ego was driving too hard. Then he dropped a pair of socks. Fuming, he picked them up and slammed them into a suitcase. Then he walked over to an open closet door, kicked it, and rammed it shut with his shoulder. He felt much better. That accomplished, he began to chastise himself and scold his overzealous ego. *Okay, that's enough, ego. You're doing a good job, but you can back off now. Settle down; get some rest. I'm on it.* He slowly became aware that his mood was changing, and once again he was consumed with overwhelming sadness. He began to wonder how Lorrie Dean felt at this hour.

Lorrie Dean didn't have the heart to watch her man pack, even though she had given him a de facto order to move out. Still, she couldn't sit down. It was all too enormous to comprehend. *What am I doing?* she asked herself. Sadness so gripped her that she wanted to double over and drop to the floor, bawling her heart out. She steeled herself, but the effort was crushing her where she stood in the middle of the front room. She drifted toward the bedroom where Andy was packing. "Need any help?" she murmured.

Andy glanced up and smiled meekly. He started to answer, but his voice faltered, so he just shook his head in a surrendering kind of way. Momentarily, he closed the suitcase, turned to his beloved, and they embraced, holding tightly, summoning all the strength they could, in respect for each other. Then they broke away, and Andy headed for the front door with his suitcase and a little bag of shaving gear.

Lorrie Dean stood at the window, tears spilling over her face and slipping into the corners of her mouth, as she watched Andy pitch his shaving gear onto the passenger seat. She tried simply to blink away the tears, as she watched him linger by the car, his arm draped across the roof of it, looking toward the house. He looked like a little boy who'd just been kicked off the soccer team.

It seemed that Andy would stand there beside his packed car forever. Finally he slapped the roof of it, stepped away, and poked around to the driver's side. All too soon, he backed out and drifted away, leaving Lorrie Dean alone in the house, once intended to harbor them as wife and husband.

She stood at the window, frozen, trying to reckon with it all. In this compelling moment, she didn't care about anything in the world but Andy. After what seemed like an eternity, she turned from the window and started away. Then she stopped abruptly and her mind started to clear. "Okay, Andy," she whispered, "I'll see a doctor—for you, sweetheart, for you." She looked up toward the ceiling, tightened her lips and proclaimed aloud, "Okay, Lorrie Dean, you've got some writing to do."

Another night passed, and the next day was lonely and confused for two denied lovers. Nevertheless, that evening, Lorrie Dean picked up the phone and listened to a familiar, very upbeat voice: "How about dinner tomorrow night at Lawry's?"

"Yes, I'd like that."

"I'll pick you up at six."

21

They stared past the flickering candle between them, half-looking away, their faint smiles the penance of sadness. They were alone in a quiet corner of Lawry's, lost in their quandary, oblivious to the murmur of the other diners. The bond of Andy and Lorrie Dean, so carefree and natural when it began four months ago, had grown into an ominous burden.

They waited for inspiration, unflinching, acutely aware of their breathing. In time, Andy leaned forward and sighed. He started to talk, but no sound came. He shook his head and grinned uneasily. He cleared his throat and tried again. "Are you telling me it's never to be? I mean, now or ever?"

Lorrie Dean nodded lightly. She glanced down at the saucer in front of her and stared into the square of cheese cake until it became a diffused little mass. She could barely hear her own words as she murmured, "No, Andy, it's never to be."

Again, they sat in silence, picking at the edges of their desserts. At once, Andy grabbed his cheesecake two-handed, lifted it up, and bombed it back into the saucer. "This is stupid," he grumbled. "Whatever happened to love, the hero? Love is supposed to be the great liberator. For us, it's the villain."

"Andy, please don't get started again. It only makes it harder. What we're doing is the right thing for both of us. You'll be free, and I won't feel quite so guilty. You've already agreed to separate and so forth, so please don't be difficult."

"Well, if this is so right, why are we sitting here like two spanked kids, raking through this forsaken, damn cheesecake?"

"Because it's sad. I never said it wasn't heartbreaking. Right things are sad . . . sometimes."

"Bull!"

"Andy, you promised."

"I never promised I wouldn't try."

"Well, your trying only makes it worse for you. Don't you get exhausted, trying? I just can't hold out any longer." She bowed her head in both hands as she talked, fighting hard to keep from crying. Why couldn't Andy understand? Why did he try so hard to hurt her, pleading so stubbornly? "I'm scared," she said, dropping her hands to look straight at him. "It would eventually destroy both of us. The richer our love grows, the more threatening this thing gets."

The unaffected waiter was suddenly in the shadow of their table as if summoned to referee. But the only consolation he brought was a polite smile and a softly-spoken offer of more coffee. They nodded and stared after him as he drifted away. Too bad he couldn't take with him whatever they had. That would be the truly merciful intervention, for something to come along and just steal their love.

Andy was leaning over the table, pushing a wrinkle into his forehead with two fingers, his eyes closed. Lorrie Dean smiled faintly, knowing that the wheels were still turning in his little-boy head. Her love for him welled inside. She thought of how easily and naturally they had fallen in love, even before he realized who she was, namely the childhood sweetheart for whom he had searched relentlessly. She tingled at the memory of their sexual experiences, so profoundly intimate—those exhilarating times when they were fully given to each other and when afterward they felt enormous gratitude for the loving promise that would hold their lives as one, forever.

Andy stirred and caught Lorrie Dean's intense gaze. "You know, Lorrie Dean, we need something different to overcome, something to take the place of this stupid monster. Maybe I could try to rob a bank and get myself caught and arrested. Would you bail me out?"

"That's not even funny."

"Well then, let's join that couple over there. They seem to be having a good time."

"I don't want to have a good time. I want to be sad—miserable. Serves me right."

"Sure it does. Pain power! I'm tired of being resident droop; let's play something else."

"Don't be so cavalier. All that platitude stuff is easy for you to say. You weren't raped." She squeezed her clinched hands to keep from pounding the table. She glanced down at them as she argued. Her locked fingers were strained white. She tried to relax them, and she drew a deep, quivering breath.

They fell silent and instinctively stared vaguely past each other. Lorrie Dean continued to think, and it hit her that she was living a paradox, that the repeated inconsistencies in her behavior were inexplicable. Throughout their merciless ordeal, she would argue vehemently with Andy one minute and in the next ponder her rich, undeniable love her him. How could this be? In that moment, it occurred to her that in those hateful times, when she was so verbally mean to her man, she was under the power of her inscrutable sense of guilt. *Maybe Andy's right. That's what he's working so hard to help me understand. I am letting a rapist control my life.*

Andy broke the silence. "Wow! This is really some war. This struggle is not between right and wrong. It's between love and hate. They are the contestants in your war with yourself, our love for each other, and your hatred for that monster who raped you and for yourself because you think you were bad and deserved it. Well, let me tell you, I'm not going to let that worm have the victory here."

"Dear Andy, you just may have a point there. It is something that I seem unable to keep out of my mind, that horrible nightmare and my own stupid behavior that I feel led up to it. Sure, I can deliberately tune it out by sheer force of will at times, like when I'm at work. But I really can't shake it except for those very brief moments. It pulls back on me; I'm a prisoner of it. Every time I change anything about what I'm doing, it jumps up in front of me. When I sit down or stand up, it's there. When I change TV channels, it's there. If I try to read, it flashes whenever I turn a page. And when . . . and when I think of you, it bores in on me. Our love draws it to the surface like fever in a sore."

"We have to change that. You can win this. Take your time and keep on thinking. And let us pray for God's help in this ugly battle."

"Thank you, my dear Andy, and I assure you, I will pray. For now, I guess we ought to go."

Back home, at Lorrie Dean's front door, they stood in silence. To Lorrie Dean, Andy seemed a little unlike himself. She searched his eyes, trying to fathom his faraway look. She tightened her jaw, gathering all the grit she could summon to keep from breaking down. Finally she said, "It's probably better if you don't come in."

"I know," said Andy. They began to shift around nervously. Atypically, Andy didn't reach to embrace her. Instead, he took her hands, folded them together and brought them up to their chests. He squeezed them and held them that way for a long time, until her hands ached. Finally he set them free and walked back to his car.

Early the next morning, Lorrie Dean shuffled over to the park. It was Saturday, which meant she didn't have to wait until the end of her workday for her visit. It was busy, and that was good. Andy had said it was safer that way. This time, she wandered a little deeper into the woods, beyond Big Red. She stomped along, ducking under low-hanging limbs, twisting vines out of her path, taking deep, deliberate breaths and lifting her chin into the morning breeze that somehow found its way around the trees and scrubs and through the undergrowth.

It felt right, as always it did, inside this wooded paradise. She leaned back into the trunk of a pine tree and picked at the petals of a white daisy, smiling into it, trying to capture its innocence.

Lorrie Dean opened her eyes, startled by a sense that she had been asleep, still propped against the tree. She cocked her head and smiled to herself. Then melancholy swept over her, and she began to tramp back toward her usual spot. As she drew near Big Red, she stopped abruptly, startled at the sight of someone standing a ways off, back toward the beaten path. Instinctively, she slipped behind a juniper and peeked through its branches. She gasped. Her hands flew up to cover her mouth and then slowly dropped away as she stared in disbelief.

The intruder started on in, slowly, looking up through the treetops, as though plotting his course from glimpses of the sky. He stopped at a little sapling and shook its thin trunk with one hand. In a while, he turned away, stuffed his hands into his pockets, and slowly retreated.

Lorrie Dean cramped her lips as she watched. She thought of how Andy had tried to be funny at times to ease her pain. He'd worked so hard on her—always. He had really tried. He seemed so out of character, now, slinking away, his hands in his pockets, shoulders drooped, looking down as he trudged on. She felt closer to him in that instant than ever before—just seeing him out there, gone from her life, but still out there.

She started to follow, keeping her distance. Soon she was conscious of walking faster. She lifted a hand in the air and called out, "Hi Andy." He stopped instantly, but he didn't turn around.

They were only about fifteen yards apart. Then he slowly turned around, hands still in his pockets. They stared at each other across the underbrush. In a few moments, Andy turned and started again on his way. Lorrie Dean sobbed quietly where she stood. Giving him up was one thing, but losing him was quite another.

Andy plodded along the path back toward his car. There was no reason to hurry. He wasn't running away; he was just leaving. In time, he left the park and headed back to his motel. He had plans, and they began with a phone call to his morning light, Kelly Surrat, at the farm.

"Hi, Boone Woo. What's up?"

Andy groped for the right words as he related the incident with Lorrie Dean at the park. Somehow the right words just wouldn't show up, so he conceded to stumbling his way through it, as best he could. He explained that when Lorrie Dean failed to answer the ring of her doorbell, he knew instantly where she was.

"I was in complete limbo when I got to the park. I didn't have the foggiest idea of what I was doing or what I was *going* to do."

"You didn't know why you went there, Boone Woo?"

"It was sort of that way, I guess. All I knew was that I had to go see about her. But after I got there, something came over me. I can't explain it. I just seemed to take on a different purpose than just seeing if she was safe. I was flooded with a whole new set of impulses."

"Weird."

"It was indeed weird, yet strangely it seemed right. When I saw her, I didn't rush to her as I would have expected of myself. I just dillydallied and then abruptly turned back and headed out of there."

"Did she ever see you?"

"Yes. In fact, she hastened after me at first, and when she got close enough, she called my name. Kelly, I stopped in place, but I didn't turn around. Finally, I turned partly around, and all I did was look at her. I said nothing. Then I whirled around and walked away, leaving her alone there in the woods."

Neither said anything for a while. Andy waited for Kelly to respond, but didn't hear any hint that she was about to speak. So, he waited—and waited. Finally, he said, "Kelly? Are you there?"

"Boone Woo . . ." That's all she got out. Now he could hear her crying. In a moment, she started trying to babble through her sobbing. In a while, she calmed enough to get out a few words.

"Why, Boone Woo? Why did you leave her alone like that? Oh, please, please, dear God, help us."

"Why did I leave her alone there? Well, she went there to *be* alone. But really, as best I can figure myself, I think I was trying to shock her—shake her off dead center. She's at a standstill in that crippling guilt complex she's suffering under. I guess I thought shocking her would help."

"Okay, but it's so heartbreaking, not just for her, but for both of you. You're my friends, and I need you united. I'm sorry, Boone Woo. I can see both sides. You're trying and she's suffering." She said nothing more for a few moments. Then she murmured, "But it's all so painful." She started sobbing and broke down again.

Ultimately, there was nothing more to be said, and they both realized that. They braced up, ended their call lovingly, and bade one another good-bye. Rightfully, Kelly got in the last word.

"Let's keep trying, Boone Woo."

Later in the morning, Andy called Lorrie Dean to ensure that she was safely back from the park. She was. They spoke only briefly. Neither said anything about what had happened at the park. Andy fully expected her to ask why he had walked away from her, but she didn't. Likewise, he didn't bring up the subject of their encounter. They ended their brief call on a polite but reserved note.

The rest of the weekend was uneventful. Andy asked Lorrie Dean to join him in church Sunday morning, but she declined, explaining, "I'm not quite ready for church yet, but you go on. I'm sorry, Andy, but I would feel like such a hypocrite there." Andy wanted to argue, but he didn't. After he hung up, he prayed. A couple of miles away, Lorrie Dean prayed.

*   *   *

Monday morning at Clay Cutter Industries was conspicuous by the impact of Andy Boone. He swung into his work like a runaway bus. This was another step in his plan. He felt that professional achievement was an investment he had to make. He reckoned that the payoff would be his employer's implicit support for his personal needs as they developed.

At this hour, Andy's all-consuming mission in life was to find a way to rescue his soul mate from the crushing sense of guilt that dominated her every waking moment and threatened to destroy her altogether. If they could conquer that vicious enemy, then they could work on restoring her self-esteem. In his mind and heart, this innocent, gracious, beautiful woman was deserving of every ounce of energy and dedication they all could give.

So, he did his job. He was electric—indefatigable. He was running after his work like it was trying to get away. On this Monday, he was at work an hour early so he wouldn't be interrupted while he pounded out two critical reports abandoned by a coworker who had been out sick the previous week.

"You owe me big-time for this one, dear boss," he said, as he tapped away. *If I can knock out both of these suckers before the staff meeting and finish my own stuff by noon, then I can tend to—ahem—other pressing business.*

"Damn, who else could possibly be around here at this ungodly hour?" he barked as he grabbed the phone. "Good morning, Employee Relations."

"Thank God you're there, Andy. This is Brewster at the Burleson plant. Got a problem. One of the new guys has gone berserk, screaming about invasion of privacy and disturbing everybody. I wouldn't bother you, but he's really raising hell. As you know, this issue is outside the contract. Can you get over here and explain some things?"

"Is he there, now?"

"Oh yeah; his shift started at six."

"I'll be right there, but I'll only have a minute. I have a staff meeting at nine thirty."

"I think that'll probably be enough. Nobody can handle this like you."

"I'm on my way." *So fire the guy! Shit!*

Andy took another ten minutes to finish one of his reports and then sprinted out to the parking lot, griping all the way: "Thirty minutes over and thirty minutes back. That'll leave me ten minutes to deal with this fiasco—just enough time to say to the supervisor and his employee, *you gotta be kiddin'.* Eye contact will be the key to making this work."

It worked, and he was soon back in his office, still griping. "Now I've got to boot up again. Damn!"

He finished his other report and dashed off to the staff meeting with the eminent Kirk Daniels, his laughable boss, who just weeks earlier had tormented him in some way every day. But of late, he had won Kirk's unprecedented support by the sheer force of politically correct behavior.

It's working, and I'll keep it up, thought Andy. *Sometimes, you just have to do what works, even when it violates personal principles.* At that reminder, he chuckled, recalling a piece of sage advice handed down by Grandpa, the farm's erudite professor. "Andy, my boy," he had once said, "always be nice to the people who treat you poorly; you may need them some day, and if you do, you won't give a hoot whether they're good or bad."

Andy took a chair at the conference table and mentally ran through the points of politically correct behavior for company staff meetings. *Actually, all you have to do is show up on time, ask easy questions, and appear to be taking notes. Staff meetings usually accomplish very little except to remind employees that they're subordinates.*

"Okay, everybody," began Kirk, "just a quick reminder: don't forget we've been gigged on omitting certain company policy statements from our supervisory training classes. Any questions on that?"

Lifting the pen above his note pad, ostentatiously, and looking really serious, Andy asked, "Should we undertake some revisions well ahead of the next session?" *Good one, Boone Woo, really easy.*

"Oh, absolutely. Any other thoughts?" After a moment of silence, Kirk continued, "Okay, moving right along, the union has a new, upstart officer they're sending over on this latest overtime proposal. Morris, you'll be on that one. I'd say just be cool; I understand this guy's a bit cocky. Andy, you want to sit in with Morris on that one?"

"Whatever you want, boss."

The meeting continued with other compelling issues and ended when Kirk, himself, started to yawn.

On the way back to their offices, Andy and Morris Allgate talked about Kirk's suggestion that they both sit in on the meeting with the union's new guy. "Morris, we don't need that," insisted Andy. "You, of all people, don't need any help. But so we can show compliance, suppose I appear for just a minute under the pretense of meeting the guy, you know, sort of as a matter of courtesy. Then I'll leave. Does that comply? We can always plead that I didn't stay longer because everything was clearly under control."

"Right on," said Morris. "This is no big deal."

*   *   *

By midafternoon, Andy was caught up on everything. Now he returned to what he regarded as the more pressing business, his campaign to rescue his sweetheart. His ultimate goal was to rally Lorrie Dean's support group, which was already out there but needed a clarion call to action. He wasn't sure just yet how he would accomplish this rallying effort, but he was on fire. That alone—the solving of pressing challenges through unrelenting creative effort—put him in his element.

Andy's plan also called for a couple of crucial phone calls, one to his counselor at the Rape Crisis Center and one to his friend, FBI Agent Chad Jarrigan. He'd been so busy the previous week that these two vital steps hadn't been taken. Now he felt that he was clear to go on these.

His contact at the Rape Crisis Center, Debbie Sills, was fully responsive, as she had been during their first meeting. Andy's question this time was how he should react to Lorrie Dean's self-punitive behavior. "I'm at my wit's end on this part, Mrs. Sills. Lorrie Dean seems determined not only to blame herself but to inflict her own punishment."

"Not uncommon," the counselor assured him. "This self-punishment syndrome is actually a form of neurosis, hopefully temporary. I know that's probably not very comforting to you, Andy. What it really means is that your Lorrie Dean is still a victim. It just emphasizes that there's much work to be done to convert her to survivor. It's right for you to be concerned about this, but just remember that your primary role must continue to be that of listener, not analyst. Somehow, we have to get her in here!"

Andy's conversation with the FBI agent, though informative, was not particularly decisive. After a couple of pleasant exchanges relating to nothing that really mattered to either one of them, but which represented social protocols, Andy asked his operative question.

"Chad, where is this guy, ah, Jarred something?"

"Jarred Lynch. So far as I know, Andy, he's still in the hospital, at Parkland. The last I heard was that he had contracted a very serious infection."

"Can he have visitors?"

"That's all under very tight control. A person would have to establish a compelling need to see him and provide justification acceptable to us as well as the medical authorities."

"Okay, I see. I think Lorrie Dean would have a compelling need."

"What are you thinking, Andy?"

"Well, Chad, my Lorrie Dean is in terrible shape right now. She is destroying herself emotionally—intense, unshakable guilt feelings, complete loss of self-esteem, and just outright depression."

"How would it help her to see this guy?"

"In my imagination, I see some kind of indifferent, unemotional exchange between the two. Somehow, we have to burn the passion out of this crisis for Lorrie Dean. Chad, there is no way I can describe to you the horrible shape she's in."

"What does she say about this proposition?"

"I haven't talked to her about it, yet. I wanted to see what the chances were before I bother her with it."

"Hmm. I don't know, Andy. I'm not sure this is tenable. It sounds too vague, or rather, too uncertain."

"I understand. I just . . . I can't stop trying." With that plea, he slapped his forehead. *Go away, tears; I don't have time for you!*

"Okay, why don't you talk to Lorrie Dean about this issue and let me know her reaction?"

"Chad, thank you for that; I was so afraid you would turn me down outright. She has a devoted young friend who can really help me in this. That's Kelly. You probably remember that name from the days of protective custody."

"Right, I do indeed. Okay, Andy, I'll try to work with you. I feel we owe Lorrie Dean one, because of the excellent work she did in collecting clues that expedited our investigation of the kidnapping. So, count me in. But one caution: it has to be right. You know, we can't let her go in there and confront the guy."

"Absolutely. Thanks again."

Now Andy's excitement was bubbling over as to the possibilities he envisioned in his plans. This ecstasy led him to make one more call. He had to share his plans and the promises inherent in them with his morning light. As it developed, she was as exhilarated as he. As he talked, he could hear Kelly gasping with glee, just listening and letting his enthusiasm fill her.

"Way to go, Boone Woo! Count me in. We're in a rally, right?"

"Right on. And sweetheart, I'm convinced it's up to you and me. Somehow, we have to get Lorrie Dean out of her routine. Right now her routine is brooding over her self-proclaimed guilt."

"Okay, concerning that guy in the hospital that you mentioned, I can tell you that Lorrie Dean and I have raised a solemn question with each other relating to our individual situations. I'll tell you more about that some time. For now, let's hit it with the rally!"

"You are indeed my morning light. Now, there's one other thing I want you to know. Dear friend, I wish you the best with the meeting of your mother and so does Lorrie Dean."

"Thanks. I'll give you a report" she chortled.

22

Kelly hung up the phone and snickered into her hands. Mom and Uncle Dub looked at her expectantly, waiting patiently for an explanation. In a while, their expressions turned to chagrin, as Kelly let the suspense ride, shaking her head and giggling.

"Okay, Kelly. Enough!" exclaimed Mom. "Come on; spill it!"

Kelly sat down at the table with them, lifted her eyebrows and said, "You won't believe what she'll be wearing for our rendezvous tomorrow."

"I'll believe anything," chuckled Dub. "I know how my sister dresses. Do tell us."

"She says—very matter-of-factly, by the way—that she'll have on a full-length, mauve dress. Okay so far, right? Well, from there, it goes downhill." She laughed and slapped the table. "This long dress, mauve, mind you, has little wine-colored circles about the size of jar lids spread over the entire garment."

Dub and Mom threw their heads back and guffawed, while Kelly continued trying to hold their attention.

"Listen, y'all. It gets better. The last thing she said about it was . . . well, she said, 'Kelly, dear, it's kind of a loud dress,' like I couldn't have figured that out." She giggled and raised a finger in the air, signaling that she was about to make a vital point. "Wine on mauve. Really now. When did you last see a long mauve dress with wine circles?"

"Never in my life," said Mom.

Kelly squinted and pursed her lips, "What's the difference between mauve and wine color, anyway?"

"I think mauve is browner," said Mom.

"Browner?" posed Dub.

The three jokesters jabbered on about their family cliff-hanger until, in time, Kelly became very serious. "I hope it comes off this time," she moaned, "and if she runs again, she can just keep running, because that'll be the end of it."

"Agreed," said Dub. "Somehow, though, I feel like it'll work this time. Her persistence makes me think it isn't a joke—that she really wants to talk to you about somethin' important to her."

Kelly nodded. In a moment, she took a deep breath and grinned modestly. "We'll see."

"Where exactly are you to meet?" asked Mom.

"On Fourth Street, north of the tracks in the old town part. I'm supposed to stand directly across the street from the Rose Dry Goods building. Then she'll come out of one of the shops in there and face me. She'll raise her hand, and I'm to cross over and join her."

Dub was shaking his head. "I just don't understand why it all has to be such a mystery. Anyway, dear Kelly, our prayers and hearts will be with you." Mom nodded her concurrence.

"I know that, dear ones," said Kelly. "Knowing that will get me through it. I feel blessed. Boone Woo called me Wednesday and gave his blessings, and Lorrie Dean called me yesterday with hers. I know I am loved. Thank you, dear God."

In a while, they all agreed that it was bedtime and headed toward the hallway leading to the bedrooms. Minutes later, Dub slipped back down the hall to the den, lifted the phone, and started dialing.

*   *   *

Things were looking up. It was a bright, sunny day in Wills Point, with no hint of any inclement weather to come. Kelly had hardly paid attention to the town during her previous visit. This time, however, she was somewhat early and, surprisingly, more relaxed, so she started looking around.

After a casual cruise around the active area of Wills Point, including several residential streets, Kelly returned to the main downtown section and parked on Commerce Street, about a block from the designated meeting place. She was still a few minutes early, so she decided to lock the car and go piddle around in the vicinity of their meeting site. She had suddenly become a little nervous again, so that waiting in the car would be frustrating.

Downtown was absolutely fascinating. It was a busy little commercial center with brick streets and nineteenth-century storefronts. Sidewalks and stores were elevated some two feet above the streets. There, in a range of four short blocks, this historic old East Texas town offered a telling picture of modern American culture—fitness centers, computer stores, electrolysis spas, appliance stores, gift shops, barbers, beauty shops, nail salons, pharmacies, furniture stores, cafes, sandwich shops, investment services, CPAs, insurance agents, doctors' offices, a municipal court, a church, a bank, and the newspaper.

Kelly continued to amble along the sidewalk, looking all around, mesmerized by her surroundings. Clearly, downtown Wills Point had the ambience of strength. One could not be in it without reading a little history. Perhaps it had weathered a few storms. If so, it had survived them admirably.

Now, she was on the side of the street where she was to position herself for the long-awaited, much-dreaded confrontation. As hard as she tried to diffuse her anxiety by engaging with the novelty of her surroundings, she was knotting up inside and breathing heavily. She tried peeking inside show windows and concentrating on the unique fascination they held, but that wasn't working, either. She was so absorbed in the mystery and anticipation of the imminent showdown that no intervention had any chance to work.

Then, as if by divine providence, she spotted a young slap-happy couple frolicking at the end of the block across the street. They appeared to be having a merry old time. They were really kind of cute—but zany. In a moment, the couple started down the walk where Kelly's mystery woman was to appear in just about three minutes. On they came, clowning all the way, bumping along the sidewalk, poking the air with their little fingers and bopping their heads with their thumbs. They looked like a couple of vaudeville dropouts.

As the pranksters neared the Rose Dry Goods building, their appearance gave them away. They had turned themselves into wacky clowns with wigs and makeup. This was truly a pair of bona fide doodles—Punch and Judy. The young woman was quite pretty, in spite of her bright-red, bushy wig, face paint, and purple lips. The boy, who couldn't quit grinning, was a model bumpkin in his long-waisted, striped pants, pulled almost up to his armpits. Somebody should have told him his fake mustache was crooked and his heavy eyebrows were drooping. Still, the young sweethearts looked blissfully happy, oblivious to all the worries of the world.

Now was the hour. Where's the lady? In that moment, the goofy couple separated, as the boy skipped on down the sidewalk a ways, leaving his girlfriend to stand waving and shouting in her silly falsetto voice, "Oh, oh, I've lost my man." Then the two began to mosey back toward each other.

In that instant, a long, loud dress began to materialize in the doorway directly across the street from Kelly. It just sort of floated out, as if fanned by a light breeze. As it took on more definition, there was clearly the head of a woman at the top of it. Now, the two goofballs started to saunter aimlessly toward the new visitor. The mystery lady glanced from one to the other, looking somewhat apprehensive. Then she stared across the street at Kelly and raised her hand. It would be hard for the woman to run, now, with Kelly right in front of her and the two clowns on either side of her.

As Kelly approached, she eyed the two quirky characters. There was something uniquely familiar about the boy's grin. She looked ahead to greet the woman and then instinctively glanced back at the grinning young clown. Suddenly, it hit her, and the heretofore wholly composed Kelly Surrat just lost it and doubled over laughing. As she tentatively regained a little control, she looked back and forth from the girl to the grinning boy and tried hard to brace herself against the momentous temptation to laugh herself right into crying.

The mystery woman clearly was fed up with the whole charade and snorted, "What *is* this?"

Kelly pointed to each of the intruders in turn but couldn't speak for laughing.

The woman pleaded, "Kelly? You're Kelly, right?"

"Yes, Rosalea, I'm Kelly."

"So, what is this with these two people here?"

"It's love."

"Should we get the police?"

"No, no. They're harmless. They're just having one of their periodic benders."

"Well, okay, come on, let's go. There's a coffee shop around the corner where we can talk."

Off they went, leaving the two zany characters jesting with each other. In a few steps, Kelly glanced back over her shoulder and smiled at the sight of Lorrie Dean and Andy high-fiving.

Rosalea and Kelly sat quietly at a small table next to a windowless wall. They both ordered coffee and Danish, but left them untouched for a while. Each was trying to gauge the other and also trying to measure the situation they were in. Clearly, each was groping for an opening line. Finally, Kelly decided to get things underway.

"Why are we here after eleven long years? I mean, what's different?"

"I understand what you're asking. I would ask the same thing if I were in your shoes. And, my dear daughter, that is exactly why I'm here. I'm at a place in my life where I need you to know the answer to that question."

"What do you mean, *place in your life?*"

The woman laughed nervously and said, "You're just full of questions, but I would be, too. So, let me get started . . ."

"Don't you want to know how I am?"

"You're looking good; I can see that, and my brother has indicated you're doing well, after healing from that horrible fall in your garage."

Kelly said no more. It was clear that Rosalea Surrat was there to talk about herself.

"First of all, Kelly, I want you to know that I'm not crazy. I have to admit I'm a bit eccentric because I have lost some control . . . and frankly, some brain cells."

"At thirty-five you've lost brain cells?"

"Yes, that's a hard fact. You'll understand as we go along. Before I get into the particulars of that, I want you to know that I had to come to you and tell you I'm sorry." She fell silent, and Kelly waited.

After a while, Kelly said, "Is that all?"

"I know what you're wanting to hear, and I'm getting to that." She paused again, obviously struggling, but for what? She touched her eyes, trembling, and lowered her head. In a few moments, she lifted her head and tried to smile, but it looked painful and weak.

In this hour, Kelly's anguish and long-standing grievance against her mother yielded to the immensity of the moment and to the woman's obviously pitiful circumstances, whatever they were. Kelly actually felt for the troubled woman who had sent her into exile when she was six years old. She felt tears gathering in her eyes as she gradually came to accept that she was feeling sorry for her estranged mother. It was jolting just being aware of the word *mother* and of her sudden ability to use that word. She jumped at her mother's sudden outburst.

"Kelly, I'm your mother," she blurted. "Nothing can change that, no matter how terrible I am, or what horrible thing I did to you. Please, can you just grant me that? I don't expect you to have loving feelings for me, but could you please call me 'Mother'? I so need to hear that."

"Okay, Mother. I'm sorry you're going through whatever you're going through, so welcome to the club . . ."

"Ouch! Okay, I had that 'welcome to the club' part coming, but thank you for saying 'Mother.'"

"Well, but you have to know this. In all honesty, I can call you my mother, and I can care that you are suffering—just as a human being—but you have to know that I don't have feelings for you as my mother."

"I know. When you were little, you called me Mommy."

"When I was little, you held me in your arms."

"Ouch again. That's okay. I've got it all coming to me. So, I don't know how this is going to turn out, Kelly, but I want you to know I love you. I wouldn't be here if I didn't."

"So, what have you felt for me in the last eleven years, or need I ask?"

"Love . . . yes, all that time. And I felt the guilt, but I was worried that you wouldn't get the care you needed from me simply because I wouldn't be around long enough to provide it."

"Okay, let me say the word: Mother. Now, I must say, I don't understand a word you're saying. What, in all God's creation, could make a mother throw away her child?"

"Didn't throw you away. I set you free. I don't know if you'll ever understand, much less accept it, but it's true. I didn't throw you out; I let you go—and it was mortally painful."

Kelly's emotions were distressingly mixed, and she was sobbing as she tried to answer. "The fact is you sent me shopping for someone else to have me."

"There's no excuse for it. But you deserved to have a chance at a promising and happy life, and I couldn't give that, and I'm sorry." She broke down completely, bawling and pressing her head between her hands. Mercifully, the astute server stayed away and left them to their own discretion.

Kelly's throat was cramping and her heart pounding as she gradually came to understand that she was feeling empathy and genuine caring for the misery of . . . her mother. It was not in her to remain indifferent to the plight of anyone, especially one who had been a part of her life. There was no way she could just sit before this pleading human soul and look at it academically. All the consternation she'd harbored for eleven years was suppressed during these gripping moments. She had to do something. She had it within her power to ease the torture of this woman, at least to some degree. Refusing to do so would have been a heinous sin.

So, Kelly laid her arms out across the table and patted the woman's hands. "Mother, my dear mother, I don't understand. I don't understand at all, but I'm sorry. Do you hear that, Mother?"

"Thank you from the bottom of my heart. I know you didn't even have to say that. Thanks for calling me your mother. Now, if I could only get you to say you love me."

"How can I, Mother? I don't have any basis for loving you. How can I love someone who didn't want me? Now, I care about how you're doing, but I've had nothing for love to grow on."

"I see. Well, I'm sure you aren't going to be able to grant me the one other wish I have, either."

Kelly nodded but said nothing.

"So," began her mother, "I guess it'd be futile to ask you to forgive me."

"I would have to think long and hard before I could make any such leap as that."

"I understand, Kelly, and I don't blame you a bit. You have to be thinking, like, 'The nerve of this woman to ask forgiveness after apparently not giving a damn about me for eleven years.' Right?"

"That's kind of it, all right." Even as Kelly said those words, her heart was breaking, just out of pure sympathy for this defeated woman who happened to be her mother.

"All right. At least I owe you an explanation of why I did what I did. The fact is that just before you turned six, I got some staggering news from the doctor. I had gone to him to see if there was anything at all that could be done to relieve the excruciating headaches I'd been having for at least two years. Sometimes, it hurt so bad that I literally couldn't see. Your dad said I should adjust to it, but the pain was so dreadful and agonizing that I couldn't adjust."

"I'm so sorry, Mother." As Kelly thought back, she recalled seeing flashes of stunned expressions when her mother would grab for her head and hold it, as if trying to get it to mind her or something. At that time, she had just dismissed it as normal for a grown-up.

"Thanks for your caring. So that's why I went to the doctor. He was able to help with the pain, all right, but there was absolutely nothing he could do to correct the cause of it. They did a bunch of tests on me—some of them pretty uncomfortable—and found . . . I'm sorry, bear with me . . ."

Kelly reached for her mother's hands and held them until she regained a measure of composure.

Sniffling, her mother continued falteringly. "They found an inoperative brain tumor. They said because of where it was, any surgery to remove it would damage other parts of my brain, and I would probably suffer an early death because of it."

"Mother, that's horrible. I can't imagine getting news like that. I'm so very sorry."

"But you don't forgive me."

"I just can't reckon with this whole thing to that point, not yet anyway. I mean, you still could have kept me around you."

"They gave me five to seven years to live—said it would grow, but they had no way of knowing how fast. So, with that news, Kelly, I knew I couldn't give you the care and grooming you needed, and I knew you would anguish just watching me get worse."

"Mother, there's just one thing I don't understand. If you loved me, looks like you would have wanted to care for me as long as possible—again, that's only if you loved me."

"Believe me, I loved you. My Kelly, you were the most adorable child I'd ever been around. You had such promise. I saw unlimited potential in you, but I knew I couldn't help you develop it. Although I outlived their prediction, I am aware that time is running out."

"It's too much for me to grasp, I guess," said Kelly, as she rubbed the back of her neck and stretched her shoulders.

Her mother nodded. "And I thought maybe you could forgive me. I've explained my situation to you only so you'd understand. So, I'm not asking for pity. I'm here just asking for forgiveness. If, in your heart, you can't, I certainly understand why."

"Are you in constant pain, Mother?"

"Pretty much, but I'm rapidly losing mental stability. The doctors warned of this, that it would be a sign that the end might be drawing near. They said I would become confused a lot and disoriented. They were right. I've gotten real jumpy, and sometimes I forget where I am. That's what happened the last time we came here. I got afraid. All at once, I didn't know what I was doing here. Forgive me, I shouldn't burden you with this, but I thought I saw this coming when you were six years old."

"Mother, why don't you come to the farm one day, and we can all get reacquainted. They would all treat you right. They are fabulous people."

"It wouldn't work. My brother, Dub, doesn't want to have anything to do with me."

"Really, now. Does he know all that you told me?"

"He knows certain essential points of it. Nobody but me, and now you, knows all of it. But Dub still thinks my giving you up was inexcusable."

"Well, okay, let me work on this. Meanwhile, whatever happened to my daddy?"

"I haven't heard a word from him or about him in years. I'm sorry, Kelly, but the truth is I couldn't care less."

Thereupon, they paid out, and Kelly walked her mother to her car. They embraced awkwardly, but tearfully, and Rosalea Grimes Surrat drove away. Kelly sniffled her way back to Tillman, thinking about her mother—and caring, but not forgiving.

23

The clowns of Wills Point were back in Dallas, holding conference in the home of Lorrie Dean LeMay. They had already resolved that their operation in Wills Point was a bull's-eye. They also agreed, unanimously, that the extraordinary success of this mission was the result of consummate teamwork by the two seasoned performers. On a more contentious issue, after some scrappy debate, Lorrie Dean ultimately conceded that the teaming in question was natural. Therefore, the crucial mission achievement would go in the official record as the masterwork of a natural team.

"But that doesn't change the way things are with us, Andy," said Lorrie Dean. "We may be a natural team in getting certain specific things done, but we still have to face the reality of what happened to me, and my own indiscretion in causing it."

"Well, let's face it and get on with living."

"You always make things seem so simple."

"I love you; that's how simple it is. You may try to run me off . . . but I'm not leaving you—ever."

"But that's the whole point, Andy; I can't do that to you . . . because . . . because I love you, too. Please let's don't talk about this anymore, right now."

"Okay." After a few minutes of uneasy silence, Andy said, "Guess I better be shoving off. Are you going to call Kelly?"

Lorrie Dean nodded, accepted his kiss, and walked to the door with him.

Andy looked back as he reached his car. The front door was already closed. He'd hoped Lorrie Dean would have waited for him to wave.

As he drove toward his motel, he tapped the steering wheel, trying to fight off a little rush of unwelcome anger. Then, as often he did when frustrated or perplexed, he started talking aloud to himself.

"Nothing's working. Lorrie Dean seems to have lost her mind. Yep—lost her mind—still punishing herself. So, just have to step it up. Dammit, I'll get her to the Rape Crisis Center if I have to threaten her. Yeah, threaten her with what, Andy Boone? Okay, forget that one—but I'll get her there!"

Soon, Andy pulled into the parking lot of his motel, shut off the engine, and slumped over the steering wheel, still fussing. "What must God think of our faith? Our prayers are all so shallow and perfunctory, especially mine—nothing more than frantic, desperate cries for help. Where's the thanks for being alive and well? Oh, shut up, Andy!"

In his room, he prepared for bed, still frightened and feeling helpless. At bedside, he prayed, "Oh, God, please forgive our prayers, but whatever you decide, thanks—thank you for giving us life and for rescuing us from our sins, so that we could live on."

In bed, still tense, he continued to think, on and on. *Lorrie Dean, why couldn't you have waited for just one minute, so I could wave? My pretty symphony, a wave is a promise, a sign of loyalty . . . oh well . . .* He was just beginning to key down, when it occurred to him that there was one measure of support he hadn't given his Lorrie Dean. It hit him suddenly and firmly. How could he have missed it—the most basic component of love there is? *I have to apologize.*

*   *   *

Lorrie Dean decided to relax a little before calling Kelly. She strolled into the parlor, deep in thought, settled into her recliner, pulled to the edge of the seat, and leaned forward over folded arms. She was at once conscious of a slight, involuntary shaking of her head. In a moment, her knees were quivering also. It seemed so ironic that with all this trembling, she felt practically immobile. She wanted to just crawl under a bush somewhere, like a sick cat, lie on the bare dirt, and wait for something to happen—and she didn't much care what. *This can't go on. Something just has to change.* She pushed back and set her chin. She needed to call her friend.

After a few giggling exchanges about the surprise appearance of Lorrie Dean and Andy as slapstick reinforcement for the meeting with her mother, Kelly turned serious. She said, uneasily, that the meeting with her mother had gone all right but had left a lot of questions. They agreed to get together with Andy and maybe her Uncle Dub and hash over the whole thing. Lorrie Dean indicated that she and Andy would work out something right away.

After she hung up, Lorrie Dean reflected on the phone call for a while and then began chastising herself for what she now felt was a very perfunctory effort on her part. She had failed to show any real enthusiasm during the call with her best friend. *Please forgive me, Kelly; you deserve the best, and I didn't give you my best. Oh, if I could just be Lorrie Dean again.*

She moseyed to the kitchen and haphazardly mashed together an egg sandwich, poured a glass of wine, and retired to her easy chair, where she hoped she could relax, in spite of all that was weighing on her. Then came the night, and she poured another glass of wine. She turned out all the lights and sat in the dark. She was hoping the darkness would gather her in and absorb all the ugliness and distraction—all the crippling guilt feelings. But it didn't.

In a while, Andy's words echoed back to her: "I'm not leaving you—ever." *What greater consolation should anyone ever hope for in all their life?* she thought. *And, oh, my God, I love that man so very much. If he still wants me like I am, why am I resisting? But I seem powerless in everything.* Lorrie Dean started to pray silently, on her knees. In a few minutes, she returned to her chair and continued praying. Then she began to drift. Soon, she found herself in the park somewhere near Mr. Red, her companion, the mighty red oak.

Now the dreamer wanders away from Mr. Red farther into the woods. She creeps over to a tree, sits down on the ground, and leans back against it. It is nighttime, but the night appears to be a friend. It seems so easy, so natural, so totally unthreatening to sit in the woods by a friendly tree, protected by the darkness.

In a while, the dreamer hears a cracking sound that seems totally out of place on this quiet night in the still woods. It sounds like footsteps over brittle underbrush. It fades and then comes again, this time closer—the sound of people stomping their way around trees and bushes. Suddenly they are right before her.

Lorrie Dean is startled stock-still. She gulps and garners all the grit and will she can squeeze into her helpless body and stifles the overwhelming temptation to scream. It works, but her throat aches from the unprecedented tension in it. She calls on the power of God working within her to mask her crushing fear and help her confront confidently the two young men standing just a few feet away.

The two immature, smart-aleck-looking boys are just standing there, shoulder to shoulder, glaring down at her with perverted grins. Then they start slithering their tongues around over their lips. At once they flex as though ready to move in on her.

"Hi, guys," smirks Lorrie Dean. "Are you lost?" As she speaks, she hears the tone of sarcasm in her voice and at once remembers running for her life. *Oh, God, how I remember running.*

The two young men snicker and slap their legs. "What you think, huh, young lady? What are you thinkin'? Are you 'bout ready for somethin'?"

"Oh, I see, you're planning to rape me, right? Well, okay, but just one thing, so you'll know. See, I've been raped before." While the two jerks look goggle-eyed at each other, Lorrie Dean continues to leer at them and babble on. "Now, okay, the guy who raped me is lying in a hospital, dying—and if it matters, I am also dying."

The boys cock their heads and restore their foolish grins. But they seem to be having trouble sustaining them, and finally, their smirks slowly twist themselves into scowls. They shake as though to shed the unwelcome signs of uncertainty and take one lame step toward her. They pause, just as Lorrie Dean raises her hand.

"By the way, while you're thinking about this, would you like to hear my award-winning, earth-shattering scream?"

The boys suddenly look dead serious—maybe a little afraid. In the next instant, they swing around and scamper away.

After giving the two dodoes time to clear the woods, the dreamer struggles to her feet and begins running for her life. It's getting harder and harder to run, and at once, the trees begin to shake violently and threaten to come down. The whole forest is a mad, raging tiger.

Now the ground is heaving, and huge tree roots are erupting out of it. Lorrie Dean tries to speed up, but the harder she tries, the slower she goes. The heaving of the earth is so fierce that the trees are screaming and starting to uproot. Suddenly, fire breaks out in the treetops, and the ground continues to roar. The horrified dreamer is trying to run for her life, but her legs are so, so heavy and won't move. Now, while the ground heaves and rumbles, trees are falling, and the fire starts to spread across the ground, headed right for the runner. Then she makes one more, all-out stretch for whatever power is left in her human life and lunges forward. In that instant, the frightened runner stumbles over a root and plunges to the ground.

She wants to scream, but she can't. She tries to rise, hoping she can run again, but she is paralyzed. She can't even wiggle her fingers. She lies perfectly still and waits for redeeming power. Her heart is pounding as though it will explode through her chest. Then in one all-out effort, she screams, "Andeeee!"

"Andeeee!" Lorie Dean tumbled out of her chair, as she cried out for Andy Boone. Then she looked all around, peering into the dark. Ever so quietly, she murmured, "Oh, God, I was gone—gone. The dream almost killed me. Thank you for saving me. Please help me know what to do, for once again I am burdened with the memory of running."

Still sitting on the floor, arms folded around her knees, Lorrie Dean started looking all around, through the darkness, surveying the room, as though she'd never seen it before. Her heart started to flutter, and her breathing was so labored that she was becoming frightened over the abrupt changes in her physical condition. She'd never had such symptoms in her life, and she felt on the verge of some kind of attack.

Lorrie Dean strained her way up from the floor, crept across the room, found a light switch, and headed back for the telephone on a table beside her chair. She glanced at her watch and winced when she saw how late it was—ten thirty on a Saturday night. She felt some reluctance about making the phone call, but she shook it off and dialed Andy's number.

"Andy Boone."

"Oh, Andy." Just the sound of his voice was heartening, and she started sobbing.

"Sweetheart, what's wrong?"

"I just had . . . I just had . . ." Now she was crying full tilt but pushed on. "I just had the most horrible nightmare!"

"I'll be right there."

"No, Andy, it's okay, no, no, no, it's okay. I just wanted to make sure my real world is still intact. I'll be all right, now."

"Does that mean I'm your real world?"

"Yea-yus." Now she was bawling; the kindness in his voice hurt as much as it helped.

Andy waited. When it sounded like she was calming down some, he said, "I know the feeling; I had them fairly often my first two years at our headquarters in McLean, Virginia."

"I've had nightmares before, too, but nothing like this."

"Please, sweetheart, why don't I come over for a little while?"

"I'm okay, now. Thanks, my dear Andy."

"Sure. Do you want to tell me about your dream? Maybe you could get back to sleep faster if you put that to rest. You know, it's kind of like kicking it out when you tell someone a bad dream."

"I guess so; I can see the logic in that. Okay, I'll just give you a little bit of it, you know, sort of like an outline."

"Let 'er roll."

"I was alone in the woods one night when two boys appeared, ready to do damage, if you know what I mean."

"I take it they were there to rape." He was careful not to add the word *you*.

"Right. Well, to make a long story short—and it was a kind of a long dream—I started toying with these two pathetic perverts, just like I did that time with old Jarred, my guard. I mean, I taunted them just like I did him, raising myself above him, talking down to him like I'm all smart and he's an idiot." She stopped and was about to leave it there when Andy blurted out.

"Great! It worked."

"Yeah, it worked all right."

"Want to tell me any more?"

"Well, there are a lot of details, like me running through the woods that were exploding all around me, but this much is probably enough to help me."

"Okay, tell you what; why don't you get a pad and write down all you can remember. Maybe that'll serve a couple of purposes: one, getting it off your chest, and two, possibly making you sleepy."

"Andy, you're a gem." She owed him that, but she was not about to make a commitment on his suggestion.

"Err . . . well, okay, ah . . ."

"Oh, Andy, I almost forgot; I talked to Kelly, and she said the meeting with her mother came off okay, but it left her with questions. She wants to get together with us and talk about it."

"Good idea. I'm ready when you are."

"How about we grab lunch at a cafeteria and drive down to the farm tomorrow afternoon? They keep saying, 'Come anytime.'"

"Super. Ah . . . how about church in the morning? We could go to the late service at First Methodist and then . . . and then, here's what we could do; we could stop for lunch, en route, at the Cotton Gin Restaurant in Crandall."

Lorrie Dean opened her mouth to decline, but Andy's little-boy enthusiasm didn't leave her with the heart to disappoint him. She tried really hard to sound elated when she said, finally, "That's a deal."

Lorrie Dean was back in her chair with her eyes closed, waiting to get sleepy enough to go to bed. In a while, she frowned, as obviously it wasn't working. Then she thought of Andy's suggestion. *Oh well, it can't hurt anything.* On that impulse, she scurried around, found a pad and writing pen, and fell back into her chair.

She did not know where to begin. It was several minutes before she wrote anything. After she got started, it moved along pretty well, but she caught herself switching stories, unconsciously jumping from her nightmarish dream to her real-life tragic torture at the hands of three worthless hoodlums. She tried to force herself to stick with the horrible dream but seemed unable to control what she was writing about. It was just out of her hands. This went on until she started to nod and her pen kept falling out of her fingers.

Lorrie Dean awoke and discovered she was still in the chair. As she pushed back against the seat in readiness to get up, she spied the writing pad on the floor by her feet. She picked it up, laid it on the little side table, and went to bed.

The next morning, she picked up the pad and started to read. The first words on it were: "I remember running."

24

As they were about to enter the church Sunday morning, Andy took Lorrie Dean's arm and guided them aside for a few moments. "Just a short delay, sweetheart," he murmured. "I owe you one big apology. I don't ask forgiveness for missing this one, but I must tell you I'm sorry. I'm so very sorry."

"Andy, what in the world? You have done nothing wrong, nothing against me. You've tried really hard with me, and I am grateful. I can't imagine what you could possibly have in mind."

"My Lorrie Dean, I've given you everything but patience. I apologize with all my heart."

*　　　*　　　*

Lorrie Dean and Andy left the First United Methodist Church of Mesquite feeling restored and confident. They agreed simultaneously that it was a wonderful and inspiring worship service, and they talked of little else as they cruised down US Highway 175, headed for the farm.

When Lorrie Dean noticed a glowing smile sweeping across Andy's face, she blurted out, "What's up, Andy?"

"Wow!" he whooped.

"Wow what?"

"Awesome choir!"

"Agree. Why don't you audition?"

"Can't. I sing flat."

They were still reflecting on their uplifting spiritual experience when they pulled into the gravel parking lot of the restaurant. The Crandall Cotton Gin Restaurant and Club sat just off the highway alongside a trail left by the railroad tracks of earlier times. It was a huge, weather-worn, metal building, left intact, just as it had stood in its cotton days.

As Lorrie Dean and Andy stepped inside, they were at once absorbed in fascination and wonder at their new surroundings. A smiling, confident-looking hostess greeted them and escorted them to a table, speaking graciously as she drifted along the way. Instantaneously, a server was before them, calmly offering her services. After she eased away to get their drinks, Andy and Lorrie Dean looked at each other and shook their heads in amusement. It was a captivating world to be in, a welcome refuge from the toils of fast, impatient living.

Their hands still rested on unopened menus while they looked around the huge interior. Murals depicting country living in the age of cotton fields covered the walls all around. They showed people at work, children at play, and families resting on the porches of colonial homes. Also scattered along the walls were pictures of mule-drawn cotton wagons, locomotives towing flatbed cars laden with bales, as well as lakes and streams and cotton fields.

Amazingly, the massive facility was still a gin, ready to go with but a few days' notice. All the machinery was still in place, scattered throughout the building. In fact, the bar surface inside the club section, known as the Cotton Patch, was part of the original cotton press.

Dining was pleasant and quiet. The food was delicious. The servers were calm and serious, but they smiled easily, and when they did, it was genuine, and you knew it was for you. The appealing personality of the restaurant clearly reflected the character of its clientele—proud, hard-working, sensible people with admirable bearing and a sense of good will. It would hardly have been possible to spend a few relaxed moments there without mentally drifting back to the early days, to the cotton fields of Texas and to the spirit, faith, and tenacity of the families who had tended them.

After they finished lunch, Andy and Lorrie Dean rested calmly with little talk for several minutes. When they did speak, it was about Kelly, their dear friend. Their minds instinctively turned to her as they contemplated their imminent return to the highway and their mission. When they finally started shoving away from the table, Andy raised a hand, obviously hit with a sudden impulse.

"Oh, by the way," he said, "they have an open-air extension of the club out back. It's sort of a pavilion with tables and chairs, and it even has some theater-style seating. Maybe you all at We Party should add this place to your list of facilities."

"Good of you to think of us, Andy; I think that's a great idea."

Back on the highway, after a few remarks reflecting on their dining experience, they fell silent. Lorrie Dean was thinking that Andy's silence was deeper than hers. She eyed him a couple of times without turning her head. Obviously, something was on in his mind, something he couldn't suppress but so far was able to inhibit. In a while, it seemed he was priming himself to say something. He had both hands on the steering wheel, an unusual driving posture for him, and she could tell, by the tilt of his head and the occasional working of his lips, that something was forming in his mind.

Andy was aware that Lorrie Dean had noticed him in his deep reverie. Little did she know that he was trying to figure out how to say what he wanted her to think about without sounding smart-aleck or judgmental. He wanted to raise the issue in a way that signaled his love for her, rather than criticism.

Finally, Lorrie Dean broke the spell. "You're awfully quiet, Andy."

"Yeah."

"Did you want to say something?"

"I was just wondering if, now, you may have given up the notion that you're not fit to be in church—as you put it some time back."

"Well, it was encouraging in church today, and I felt some peace, but, Andy, my mind kept wandering to my horrible ordeal."

"I thought maybe you might have found Lorrie Dean in church today."

"Actually, the only time I feel like Lorrie Dean is when I go to my job. I enjoy putting on makeup, getting my hair and nails done from time to time, dressing up, and going to work with the other women who have pride and who also have decent self-esteem. You know, like, when I strive to present myself as a lady, instead of a tramp, it encourages me. I come closer to Lorrie Dean at those times. I think that's why I do so well in my job."

"Sweetheart, I'm glad you have that, believe me. By the same token, you got all dressed up and pretty and ladylike for church today."

"You're right, but when I got in there, the old guilt feelings hit me again. Bam! I didn't want it to happen; it just did."

"I see. I was just thinking that, when you're in church, learning of the love and forgiving nature of the Lord, that this is the real you, sitting there."

"I know, I know; what you say is entirely logical. I can't argue with that, but at the same time, I don't seem able to control myself."

"Truly, I'm sorry, sweetheart. Do you see a time when maybe you will forgive yourself?"

"I don't know where to start."

"Ask my morning light; she's facing a forgiveness issue also."

*   *   *

At the farm, the three visitors agreed that Kelly and Lorrie Dean would visit privately while Andy went to find Dub and Grandpa, who reportedly were knocking down dead corn stalks in the field. Leah was in her room, and Mom sat in the den, methodically thumbing through a recipe book.

Kelly and Lorrie Dean opted for the front porch instead of the cove for a change. They wanted the reality of bright light to enhance their indulgence in some serious business. They sat together in a swing that hung from the porch ceiling and looked out over the range as they talked. The cattle were grazing peacefully, unhurried, very nearly motionless, their heads bowed just into the lush grass. The two girls sat for a few moments, just taking it in, letting this tranquil scene transcend their problems. In a while, they looked at each other and smiled humbly. Then they began rocking leisurely.

"That's interesting," began Lorrie Dean. "Look how all the cows are grazing in the same direction. I mean, absolutely every one of them is pointed east. There's no exception. I've never noticed that before."

"Yeah," said Kelly, "Personally, I have no idea what really explains that. I figured they were just being sociable, that it gave them a feeling of togetherness, but Grandpa says it's instinctive animal behavior. He assumes that it gives them a sense of security."

Lorrie Dean chuckled. "Security? Well, if that's so, somebody ought to tell them there's no one guarding the rear."

Kelly laughed and slapped her knees. "Good one, Lorrie Dean. That sounds exactly like something Boone Woo would come up with."

With that little offhand reference to Andy, both sobered immediately. Then Lorrie Dean said, "What about your mother, Kelly?"

"Well, she's . . . what can I say? She's disturbed and not in good health, physically or mentally."

"What does that mean for you?"

"I don't even know. I do care about that, but I'm still . . . I guess I'm angry and frustrated and hurt. I lived without her for eleven years, all that time knowing she regarded me as a burden rather than her child."

"Does she work?"

"She works for the woman she rents from. She sews for her—the woman has a shop, selling stuff."

"What's with Wills Point? Has she lost something there?"

"Don't know what her thing is with Wills Point except she knows her way there. That's because the woman she works for has family there."

"So, what is she after?"

"Forgiveness." When, after a few awkward moments, Lorrie Dean didn't respond, she continued. "I don't know if she wants anything beyond that or not. I do know this all started after Uncle Dub called her to tell her about my accident. Her first move was to come to the hospital when I was in a coma."

"Sounds like more than idle curiosity."

"What do you mean?"

"Well, I wonder if this means she has some feelings for you, maybe deep feelings that have been repressed for some reason we don't know about."

"Okay, here's the story on that. She told me at Wills Point that when she found out she had an inoperative tumor, she wept at what it would do to me. She said she wept for days. She said she finally shook all that off and tried to look at it realistically with my best interests in mind. On that point, she claims she realized she would die before she could teach me all that I would need in order to continue my life on solid footing. So, she finally decided she had to place me where I could be taken care of. The way I look at it, she didn't think I was worth her time and just put me up for grabs. What do you think?"

"Hmm, I'm trying to picture how I would respond if given the devastating news the doctors gave her. What would I think? What would I do if suddenly I was told I had an incurable disease and that my life would be drastically shortened? I mean, all your points are reasonable, Kelly, but your mother probably wasn't thinking of anything but dying. It would be hard to think rationally when you've just been hit with a bomb like that. So, I think the bare question is: did she give you up out of love for you or out of pity for herself? And, my dear Kelly, we'll never know, will we? We *do* know that she was staring right square into the hideous face of a humongous enemy."

"I think you're taking up for her."

"Not at all. I'm just trying to help you look at it."

"So, okay, if we're just looking at it, how about this: as it turned out, we could have had eleven-plus years together, and she could have taught me, as only a mother can do. She could have given me principles to live by; she could have taught me how to make life work, things I could do to take care of myself for the future, how to be independent, and all that. She could have given me what she had. But I guess she didn't have the courage to give it all that effort. Any way you look at it, I was forsaken."

"Inexcusably, unforgivably forsaken, right?"

"Okay, I hear you, but I don't think she really loved me. Was she really thinking of my welfare? I mean, *really*? Or did she just want to be unencumbered while she suffered. I could have been a joy for her, an alternative to concentrating on her pain and illness. I could have been some therapy for her."

"That's a point."

They looked at each other for a few moments and started swinging again. In a while, Kelly repeated Lorrie Dean's last remark. "That's a point? Is that all of it?"

"It's probably enough to think through, to study about, for now. Seems like you have two questions to answer for yourself: Should I tell my mother I forgive her, and should I try to continue an active relationship with her?"

"I still don't know why it's so important to her to have me forgive her, now."

"Does it matter?"

"Does what matter?"

"Do you feel she has to earn your forgiveness?"

"I don't know; I'm thinking."

"It didn't matter to Jesus, did it?"

On that note, they fell silent again, taking a little pause to reflect on the compelling questions in their lives. They gazed out across the range, swinging lightly. Lorrie Dean was beginning to feel a little queasy, which made her vulnerable to creeping anxiety over the crises in their lives, hers and Kelly's. Then Kelly stopped the swing and looked directly at her friend.

"Speaking of forgiveness, Lorrie Dean, how are you feeling about yourself of late?"

"Nothing has changed. I guess I'm still running. I seem obsessed with it, as if it's what I want to do—you know, to punish myself. I just keep clobbering myself with the memory of that run. I think I'm getting punch-drunk from it."

"You're so innocent, Lorrie Dean; I just don't understand it."

"I know. If this is a survival instinct, I think sometimes I was born with too much of it. Seems like I'm destined to run. That's the story of my life. I was running when we escaped to our hideouts in the Witness Protection Program; I had to run for my life after I shot my rapist, and now I'm running from . . . I don't know what. You know, Kelly, that may be what struck your mother in the beginning—an instinctive urge to run. In a way, that's what she did after she got that staggering news."

"Maybe so."

"Know what else? We're all alike in some ways, and we're all different in other ways. Everybody has to solve their problems with the tools they have. In fact, there are a lot of people who'd say it would have been selfish and irresponsible of her not to give you to someone who could take care of you."

"How did we get back on my mother?"

"Okay, okay; you're right. I think . . . I guess you and I are both locked in."

"Yes . . . yes we are. But you've made me think, because all I've had over the years are gut feelings. I guess, as friends, that's the very best thing we can give each other, raising questions for us to think about." She paused briefly. "So, that brings me back to my question for *you*. Are you working on forgiving your rapist—and, I dare say, yourself?"

"Honestly, I can't picture myself forgiving my rapist."

"I positively agree with you on one thing: he doesn't deserve it, and there's simply no way he can ever earn it. I guess that takes us back to our earlier remarks on this pesky question of forgiveness."

"I guess I should go find the guy and say, 'That's okay what you did. I'm over it now.'"

"No, no, no. It's not okay what he did; it'll never be okay. As they say, 'You can't unring a bell,' but you've helped me see where none of that is the point of forgiveness. And, Lorrie Dean, I thank you for putting questions in my mind that led me to understand the issue this way."

Lorrie Dean beamed as she felt unadulterated pride for her young, steadfast friend. Her smile broadened, and she chimed, "My Kelly, we are really good for each other. Right on?"

"Right on!" whooped Kelly, and they almost fell out of the swing high-fiving. When they finally quit giggling about that, Kelly sobered and cleared her throat. "Now, ladies and gentlemen, the question is: 'When will the beautiful, innocent Lorrie Dean forgive herself?' Stay tuned."

Lorrie Dean laughed and muttered, "I'm thinkin'. I'm thinkin'. Okay?"

"But it's so sad, Lorrie Dean," sobbed Kelly. "Sorry, I didn't mean to cry. All this made me think about Boone Woo. And, as I guess you know, your life is his life. He does not want, and he'll never have, a life without you." She was sobbing harder now. "But this old monster is pulling you two apart." She gripped the slats in the seat of the swing and braced up. "Now, see there? I'm okay, now."

"I'm so sorry, Kelly. I wish I could say right now that I forgive me, and I forgive the miserable wretch who raped me. But it's just so inconceivable that I could ever forgive him."

"I understand. That's the way it is with me about my mother. I keep thinking what she did was so hurtful that it's just inexcusable under any circumstances. I guess my hang-up is my stubborn opinion that it's unforgivable. Is that it? Am I just being stubborn?"

"I don't think the issue reduces itself to that question. Be assured, I understand your view of it, because I have the same reaction to the jerk who assaulted me."

They stared at each other in astonishment for a long time, forgetting to blink until their eyes dried out and started itching. All at once, they were saved by the clamor of men frolicking in the den, brave men, back from their awesome mission in the fields.

"Guess we better strike an upbeat pose," said Lorrie Dean. "If we don't, the despair in our faces will make them ask all kinds of questions. And I don't know about you, but right now, I'm not up to any more questions."

"Absolutely." On that note, Kelly twisted around to face her buddy and made a goofy-looking face, pulling her jaws out wide with an index finger from each hand. Lorrie Dean immediately did the same thing. This compelling drama ended with both of them laughing and slapping their hands.

Enter the men of the world, fresh from decisive victory in the far-flung fields of the farm. "Well," whooped Grandpa, "sure looks like we entered on a cheery note."

By then Lorrie Dean and Kelly were already applauding, lifting their hands high.

"Here-here," chimed Dub, "they are toasting our arrival."

"Out of pity, I would tender," mused Andy.

"Cute, Boone Woo," chortled Kelly.

After the banter, the girls settled again in their swing, while the men pulled rockers forward to form a kind of lopsided circle facing them.

Let the chatter begin! And so it did. Most of the conversation was about Kelly and her situation with her mother. There were really no new nuggets of wisdom coming forth on that subject, but the effort, in itself, demonstrated sound support for Kelly in whatever she decided to do. When asked if his regard for his sister had changed any, Dub indicated he now had more information to go on and was willing to release his grudge if future developments indicated a reason for doing so. He said that, at the least, some compassion for her circumstances was clearly in order.

It was nearing sundown when Andy and Lorrie Dean prepared to head back to their big-city life. Mom had fixed sandwiches for them and lingered at their car as they were bidding their last words of love and goodwill.

Lorrie Dean and Andy had little to say during the trip back. It appeared to Lorrie Dean that Andy might be a little peeved. Still, she decided it was only right to give him the benefit of the doubt, because perhaps he was just tired.

At one point, Andy asked, "Did you and Kelly resolve the issues you share, you know, her with her mother and you with yourself?"

"If I understand the question, I can say that we raised a lot of important matters for each of us to consider, but we didn't decide on any new course at this point. But we're thinking, Andy, we're thinking."

When Andy didn't respond, Lorrie Dean let the subject drop, and they cruised quietly on into Mesquite.

At her door, they said good night to each other, and that seemed to be it until Andy shuffled in place for a moment and then looked her straight in the eye and said, "There's just one more thing that I need to say, and I have to say it rather emphatically."

"Well?"

"Get over it!"

"Good-bye, Andy."

25

At his desk Monday morning, Andy wrestled with a daunting question: what did she mean by "Good-bye, Andy"? It sounded a bit final, the way she said it. Lorrie Dean had never before said good-bye that way. It was always "Bye now" or "Good night, dear," or some warm expression like that. This time, she had not only said "Good-bye, Andy," she had emphasized it, as though dismissing him—for good. It was almost as if she was saying, "Good-bye, Andy; it's over."

A faint tap at the door beckoned him from his dilemma. "Come in," he said. A moment later, he rose as his dear friend and colleague, Paige Ivy, strolled into his office. "What a welcome change of fare," he chimed.

"Uh-oh, aren't we having a good day?"

"We are, now," said Andy, motioning her to a chair.

"Well, I've just been thinking about your Lorrie Dean. I'd like to call her, but I thought I'd check with you first. How's she doing?"

"It's really good of you to ask and to care, my friend. Yes, call her—yes, yes, yes. How timely. At this very moment, I'm underway with plans to rally her support group. See, they're all out there already, but I need to energize them, so I'm going to be putting a lot of things in motion over the next few days. I have specific plans, and I will work on them every minute I get. We just have to . . ."

"Goodness, Andy, rarely have I heard such little-boy enthusiasm and excitement out of you. You are really into this." She paused, smiling broadly, and added, "And, I dare say, it becomes you, and it's very refreshing. Press on, valiant one!"

"Okay, thanks. To begin with, my Lorrie Dean is not well. She has completely lost any semblance of self-esteem; she's sorely depressed, and she's strapped with guilt feelings over supposed misdeeds during her captivity, and she tends to swing a little. I mean, one hour, she's kidding around with me, and in the next, she's sullen and sometimes, even a little contentious. She . . . She needs us, Paige."

"I'm in. Just call me any time and tell me what you need of me. Meanwhile, I'll call her tonight."

"That'll mean more to her than anything I can do."

"Well, all right, then. For now, I guess I better get back to my cell."

They laughed, and Paige left. Andy continued to think, trying to reckon with his situation. At once, he shook free of his perplexity, jumped up, and started pacing the floor, mumbling out loud about his rallying strategy. With each step, he checked off a point in his scheme: Get Kelly lined out on her role, maybe zip down to the farm and back in one evening after work and get all of them primed. Call We Party Tuesday while Lorrie Dean is on assignment in Fort Worth and talk to her coworkers. Call home. Check with FBI agent Chad Jarrigan. Check with the Rape Crisis Center. Stockpile some cardboard—do my job. With that, he bounced back to his desk and slipped into his chair.

Seconds later, there was a knock at the door, and his boss, Kirk Daniels, hustled in and pulled up a chair. *Time for the job part.* Kirk was the epitome of diplomacy, a rare tactic for him, as he solicited Andy's help on a faltering program assigned to another action officer. Andy agreed, outlined his approach, and Kirk sailed away, happy. *Piece o' cake.*

Andy worked late that day, plunging himself into his add-on assignment, which he really didn't have time for, in light of his regular duties. He had sworn to himself that he would continue to do all the right things, so he wouldn't be a target for anything that might interfere with his efforts to save his sweetheart. This was no time to make a wave at Clay Cutter Industries.

After work, he plodded into a nearby cafeteria and methodically worked his way through dinner, hardly aware of what he was eating. Back at the motel, his (he hoped) temporary quarters, he rested for a few moments and then pulled the telephone into his lap and let his hand rest on it for a while. Finally, he dialed Lorrie Dean's number.

"Hello."

"You okay?"

"Uh-huh."

"You, ah . . . you really *are* okay?"

"I'm okay."

"You need anything?"

"No."

"You're working in Fort Worth tomorrow, aren't you?"

"Right."

"Please drive carefully."

"Yes."

"Can't I do anything for you?"

"I don't need anything."

"Well, I guess . . . I guess that's all for now, huh?"

"Right."

"Okay, good night, sweetheart."

"Night."

*   *   *

Lorrie Dean sat at one end of her couch, crying softly. She just caved in to it—let it go, for whatever its purpose, for whatever crying is supposed to do. She looked at her hands, which were wet from wiping tears, and said to them, "I think I'm feeling sorry for myself."

In a while, the crying eased up a little, and her mind drifted back to the jolting nightmare she'd had last week. It had taken away the only source of cleansing she had. She could no longer tell her problems to the trees, lay her feelings on them, sit under them, and feel the peace. Even though it was just a dream, it had frightened her just as though it were real—so real, in fact, it had left her afraid to venture again into the woods.

With that option gone, she searched her mind for things Andy had encouraged her to do for herself, like writing a journal or a letter. At once, she recalled the impulse to write a letter that had occurred to her a few days ago—a letter from her to herself, describing what happened to her and how each event made her feel. Kelly had also mentioned this subject to her at some point.

She gazed at the writing pad in her hand for a long time, holding the pen in readiness above it, recalling her earlier botched attempt to write about the horrible dream. She'd been unable to keep that story focused and, in the end, wound up with nothing that made sense. This would be different—she hoped. She continued to stare at the writing pad until she felt herself floating into a trance. *Maybe that's what you're supposed to do,* she thought.

At once, she shook her head, huffed rowdily, and started to write. It was very hard at first. *What's to be said about endless horror?* Finally, she decided just to write something—anything, whatever entered her mind. Still, she struggled at times. Occasionally, she stopped completely and laid down her pen. Invariably, she would grit her teeth and start back into it.

After a time, something seemed to be pulling her along. *I think I'm on to this thing. Go, me! I'm on a roll, but this thing is keeping me awake. It's like I'm creating a nightmare that hasn't happened yet. Will I ever get to sleep tonight? No matter. Got to finish.*

When she decided she had written enough for one sitting, she capped her pen and laid her composition aside. After she brushed her teeth and dressed for bed, curiosity drew her back to her work. She picked it up, retired to her recliner, and began to read:

Dear me,

So, okay, I'm in the old house, right? The forsaken old house, my prison. That's where I am. So, what's to say? Oh, and there sits old Stupid, looking at me stupidly, making me feel stupid. He looks like a guy totally out of tune with what he was raised to be like. What went wrong there? Stupid!

Okay, it's time for that stupid soup, that abominable, nauseating broth. Ugh! One more swallow and I'll vomit all over myself.

Now, I'm sitting up in this dreadful chair. All night, I'm sitting up, while that miserable idiot sleeps on a couch. I'm aching. Oh, how it hurts, and it's making me weary, so very tired, but I have to stay in shape, because somehow, I will have to do something. I have to, or I'll die here. I'm going to the bathroom as much as I can and exercising in there. Stupid doesn't have sense enough to figure it out. He's dumb enough that there's got to be a way to trick him.

Oh my, what would Andy do? What would Kelly do?

Andy, dear Andy, please find me; please come get me, look for me, find me. Search, Andy, search! I'll be your Lorrie Dean, or my old alias, your Kimberly Malveaux, whoever you want me to be. Please, Andy, find me again.

No, no, no! Oh God, he's beating on me. He knocked me to the floor. It's my fault for thinking him stupid enough I could trick him with clever talk. He didn't take the bait. It's my fault, Andy.

Now, he's on top of me. He's so heavy, and he stinks. He's trying to tear my hair out. Merciful God, please make it quick. Now, he leers above me, smarting from his cowardly conquest of a helpless prisoner. Andy, I have betrayed you!

Oh, the scream, the harrowing scream! Okay, it worked, didn't it? Aieeeeee! Whop-ugh! Whop again-ugh!—Clonk-rattle. Whop from behind-ugh!—pause—Bam!—pause—Bam!

I'm running! I can barely run, but I'm running. Got to run. If God has me live, I'll always remember this run because of all it stands for—all that it exemplifies of four horrible days of hell. Run, Lorrie Dean!

The rape! Ohhh, dear God, thy will be done.

The rape did it.

*   *   *

Tuesday at Clay Cutter was a bummer. Andy's plate was loaded with priority items, leaving no time for personal business. He wouldn't even be able to wedge in a short phone call. So, he decided to work his tail off, skip lunch, and get back to Lorrie Dean. It seemed that's the way it had always been, most notably when he was pouring his heart into the search for her. Even then, bizarre as it might be, it was as if she had been beckoning him, crying out to be found.

In the early afternoon, Andy had his business settled to the point that he could spare a few minutes for a couple of phone calls included in his rallying plan. The question in his mind was who to call first, rape crisis or We Party. He decided to call We Party first in case Lorrie Dean should return early from Fort Worth and literally walk in on his phone call. He dialed their number.

"We Party. This is Shirley; let me help."

"Hi, Shirley, this is Andy Boone and I . . ."

"Oh hi, Mr. Boone, you're Lorrie's man."

"Right you are. I hope so, anyway. Thanks for acknowledging that. Oh, and call me Andy."

"Sure, thanks, Andy. You know, Lorrie's not here today; she's in Fort Worth doing a sports club banquet."

"Oh yeah, she mentioned that. Actually, that's why I picked today to call you. First, I just want to bow to you all for . . . well, for just being a class act. I can't tell you . . ."

"Wow! Thanks, Mr. . . . . I mean, Andy."

"You're sure welcome. Let me try to tell you what all you mean to my Lorrie Dean."

"Listen, Andy, let me get our boss, Jan Merrit, on with us. Hold on. Okay? Hold on."

"Hello, Mr. Boone, this is Jan. Thank you for calling."

"Hi, Jan, I remember you and Shirley from the wedding—oh, and call me Andy."

"I will, and Andy, I'm so sorry about the wedding."

"Thanks. As you probably know, we're sort of in limbo right now. Anyway, I called to thank you for what you've done for Lorrie Dean. Jan, you are the only influence that is really making any difference in her adjustment. You all are the only rehab she has. Nothing else is working, not me, not church, not anything. So, thanks, Jan and Shirley and all of you for being who you are and for providing Lorrie Dean an atmosphere of grace and professionalism. You are absolutely the best thing going for her right now, and I salute you, and I thank you from the bottom of my heart."

"Andy, you're putting tears in my eyes," said Jan.

"Mine, too," chimed Shirley.

"We can tell you why that is," said Jan. "First of all, Andy, your Lorrie is a lady. Believe me; she brings class to this operation."

"Thanks. As a matter of fact, you don't have any way to know this, but the time she spends working with you all is the only time that she is Lorrie Dean in person. The rest of the time, she's somebody else, a person she despises. Oh, and please, I'm telling you this secret only to help her."

"I know, I know. I pray God will bring her back."

"Me, too, and thanks for your prayers. That brings me to the other reason I called, which is to recognize and seal your support for her. It happens that I have put in motion an undertaking that I call a rally. I'm out to energize all of her support group."

"Count us in. What can we do?"

Thereupon, Andy outlined his plans for rallying Lorrie Dean's support team toward one big push, an all-out effort. He emphasized that, at some point, he would get everybody together in one place to honor her. He mentioned that nobody would have to spend any money on their participation, that he would cover the costs. At that point, he chuckled and said, "Plus, I'll have all the cardboard and paint you need."

"All of that sounds great," said Jan. "We are with you in full force here. One other thing, Andy. Here's to you for trying. Just let us know when and what."

"I will, indeed. I want you to have my phone number here at work and at my . . . err . . . temporary residence."

"Good. Before you go, I have something I think will lift your spirits. Of course, you already know what a super human being Lorrie is. Well, Andy, I have two letters at my desk right now, sent by two very satisfied, very happy clients. Both of them praise your Lorrie for her professional and gracious style and for her expert manner of planning their parties. The qualities they mention about her are assets you already know about. But isn't that absolutely super?"

"Yes, that's my girl, and that's the lady she claims to be when she's there in your environment, but that she fails to acknowledge when she's out of it."

"Perhaps there's some hope in your rally program. Now, let me tell you one other thing about your Lorrie—well, Lorrie Dean as you call her—see, I called her in after each of these letters and thanked her, and just commended her with all the best words I could think of. When I finished each time, she just smiled modestly and said, very humbly, 'Thank you, Jan, these clients were really wonderful people to work with.'"

Andy was busy suppressing tears, so he was unable to answer right away.

"Andy? Andy, are you still on?"

"Yes, yes. It's that she just never told me about it. Part of her beautiful grace involves never seeking recognition. How can I ever thank you all enough?"

"Hey, we're the winners here. And it's rewarding to us to see her bubble with enthusiasm like, for example, the way she did after she finished the serenade assignment. She was just all aglow on that one."

"Serenade? Oh yeah, I remember now; she mentioned something about that, but I forgot all about it."

"Right. One of her first assignments when she returned was organizing a serenade for a young man honoring his new wife on their one-month anniversary."

"That is creative. I salute the young man. Did she get the singers and everything?"

"Oh yes, she found a young male trio, just getting started. Apparently they're outstanding, and at this early stage of their career, they're pretty inexpensive."

"Hmm. I wonder if I might have their number."

"Sure. We'll dig it up and call you. I want you to know your phone call has been very reassuring to us."

"I owe you big-time."

After he hung up, Andy gave some time to the urging of his heart. He felt both pride and sorrow for his sweetheart. He could not shake the poignant image of Lorrie Dean modestly accepting praise, and not telling anyone. When he had settled a little, he prayed aloud, "Please, dear God, reach to our Lorrie Dean."

Step 2. Andy's next move was to check with the Rape Crisis Center and test his plan against their guidelines and counsel. When he called, he asked for Debbie Sills.

"Hi, Mr. Boone, how's it going?"

"Not much headway, really, but thanks for asking—oh, and call me Andy. Anyway, let me bring you up to date on the status of my sweetheart who, except for a technicality, would be my wife now. Debbie, she's totally the same, still laden with guilt feelings and still punishing herself."

"I'm sorry; you still don't think there's any way you can get her in to talk to us?"

"Not at all. In fact, I've quit trying." Andy proceeded to tell her about his trying to shock Lorrie Dean on two occasions, one when he turned his back on her and left her alone in the park and the other when he told her somewhat hatefully to "Get over it!"

"What was her reaction?"

"It didn't work either time. It may even have backfired. Am I never to try that again?"

"As for telling her to 'get over it,' that's probably the only directive type counseling that has a chance of working. Remember that we talked about nondirective counseling when you were here?"

"Yes, I have my notes on that, and I bought a couple of books."

"So, it's very human and natural for family and friends to want to help. Sadly, the direct advice they often give—while conveying love and caring—is not all that useful. But we all do it, again, just honestly trying to help."

"I understand. I hadn't thought of that prior to our contact—namely, that usually we're too directive."

"Yes—well-meaning, mind you, but not very effective—you know, things like *forget about it, hold your head up, put it behind you, don't dwell on it,* and the granddaddy of them all, *don't worry.*"

"Guess I really blew it with my 'Get over it!'"

"Andy, as a matter of fact, that's one that has some potential to help. By saying 'Get over it,' you're putting her in control without telling her what to do. In effect, you're saying, 'Use what you have to solve this.' Now, on the other thing, Andy, I'm sorry, but I have to give you a minus-one for turning your back on her and walking away from her in the park, essentially withdrawing your support."

"I was already regretting that boo-boo. Be assured, I will never again knowingly do anything that has the slightest appearance of withholding my support."

"Well, you know, don't discredit yourself. You reached for something that you hoped would shake her out of her fixation. So, don't condemn yourself for trying. At least you're not letting it go, and there's a lot to be said for perseverance with rape victims. But remember: *time* is a factor in any recovery, so we need to be patient."

"Thanks for your time. May I mention just one more thing . . . well, actually two things?" At that point, Andy told Debbie about his support group rallying plan. The counselor praised him for that effort and said it was right on target. Next, Andy related to her Lorrie Dean's confession that the environment of her job was the only place where she felt like her old self, partly because she would prepare herself as a lady, dress up, and go among other women who were self-assured and happy. He ended by asking the counselor what she thought of that.

"It's great. I mean, that's at least one positive we have working for us. It's good that she has that, and here's where you might tap into it. You get dressed up with her and go out, both of you looking sharp. Get into positive social situations sometimes, indulge in a little fine dining out, take in some formal concerts like those given at the Meyerson Symphony Center, that sort of thing. That should be good conditioning for her in the same way her job is."

"How can I possibly thank you enough for your time and expertise?"

"Knowing it might help is my reward. Keep on trying; never give up. Someday, when you least expect it, you may see her lift her head and set her jaw and look alive. I wish you all the luck."

The demands of Andy's job took over after the two somewhat lengthy, but very productive, phone calls.

That night, he called the farm to arrange for his down-and-back flying visit the next day after work. Mom answered and warmly agreed but chastised him for opting to eat early before getting on the road. That settled, Andy asked to speak to his morning light, to which Mom replied, "You bet. She's standing right here, looking expectantly at this phone in my hand. Take care, Andy."

"Hi, Boone Woo. Guess who I just got off the phone with a minute before you called?"

"Err, I don't have a clue. Anybody I know?"

"Lorrie Dean. We had a good talk, as always we do, but she sounded really down. What can we do?"

"That takes me right to my reason for calling. I'm coming down tomorrow evening on a whirlwind trip to talk to everybody about Operation Rally. You with me on that, sweetheart?"

"I'm primed and ready to fire."

"Okay, you know, you are sort of the focal point for this campaign. I hope that's all right, because I have a lot in mind for you to do. Still, my dear Kelly, I don't want to take advantage of you."

"Not at all, Boone Woo. You two are the center of my life. Press me into action. I'm set to go."

"You are the center of our lives, too. Thanks for all you are. Oh, I should mention right now that it will involve two or three trips into Dallas for you, each of which will probably involve an overnight stay with Lorrie Dean, but we'll always arrange that for the end of a school week."

"That's fine. School is a piece of cake, and the homework is really light, for one thing, because school just started. As Grandpa says, 'It's as easy as falling off a log.'"

"Okay then, I'll see y'all tomorrow evening. Before I go, Kelly, tell me about your mother."

"I'm still working on it, and . . . I guess . . . well, let me just say that—still working on it."

Andy realized that discretion was in order here, so he didn't press the question any further, and they ended their call. He was feeling disheartened himself. He guessed he was in good company: Kelly sounded downcast when he asked about her mother, and she had said Lorrie Dean sounded down during their conversation. "Oh, Lord, what would you have us do?"

26

There is a dream. It's frightening. Three little children are lost in a vast, barren field. Somehow, they've wandered away from their homes. They turn round and round, looking for a sign. They could start running, but which way would they go? They keep scanning the endless chasm, looking often at each other for any sign of an idea. Once more, they turn, looking out across the clueless field. Again, they face each other and shrug. They're scared to death, yet they cling together in their cruel dilemma—and wait.

The little boy thinks it's his job to be the leader, but he doesn't know what to do, and the two little girls seem to know as much as he does, maybe more. There's nothing around they can plug in and watch it solve their needs, no icon to click on for a pop-up menu giving them choices. All they have is their simple faith and their instincts. In a while, the youngest one, a little girl, says, "Let's pray and ask Jesus for an angel." Now, they huddle together, holding hands, in the tall grass—and pray. The dream fades.

*　　　*　　　*

The farmhouse front door swung open just as Andy stepped up to the porch. "Hello there," he said, "It's me again, Andrew Boone."

"Well, come on in anyway," replied the cute little heckler holding the door. "We'll try to bear up somehow."

As Andy entered the family den, Grandpa called out, "Gather 'round, everybody. The Boone is in the building."

On that note, the little band of chuckling devotees shuffled up to the table and leaned in, ready to listen to their esteemed visitor.

"Wow, look at that speedy action," exclaimed Andy. "Grandpa, you've got influence in this place."

"Well, I'm afraid it's not very consistent, but thanks for that little bit of recognition. Maybe it will improve my image around here."

"Right on," said Andy. "Now, seriously, please accept my thanks to all of you for . . ."

"What do you mean, *seriously?*" piped Kelly. "Does that mean the other part wasn't serious?"

When the laughter died a little, Andy gestured toward Kelly and announced, "Let me present my assistant, ladies and gentlemen."

"You do mean *boss*, don't you, sir?" teased Uncle Dub.

"Yes. Boss—definitely boss."

With all the banter aside, they took up the very urgent and fully supported cause that Andy had dashed to the farm to present. All eyes were on him as he began again, in earnest.

"I'm not here to run a meeting with you. This is your affair as much as it is mine. Lorrie Dean is ours. I just want to outline some things I thought of that might help bring back our dear, lost friend. These are just things for you to think about, y'all. I'm not trying to be the authority here."

"As far as we're concerned, Andy, you can be the authority," said Mom, and all nodded agreement.

"Thanks. Okay, what I'm trying to do is rally one all-out surge of support for Lorrie Dean—support that she already has. Essentially, I want to unite that support into one big push. My plan is already underway, meaning, among other things, that I have wholehearted commitments from people at Lorrie Dean's job and colleagues from my job, my parents, and now, you. Our Kelly does indeed have a key role in all this. As you know, the bond of acceptance and caring between these two incredible women is unsurpassed."

"Hear! Hear!" blurted Grandpa. "This one is for you, Kelly."

Kelly scooted back from the table, stood up, and bowed. "As Boone Woo's assistant, let me add that one key element in this effort will be our prayers." It seemed she wanted to say more, but her voice had started to quiver, so she sat down again.

Now, a little patter of agreement ran through the crowd, as a vigorously nodding Andy raised a thumbs-up high in the air. He cleared his throat and began again.

"How right you are, my morning light. Do you all see why she's my boss? All right—main target: we will have an all-hands gathering to honor Lorrie Dean in two or three weeks, whenever we're all available. I'd like for this to come off as a surprise to her, if possible, and Kelly's going to be a key factor in that effort." He started to say more but held up abruptly.

Turning to face the always reserved Aunt Leah, he said, "Dearest Aunt Leah, you don't have to raise your hand. You can jump in just any time, like the rest of us. We need you, and we need your input. What do you think?"

Aunt Leah smiled timidly and said softly, "Well, I'm trying to be as quiet as Uncle Dub. But here's what I was thinking. Grandpa made me think of it when he said a minute ago, 'This one's for you, Kelly.' So, I thought maybe we could have a marquee at the gathering place that reads: THIS ONE'S FOR YOU, LORRIE DEAN."

That meekly proffered suggestion got an instant, voice vote of "Yes." Andy mused about this event, as spontaneous crowd babble took over the moment. *A more powerful endorsement of Lorrie Dean's character and bearing would hardly be possible. This unprecedented outward thrust by a shy, highly introverted, normally noncommittal person, shows, in an instant, the widely held regard for Lorrie Dean and her natural capacity for commanding love.*

"I want everybody, I mean everybody, to come to this. We may be able to have a little entertainment and some food, but the main thing is for us to mingle among each other and with Lorrie Dean. And, Aunt Leah, speaking of marquees, I have already bought a big supply of cardboard and paint that I will furnish to each one. See, we'll make signs to hold up when Lorrie Dean takes the stage, so to speak. Each participant can decide what their sign will say, and I'm thinking it'll be fun to keep them secret from each other until the big day. But they should be brief and essentially just show support."

"Boone Woo, may I offer something here?" Kelly interposed. "I really don't think paint and cardboard is the thing. I think the visual support idea is great, but not big, gawky signs, huh? That's just not Lorrie Dean. Don't you know, Boone Woo? Okay, *you* are paint and cardboard, and that's okay, because you're a man. But, really, Lorrie Dean is more lace and polish. I think big signs would shock her. It's just not her character—this gentle, gracious lady."

Silence! Andy listened intently, and before Kelly could finish, his countenance had started to fill in with the trademark glow of adoration he had for his morning light. When the others saw Andy's acceptance of Kelly's observations, they began nodding approval.

"Oh my goodness, Kelly, I dread to think how it would have turned out if I didn't have you, sobering me when I need it the most. I'm afraid I was just letting my rampant enthusiasm get away with me. The signs are hereby deleted from the plan."

"Oh, wait, Boone Woo. You're thinking is sound, very good. Your idea for some visual show of support is great. I'm handing that to you. How about we just amend it a little? Instead of signs, why not have each person pin a little tag up near their shoulder, sort of where a name tag is usually placed. It can have a very brief expression, one or two words. Maybe each one should start out the same, you know, just have her name followed by a dash. Then, after the dash, we can add our personal message. Say, okay, here's an example: one little tag might read, 'Lorrie Dean—Thank you.'"

"I'm already thinking of what mine will be," said Uncle Dub.

"Me, too," echoed Mom.

"It's settled," said Andy, enthusiastically. He thought for a moment and then smiled mischievously and said, "Guess I ought to look for a salvage yard for my mountain of cardboard."

"We can have a yard sale," offered Leah.

At that, everybody cheered, and Dub blurted out, "Hey, look sharp, everybody. Our Leah is in there tonight; she is *on!*"

After a round of laughter, Andy decided to add a caution that closely paralleled Kelly's comments about the uniquely feminine and gracious bearing of Lorrie Dean. "Picking up on Kelly's point, let me urge against swarming around Lorrie Dean. Somehow, that seems to be the conventional method of showing support, but again, that won't work with Lorrie Dean. So, don't line up in front of her like a receiving line or bunch up around her, waiting your turn to say something. All that would look terribly contrived. Believe me, Lorrie Dean can detect pretense in a heartbeat. Let's do whatever we can to ensure that it doesn't come across as phony. Remember that we are there to honor her, not to patronize her."

"Well said," agreed Dub. "One day, she told me that of the many things she admired about us was our realness. In fact, she said to me one day, 'You all are truly genuine people.'"

"So, be yourselves," said Andy. "Let's all just mill around, visit with each other, and at times, meet up with Lorrie Dean, smiling and pausing to let her read the sentiments on our lapel tags."

"Yeah," said Mom, "we need to just treat her exactly the way we always have. If we change ourselves, she'll see it as artificial. Let her read the love in our smiles, the twinkle of acceptance in our eyes."

The meeting ended on a high note, and the participants began to peel away to other activities. Andy remained at the table, his head bowed just slightly. Kelly stood a ways from the table, folding cup towels. In a while, she felt the essence of Andy and looked toward him.

"Boone Woo, why are you so quiet?"

"Thinking about you."

"Thinking about me makes you quiet?"

Andy just nodded.

Kelly waited for a while, giving him a chance to speak, and finally said, "Well, duh! What about me plunges you into such endless silence?"

"It's just you being you. Kelly, I love you more than I will ever figure out how to show or say. I thank God for you."

"And I thank God for you, my dear Boone Woo, and I thank God for my friend, Lorrie Dean. Somehow, someday, we three will figure it out—someday. We *will*, Boone Woo! Right now, we have to pray for divine intervention."

"And so we will," said Andy.

And so they did, holding hands. When they finished, they visited privately for a few minutes, until it was near time for Andy to leave. During that time, Andy told her he was planning an evening serenade, honoring Lorrie Dean, and he needed Kelly to be with her that night to assure she stayed put and urge her to the front porch when the racket started. Another matter, always uppermost in Andy's mind, concerned the issue of Kelly and her mother.

To that question, Kelly said, "Well, in my phone conversation with Lorrie Dean last night, I told her I was about ready to forgive my mother. I could tell all along that's what she hoped I would do, but she would never say so. When I told her I was going to do it by phone, Lorrie Dean sounded disappointed. I'm pretty sure she believes it won't be genuine unless I say it to my mother, face-to-face. The way I know that's how Lorrie Dean feels is her comment to the effect that if I changed my mind, she'd be glad to go with me to meet with my mother."

"You two are really good for each other," said Andy. "Speaking of forgiveness, I need to get back to that issue as it involves Lorrie Dean. I broached it about ten days ago, with no luck, and I need to get busy and follow up on it. Thanks for reminding me."

Just before he left, Dub and Andy chatted briefly. In that time, Dub indicated that he wanted to reconcile with his sister, but was reluctant to make a move in that direction until after Kelly resolved her situation with her.

It was after dark when Andy headed back to Mesquite.

*   *   *

It was still a little early for bed, and Kelly was too worked up to attempt sleep anyway. She returned to sit at the table—and meditated. She was both excited about Andy's plans and apprehensive that something might go wrong. She was also wrestling with the issue of her loyalties concerning her two best friends in all the world. Ultimately, she resolved that her loyalties would always be united into one steadfast dedication to both Lorrie Dean and Andy, that her loyalty to each of them would always be equal. She laughed aloud as she thought, *Now, you guys gotta understand, my loyalty may require me to keep each of you informed about what the other is doing. Just remember, this is out of love, y'all. After all, neither of you has pledged me to any secrets.*

With that resolution firmly declared and tucked away, Kelly picked up the phone and dialed Lorrie Dean.

"Hello."

"Hi, Lorrie Dean, what's happening?"

"Well, I can say that I had a very rewarding day at the office; everybody there is so really good to me."

"As well they should be."

"I don't know. It's true I work hard for them, but that doesn't seem to be enough to explain it. I thank my God for them, because they interrupt this stubborn curse I'm under, at least for a little while each day. But enough of that. What's going on with you?"

"Just had a short visit with Boone Woo; he was really here to meet with the family to enlist our support for something he's doing. But more about that in a minute. Right now, let me tell you about my forgiven mother."

"Dear Kelly, I'm so glad to hear you use that word."

"I know. The reason I said it that way is that I realize I have already forgiven, even though I haven't told her so. And, Lorrie Dean, I can't begin to tell you what a feeling of peace, what a sense of cleansing, it has given me."

"I can imagine. Are you going to see her?"

"I am, indeed, now that I've thought it through and put myself in her place. I plan to call her tomorrow afternoon and get it set up. I'm going to offer to come to Shreveport and meet with her in her apartment. I'll let you know."

"This thrills me, Kelly, and remember, I want to go with you and be at your side at this crucial time in your life"

"Thank you. This time, I'll take you up on that offer. But, just one thing . . ."

"Oh?"

"No clowning around, okay?"

Two ardent friends shared a spontaneous, get-down laugh. When they sobered, Kelly said, "Now, I need to change the subject. Okay?"

"Roll on," said Lorrie Dean.

"Andy just spent a couple of hours with the whole family, sitting around the table. I'm telling you about this, not to break confidence with him, but because I love you both. For that matter, he didn't swear me to secrecy, although he probably figured I'd never mention it to you."

"You've really aroused my curiosity."

"I won't tell you any details of what he's up to, but I think I ought to let you know in general where he's headed. It's just . . . well, Lorrie Dean, I'm really excited about it, and if you already knew, I'm positive you would be, too, and also, you would be touched, as I am. Everything about it says uncompromising love."

Thereupon, Kelly described Andy's project in very broad terms, indicating essentially that he planned to stage something in Lorrie Dean's honor before a gathering of people who supported her unequivocally. That's all she revealed, and she kept secret Andy's plan for a serenade. *That one really needs to be a surprise,* she thought.

Lorrie Dean listened attentively without a single interruption. When it was clear that Kelly was finished, she said simply, "I can't wait."

"We need to get together some time, and I can give you a little bit more."

"Yes, yes, let's do. I need your wisdom on some sticky issues that are beginning to nag me more than ever. My problem seems to be mushrooming to the point I feel like I'm about to go under."

"We have to talk. Boone Woo and I absolutely will not let you go under."

"Thank God for you two. I don't deserve either of you."

"Bullshit! Excuse me; I don't usually talk that way, but I don't ever want to hear any such nonsense as that come out of your mouth again. You dig?"

A distraught Lorrie Dean mumbled, "I dig." She took a moment to regain some composure and then said, resolutely, "Here's something that will give you an idea as to how things have turned: I started writing a journal—actually a letter to myself—as both you and Andy suggested. Kelly, I want to show it to you. Even though I wrote it, there's something in it that baffles me."

27

Three days later, early Saturday morning, the two girls cruised toward Wills Point. Kelly's mother had elected to meet there instead of Shreveport for reasons known only to her.

"I think my mother just likes to come here," said Kelly. "I didn't realize it before, but I've learned that she has been here often with the woman she works for and rents from. My mother says the woman has family here."

"So, I guess she's just comfortable here," said Lorrie Dean. "Perhaps she feels more secure here and that it gives her a chance to get out—way out—of her usual confinement. And, you know, we all need that."

"Exactly, and it's fine with me. I like Wills Point, too."

"So do I. For that matter, I like getting away sometimes, too. Tell me, did your mother express any reservations about my coming along?"

"Not at all. In fact, she said she was glad I had friendship and that she was looking forward to meeting you. By the way, did you bring your letter with you?"

"No, I didn't want to take the edge off this meeting with your mother."

Minutes later, they were passing the ages-old train station that sat along the railroad tracks near the downtown center. They turned on Fourth Street at the next light and parked just around the corner on Commerce, less than a block from their meeting place. Everything in their venture was out in the open this time—no covert maneuvering. They were to meet inside the Quilt Store on the first floor of the old Rose Dry Goods Company building.

As they drew near the Quilt Store, Lorrie Dean laid a hand on Kelly's shoulder and said, "Why don't we go in separately, and I'll mill around while you have some private time with your mother? Then we can get together when you all are ready?"

"That's very discreet of you, Lorrie Dean. Good idea—let's do it."

With that, Kelly pulled away and hustled into the store. At once, she spied her mother, poking along two aisles over. Seconds later, mother and daughter, painfully estranged for eleven years, walked freely into a warm, willing embrace. When they slowly pulled apart, teary-eyed, holding hands, Kelly said, firmly, "My dear mother, I want you to know, that if you've done anything wrong at all, I forgive you. Will you forgive me for taking so long?"

"Oh, my darling Kelly, of course I . . ."

She was cut off by another spontaneous embrace. Just an aisle away, Lorrie Dean witnessed these poignant moments and whispered, "Thank you, dear God." She walked on to another part of the store to wait for Kelly's signal.

Soon, a smiling mother and daughter walked resolutely to Lorrie Dean, and the spirit of their introduction was friendly and genuine.

"Dear mother, I want you to meet my very best friend. Lorrie Dean, this is Rosalea Surrat."

"This is a genuine privilege," said Rosalea. "Thank you for being my daughter's friend."

"It's my privilege to meet you; thank you for having her and finding her. She's an absolute jewel and incomparable friend."

"I guess Kelly's told you all about us," quizzed Rosalea.

"Sure, she's mentioned some things of concern. But, you know, we all have some of that. The only thing that matters, now, is that you two are reunited in love and acceptance. Praise God for that!"

"Praise God, indeed," echoed Rosalea. Then, looking somewhat glassy-eyed at Lorrie Dean, she said, "Would you like to sit down?"

Lorrie Dean glanced all around, confirming to herself that there was no sitting area, shrugged instinctively, and said, "That's okay; we've been riding for a while . . . I'm fine, thanks."

"Okay, whatever you'd like, but there's a Subway sandwich store across the street where we can sit and talk, if you want, and, for that matter, even grab a bite to eat."

"Oh . . . yes, right. That would be pleasant."

Thereupon, the three headed out. Lorrie Dean, comfortably trailing behind, feeling a little mischievous, smiled and thought, *So there! Guess she's not as crazy as you thought.*

In the Subway shop, they chatted amiably as if they'd been companions for years, waxing ever more spirited as they continued their historic visit. Mother and daughter, though a little nervous, were clearly on their way to a healthy relationship. After all, they were just getting started. Full reconciliation would take some time, but mercifully, it would happen.

In the course of their patter, Kelly said to her mother, "Oh, before I forget, Uncle Dub said to tell you that he wishes you well."

"Oh. My Dubby," sobbed Rosalea. "I'm sorry about us. We were bosom buddies when we were little kids. But . . ." She hesitated, sniffled a little, blotted her tears, and went on. "But I understand. Please tell Dubby . . . err . . . your Uncle Dub, that I wish him well, too."

They all continued to chat merrily for a good hour and parted, smiling, with pledges to meet again.

The two girls were mostly thoughtful along the way to Tillman, where Lorrie Dean would pick up her car and head back to Mesquite. However, they did share their thoughts, solemnly, from time to time. At one point, Kelly offered, "You know, Mother seemed to be in a little better touch with reality today. Of course, she had a few spells of confusion, but all in all, she held together pretty well, I thought."

"I agree. Give her credit; she was really trying. She was giving it her best."

"Right. Even so, I do worry a little about her driving."

"I know."

"You think I've been too hard on my mother, don't you?"

"Absolutely not. There's a perfectly good reason to your reluctance—in fact, all of your reaction. I would have been exactly like you."

"But this was right, wasn't it?"

"It sure was. I can say that with full assurance, because I've come to look at all sides of it, and I know you've had some really hurtful times, and I'm sorry, my Kelly. But I can see, now, where your mother's decision to give you up might have been an act of running for her life. When the possible end of your life is staring you in the face, it's very human to think mostly of yourself. I don't say that's an excuse, but it's very human. I realize, as I think you do, that we just have to let her be human."

"I guess she did what she knew to do."

"Right. Sure, it probably would have been less selfish, certainly more responsible, if she'd given you whatever time she had left, but this was her way of responding to the death sentence with a daughter in the picture."

"I understand it all so much better, now. Lorrie Dean, thanks for coming with me. That meant everything to me."

"We're friends. You'd do the same for me. In fact, I need your help and support for this troubling situation I'm in."

"I'm yours."

"Well, you asked me if I brought that letter I wrote to myself. I want you to read it, and we can talk about it together, not on the phone."

"Sure. I want to. Shall I just come on, sometime, maybe even next week, and we can spend some serious time together and—" She chuckled. "—And maybe even a little frivolous time?"

"Yes, yes, if you can do that, it would be great. How about next Friday evening, and you can spend the night? We can tackle the ugly business first, get that over with, and then frolic around on Saturday."

"It's done."

They fell comfortably silent for the rest of the trip and parted in good spirits shortly after arriving in Tillman.

Moments after Lorrie Dean left, Kelly phoned Andy and gave him a brief, very general summary of the day's events with her mother. At the end, she mentioned that she would be spending the next Friday night at Lorrie Dean's place.

"I was just wondering, Boone Woo, if you'd like to do your serenade then?"

"Great idea. Let's shoot for about eight thirty Friday night on the front lawn."

*   *   *

Suddenly, there was a new demon loose in the life of Lorrie Dean LeMay. She was so nervous as she waited for Kelly that pacing the floor only made it worse. So, she sat fidgeting in her chair, certain that she was on the brink of a disastrous showdown. It seemed everything was weighing down on her—*hurry, Kelly*—that her ordeal was coming to a head. She couldn't sit still. She bounced up and started going back and forth to the kitchen and her bedroom and to the front window to look out—for what, she had no idea.

She was shaking, and at the same time, bracing against the strain in her shoulders; her breathing was conspicuous, yet shallow. There seemed to be contradiction all about her. She picked up a magazine and, in a moment, caught herself just thumbing pages with no thought of anything she was looking for, and the whole exercise served no cause but to make her ever more desperate.

In this hour, naked fear ruled Lorrie Dean's world—a daunting fear of the unknown, a morbid dread of what might be just around the corner. Maybe it was a fear of losing her tragedy, as though she was attached to it, woefully unprepared for freedom—for a normal, guilt-free life. How could she deal with liking herself again? Maybe she should just go to pieces and get it over with. She had an eerie feeling that if she were at the edge of a cliff in that moment, she would jump. Her own words came floating back to her: *Please, Andy, find me again.* At once, she cried out, "Hurry, Kelly!" In the next moment, she heard a car drive up.

The two best friends embraced quickly at the door and turned to head in.

"Lorrie Dean, what's wrong?"

"Oh, I'm just a bit nervous, today. We'll work it out."

Kelly, still feeling uncomfortable about the look of anguish on Lorrie Dean's face, frowned but let the subject drop. "Nice day," she submitted.

"Isn't it, though? What say we go out for a leisurely dinner? Maybe there'll be some catharsis in that for both of us."

"Oh, ah . . . well, I mean . . . I hadn't thought of that. It has a good ring to it."

"Okay, let me get on some makeup and brush a couple of strokes in my hair, and we'll take off. Have a seat. I won't be long."

As Lorrie Dean stepped away, Kelly glanced at her watch. *Hoo, boy. What now? Andy's thing is supposed to come off at eight thirty, and it's already six thirty.* She took a deep, noisy breath and blew it through loose lips. Now, she was reminded of a drama course she took during her junior year. She recalled that they were taught to convey emotions and all kinds of human conditions through postures, facial expressions, and gestures rather than words. If you were exhausted, you had to show it, not say it.

Abruptly, Kelly collapsed into the nearest chair, slid way down in it, spread her knees far apart, and let her shoulders sag, her head flop to one side, and her tongue hang out. Then she aborted that last part. *There's no way I'm going to do the tongue thing.*

When Lorrie Dean walked in, she stopped suddenly. "Oh Kelly, you're so exhausted. I'm sorry. Tell you what . . . plan B: let's just pick up some Chinese to go."

"No, no, Lorrie Dean. I'll be all right. I was just taking a quick break. We'll be on our way." She began squirming to get out of the chair, dramatizing every piece of the effort, all the while trying to make her grin look awkward.

"No, no. That's okay. You've been through a lot lately, plus you were in school all day, and without stopping, you drove in here. I perfectly understand."

As hard as Lorrie Dean tried to sound contrite, Kelly could detect a little prickle in her voice. *Two colossal actors,* she thought. *But that's okay. Friends do that, not to be pretentious, but because they're friends.*

"Actually, let's be real," continued Lorrie Dean. "Neither one of us needs to get cranked up right now. Let's just call in pizza, and we won't have to go hopping around." She giggled.

When they finished their pizza, they agreed that it was a good time to deal with Lorrie Dean's letter to herself. They returned to the parlor to relax—if that was possible—in the recliners.

Kelly began to read the letter, ever so slowly. Halfway through it, she blinked away tears and spoke softly to her friend. "I feel this so deeply for you. I'm so sorry you had to suffer all that humiliation and pain."

Lorrie Dean nodded, and Kelly continued to read. When she finished reading, she held the letter by one end and let it flop down in her lap. She continued to hold to the edge of it while she stared at the floor, motionless. Finally, she sat up straight, started waving the letter about, and said, "I just don't know, Lorrie Dean."

"I know. That was my reaction, exactly, and I wrote the thing."

"I just thank God you did what you did, because it means you're here now."

"Really."

"I can say this much, my impression is, that you're on the verge of stopping the run. I get that, not only from the content of the letter, but also by the simple fact that you brought yourself to write it. Orchids to you!"

"Thanks. Maybe that's the thing making me so nervous, the idea that I may be about to give up the run."

"Yes. There's one part here that I believe has some very real significance, the part about the rape—you say, 'The rape did it.'"

"Amazing, Kelly. I'm hung up on that part, too."

"Okay, you ready, dear friend?"

"Go."

"I know you don't want to hear this, but I can't help it; you're going to hear it. We're friends, and this is tough, but it has to be. Lorrie Dean, get your butt to a counselor! This part about the rape has to be presented to a professional. You and I can try all day to guess what it means, but they have experience that will tell them what it means. They've seen this hundreds of thousands of times."

"I hear you. Andy's been trying to get me to the Rape Crisis Center."

"Good for him. The stuff you have in this letter shows the feelings inside you and your reactions, and that's what crisis counselors are trained to do—to help you interpret these feelings and reactions."

"Maybe so. Perhaps I'm going to have to give in on that. I'll just think about it, and, who knows . . . wait a minute, how did you come to know all this about rape crisis counseling?"

"Boone Woo told me. At this point, you might as well know, he's been educating himself so he can help you. He has talked to people at the Rape Crisis Center here, and he ordered books on the subject, all so he could teach himself how to help you. And that time he dropped by on his way to see his parents, he gave me his notes to teach me, and the books came direct to me in the mail."

"Andy did all that?"

"Yes. I don't think he wanted me to tell you about it, but the time has come. He'll understand, and he'll agree." She glanced at her watch—8:20.

For a few minutes, they sat quietly, occasionally looking at each other and nodding. Oh, the untainted rapport between two friends. Their spell was broken by the sound of shuffling on the front sidewalk.

As Lorrie Dean pushed to start up, Kelly sprang out of her chair and darted for the front. "You rest. I'll check it out."

"Gosh, what energy. Amazing how fast you have recovered." She sat back.

Kelly returned promptly and said, "It's just some people scuffling along the walk out there—looks like a family. They seem happy."

"Oh."

In a few minutes, they heard other noise, and Lorrie Dean remarked, "Sounds like somebody's playing a radio loud."

At that, Kelly stood, walked over to stand in front of her friend, and held out her hands. Lorrie Dean cocked her head like a suspicious little girl

221

and took her friend's hands. They walked onto the front porch to behold Andy Boone and three other young men, standing abreast, applauding politely. All were dressed in suits, including Andy. One of the men stepped forward and said, "For you, Lorrie Dean" and then stepped back in line. At that moment, the foursome raised their voices in tuneful harmony, singing "All the Things You Are."

When they finished, Kelly and Lorrie Dean bowed and applauded gently.

Andy raised a hand in the air as though to silence an excited audience. When all was quiet, he stepped forward and placed his hands together, about belly-button high, while the hired singers started humming a pretty melody. It was evident that this group would now serve as backup for an obvious solo by Andy Boone. While they hummed—wooed, actually—Andy sang, somewhat strongly, "Have I Told You Lately That I Love You?"

When Andy finished and the raucous applause subsided, he stepped back in line, and they all started singing, "Three Times a Lady." After one verse, and while the professional group continued to sing, Andy faded into the background. In a few moments he reemerged out of the dark, strolled proudly up to the porch, and handed Lorrie Dean a bouquet of flowers. She took the flowers, held them to her chest, sobbing, and smiled sweetly. Andy took a step backward, blew her a kiss, and returned to help the struggling pros finish the song.

As Kelly and Lorrie Dean applauded, Andy said, "Gotta take my men back. I'll call you." They loaded into Andy's car and pulled away.

On the porch, Kelly and a shocked, yet thoroughly humbled Lorrie Dean tarried for a while, staring at the spot where Andy and his fellow musicians had stood. In a few moments, Kelly chuckled and, frowning at the vase of flowers in her friend's hands, said, "A bouquet of snapdragons. Is that romantic or what?"

"It's Andy Boone. That's what it is," said Lorrie Dean.

"Yeah, you're right. Snapdragons are Boone Woo."

They continued to peer into the dark. Kelly said, with a touch of sadness, "There goes our dreamer boy."

Lorrie Dean, still gazing into the darkness, began to murmur in a voice that was steady and a bit melancholy, "Yes, there goes little-boy dreamer: chases cars, gives me snapdragons, burns the steak and fries, sings flat . . . and loud—never gives up."

At that instant, Kelly could no longer hold back. She just lost it, bending to her knees, crying uncontrollably. Her heart was broken for her two beloved friends, the dearest people in her world. Lorrie Dean knelt beside her, cuddled close to her, trying to console her, but not wanting to have her stop crying. She knew what was going on with Kelly, for she felt the same things—helplessness and sorrow. She braced hard against her own temptation to let go. She had to hold steady, for it would not do for them to cry together. That would only weaken both of them.

Then it came to Lorrie Dean, in that moment while she was reassuring her friend—a sense of strength she hadn't felt since the kidnapping and brutal assault on her. With that new consciousness, she lifted her head, and started to stand, hoisting Kelly with her, and continued to stretch tall. At once, in that resurrected stance, she even felt a tinge of the grace she had come to believe was lost forever. *Andy would be proud of me.*

Kelly pulled away, almost toppling over, as she cried out between sobs, "How could you just let him go like that?"

It was several moments before Lorrie Dean could answer. Finally, she said, "Good question." She paused a few more moments and then added, "I think maybe it's part of my punishment."

"Well, punishment be damned!" In a moment, Kelly took Lorrie Dean's shoulders in her hands and said, "Sorry about that outburst."

"It's okay. Oh, precious Kelly, it's okay. I think, now, the certainty that this hour was at hand is what had me so nervous today. But that's only part of the unknown. One thing is clear, however: I must walk boldly into that unknown. My Kelly, I will!"

Kelly was smiling and even managed a little giggle as she said, "I bet you can't wait to see what yourself is going to do."

"Right you are. Give me five!"

Back in the parlor, sitting calmly, intermittently regarding the flowers resting on a table before them, the dear friends continued to mull over the evening's events, muttering little tidbits of insight from time to time. A little while later, Lorrie Dean punched the air with her fist and called out, "Let's really tie one on tomorrow. We can shop and gorge and play and raise hell and whatever. What about it?"

Kelly fisted the air in like manner and sang, "We're on!"

As matters were winding down for bedtime, Lorrie Dean asked, "What else can you tell me about this big gathering Andy has up his sleeve?"

28

Lorrie Dean was about to make an unprecedented move. She would not wait for Andy's call; she would take the initiative to call him. Kelly had left an hour earlier in time to get back to the farm in daylight. Lorrie Dean waited, composing her thoughts, her hand resting on the phone in her lap. She sighed and dialed his number.

"Hello."

"Is this Boone Woo, the crooner?"

Andy chuckled. "I can tell who you've been around for a few hours. How *are* you, sweetheart?"

"My dear Andy, I'm fine, and I want you to know that I've never been so touched by anyone's kindness as I am now, thinking of your beautiful gesture. Andy, I'm honored. And you know what?"

"What?"

"I'm honored because it was you who did it. I've never been serenaded in my life, and if it was destined to happen, I'm just glad it was you."

"Lorrie Dean, I'm humbled."

"No, Andy dear, I'm humbled. Really, what made you do it?"

"The power of love."

Lorrie Dean waited, thinking he'd say more. When, after an awkward period, he didn't, she thought, *Actually, that says it all: the power of love. If you try to embellish that, you diminish it. Andy knows that.* As much as she still believed she didn't deserve his love, she suppressed that notion—another unprecedented move—and said to him, "Thanks again, Andy, you're pretty special."

"*We* are."

"Okay, now, there's another reason I called. May I attend church with you tomorrow?"

"Wow, yes! That's fantastic; I'll pick you up at 10:30 in the morning."

"You got it."

They rambled on, good-naturedly, over little irrelevant, innocuous matters, relaxed and enjoying the banter. Finally, Lorrie Dean pleaded it was bedtime, and they said good night sweetly.

*   *   *

The tranquillity of City Lake Park on a cool September afternoon would seem a fitting touch, following worship services at their church. Although these inspirations did offer some redemption individually for Lorrie Dean and Andy, they fell short of firmly reuniting their lives. Nevertheless, the setting placed them in the best possible atmosphere for a little peaceful deliberation on some very difficult, nagging issues. So, as they sat relaxed on a park bench overlooking the lake, they accepted their situation, and debated their dilemma.

"What better time," began Andy, "to look at this whole question of forgiveness."

"Guess so," jumped in Lorrie Dean.

"Well, I think the monumental effort of our friend to forgive her mother, and our commitment to that basic element in our Christian faith, are a harbinger."

"I read you, Andy. You're thinking I should leap forward without further ado and forgive old Jarred what's-his-face for assaulting me."

"Yes. If you'll forgive him, I will."

"Whoa. Why are you putting a condition on it: *I will if you will?* Come on. Kelly didn't impose any such reservation when she forgave her mother, and it certainly doesn't track with our faith, you know, our fundamental belief."

Andy slumped forward and started shaking his head. He seemed physically and spiritually unable to move. He fell deep into thought, very nearly paralyzed by Lorrie Dean's trump. He felt no temptation to hurry as he wrestled with what her objection told him about himself.

Lorrie Dean waited quietly. This was no time to rush. She had come to regard impatient behavior with great disdain, believing it a needless opponent in most cases. It was her fear that, without some extraordinary intervention, humankind would eventually annihilate itself through sheer impatience. She refused to be a party to that sad, preventable demise. Now, in these absorbing moments, her love for Andy Boone began to well inside. Even though some might think him immature and a little crazy at times, he would always listen to reason, and he always held sway over his ego.

Andy finally sat up, twisted around and looked squarely into the beautiful eyes of his soul mate. With his trademark grin, a little sheepish this time, he said, "You got me on that one. It makes me realize what a hypocrite I am. I want to be an honest believer, but that little gaffe of mine makes me look pretty phony—like I'm ready to love only the lovable."

"My Andy—yes, you are my Andy, even if we can't fulfill it—there's a measure of hypocrisy in all of us. It's not willful, but again, it's one of those human things. I don't see you as a hypocrite. A hypocrite is someone who isn't even trying to grow."

"Thanks, *my* Lorrie Dean. So, even though it may be for the wrong reasons, I say categorically, I forgive Jarred what's-his-face, whatever you decide to do."

It was Lorrie Dean's time to slump over and think. Mercifully, Andy took a cue from her earlier concession to him and waited patiently. She looked up and said, "Okay, here's what I'm willing to do. I would go and stand somewhere within the general presence of that . . . okay, that man—see how nice I am this time, inhibiting what I really want to call him? Anyway, I will stand in his presence and look him in the eye and then decide what to do."

"That's reasonable and, by golly, it's fair."

"Will the FBI man, Chad, help us on this?"

"Yes. I'll call him tomorrow."

At that, they looked at each other and shrugged; the question was settled.

After this somewhat grueling exercise, they turned their attention away from tribulation and started talking about the park and drinking its peace. Indeed, it was so alluring and innocent that it could not long be ignored on its own merits. After a healthy round of indulgence in that welcome respite, they turned again to another compelling issue, one that, though it could be stifled for a brief period, could never be defeated or held down for long.

"Andy, our sweet friend has ordered me to, as she put it, get my butt to a rape crisis counselor."

"Only because she cares about you. We want that for you, not to cause you unpleasant moments, but because we want you back. I know, I know, that's selfish, but so be it. We both need you—and only you. There is no substitute. So go, dammit!"

"Wow! Such fervor from one normally so composed."

Andy grinned.

"Okay, the grin got me." She laughed and jumped ahead. "How can I win with you two hanging together against me like that?"

"We're not against you; we are your biggest fans."

"Okay, *fan*, can you call them for me?"

"Consider it done."

*   *   *

Andy called the Rape Crisis Center early Monday morning and made an appointment for Lorrie Dean with a delighted Debbie Sills. On his noon hour, he delivered a little sack of name-tag holders to We Party, meeting covertly with Shirley on the sidewalk near their building.

"Shirley, I put two or three extra in here. If you all think of any happy clients who might want to be a part of this expression, feel free to call them."

"Oh, good. I think Jan has at least two she would want to call."

"We're looking to hold this in the old stone house at Westlake Park on Saturday, October 2. Call me if you have any conflicts."

"Will do."

Andy's call to the office of FBI agent Chad Jarrigan was not as productive as his first two contacts—only because Chad wasn't in. Though this meant a little gap in his momentum, Andy wasn't worried. Chad had an unblemished record of returning his calls.

About midafternoon, he was handed what he regarded as the surprise thrill of a lifetime. Lorrie Dean called and invited him to dinner at the house. He mused at her deliberate reference to the dwelling as *the* house, rather than *her* house.

Andy was so excited that he showed up early and helped with a few incidental kitchen chores. During the course of their dinner, Lorrie Dean reflected with fascination on those few moments when they were breezing around in the kitchen together, getting things done. There was harmony to it; little boys make good helpers. They discussed very briefly Lorrie

Dean's appointment with the crisis counselor and the expected trip to Parkland for a visit with one Jarred Lynch.

"I'll be able to get away and go with you to your three o'clock appointment with the counselor tomorrow."

"Oh, Andy, you don't have to do that."

"I could be moral support for you, and I wouldn't attend your meeting. I could wait in the lobby."

"You know, Andy, that does sound good. I think it would encourage me, knowing you'd be there when I get out."

They enjoyed an unusually pleasant, relaxing visit after dinner and parted shortly after they both started yawning. It had been a long, busy day for them.

FBI agent Jarrigan returned Andy's call early the next morning and agreed to arrange for Lorrie Dean's visit to the hospital.

"Keep in mind, Andy, that I'm not the ultimate decider in this matter. Hospital officials will have the final say, but I think they'll look at it favorably, considering the positive nature of the intended visit. They may impose some restrictions, but I think, in general, they will support it."

"I understand, and thanks for all you're doing. I feel confident with this matter in your hands."

"Good. I'm sure we'll get it done."

"So am I, and, you know Chad, just between you and me, this may well turn out to be the single most decisive event in Lorrie Dean's recovery."

Minutes before it was time for Andy to leave the job and meet Lorrie Dean at the crisis center, Chad called and said everything was set to go at the Parkland Hospital on Thursday afternoon at five thirty.

*　　　*　　　*

At the Rape Crisis Center, Lorrie Dean was met by a smiling, fashionably dressed Debbie Sills. Andy remained in the waiting room while the two women headed for a private office.

Debbie Sills and Lorrie Dean chatted amiably for a little while. Plainly, the counselor had no intention of forcing anything or rushing their conference. Lorrie Dean could already feel the fear and anxiety dissipating as they continued their nonthreatening interview. The stress just seemed to be evaporating from her body and she was thinking, *This woman is a professional, and she cares.*

When they seemed to have wound down, the counselor said, "Tell me about your experience; tell me what you want me to know."

Lorrie Dean began. It was pretty slow at first, and at times, a little jumbled. Clearly, the counselor was content to let her go at her own pace. She just listened. Even during long lapses, she didn't push. Now, within that very conducive atmosphere, Lorrie Dean began to take off, and in a while, unloaded the whole grim story. When she seemed finished, Debbie Sills let the ensuing silence prevail, giving Lorrie Dean an opportunity to think further and a chance to rest. In a while, Lorrie Dean said, "I guess that's about it."

"Lorrie Dean, I must say, you are to be commended. You did well, really well. Thank you for going through that with me, and I want you to know this: I am truly sorry you had to suffer through that brutal experience."

Then the counselor went on to make some observations about points that came out in Lorrie Dean's account and to suggest how they led to her feelings and to emphasize how the whole ordeal was history. She was very adamant at the end of her comments when she insisted, "Nothing about it really changed who you are, Lorrie Dean. Be assured, you handled it correctly. You survived it. You are a survivor. That has to be your new motto. Don't forget it!"

"Thank you. Thank you for listening and for everything."

"Did you say you had a journal you wanted me to look at?"

"Oh, yeah, I almost forgot," said Lorrie Dean, fishing some papers out of her purse. "This is a letter from me to me that Andy and my close friend encouraged me to write."

The counselor accepted Lorrie Dean's letter and read through it, obviously taking the time to attend meticulously to every detail of it. When she finished, she held on to it, looked warmly at her client and said, "You did a good job here. How do you feel about it? Do you think it helped you to write these feelings?"

"I really don't know. All I do know is that I can't quit thinking about it, and I have to admit that when I do, it doesn't upset me as much as it confuses me."

"Remarkable. Don't worry about the confusion; that's normal. Shall we talk about it for a few minutes?"

"Sure, that's fine."

Thereupon, Debbie Sills went through each point of the letter, offering brief comments and mostly asking questions, prompting Lorrie Dean to come to grips with her own writings.

When they appeared to be finished with the letter, Lorrie Dean said, "I still don't know what I was trying to say when I wrote that the rape did it. What do you think, Ms. Sills? What was I driving at?"

"Good question. Here's what I think: when you say 'the rape did it,' that is all encompassing. It did everything to you—your life, your regard for yourself and, in this case, your escape."

"My escape?"

"Yes. That ugly, hideous rape was very likely the last shot of desperation you needed."

"I think I understand what you're saying."

"Yes. Sad to say, but who knows, it is entirely possible that the rape saved your life." She paused, giving Lorrie Dean time to grasp that statement, and continued, "Because it was right after the rape, that you got busy and, with absolutely remarkable ingenuity, got yourself out of there. Praise God!"

"Yes, praise God!"

"You're going to make it, Lorrie Dean. I can tell. You've got a lot working for you. For one thing, you brought yourself in for help. For another, you have a man in your life who is devoted to your cause."

"Yes, I think you're right. I have to admit, though, I have asked myself at times: Is Andy standing by me for love or out of pity?"

"Surely, it must be love—pity gives up after a bit."

Lorrie Dean nodded. At once, she felt the teasing of a little smile easing across her face and kept nodding.

They talked a while longer, during which time, the counselor advised that they would be Lorrie Dean's advocate, and the first step in serving that role was to have her see a doctor. From there, they ended their meeting on a high note.

Before leaving, Lorrie Dean said, "I don't know how to thank you enough." While she was saying these last words to her counselor, she became vaguely aware of herself physically. She noticed that she was standing tall, holding her head up and again, as she briefly had once before, she felt a tiny sense of the grace that previously had been so natural for her. She smiled and said, "Thank you again."

Andy stood up as Lorrie Dean stepped into the waiting room. She walked straight to him, embraced him briefly, stepped back, and let her hands rest gently against his chest. Looking very serious, she said, "You're always here, aren't you, buddy?"

*   *   *

There's always time for one more ordeal, thought Lorrie Dean, as she and Andy walked into Parkland Hospital late Thursday afternoon. They learned promptly that they were expected. They followed a nurse who had been assigned to them, as she led the way.

This has to be the busiest hospital in the world, thought Lorrie Dean. Parkland was a sprawling medical complex, anchoring several medical centers and specialty hospitals in the area. Inside, it was a teeming community of effort—nurses, doctors, and staff—scurrying about simply getting things done. They were in the huge, older section, the original building. For the staff, getting about, tending to business was especially challenging here, because these narrow hallways and small rooms had not been designed to accommodate such sweeping, intense effort.

In any event, this remarkable medical facility was a hive of clearly dedicated human effort. Indeed, the demands of a mushrooming population of patients begged a much larger staff than was practically possible. It seemed that, throughout the world, the medical needs of so many fell on the shoulders of so few.

Soon, they stopped outside a room at the very end of a hallway. The nurse held up her hand to hold them and said, "Wait here while I go in and find out if Mr. Lynch is willing and ready to see you."

The nurse returned promptly and, holding the door, said, "I'll wait out here while you go in." As Lorrie Dean started in, Andy headed back to the main waiting room, as previously agreed.

Lorrie Dean strolled in, looking away from the bed as she poked along. In a moment, she stopped several feet from the foot of it and lingered there, still looking straight ahead. Slowly, she turned to face her adversary.

Jarred Lynch was a sick, sick man, thoroughly defeated, barely able to lift his head a few inches to see his visitor. His face was dark and contorted. Lorrie Dean and the victim stared at each other, neither seemingly the least interested in speaking. Lorrie Dean twisted in place a few times and then took a couple of steps to the side, glancing from time to time at her rapist. Finally, she stopped and, looking haughtily at the disabled man, said, "How's the soup here?"

For a moment, it looked as though Jarred was trying to create a smile. He said nothing. He looked as though he was trying to shake his head, but he seemed unable to do so. Finally, it did move ever so slightly. He started to cough and then he was trying to cough and say something at the same time. Finally, he was able to mutter, "Well, little lady, you win."

Lorrie Dean pursed her lips and looked at the ceiling as she answered, "No I didn't. I didn't win anything. Nobody wins in the kinds of games we played."

Time passed, and they continued to look at each other. After a while, Lorrie Dean said, almost to the side, "I'm sorry I blasted your knees."

Jarred's lips began to work and in a moment, he said, with surprising clarity, "I forgive you."

Lorrie Dean stood in place, stoically, unable to respond in any way. After a long time, she turned and started toward the door. As she reached for the handle, she heard the patient hacking, obviously trying to speak. She paused.

"Do you forgive me?"

Lorrie Dean started to open the door and then dropped her hand, looked at Jarred, and nodded. She turned back to the door.

"Can't you say it?"

She hesitated and started to turn the door handle. Then she let it go and looked at the man one last time. They said nothing but continued to hold eye contact. Lorrie Dean looked again at the door and then stared into the eyes of her rapist and said, "I forgive you." She walked out.

Outside the room, she heaved a long, deep breath and leaned back against the door. There, with her chin resting on prayerful hands, she whispered, "Oh God, bless that man."

The nurse, standing nearby, said to her, "And God bless you."

When Lorrie Dean entered the waiting room, Andy rose in place, and she walked straight to him, paused briefly, and fell wholly into his outstretched arms. They embraced, holding tight, for a long time. Finally they walked away, holding hands.

29

Get ready, Andy Boone! You are in for one big shocker. This will come at the hands of two conniving women, well known to you. So, this is fair warning. Just get set, young warrior. While you wait, dream on—for what it's worth.

*   *   *

An emotionally demanding week had left Lorrie Dean very tired, but it felt like a good tired. She was actually pleased with herself for the first time in almost eight weeks, proud of definitive achievements in reckoning with the tragic changes in her life, specifically with her self-image. Although she didn't feel she was yet a fully deserving, whole woman, she had the sensation of being on the way.

Now, she yearned to tell her best friend the good news. Even though it was Friday evening, she was ready to gamble that Kelly wasn't out on a date. In any event, she dialed her number, and Aunt Leah answered. It was gratifying to visit with her for a few minutes. Of late, Aunt Leah seemed to be reaching out to those in her circle and finding a new level of rapport with everyone. After talking genially for a while, Leah called Kelly to the phone.

"Hi, Lorrie Dean, I was just thinking about you."

"Maybe I felt the vibrations. I have some very promising news for you, but first, how about your mother? Did she get back home all right?"

"She did. She did, and I have talked to her three times in the last two weeks. Oh, Lorrie Dean, this is so much better."

"I'm so grateful for that, and very proud of you, Kelly."

"Thanks. Oh, let me tell you what we're doing around here. We have this really big greeting card we're sending Mother. Everybody here is signing it and, you know, writing friendly blurbs in it. I'm excited about it. Isn't that great?"

"It is indeed. Sorry to say, that's something I should have already done as a follow-up to my meeting her. But, I've been so wrapped up in my personal life that I've neglected important things in the lives of those around me. Darn!"

"Hey, Lorrie Dean, now don't you go berating yourself. You've been gracious to everyone, and your burden has been heavy."

"I'll get a card tomorrow, and I'll have Andy do likewise. We'll deluge your mother with friendly support."

"Super. What's this news you have?"

At that question, Lorrie Dean eagerly recounted the full story, with details, of the two strategic events of her week. She quivered at the sound of excitement in her voice, and pressed on until she got it all out. Kelly was absolutely overjoyed, and she showed it, applauding vigorously when Lorrie Dean finished.

Then the two devoted friends gabbed on and on, with little concern for the passing of time. Among other things, they discussed at length the upcoming get-together in honor of Lorrie Dean. Since she was not under an expressed pledge of confidence, Kelly spilled the beans about the name-tag plans and a few other details. Lorrie Dean responded enthusiastically and even vowed that she would seize some initiative of her own in the matter. In fact, these two veteran conspirators agreed to join forces and have some surprises of their own for the big gathering.

"We'll one-up Mr. Andrew Boone . . . excuse me, I mean Crooner Boone Woo," said Lorrie Dean.

"Crooner Boone Woo. I like that," crowed Kelly. "Right on, we'll show him."

"I think I'll have a lapel sign of my own," hooted Lorrie Dean. "Are you going to wear one?"

"You bet. All of us here will have one. They'll be personalized."

"Do you think you can find out what Andy's will say? Never mind; on second thought, I think I'd rather be surprised. It'll be more fun that way. Don't tell me yours, either."

As they neared the end of their exhilarating session, Lorrie Dean was plainly on a high, practically singing her part in the dialogue. Kelly was equally animated.

"Okay," began Lorrie Dean, "I'm thinking of one more thing, and if I can pull this off, it will be the crowning touch. Here's what: I'll have to make some phone calls because this whole thing would require the cooperation of specific others. I don't want to tell you what it is until I find out if I can swing it."

"I can't wait; I'm about to explode with curiosity."

"Oh, on that note, I need to . . . well, on this one, I'd like you to keep it a secret. I'm sorry to ask that, because I know Andy's going to be picking your brain also . . . but, please, just on this one?"

"What are friends for?"

"Deal! I'll make my calls and let you know."

*   *   *

Back to you, Andy!

The line was busy when Andy tried to call Lorrie Dean Friday night. In fact, it was busy when he tried to call the next six times. It dawned on him that she probably was talking to their friend about her very eventful and gratifying week. When he finally reached her at nine fifteen, she confirmed his hunch.

"Andy, they're all getting together and sending Kelly's mother a friendship greeting card. I think we should do the same thing."

"Absolutely."

"Do you want to go together on a card or do it individually on separate cards?"

"I like doing anything where we are united. Let's use just one card."

"That's settled. I'll get a card tomorrow."

"Good deal. Thank you for taking care of it. Speaking of tomorrow, I'm going to make a flying trip to see my mom and dad. Assuming I get back in time, would you have dinner with me, and maybe we could take in a movie afterward?"

"Yes, Andy, I'd like that."

Andy spent a very uplifting three hours with his parents in Dibol the next day. After lunch, they talked about the upcoming big get-together, just one week away, and Andy left them a couple of name-tag holders with instructions. Hugs and sweet words, and he was away.

He stopped off briefly at the farm, to coach the principals there and remind them of their roles. Before leaving, he and Dub talked about the rebirth of Kelly's relationship with her mother. The best news of all on that subject was Dub's revelation that he and Kelly were teaming up to try and have Rosalea come to the farm for a visit with all of them.

Dub's last words on that subject were, "Through Kelly, she's in our lives again, and we want to open our arms to her."

Andy and Kelly also got together for a few minutes to check their signals and make sure everything was on course. They talked a little about her mother, at Andy's prompting, and Andy let her know he and Lorrie Dean were getting together to send her a card.

"That's good of you guys," said Kelly. "Thanks for your support and good will."

"We love you, my morning light."

"I know, and I love you, too."

"Okay, now when we send our card to your mother, I will, in all humility, have to identify myself as the lead clown."

"Yeah; you'd do that," grumbled Kelly.

After he visited briefly with Leah and Mom, Andy headed away. He missed Grandpa, who reportedly was in the hen house reading the riot act to the somewhat unproductive, plainly ungrateful chickens—having one of his off days.

Dining was relaxing and pleasant. Lorrie Dean smiled easily and seemed unusually carefree, and that put Andy on cloud nine. After a dull movie—who cares, they agreed—Andy lingered at Lorrie Dean's place for about an hour. Assuming a somewhat mischievous expression, Lorrie Dean opened the box.

"I hear there's a big shindig coming up next Saturday. Know anything about it, Andy?"

"Some."

"Wow. Try to contain all that unabated enthusiasm. Anyway, I just mentioned it because I heard you were sort of hosting it."

"Yep."

"A gathering of friends, right?"

"Uh-huh."

"Is that all there is to it?"

Andy shrugged

"Andy Boone, out with it!"

"We're just having a reunion of friends, you know, a revival of spirit and camaraderie. You're included. I'll pick you up, and we'll drive over together."

Lorrie Dean chortled, "Andy Boone, I'm sorry to have to tell you this, but you don't make a very convincing fibber."

"Okay, here's what we're doing. At this late hour, I think it's okay—it's time, actually—for you to know the whole scoop. Just about all the people who feel really close to you are getting together at Westlake Park, in the old stone house there, specifically to honor you—to show their totally united support for you, my Lorrie Dean. Maybe, you could consider it an extension of support for you that began with the events of last week."

"Question."

"Shoot."

"Have I told you lately . . . that I love you?"

"You just made this the happiest day of my life."

"I'm glad. Now, let me hasten to add that this doesn't change anything about our arrangements, but it's a fact, even under these circumstances."

"Whatever."

"Yeah, right, whatever. Otherwise, shall we join again for church tomorrow?"

"Sure."

In a while, they kissed and hugged—an academic sort of hug—and bade one another good night.

Sunday church was its dependable self, and the two seemingly denied lovers parted amicably after a scintillating cafeteria lunch.

Monday at Clay Cutter Industries was a frenzy—a fun frenzy, not a hectic one. Andy was going full tilt, a whirlwind, taking care of business, doing his job—his inside job, as he called it—and making commitments and arranging affairs outside his corporate assignments. He felt at ease with these divided interests, working unpaid overtime as needed, ensuring fully responsible coverage of his job.

He called Chad Jarrigan early, offering feedback on Lorrie Dean's visit to the hospital and thanking him for his efforts in making the arrangements. He also invited him to the big gathering on the upcoming Saturday. Chad said he'd definitely be there, that he could think of no more honorable cause than paying tribute to Lorrie Dean. When Andy told him that she had expressly forgiven Jarred Lynch to his face, the agent said he wasn't surprised. As he put it, "she's all class."

Andy skipped lunch, raced over to the Rape Crisis Center, and handed counselor Debbie Sills a personal invitation to the Saturday celebration. He left some name tag holders and invited her to bring along anyone else at her discretion. He also briefed her on Lorrie Dean's visit with her rapist to offer her forgiveness. Debbie's last words, before Andy zipped away, were "I couldn't be prouder. See you Saturday."

*   *   *

Early Tuesday evening, Kelly was just finishing up with supper dishes when the phone rang. Somehow, she had an odd sense that it was for her, so she picked it up and answered. At that instant, Dub showed up for coffee and Mom wobbled in and started rooting around in the pantry.

"It's me again," chuckled Lorrie Dean.

"Amazing! I had this strange sensation that it was you calling the minute the phone rang. What's up, girl?"

"It's done. I got it done. Don't answer. Actually, Kelly, let me do the talking. Don't repeat anything I say in case others are listening there. This is the secret—I mean the really big secret."

"Yes, Lorrie Dean, it was a good day at school."

"Way to go. I knew I could count on you. Okay, I completed my phone calls and everything just fell amazingly right in place. It was really miraculous. Anyway, this one is going to stun the whole crowd at the gathering. But I wanted you to know in advance because you've always confided in me, and we're best friends. Remember, don't say anything while I'm talking."

"Yeah, everybody's okay. We're hoping to get my mother to the farm soon."

"You are a genius, Kelly. So here's the whole plan. When I finish, just say something like 'We'll all be there. Bye.'"

As she hung up, Kelly slapped a hand to her mouth and gasped. Then she dropped her hand and began to creep toward the dinner table, staring vaguely at the ceiling. Dub leaned in, and Mom abandoned the pantry and padded over to stand at the table, holding to the back of a chair.

Kelly dragged out a chair, dropped into it, and pulled up to the table. She smiled at her two cronies and then laid her head over and stretched an arm full-length across the table and started tapping on it. In a minute, she sat up and looked mischievously at two startled companions. Their eyes begged for a word, anything she could say.

"You're not going to believe this one. Unfortunately, it's a secret and I can't tell you what it is—but get ready."

30

A wide banner hung above the front steps of the stone house at Westlake Park: THIS ONE'S FOR YOU, LORRIE DEAN. Just in front of the steps, Andy and Kelly paused to compare the messages printed on their name tags. Kelly's read: *Lorrie Dean, Always*. Andy's had: *Lorrie Dean, My Symphony*. They smiled affectionately and joined in a thumbs-up. Lorrie Dean had not stayed for this exercise, opting instead to proceed tagless into the house.

Andy pondered that development, as he and Kelly climbed up to the front porch. Before they went inside, he asked Kelly, "Doesn't she plan to wear a tag message?"

"She does, but she wasn't ready for you to see it quite yet. Be patient, Boone Woo; it's all coming down okay."

"Do you know what her tag will say?"

"Yes, but I can't tell. What do you want it to say?"

"I'm hoping it'll say simply, 'Lorrie Dean.' Let's go in."

Inside the large front room, a half dozen people mingled quietly, speaking calmly and politely. Others had scattered along the wide hallway and into other rooms. As Andy looked toward the hallway, he spotted his mom and dad talking to FBI agent Chad Jarrigan. When they chanced to look toward him, he waved, and all three waved back.

Close by, Lorrie Dean was smiling and gesturing eagerly as she greeted each one of the women from We Party. The instant she stepped away toward another couple, Kelly rushed up and took her arm. For a few moments, they seemed to be whispering. Then Kelly hurried away to the front entrance, apparently to watch for an expected event there.

Andy strayed into one of the rooms and greeted the We Party folks, who accepted him with giggles and curtsies. He, too, bowed and lauded their presence. Their tags all read the same: *Lorrie, Our Lady*. They introduced him to two of their clients, a young man and an older woman. Their messages were perfect: *Lorrie, Thanks.* Andy felt instant rapport with these two, and lingered a while with them, chatting cordially.

As Andy stepped back into the hall, there was a sudden clamor at the front door, and he instinctively glanced in that direction. All four of the remaining members of the farm group streamed in, led by the so-called resident professor, Grandpa, grinning full tilt. When he spotted Lorrie Dean coming toward them, he broke away and scampered over to intercept her. As he saluted her, Lorrie Dean lifted her arms out toward the crowd as if presenting him for special recognition.

From a distance, Andy watched with admiration as Lorrie Dean and Grandpa interacted playfully. She touched his name tag and then poked a finger in the air as if to underscore a point. Now, as Grandpa was shifting around like an adolescent on his first date, she pretended to write in the palm of her hand.

While Andy gazed at this remarkable episode, he was shaking his head with pride, watching Lorrie Dean brighten into her old trademark unassuming smile, the incomparable glow of full acceptance. In that magical moment, he was aware of his heart tapping rhythmically against his chest and a little moisture in his eyes. This time, his soul mate did not slump toward the imaginary writing pad as he would have expected. Rather, she was standing tall, holding her head high, keeping her hand at eye level as she pretended to scribble on it. There was the old poise, the inimitable bearing of this amazing lady. *She's back,* thought Andy.

Kelly entered the scene for a moment, apparently delivering a quick message to Lorrie Dean. When she spotted Andy, she walked toward him, swaying and swinging her butt like a prissy little teaser. As she finally twisted her way on up to him, she bowed and gushed, "Want to know what Grandpa's tag says?"

"I'm burning with curiosity, especially in light of Lorrie Dean's unprecedented theatrics over there."

"It says, *Lorrie Dean, Call me.*"

Andy shook his head and laughed out. "That's Grandpa all right. He better watch out, or I'll exile his butt back to the hen house." On one wide swing of his head, still shaking, he spied Debbie Sills, just entering. He started to break away and proceed to greet her when she was intercepted by his mom, who had an enviable ease with strangers. In a moment, he noticed that a little girl had come in behind the crisis counselor.

"Wonder who the little girl is?" he said to Kelly.

"Wonder?"

"Guess I could ease over there and find out, but I don't want to interrupt Mom; she seems to be really enjoying the encounter, and so does Debbie Sills. Best I leave those two alone for now."

Said Kelly, "The little girl looks to be about eleven or twelve years old. Maybe that's *her* little girl."

"Don't think so. She mentioned one time that her kids are all grown."

While they were pondering the question, Leah came up and button-holed Kelly. At once, they started talking intellectual stuff. At that, Andy pulled away and strolled toward the front. As he approached, his mom was distracted by a peal of laughter in another area and left.

"Hi, Debbie," said Andy. "It means a lot to me that you're here. How can I ever thank you?"

"Andy, you just did; we're on the same team, you know. By the way, I like your mom."

"She's a jewel. And you're right; we are on the same team. You'll be gratified to know that I honestly believe Lorrie Dean is on her way back. Look at her over there, talking to that man. Notice her posture. See how she lifts her chin when she talks, and is that a thrilling smile or what?"

"This is just beautiful to behold, and Andy, just try to imagine what all this support means to her, all these people, singing the same song and singing it for her. I feel very humble."

"Me, too. I see you have a little friend with you."

"And that's exactly what she is. We are the best of buddies," she said, as she looked at the smiling young lady. "Sarah, I want you to meet another friend of mine. This is Mr. Andy Boone."

Andy leaned a little to take her hand and, as they smiled bashfully at each other, he spotted her name tag. Dumbfounded, he stammered out a few difficult words, praising her attendance and complimenting her good looks and pretty dress.

At that moment, Debbie Sills started toward a beaming Lorrie Dean, and the little girl followed. Andy was very nearly immobile, stunned by what he had read on Sarah's name tag. He looked up, straining, woefully lost, and saw two friends from his office—Paige Ivy and coworker Morris Allgate—coming toward him. He hurried to them and visited for a few minutes. Then he flagged Lorrie Dean, who obviously recognized his look of desperation, because she hustled on over.

As she drew near, Andy noticed that she was now wearing a name tag. He smiled and nodded, thankfully, as he read it: I AM LORRIE DEAN.

"Well, it's a relief to see a smile break up that anxious look you had on your face? Is anything wrong?"

"Have you met Sarah, the little girl who came in with Debbie Sills?" asked Andy.

"Not yet, but I've been trying to work myself in their direction."

"I want to be good to her; I want to do everything for her. Will you go to her? Look at her name tag?"

"Sure, Andy, I'm on my way."

Moments later, Lorrie Dean came near the little girl. Since Debbie Sills was heavy into conversation with Paige Ivy, she leaned in and introduced herself to Sarah, who smiled graciously. When she read Sarah's name tag, she asked if they could talk for a few minutes. Sarah agreed readily, and they strolled into an unoccupied room and sat down.

"First of all, Sarah, thanks for coming to be with me."

"You're welcome; I thought it would help."

"Sarah, it has already helped, but I need still more help from a strong person like you. Do you think you could be my friend and help me? I have a ways to go with my problems."

"Oh, Ms. Lorrie Dean, I would. Yes. We can talk a lot."

Smiling cheerfully, Lorrie Dean clapped and blurted, "Sarah, we're on—you and I."

Now Sarah was swinging her legs, nodding in rhythm, and smiling sweetly. The two women talked for a couple of minutes, mostly about the party, and then visited nonverbally for a little while, until Lorrie Dean spotted Kelly motioning for her.

"Sarah, I have to go attend to something right now. I'm sorry. Heck. Anyway, we were just getting started. Please, when this shindig is over, don't get away until I see you. Also, we can exchange phone numbers. Okay?"

Sarah nodded, smiling. Lorrie Dean squeezed her hand, stood in place for a moment, and started away, glancing again at the girl's name tag: *Lorrie Dean, Me too.*

As Lorrie Dean stepped into the hallway, Kelly came skipping to meet her, took her hand, and said, "The chairs are all in place in front of the porch, and it's time. Hurry."

The two women walked briskly toward the front, motioning for the guests to follow. Just inside the front room, near the head of the hall, Lorrie Dean jiggled a little bell that she found on a nearby table, and a hush fell over the jaunty little crowd.

"Everybody, find a seat outside, please," announced Lorrie Dean. "I have a few things I want to say to you."

They all scurried out and took seats that had materialized in the front yard while they visited inside. Kelly and Andy sat on the front row, at Kelly's insistence. Everybody was quiet as Lorrie Dean began.

"Dear ones, this is friendship." She paused. "This is friendship at its highest level. And today, right here, much to my very pleasant surprise, I have found a brand new friend, and I want to thank her for coming," she said, looking straight at Sarah. "Honestly, I don't know how I can ever thank you enough for this stirring support, each one of you. But at least, please know this: I love you."

"All of you know generally what happened to me, that I was kidnapped and held captive by merciless thugs. Some of you may not be aware of some other things that happened. But, you know what? It doesn't matter, because it's all over." The instant, vigorous applause halted her briefly and then she continued: "Thank you. Yes, it's over. I am free!" She held up again for the applause. "So, the run stops here. Oh, I may remember running, but the memory of it will no longer control my life. The fact is that I have a new memory for my life: this day—and you." A little wave of *aahhh* swept through the audience.

"I have a few more things to say to you, but before I continue, I'd like to ask . . ." She tried to finish, but emotion took over, and she rested her tear-stained face in her hands for a few moments and then tried again. "I'm sorry, everyone; thank you for your indulgence. Now, here I go; just marvel at how strong I'm going to be," she said, giggling and sobbing at the same time. "I'd . . . please, I'd like for my sweetheart, Andy, to come stand beside me." The friends applauded as Andy made his way up to the porch. He, too, was straining against the force of emotion and fighting tears.

"I would also like to ask my buddy, the dearest friend anyone could ever hope to have, Kelly, to stand with us." A beaming Kelly bounded up to the porch as applause rose again.

"Love has set me free—your love, and the undying love and ardent devotion of this dear man, and this extraordinary woman. All of you dear, special friends have given me something eternal. So, with . . ."

Suddenly, a noisy car stopped just behind the crowd. The driver got out, slammed the door, and moved toward the house. Andy started to step forward, but Lorrie Dean restrained him with her arm. Now, this rather tall man was stomping straight toward the front, holding his head awkwardly down and sideways, as though to hide his identity. He kept coming.

Andy was aghast, frozen. Kelly and Lorrie Dean were smiling and exchanging winks. On stalked the intruder. Finally, he was right upon them. He lifted his head, and Andy blurted, "Reverend Woodard!"

"Yes, thank you, Andy, for that honored recognition." Now the reverend looked out at the stunned audience and said, "Excuse me, folks. I apologize for this unruly intrusion, but I have just a little unfinished business to attend to. Bear with me; it'll only take a couple of minutes."

Reverend Woodard turned again to Andy and Lorrie Dean and demanded, "Andrew Woodson Boone and Lorrie Dean LeMay, please face each other and join hands." They complied.

Now the reverend held his hands above their heads and said confidently, "I now pronounce you husband and wife. Andy, you may kiss your wife."

The newlyweds kissed and then embraced and held it, both weeping but gaining strength all the while. They held to each other for a seeming eternity. During that time, they broke away only long enough to reach out and draw Kelly into their embrace.

By this time, the dear friends were all on their feet, excitedly waiting, while Grandpa stretched his arms high in the air, signaling Touchdown!

*   *   *

Now, the dream emerges again, out of the vapors of dawn, as the sun pushes in to caress a green pasture and bathe three lost children in the promise of morning. Still they huddle in the tall grass, trusting, looking hopefully at each other. At once, they hear a faint sound. They rise up and wave to the shepherd walking toward them.